"Are you all right?"
Charlotte asked.

She searched Lord Wycliffe's face and noticed that under the dirt, he was beginning to bruise. One eye had started to swell, as had his lip, but she certainly was not going to tell him that. Happily, she had no mirror with her.

"My head is splitting, and I ache all over. Do I look all right?" he asked, his voice heavy with sarcasm. He stood up, glanced down at himself and groaned anew. "Look at me. Just look at me!" he demanded.

Charlotte's gaze swept up and down his tall frame, taking in his muscular thighs, his trim waist, his broad shoulders, his handsome if rather bedraggled features, and her heart hammered irregularly. There was something rakish about his torn clothing and his less-than-perfect appearance that made him seem more desirable, more accessible... "I think you are even more attractive than usual..."

Dear Reader,

Deborah Simmons's *The Vicar's Daughter* is a frothy Regency romp. When the stuffy earl of Wycliffe decides to take Charlotte Trowbridge under his wing, little does he know that the naive vicar's daughter will do everything within her power to disrupt his well-ordered life, and capture his heart.

Also this month, we are pleased to have another Mary McBride Western, *The Gunslinger*. Set in Glory, Kansas, it's the story of a reclusive gunfighter who finally discovers someone who sees him as a man, not a legend, yet can't escape from his dangerous reputation.

Our other titles for February include *Sweet Surrender* by Julie Tetel, the next installment of her popular North Point series, and *Lord Liar*, a medieval tale of secrets and deception by Laurie Grant.

We hope you will enjoy all four books this month and keep an eye out for all our titles, wherever Harlequin Historicals are sold.

Sincerely,

Tracy Farrell
Senior Editor

Please address questions and book requests to:
Harlequin Reader Service
U.S.: 3010 Walden Ave., P.O. Box 1325, Buffalo, NY 14269
Canadian: P.O. Box 609, Fort Erie, Ont. L2A 5X3

DEBORAH SIMMONS

THE VICAR'S DAUGHTER

Harlequin Books

TORONTO • NEW YORK • LONDON
AMSTERDAM • PARIS • SYDNEY • HAMBURG
STOCKHOLM • ATHENS • TOKYO • MILAN
MADRID • WARSAW • BUDAPEST • AUCKLAND

ISBN 0-373-28858-1

THE VICAR'S DAUGHTER

Books by Deborah Simmons

Harlequin Historicals

Fortune Hunter #132
Silent Heart #185
The Squire's Daughter #208
The Devil's Lady #241
The Vicar's Daughter #258

DEBORAH SIMMONS

A voracious reader and writer, Deborah Simmons
began her professional career as a newspaper
reporter. She turned to fiction after the birth of her
first child when a longtime love of historical
romances prompted her to pen her first book, pub-
lished in 1989. She lives with her husband, two
children and two cats on seven acres in rural Ohio,
where she divides her time between her family, reading, researching and writing.

For my father, William O. Smith

Chapter One

Wycliffe often said that had he known what awaited him that fateful day, he would never have entered the vicarage. Of course, everyone knew he was lying, and since Maximilian Alistair Wentworth Fortescue, Fifth Earl of Wycliffe, *never* lied, his statement was all the more astounding. But then everyone was astonished by what happened....

It all began simply enough in the early spring of 1816 with an innocent visit to a new property in Sussex that Maximilian had just inherited from his great-uncle. Compared to the Wycliffe seat, it was a small property, but prosperous. Unfortunately, the modest fifteen-bedroom manor house had not seen improvements in many a year, and Maximilian knew it would need refurbishing.

In his usual, methodical fashion, Maximilian began assessing the property immediately, determining what repairs were needed and ordering them. He introduced himself to the staff, the tenants and, on this bright March day, the third in a planned week-long stay, he set out to pay a call on the vicar.

Maximilian was neither looking forward to the obligation nor dreading it; he was simply performing his duty in his accustomed responsible fashion. His schedule had been painstakingly prepared before he had even left London, and he stuck to it with what some might view as excessive rigidity.

Not Maximilian. He prized order and kept himself running as regularly as the gold engraved watch given to him by his father. With the practiced gesture of habit, Maximilian removed the piece from his fob pocket and noted the time. Calculating one half hour to be sufficient for his visit, he strode up the flagstone path to the vicarage.

A small building nestled amongst a stand of ancient oaks and surrounded by thick, high box hedges, the vicarage was a little shabby around the edges. Maximilian spied some spots on the roof where slates were missing and places in the mellowed stone walls where the mortar had fallen, and he turned a critical eye on the ivy that had been allowed to run wild, climbing up one side of the building until it nearly reached the eaves.

Maximilian lifted his gloved hand to knock when the sound of ferocious yapping met him, and a small dog of indiscriminate breeding raced from under the hedgerow toward the front of the house. Assessing the animal in a glance, Maximilian assured himself that it would not dare to harry *him* and saw that it was followed by a small boy who scrambled out of the bushes adeptly.

The dog and, consequently, its human counterpart, were nearly at Maximilian's feet before they noticed him. When they did, the child hauled up short, picked up the animal with a grunt and clutched it to his small chest. "Hello!" the boy shouted over the sounds of the beast, which was still barking rather ferociously for one so small. He grinned brightly to reveal a gaping hole where his top two teeth should be. "Are you the new lord?"

"I am indeed," Maximilian answered.

"Papa's been expecting you. He is probably in the parlor." Without further ado, the youngster opened the front door and walked in, motioning for Maximilian to follow. The dog, seizing his opportunity, bolted from the prison of encircling arms and raced off down the narrow hallway.

"Patches! Hold up!" the boy cried. Racing off at top speed, he left Maximilian standing between walls hung with faded green material. Before Maximilian could decide upon his next move, an even younger child emerged from one of the rooms leading off the hall and gazed up at him solemnly. A girl, this one was wearing an overly large dress and carrying a disgusting-looking piece of material that she gripped rather fiercely. She stuck her thumb into her mouth and stared at him.

"Is your papa here?" Maximilian asked.

Without removing her eyes from him, the child pointed a fat finger, and Maximilian headed that way. His progress was impeded when the hall veered off into two different directions. He stood at the crossroads, trying to determine where the elusive parlor might lie, when he was nearly run down by two shrieking youths, chasing each other. "Oh, hello!" one yelled in passing. "Papa is in the parlor!"

Unaccustomed to such cavalier treatment, Maximilian felt like wringing their unruly necks, but he turned in the direction from whence they had come. He continued following the hallway, which opened onto various small rooms, and decided the vicarage reminded him of nothing so much as a rabbit warren. Coming upon an undraped archway, he leaned through to see a pretty little girl setting a dining table with plates. "The parlor?" he asked. Apparently used to total strangers wandering about her home, she showed no alarm but smiled and pointed across the way.

Finally! Maximilian stepped over the threadbare carpeting toward his destination, hidden away in the bowels of the building so as to discourage guests, he decided. Only the persistent made it this far, he was certain. He had counted five children. Did they all belong to the vicar?

He entered the room and was immediately irritated, for Papa was definitely not in the parlor. In fact, Maximilian thought the room deserted until a noise drew his attention to a rather worn sofa in a faded flower pattern. With extreme interest, he cocked his head slightly to one side, the better to observe a female derriere protruding from underneath the piece of furniture. Cloaked by a layer of spotted muslin, the rump nonetheless appeared quite soft and rounded.

The dictates of polite society called for him to make his presence known, and Maximilian was nothing if not well-mannered. However, some streak of wickedness, heretofore buried beneath his staid exterior, made him disregard the rules to which he normally adhered and approach the pleasing vision.

Beneath it were a pair of small feet, encased in well-worn, low-heeled kid shoes and attached to extremely shapely ankles encased in white stockings. "Oh, help me, will you?" requested the form. Far from being put out by the note of exasperation in the feminine voice, Maximilian was quite stimulated by the various ways in which he could conceivably respond to that plea.

His intriguing musings were interrupted by the appearance of one of the female's hands, pale and smooth, thrusting a tiny kitten toward him. Dropping to the floor, Maximilian took the proffered animal, though it mewled and wiggled in a frightened manner. Another was then handed to him, and he accepted it, too, although he wondered what he would do if she presented him with any more. These two filled his hands, and he had no intention of letting them ruin his green superfine coat or his elegant striped waistcoat with their sharp little claws.

Luckily, he did not have to confront this problem, for with a delightful bit of squirming, the luscious derriere backed toward him. A head emerged from underneath the sofa, and he was met with a lovely young woman cradling two kittens of her own. Maximilian noticed her hair first, a startling, thick mass of pale honey that surrounded her face like a cloud. Then he saw green eyes, the color of spring, staring out at him from a strikingly beautiful face. Her mouth was drawn up in surprise, but he could tell her pink lips were definitely lush.

Maximilian was not one to languish over a woman's charms. In truth, he usually paid them little heed, having a great deal of contempt for the mindlessness of female pursuits. He had a mistress to see to his needs, and although he must take a wife someday, it was not something that he contemplated with any relish. All of which made his reaction to this particular female all the more astonishing.

For a moment they simply sat there, she on her heels and Maximilian bent on one knee, each quietly perusing the other. Then she finally reacted. "Oh!" she said softly, releasing her grip on the two kittens she held. They immediately leapt for the safety of the sofa, while she frantically began to rise. In her haste, she backed up, knocking into a pushcart that sat nearby.

Maximilian was reaching for her, to steady her, or else he might have seen the tray of jelly tarts that balanced on the edge of the cart. As it was, he noticed them only after they had been deposited in his lap when a wet sensation seeped through to his skin. With extreme distaste, he looked down to watch a pastry slide onto the floor, leaving his formerly immaculate buff doeskin breeches dripping with dark blue ooze.

"Oh! Oh, dear!" the girl cried, her clear eyes flying wide in shock at the sight of his legs dripping jelly. She grabbed for a napkin, and an entirely different sensation crept through Maximilian as he felt a warm hand on his thigh. With no little amazement, he watched as the chit actually tried to wipe the mess from his breeches. Although he suspected that her gentle massaging was only aggravating the stain, he gave himself over to the feel of her fingers stroking him through the thin layer of his clothing.

Holding his breath, Maximilian kept a firm grip on his felines while the lovely young thing muttered her apologies and rubbed him in sweet, anxious movements. He hoped profoundly that his beauty had not noticed the bulge that appeared between his legs. It was all he could do not to lean forward just a little so that her fingers might accidently brush against it.

It was daunting, Maximilian decided, that this girl barely out of the schoolroom could move him so strongly that he felt like taking her right here on the parlor floor. Looking down at that unusual cloud of hair positioned right above his lap, he imagined it: easing her back onto the carpeting and running his hands up those slender ankles to that luscious derriere, holding it tightly as he slid inside her. With a rueful smile, he realized that should he follow his inclinations, no one in the absurd household would probably notice.

He was just wondering how long he should let her continue in her delightful but inappropriate ministrations when a noise broke into his lusty thoughts and there was, one assumed, the vicar, standing in the doorway. "Ah, you have met our dear Charlotte," he said. The man apparently saw nothing incongruous in the sight of his daughter positioned between the thighs of a stranger, which led Maximilian to wonder whether it was a vicarage or a brothel he had stumbled into.

"Oh, Papa!" the aforementioned Charlotte moaned. "Look what I've done." She glanced at Maximilian, saw that he was still clutching the kittens and gasped anew. "Oh, goodness! Let me take those." She put aside the napkin and grabbed the animals, who immediately dug their little claws into her bodice, and Maximilian discovered that her rather drab gown was stretched extremely tightly across a chest that could only be described as lush. Feeling himself harden further, he was thankful that his coat hid the evidence from the vicar.

With difficulty, Maximilian tore his gaze from the girl's straining breasts and took her hand to help her rise. He regretted his gloves in that instant and, like some besotted fool, he held her fingers just a bit longer than necessary. Annoyed with himself, he straightened, only to become aware of his breeches. They clung to him, moist with the fragrance of ripe berries....

Maximilian took a deep breath. It was time to get himself under control. Dropping her hand rather abruptly, he tried to think pious thoughts about the vicar's daughter.

"I have made a mess all over...him!" Charlotte said, all innocent consternation.

"It is quite all right, I assure you," Maximilian replied smoothly. *In fact, I rather enjoyed it.* "It was an accident, after all. I am sorry that you lost the other two creatures you struggled so hard to recover." A mistake that, because the reminder of her previously ignominious position caused her to color from her neck to the top of her head, where small strands of yellow hair curled about her temple delightfully.

That hair. It really was rather amazing, compared to the short tresses and elaborate coiffures popular in London. Maximilian had to admit he had never seen anything like it. It billowed about her, so curly as to be unrestrainable. *Unrestrainable.* Maximilian decided he liked that description and then mentally shook himself. Really, he must be getting old and cork-brained.

"Tsk, tsk," her father said. A slender man with nondescript brown hair, the vicar wore spectacles and a distracted look, but smiled in a friendly manner. "I am sure his lordship can cope with a minor spill. You are Lord Wycliffe, are you not?" he asked.

"Most assuredly," Maximilian answered.

"I am John Trowbridge. We heard you were up at the Great House, and we were hoping for a visit from you."

Charlotte looked from her father to the tall, dark stranger with no little amazement. *This* was Lord Wycliffe? Although they had been expecting him all week, she found it difficult to believe that the devastatingly handsome man before her was the earl. He did not look at all as his reputation had painted him.

Ever since Mr. Hesby's death, they had heard more than their share about Wycliffe. *When Wycliffe gets here, he'll set things aright,* they were told. And the staff up at the Great House were all aflutter, the maids all telling one another, *You had best shape up, my girl, or Wycliffe will set you out upon your ear.* By all accounts, the man was very intelligent, exacting and efficient. He was expected to have the estate running smoothly right away, and the rumors of the improvements planned for the Great House...they were such that he must be swimming in money, and yet he supposedly was the sort who knew where each penny was going—and where it had been.

Consequently, Charlotte had expected someone stuffy and stodgy and *old*, but this man did not look as if he had seen thirty. And he was so *handsome*. He was, without a doubt, the most attractive man she had ever seen. Of course, Charlotte had to admit that her experience with men was limited to the population of Upper Bidwell and its surrounding area, and among the farmers, shopkeepers, retired military men and gentry from neighboring towns, there were none like *him*.

The cut and fabric of his clothes bespoke wealth far beyond the reach of the local residents, and he held himself with a certain elegance, an air that suggested he was accustomed to having his wishes obeyed—and promptly. It lent him a quality that was alluring in itself, but there was more. Mercy, was there more…

He had a broad face balanced by wide, dark, arched brows over great brown eyes, a decent nose, and lips that were full enough to make Charlotte suppress a shiver, though she was not quite sure why. His hair was dark brown, nearly black, and he kept it long, clipped back at the nape of his neck in the most unusual fashion. The only thing that appeared in accord with his reputation was the assessing look he had about him, as if nothing ever missed his shrewd gaze.

One of the kittens climbed upon her shoulder, digging its tiny talons into her, and Charlotte realized she had probably been staring rudely. She looked away in time to see Carrie rush headlong into the room. "Did you find them?" Carrie asked breathlessly. Carrie was always breathless.

"I have two," Charlotte said, handing her younger sister the kittens. "The other two will have to… wait." Charlotte dared not glance toward Lord Wycliffe, for she could already feel the hot blush seep into her cheeks at the memory of her previous position. What he must think of her!

"Shall I see if I can nab them?" The earl's request, in a deep, soothing voice, took Charlotte by surprise. She flashed him a look, but he appeared absolutely serious. This dashing, beautiful man was willing to crawl under the sofa for a kitten.... Charlotte's heart jumped up and turned over in her chest.

"No, thank you, my lord," Charlotte said, quelling Carrie's protest. "They will come out when they grow hungry. They were frightened by Patches. He must have gotten into the house somehow. The dog," she explained.

"We have met," Wycliffe said, his lips curving slightly, and Charlotte's heart leapt again and flopped around like a landed fish. Oh, dear, this was dreadful! If she were going to let the first attractive, titled gentlemen she met turn her inside out, how would she ever get on in London?

"I had better take this tray away..." Charlotte put what was left of the tarts back where they belonged, but a stray glance led her to Wycliffe's wet breeches. Had she actually put her hands there, on his muscular thigh? Charlotte knew it was impossible for her to blush any deeper, so she ducked her head as best she could. "It was very nice to meet you, my lord," she mumbled. "I hope you have a lovely stay."

Stay. The word was on Maximilian's lips, but he called it back, knowing full well he had no business gawking at the girl. He told himself that in but a few days he would be back in London, where there were scores of females, from demireps to ton wives, who would enjoy his ogling—and more. *But they were not the vicar's daughter.*

"You will rejoin us, won't you?" Maximilian heard himself speaking and could not quite believe it. He was definitely not prone to impulsive statements, and he was definitely not the sort to trail after some female like a drooling pup. He frowned.

In response, the girl looked startled, dismayed...reluctant? Maximilian was a little stunned by that. Although he did not consider himself vain, he knew that there were very few women who were not attracted to him. But that was in town, not in an obscure part of Sussex. He reminded himself that he was dealing with a vicar's daughter, a sheltered, innocent child who, despite her lean number of years, had the good sense to be wary of a titled gentleman showing too much interest in her. Perhaps he should try harder. He gave her a charming smile. She returned it, looked decidedly flustered and fled.

Maximilian did not allow his eyes to follow her from the room, but turned his attention to the vicar. "You have seven children, Mr. Trowbridge?"

"Eight," the vicar corrected. "Please sit down. I fear we have become a little lax in our manners here, my lord." Mindful of the pets underneath the sofa and the unsteady look of it, Maximilian took a well-mended armchair. The vicar sat opposite him and beamed proudly. "You cannot have met Sarah, the eldest. She married this past winter and lives in the village now. But you saw the others?"

"Here and there," Maximilian answered dryly.

The vicar chuckled. "They are a hoydenish lot, as well I know, with a tendency to run wild. They miss Lettie's firm but gentle hand," he said, his smile drooping. "Their mother died giving birth to little Jenny."

"I am sorry," Maximilian said.

"So am I, my lord. So am I," the vicar said sadly.

John Trowbridge was a kind man, and if Maximilian was any judge, a good parson who genuinely served his flock, which was not always the case these days. Maximilian tried to keep these points in mind when the man began to exasperate him, for it soon became apparent that Mr. Trowbridge had a deal more heart than sense. He had no head for books, no grasp of the vicarage finances and very little interest in worldly matters of any type. He was just the sort with whom Maximilian had no patience whatsoever.

"Perhaps one of the children could help you with these matters," Maximilian suggested in desperation.

The vicar sighed. "Sarah managed things for years, bless her, but she has her husband's business to concern her now. I cannot expect her to mind my affairs, as well."

"And Charlotte?" Maximilian asked. A pleasant name, but far too plain for the dazzler with the amazing hair.

Trowbridge shook his head with a smile. "Alas, Charlotte has little talent for such things." Maximilian felt his estimation of the girl drop a notch, and yet, he could have sworn that those lovely green eyes brimmed with intelligence. "She is the beauty of the family, our Charlotte," Trowbridge said, as if that was all anyone expected of her. "And she will not be with us long, either."

Maximilian felt his blood rush to his head. Was the girl ill?

"She is to have a season, you know," Trowbridge announced, giving away with his sly grin the first hint of worldly pleasure.

Maximilian's life fluids dropped back into place, leaving him a bit dizzy. Of course, the chit was not going to die. She was simply going to be married off. A season? "A London season?" Maximilian asked with some disbelief.

"Yes," Trowbridge answered, grinning even more widely. "A London season. She has so much of her mother's beauty and more," he said, shaking his head fondly. "She deserves it."

Maximilian found himself both surprised and annoyed by the news—and surprised at his annoyance. Of course, every young thing aspired to a London season, the epitome of the social whirl, even drab country girls. But Charlotte was not drab, and somehow he did not care for the idea of her loose upon the town scene. He was forcibly reminded of tossing a bone to a pack of eager, hungry dogs—hungry male dogs.

"Who will sponsor her?" Maximilian asked, a little more testily than he intended.

"A cousin of mine, Miss Augusta Thurgoode."

Maximilian had never heard of the woman. He cocked his head, considering the vicar intently. "Charlotte will need clothes and money for fal-lals and tickets to sundry entertainments. Are you certain you can afford it all?" he asked bluntly.

Trowbridge smiled gently, apparently undaunted by the personal line of questioning. "Yes. I have a nest egg put by for this."

Maximilian knew, cynically, that the money the vicar had put by was probably his life savings and that it was not going to be tossed away simply to please his daughter. Oh, no, it was an investment. Charlotte was going to London to find herself a suitable husband with income enough not only to support her, but to aid her family.

Why did that rankle? Maximilian knew that even though it resembled procurement, that was the way advantageous matches were obtained. He could tell from the glow of affection in Trowbridge's eye that the vicar would not marry Charlotte off to someone she did not want, but could either the girl or her father be counted on to choose someone suitable?

Maximilian's mind flew to all the eligible bachelors he knew, and the review did nothing to ease his misgivings. He would not consider a one of them for this girl, but then, of course, Charlotte would not be aiming for his circle. She had no chance of gaining a title. A comfortable merchant or military man or a third or fourth son was the best she could hope to gain, despite her beauty.

Of course, Maximilian told himself, he was not familiar with everyone. There had to be plenty of kind, decent, reasonably wealthy young men out there. "You must be sure to give me the direction of your cousin," Maximilian said sharply. "I shall deem it my duty to have a look in on your daughter."

"Thank you, my lord," Trowbridge said, beaming. "How good of you! Of course, from all that we heard about you, we knew that the fortunes of our small corner of the world were going to improve. I cannot tell you how it heartens me to know that you have taken her under your wing."

Maximilian was hard-pressed to keep from guffawing over that one. As if he had any wings under which to take anything, let alone a succulent morsel like Charlotte Trowbridge. The vicar, it seemed, was even more blind to worldliness than Maximilian had thought.

The object of their discussion appeared in the doorway, and Maximilian allowed himself a careless glance at her, which turned into something more lingering. She had tried to restrain her hair by pinning it up, but it was untamable.

Already tiny daffodil curls were escaping, and he was certain it was only a matter of time before it all fell, billowing around her like frothy yellow cream.

If she cut it extremely short, curled it about her face and wore hats or caps she probably would be able to get by in London, but Maximilian was horrified at the thought of taking scissors to that amazing mass of hair. He wondered how it would feel in his hands. It looked soft and fuzzy as the kittens' fur. He crossed his legs uncomfortably. He was becoming a doddering idiot.

The vicar stood. "Charlotte! Imagine your luck. His lordship says he will keep an eye on you in London. You have relieved my mind no end, my lord. Although my cousin is a dear woman, one worries, especially about one's precious daughter...."

Charlotte, Maximilian judged, looked anything but relieved by the news. She looked rather alarmed. He smiled at her, trying his best to look reassuring and not seductive. She appeared flustered, but then did an admirable job of straightening and smiling back at him.

"You will stay for dinner, won't you, my lord?" the vicar asked.

Maximilian pulled out his watch and glanced at the time, surprised to find that the half hour allotted for his visit had come and gone unnoticed. However, it was not late enough to eat. The vicarage, it appeared, gave new meaning to the term "country hours." Maximilian held his smile at that and prepared to give his apologies.

When in the country, he dined every night exactly at seven o'clock. He had approved the week's menus after consultation with the cook at Casterleigh and knew that tonight he would have filet of beef in wine and fresh trout among his courses. He could hardly imagine the poor vicar offering him anything quite as tempting. Considering the state and size of the household, Maximilian pictured watery soup and brown bread.

He decided later that his mistake was in looking at the girl. She was waiting upon his answer with an air of excited expectancy that one simply did not see on the faces of the women in town, and it did something to him. "Yes," Maximilian said. "I would be delighted to join you." Outwardly he smiled; inwardly he cringed. Was someone else using his voice? He never accepted last-minute invitations. His schedule was always planned days in advance and down to the tiniest detail....

Accompanying the vicar into the dining room with as much equanimity as he could muster, Maximilian told himself that the change would do him good. His acquaintances were always complaining that he was too set in his ways, to the point of being obsessed with his own clock. An unplanned evening was just what he needed, Maximilian decided as his gaze followed the back of a blond head, where tendrils of hair were escaping their pins. It would be stimulating to dine with the vicar's family, he thought with a smile. Definitely stimulating.

Chapter Two

Stimulating, hell. It was bedlam.

Unaccustomed to children, Maximilian found the sound of so many eating and talking at once to be nearly unbearable. In his set, anyone underage was relegated to the nursery or public school; they were rarely seen and never heard.

Not so here. The family was all in attendance, and the vicar did little to quiet them. Presiding over the din with a vague smile, John Trowbridge seemed perfectly content to listen to the smallest boy play his spoon against his cup incessantly while the two youths argued in increasingly louder voices.

Maximilian had never seen such disorder. Expecting Charlotte to act like the children's mother, he was a bit surprised that she did not—until he remembered there was an older girl who was married now. Perhaps she had been the one to rein in the family's high spirits. Charlotte, much to his disappointment, did not. Either she was still too much of a girl herself or simply too fun-loving to discipline the group. And when Kit banged on the table and sent his fork flying into the air, she muffled a giggle instead of reprimanding him.

Shocking, Maximilian told himself. Then why did he envy the secret smile she shared with the boy? Charlotte seemed to be avoiding his gaze, and Maximilian found he did not care for it at all. To make matters worse, they had seated him at the opposite end of the table from the vicar, effectively preventing any civilized conversation. And Charlotte, rather than being by his side, where he wanted her, was situated far too distant for his taste.

This, Maximilian decided, was what he got for succumbing to the charms of a pretty young girl. He was surrounded by small children whom he did not even know by name until sometime during the first course when the vicar remembered to introduce them all. Sorting them out by age in his mind, Maximilian tallied them from eldest to youngest as Jane, James, Thomas, Carrie, Kit and Jenny. He put them all to memory, although they seemed to have a hard time addressing him correctly.

"This is Lord Wycliffe," the vicar said. "He owns the Great House now."

"Do you?" Thomas asked, intrigued. Thin and brown-haired, he looked much like his papa.

"You must call him my lord," James, an older version of Thomas, corrected with a superior air.

"I will not!" Thomas protested. He obviously had no intention of doing anything his brother told him to do.

"Dicky says you are richer than a nabob and are going to make the place into a palace!" Kit said.

"Kit!" Jane, who was seated beside the boy, scolded him. Although several years younger than Charlotte, she looked far more serious, perhaps because of her spectacles and the dull-colored locks that were pulled back neatly from her face. "It is not polite to repeat gossip. And you must call him my lord," she hissed under her breath.

"My lord," Kit repeated, eying daggers at his sister.

"*My* lord," said Jenny.

"He is not *your* lord," Kit argued. "He's *a* lord, an earl."

"*My* lord," Jenny repeated stubbornly.

Although not prone to megrims, Maximilian felt a headache coming on. "*My* lord," Jenny said, pushing her plate his way. He looked at her blankly.

"She wants you to cut up her meat for her," Kit explained, grinning toothlessly. After Maximilian dutifully carved up small pieces for the child, he eyed his blond beauty. Although he tried not to frown at her, silently he blamed her for this torture.

When he caught her watching him, however, his mood lifted as if by magic. The odd combination of shyness and openness in her green gaze affected him in a way he did not recognize. How long had it been since he had seen that?

Maximilian shook himself mentally and reminded himself that he saw young girls like her all the time. Marriage-minded mamas were always thrusting them at him, for, despite his orderly ways, or perhaps because of them, he was considered quite a catch. Maximilian dutifully danced once with all of them, be they pretty, plain or ugly, and never gave them another glance. Why should he feel any differently about this one?

Perhaps it was the surroundings. He was not at Almack's, where the fashionable met to dance and arrange marriages, but in a cramped room in the rabbit warren of the vicarage. The freshness of the girl's background added to her charm, Maximilian decided. His interest in her was a passing thing that he likened to viewing the local architecture or studying the flora and fauna. It would disappear soon enough when he was in London.

Meanwhile, dinner was an ordeal to be gotten through. The vicarage did boast at least one servant, Maximilian was relieved to see. Although she appeared hardly old enough to do the job, the rather plain, plump girl smiled happily as if pleased to be part of this menagerie. The food was simple country fare and not too bad, at that, thankfully.

Maximilian was trying to follow a lengthy story about the dog, Patches, as told by Kit, when the littlest one, Jenny, announced she was finished. "All gone," she said. Then she slipped from her chair, came over to him and proceeded to climb onto his lap. As the two older boys were engaged in another argument, moderated by Charlotte, no one even noticed. No one, that is, except Maximilian.

He could not remember ever holding a child, and it was decidedly odd. He gave up all efforts to eat, and sat back in his seat so that she could rest her head comfortably against his chest. What little hair she possessed wafted about her cheeks in soft, blond ringlets, and Maximilian wondered if it would grow to imitate her sister's wild mane.

Although he hesitated to imagine what filth was transferring itself from the rag in her hand to his impeccable clothing, he allowed her to drape it all over his front. She gazed at him with wide, trusting blue eyes, stuck her thumb in her mouth and promptly fell asleep with one little hand gripping both the offending blanket and the edge of his waistcoat. She smelled warm and sweet, like tarts and kittens, and Maximilian put an arm around her, just to make certain she would not fall.

When he glanced up, Charlotte's eyes were upon him, glowing with a new intensity that thoroughly distracted him. She had the oddest expression upon her face, as if she were seeing him for the very first time, but when he met her gaze, she blushed and looked away. He wondered what she had been thinking.

Charlotte was thinking about *him*.

Although she was seemingly engrossed in the dispute between James and Thomas, Charlotte's attention never strayed too far from their guest, and when she saw Jenny approach him, she cringed. Fully expecting a man of the earl's stature to discourage the little girl, Charlotte blinked in astonishment when he cradled Jenny against his chest.

She stared, and at that instant, Charlotte's heart melted into her body, spreading warmth and sweetness to every part of her. A simple, inevitable knowledge seeped through her. *Here was the man she wanted to marry.*

Was this how it happened? One suddenly just *knew*? This morning had been like any other, and yet now she was certain she had found her husband, the supposedly cold and calculating Lord Wycliffe, the same man who was gently holding her three-year-old sister on his lap.

Elated as she was, Charlotte felt dumbfounded. How was she to bring this marriage about? No one had ever really told her. They all expected her to win a proposal because of her face, but she knew there had to be more to it than sitting around looking pretty. She had imagined that during her season she would learn just how it was done, and yet she was not to leave for town until... *He planned to look in on her in London.* That remembered piece of information made Charlotte giddy.

She was well aware of her father's tendency to exaggerate or misinterpret things to reflect his own hopes and desires, yet Wycliffe had not denied his intention to visit her in town. The time that Charlotte had looked forward to all her life immediately took on all sorts of additional possibilities. A season in London... with Wycliffe. It was the stuff of dreams.

Stealing another glance at him, Charlotte marveled at his handsome features. Her eyes traveled along the smooth, clean lines of his hair. If only she could have hair like that, Charlotte thought enviously, instead of her own flyaway mop. It was pulled back from his face, distinctly showing a hairline that was boldly defined, unlike her father's receding one.

She wondered how those dark strands would look released from their thong. She had seen some of the laborers with dirty locks hanging to their shoulders, but Wycliffe's were clean, shining and altogether different. She pictured them flowing about his face and down his back, smooth to the touch...

The warmth that had trickled through her now started heating up her insides, just like a pot put on to boil. Charlotte made a strangled sound, covered it with a cough and dared not look at Wycliffe any more. Were such contemplations sinful? She had never been tempted by the pleasures of the body, as her father referred to them, although she had always been very curious as to what they involved.

When she was younger, she had even sought out kisses from the local boys in an effort to discover what all the fuss was about. She had begun early by once paying her brother James to kiss her, and then had moved on to just about every boy in the neighborhood until Sarah caught her and called her behavior most unseemly. Sarah swore that if she did not stop immediately she would surely come to a bad end like that slattern Lizzy Beaton, who lived in a hovel at the end of the village and suffered from the pox. One look at Lizzy's haggard face had put an end to Charlotte's experimentation right then.

And, in truth, she had never really found out what was so appealing about kissing. She had been on the receiving end of wet, slobbery ones, nervous ones, hard ones and quick pecks. The only one she had even liked was given to her by an older youth traveling with a fair, and he had ruined it by sticking his tongue out in the midst of it.

That memory receded to be replaced by a vision of kissing Wycliffe, which Charlotte imagined would be quite different than all her previous encounters. She thought of those generous lips upon hers, of his tongue touching her, and she was not repulsed but thrilled by the notion. Abruptly, she picked up her napkin and fanned herself.

Maximilian sat back in his chair, oddly relaxed considering the din around him. How the child on his chest could sleep was beyond him, but she was probably quite used to it. Out of the corner of his eye, he saw his beauty fan herself with her napkin. Hot, was she? Then he watched her pink tongue dart out and wet her lips, and his groin immediately leapt to life. Mindful of the child on his lap, he immediately looked away and tried to concentrate on what James and Thomas were fighting about. But deuced if his thoughts didn't keep returning to their older sister.

A banging sounded in the hallway, and he soon heard a female voice calling out, "Hello! Are we interrupting dinner?"

"Sarah!" The middle girls erupted from their seats without another word, and far from scolding them, the vicar smiled indulgently as they raced off, apparently to greet the clan's eldest member.

"We have a guest! Wait until you see him," the younger girl said breathlessly from somewhere behind Maximilian.

"Hush! He'll hear you," she was admonished by Jane. Maximilian could not help it. His lips twitching, he glanced at Charlotte and caught her attention. He was pleased to see that her green eyes seemed to have lost their wariness. They sparkled with amusement, while her mouth, that luscious pink mouth, slowly curved into the most beautiful smile he had ever seen. And it was all for him.

For one long moment, Maximilian basked in the glow of that grin before Charlotte turned away, claimed by one of her siblings. He found it strangely affecting, as if he had been granted an intimacy Charlotte allowed only to her relatives, but he definitely did not feel brotherly.

A whispering and bustling announced that Sarah was entering the room, and Maximilian watched as she moved over to her father and kissed his cheek. A large man, presumably her husband, followed close behind her with an armful of parcels and stared curiously at Maximilian.

"Ah, Sarah and Alf," the vicar said, beaming proudly. "What a nice surprise."

"I hope we are not intruding," Sarah said. She did not look at all like Charlotte, but resembled Jane, with her mousy hair, rather plain features and heavy, dark brows.

"Not at all," Trowbridge protested. "Pull up some chairs and join us for dessert. I believe Molly has some wonderful pastries prepared. Oh, and you must meet our guest, Lord Wycliffe, the new owner of the Great House."

Maximilian did not feel slighted by the vicar's afterthought introduction. Oddly enough, it made him seem a part of this big, unruly family. "I would stand, but..." he said, motioning with his free hand toward the bundle on his chest.

"Oh! Let me put her to bed," Sarah said with a startled frown. Maximilian knew a moment's disappointment when she reached toward the sleeping child. He was not sure if he liked the eldest member of the dynasty. He suspected she was a deal too serious, then caught himself. Since when did he find anyone too serious?

Something about Sussex made him as queer as Dick's hatband, Maximilian noted as he gave up his charge to the authoritative Sarah. The child hardly stirred as Sarah lifted her into capable arms, and Maximilian sat up straighter, in a position more befitting his dignity.

Sarah's husband, a strapping young man with a plain but friendly countenance, pulled up a chair near him, and Maximilian was thankful for the presence of another adult. Conversation, at least, he thought with relief. It was short-lived.

"This is Alf Smith, Sarah's husband," Charlotte said.

"Pleased to meet you, my lord," Alf said.

These were the only words he spoke.

Alf Smith nodded at his wife when she returned and then plunged into the pastry set before him as though it demanded his complete attention. Sarah sat by Charlotte, and Maximilian heard the older one complain affectionately, "Look at him. You would never know that he just put away several meat pies and a loaf of bread. The man takes in food like a furnace needs firing," she said proudly.

Maximilian gathered that Alf's appalling gluttony was looked upon with favor in this part of the country, or perhaps only by Sarah, for Charlotte, though smiling, did not look impressed. He hoped he need not display unmannerly eating habits to win his beauty, for the sight of Alf was repugnant to his sensibilities.

Win her? Now he was going around the bend. Perhaps it was the pathetic excuse for claret that Trowbridge was serving him. It made him light-headed, Maximilian decided. The girl was a vicar's daughter, nothing more, nothing less, and good for an evening's mild diversion. To prove it to himself, he sent a calculating glance her way, but it settled upon the curve of her pink lips as she gifted one of the boys with her warm smile. Delicious, he thought before dropping his gaze for the briefest of moments to where her bodice stretched tightly across breasts straining to be released. Oh, to release them . . .

"My lord!" James's insistent voice brought him from the contemplation of Charlotte, and he was drawn into a discussion of horseflesh with the youngster, precipitating many an argument with the boy's brother Thomas.

After eating three portions of pastry, Alf seemed momentarily sated, and Maximilian felt able to stand up beside him without fear of losing a digit to the fellow's wolfish appetite. They all moved into the parlor then, and in the process, Maximilian was able to maneuver himself beside the object of his attentions.

"No!"

"Yes!"

"It is not the same!"

"Yes, it is!"

The voices of James and Thomas preceded them as they made their way across the hallway. "Do they ever agree upon anything?" Maximilian asked, leaning close.

Charlotte smiled. *Oh, what a smile.* Full, smooth lips over straight white teeth... She, in turn, leaned toward him, and Maximilian was emboldened to bend nearer. "Papa has forbidden any fisticuffs and ordered them to work out their disagreements with civilized discussion," she whispered. Her green eyes glittered with laughter, and he could tell she did not share her father's opinion in this matter.

"An all-out brawl might be preferable to this incessant squabbling," Maximilian said.

"My thoughts exactly," she answered, her mouth twitching at the corner. Again, that shared bit of humor made him feel a bond with her that was pleasing, unique and rather unsettling.

When they reached the parlor, the youngest ones were sprawled upon the floor, already playing at checkers. Sarah and her husband had taken the settee, and the older children the chairs, leaving Maximilian and his beauty the sofa. Although the arrangement suited him well enough, he eyed the ancient piece critically, wondered if it would support his weight and hoped that the felines were no longer underneath it.

Maximilian eased himself down slowly. It felt sturdy. He let out a breath and answered Sarah's polite questions about the Great House. Her husband, obviously having filled his stomach, abandoned all sense of obligation and promptly fell asleep, his arm on the settee behind her and his head back. As everyone appeared to ignore it, Maximilian assumed that this was normal behavior for Alf. He suppressed any desire to laugh at the absurd but charming household.

Despite the proximity of his beauty, Maximilian found himself able to speak little to her, and for a time he simply watched the tableau unfold about him while Sarah talked about her day at the shop. Looking out over the parlor filled with children, Maximilian felt an odd sense of unity, and for the first time in his life he actually thought about his own children.

Naturally, he was expected to marry and produce an heir. It was his duty, but Maximilian felt in no hurry about the matter. He had scheduled it, as he did all the things in his life. Marriage sometime in his thirtieth year, he had planned, which meant he did not even have to begin searching for his bride for another year. At eight and twenty, he was content to let the subject lie, and he certainly had not contemplated his issue.

And yet... As he watched the faces of the Trowbridge youngsters, the interchanges between these diverse personalities intrigued him. There were arguments, but there were also loyalty and respect and great affection here. Maximilian suddenly thought of producing children, plural.

Although large families were the norm, in his there had been only himself. His mother, having done her duty, swore that she would carry no more infants. Pregnancy made her ill and fat and unable to entertain. After all, she had her priorities...

Maximilian stifled the surprising surge of bitterness that welled up inside him. Instead, he tried to imagine the family apartments at Wycliffe filled with laughing, mischievous youths. It was a very interesting image, not the least because in his mind, the girls all had flyaway blond curls.

"Oh, Charlotte, I have a book for you from Mr. Lynchworth. He stopped in today and wanted me to lend it to you," Sarah said, drawing Maximilian's attention. Digging into her parcels, she produced a slim volume for her sister.

"What is it?" Maximilian asked. To his surprise, Charlotte refused to look at him. Evidencing an obvious reluctance to show it to him, she laid the book beside her skirt, so that it was hidden from his view.

"Mr. Lynchworth often shares one of his finds with me," Charlotte explained in a strained tone.

"Ah," Maximilian said, smiling. "The newest Gothic perhaps? Is it *The Mysterious Abbey* or *The Travails of Trevlyne?*"

Apparently provoked by his teasing, Charlotte sent him a thoroughly disgusted scowl, which upon her lovely features was quite endearing. Maximilian was truly puzzled. He knew many a female who read novels, but few who took such umbrage at being discovered. What was she hiding?

Although he could easily have reached across her lap and retrieved the mysterious item, courtesy demanded that he not, so he only leaned back with a questioning gaze. Charlotte responded with a frown that projected both annoyance and dread. Then, emitting a sigh that was nothing short of exasperated, she handed him the volume.

Maximilian glanced at the title and felt a start of surprise. "*The Plays of Sophocles?*" he asked in wonder. For a moment, he suspected that she knew of his regard for classical literature, but what could she hope to gain by pretending interest in such things?

He opened the book and, to his utter astonishment, found it written in the original Greek. A jolt of excitement leapt through him. He cocked his head to one side and trained his gaze on the lovely face beside him. "You read Greek?" he asked, a little more firmly than he intended.

Charlotte lifted her chin as if she were defending a secret vice. "Yes, I do," she answered, returning his gaze with her clear one. "Papa tutors all his children well, I will have you know, whether they are sons or daughters." Her green eyes blazed with challenge, as if she expected him to argue her right to the knowledge.

"And you are interested in the work of Sophocles?" Maximilian asked. Although he kept his features schooled, he suspected that his taut voice betrayed his emotion. Was there truly a woman alive who cared about the intricacies of his study?

"Yes," Charlotte said, unflinching. "I recently read Euripides on the death of Menoeceus, which fueled my interest in Antigone." She appeared to be quite angry now, her pale cheeks flushing most becomingly.

Maximilian felt like grabbing her by the arms and kissing her soundly on the mouth. But for their audience, he might have. Instead, he grinned. "I am considered something of a scholar myself," he said. "I have an extensive library at Wycliffe Place, my family seat, and would be happy to lend you any works that you are seeking."

Charlotte blinked at him, blond lashes fluttering over her spring eyes as if she had scarcely heard him aright. He realized that she was utterly astonished by his reaction. Did she think he would frown upon her for being a bluestocking? He was not a fashionable idiot who held contempt for anyone intelligent. He loved learning and found smart women appealing.

"Oh, no," groaned Carrie. "Not another one! We shall hear nothing but babbling about ancient legends all evening. Papa, you simply must not allow it."

"Carrie!" Sarah admonished.

"But he sounds just like Charlotte—wild about all those old stories," Carrie protested. She put her hands over her ears dramatically. "I shall not listen!"

"I fear it is my fault," the vicar said, grinning happily. "I did enjoy my classic history, and I tried to pass it on to the children. So far, Charlotte seems to be the only one to share my interest."

Maximilian looked at his beauty with new eyes. And he had thought her dim because she had no head for accounts! She was anything but dim. She was everything . . . Maximilian shook himself mentally. He was letting himself be carried away. So, the chit read Greek and shared his par-

ticular affection for mythology. She was still a simple vicar's daughter, a country girl barely out of the schoolroom,
no matter how intense her instruction. Still...

"Papa, it is too late to talk about studies," James complained.

"Yes," Thomas agreed. Maximilian was so stunned to
find the two youths in accord that he stared at them, and
they took immediate advantage of his attention. "Tell us
about London, my lord. Have you ever seen a boxing
match?"

"Are you a member of the Four in Hand Club?" James
cut in.

"I expect that your horses are the finest, are they not?"
asked Thomas.

"Yes, yes and yes," Maximilian answered with a smile.
Swallowing a bit of regret at not being able to talk solely
with his beauty, he sat back and entertained the boys with
such tales of town life as were suitable to the vicarage parlor.

Although he tried to keep his gaze upon the youths, every
so often he became aware of green eyes tracing his features.
Stretching out a booted foot, Maximilian glanced at the
hands Charlotte held together in her lap. He remembered
them as pale and slim, but they were not particularly dainty.
Capable hands, he thought, capable of... He stopped his
mind from going further. Then he caught a whiff of her, a
lilac scent...

Maximilian focused firmly upon James and Thomas, and
before he knew it, Sarah was rounding the children up for
bedtime. He pulled out his watch and glanced at the time in
surprise. He often allotted himself a half hour for a visit
only to watch it tick by slowly, but tonight hours had flown
by without his notice. It was highly unusual, as the entire
evening had been. He stood. "Thank you for a delightful
dinner and lively conversation," he said to the vicar.

"It is we who must thank you," Trowbridge said with a
smile. "You have given the boys something to talk about for
weeks. We have all enjoyed your company."

"And I yours," Maximilian said politely, his gaze taking in all of them. Could he help it if his eyes lingered a bit longer on Charlotte than upon any of the others?

"You must feel free to stop in at any time, my lord," the vicar said, patting him familiarly on the arm. Maximilian looked at the hand, thin but firm, that rested upon him, and wondered if the vicar had any idea how unique his gesture was. People did not often reach out to the Earl of Wycliffe. It was oddly comforting to know that in some places, he was as warmly received as . . . Alf.

Sarah was trying to rouse her large husband, who sat up suddenly and grunted, "Good night, my lord." Restraining his amusement, Maximilian responded with a goodbye and a nod to the married couple.

He wanted to kiss Charlotte's hand, but thought it inappropriate in this informal setting, so he simply looked at her. Her earlier wariness had disappeared, and she returned his gaze with sparkling eyes. "Charlotte," he said. "It has been a . . . pleasure."

She blushed, perhaps with the memory of their meeting, but she had the boldness to smile at him anyway. It was nearly his undoing. He felt an odd, sharp stab of regret that they had not discussed their mutual interest, but there was no place in his life for the fresh-faced beauty.

Maximilian took one long, last admiring look at her. Charlotte was a remarkable combination of loveliness, innocence and intelligence, and he had enjoyed their encounter. Very rarely did a woman catch his attention so markedly, and when she did, Maximilian usually arranged to make her his mistress. In this case, unfortunately, such a possibility was not open to him. However he might wish otherwise, it was simply unthinkable.

She was, after all, the vicar's daughter.

Chapter Three

Charlotte stood staring after Wycliffe, immobilized by the elegant ease with which he moved. He possessed a particularly masculine grace that she had never seen in anyone before, and she found her gaze traveling from his broad shoulders down to the muscular legs she had wiped clean of tarts.

When he had disappeared around a bend in the hallway, Charlotte returned to the parlor, plopped down on the sofa and lifted her palms to her heated cheeks. Glancing at Sarah, who still stood in the doorway, she asked, a little breathlessly, "Is he not splendid?"

Sarah eyed her sister keenly. She had seen that look on Charlotte's face many times before. Specifically, she remembered when little Charlotte had jumped off the roof of the shed with her papa's umbrella, certain that she would float down; when Papa told Charlotte there was little more he could teach her about the classics; and when Charlotte had declared her curiosity about kissing. The last recollection dragged Sarah forcibly to the present.

Shooing Alf from the room, she instructed him to see that the boys washed up properly before bed. "Tell the girls I will be up to tuck them in a few minutes," she added. Then she turned to her sister. "Yes," she answered matter-of-factly. "Lord Wycliffe is quite splendid."

"Oh, Sarah," Charlotte said. Leaning back against the worn sofa, she raised her hands above her head in an expressive gesture. "He is beyond anything!"

"Of course he is," Sarah said, taking a chair near her sister. "He is an earl, and handsome and wealthy, as well. That would certainly qualify him on all counts as beyond our experience."

Charlotte suddenly sat up straight, as if seized by a thought, and Sarah felt a surge of trepidation. She schooled her face to calm, however, and leaned toward her sister.

"Oh, Sarah," Charlotte whispered, her lovely features aglow. "All my life I have looked forward to this spring. Even when I was little, I remember being told that if Cousin Augusta remained alive and willing, I would have a London season. You know how much I've longed for it. But Sarah," Charlotte added, her voice hushed, "I think I would even give up my season...if I could only have *him*."

Sarah hid her stab of panic well. She smiled at her sister gently. "A lovely dream, Charlotte, but a dream, all the same," she said. "Men like Lord Wycliffe do not marry the daughters of impoverished vicars."

Charlotte appeared to be stunned by that information, and Sarah knew a bit of envy for her sister's self-assurance. In truth, Charlotte had never viewed anything as impossible, but charged on ahead, supremely confident of her plans, even if she ended up with naught but a broken umbrella and a sprained ankle. "But you and Papa have always said I must find a husband to provide a handsome living for us all," Charlotte protested.

"My dear," Sarah said, "there is quite a difference between a handsome living and the boundless wealth of Lord Wycliffe." Sarah paused to choose her words carefully, for she did not wish to present Charlotte with even a hint of a challenge. She had learned a painful lesson about her sister over the years. If you told Charlotte that she *could not,* she was sure to try to prove you wrong.

Sarah had no intention of telling Charlotte that she would be unable to catch Wycliffe's interest, for Charlotte would be certain to get that determined look in her eye. And all her sister's beauty and resolve and intelligence would serve her little in such a hopeless endeavor.

Papa and Charlotte might thrive upon dreams and legends, but Sarah was the practical member of the family. She knew that the Lord Wycliffes of the world did not marry fortuneless nobodies straight from the schoolroom, no matter how lovely and nice they might be. "You can be sure that he will marry only a rich lady with an impressive lineage," Sarah said. "And that is as it should be."

Charlotte appeared to be mulling over Sarah's advice, and Sarah pressed her advantage. "Forget about our handsome visitor," she urged her sister. "You will find plenty of other fellows to suit your fancy in London. They may not have titles, but they will be good, solid, dependable men, more than willing to provide for you and your family."

Charlotte looked up at her sister and stopped herself from pulling a face just in time. *Solid. Dependable.* The terms held no allure for her, for they described Sarah's dull husband Alf and not the elegant, stimulating and oh-so-attractive Lord Wycliffe. Just the thought of him made her heart dance merrily in her chest.

What did Sarah know? Sarah had always been wary of anything beyond her experience, and she had acquired an unreasoning distrust of the nobility, probably from some of Alf's more discontented relatives.

Although Charlotte normally trusted Sarah's judgment, she did not want to believe that Wycliffe was not meant for her. She remembered kneeling between his thighs, overcome by shivers of excitement when she touched him. She had watched him hold her littlest sister with unexpected gentleness, and she had seen his handsome features grow taut with the thrill of their shared interest. He was the only man besides her father and dear, doddering Mr. Lynchworth who did not frown upon her studies!

To her mind, the entire encounter smacked of fate, but she knew better than to say as much to practical Sarah.

"Girls, are you still in the parlor?" The sound of their father's voice brought their heads up.

"I am sorry, Charlotte," Sarah said, leaning close to pat her hand, "but you had better set your sights a bit lower. Lord Wycliffe moves in circles far beyond the reach of the rest of us."

Charlotte frowned at her sister's choice of words. They made him seem so...unattainable. "Like one of the gods," she whispered.

"Yes, I suppose so," Sarah said. "Like one of the gods in the stories you like so well." She smiled, dismissing the subject of Lord Wycliffe easily as she greeted Papa.

Charlotte smiled, too, but it was a small, secret one that she hugged to herself, for she knew that even the gods were known, on occasion, to take mortal wives.

Maximilian looked at his schedule. He was to leave on the morrow, and he had accomplished all that he had intended within the allotted period of time. He had installed one of his own people to oversee the property with the help of some of the former staff. In a few months, the house would be up to his strict requirements, and the estate would be running like a well-oiled gear.

This afternoon was set aside for whatever extraneous details might need his attention, but he could think of nothing his steward could not handle. That left him with free time upon his hands, which he could use to catch up on his correspondence . . . or go out.

Abruptly, Maximilian imagined making a return visit to the vicarage. He scowled, drumming his fingers on the desk as he considered the notion. Although he had tried to dismiss Charlotte from his mind, she kept returning to his thoughts. It was ridiculous! He had wasted enough time admiring her last night while suffering through that interminable meal with all those children making so much noise. There was no earthly reason he should go back...other than to say his farewells.

The well-worn path to the vicarage door was familiar now, but Patches did not rush at him, and the yard was strangely quiet. He knocked, suddenly hoping that Charlotte would be in. He had never considered that she would not be there, and now he was struck with the possibility of spending a dull afternoon with the vicar. He pulled out his watch and checked the time. One half hour, he told himself. Then he would leave.

He did not have to worry. The door was opened by his beauty herself. Dressed in a simple sprigged muslin gown and carrying a basket, she looked fresh as morning dew. When she lighted up like a ray of sunshine at the sight of him, Maximilian felt a rush of pure pleasure. "My lord, how delightful to see you again," she said, smiling brightly.

"The pleasure is mine…Charlotte," he said, savoring her name like a bit of fine wine. She blushed rosily, but held his gaze, both of them very aware of the intimacy granted him by the use of her given name. Then the hall erupted around her.

"I'm ready!" called Kit, racing toward them and nearly plowing into Charlotte's skirts. Carrie followed a bit more sedately.

"We were just on our way to the village," Charlotte explained.

"Let me drive you," Maximilian offered, gazing into clear eyes the color of spring buds.

"That would be lovely," she said, returning his regard. The children seemed to fade into the distance, leaving just his beauty with her green eyes and luscious lips. Her hair was tucked up under a beribboned straw hat, but Maximilian's twinge of disappointment was tempered by the sensual knowledge that the blond glory so hidden could be released with just a flick of the brim.

"Are you lame?" Carrie burst out abruptly. Startled, Maximilian looked down to see her staring at his elaborately carved, silver-headed walking stick.

"Don't be a noddycock!" said Kit. "That's an af-fectation."

Before Maximilian could respond to the apparently unintentional slight, James's voice boomed out from down the hallway. "If his lordship is driving you, I want to come, too," he shouted.

"Me, too!" echoed Thomas.

"Me, too!" Carrie said, more softly.

Charlotte shook her head and turned around. "It is time for your studies, James, Thomas and Carrie," she said firmly, herding them along the hall like so many goats. "Go on now and tell Papa that his lordship is driving us to the village. Come along, Kit." Just then Jenny toddled out of a room toward them.

"*My* lord," she chanted. "*My* lord." Halting at Maximilian's knees, she raised her arms upward, her blue eyes wide.

"She wants you to pick her up," Kit explained.

Setting aside the walking stick with a grimace, Maximilian reached down and lifted Jenny, settling her into the curve of his arm where she snuggled very nicely to him. He registered her warmth and her smell and the feel of her small arms snaking around his neck. Then he glanced at Charlotte to gauge her reaction.

Somehow, Maximilian thought his odd delight in the child was noticeable—and laughable—but Charlotte was not amused. She was blinking at him in surprise. He grinned. She smiled, and that shared moment sustained him through the effort of getting everyone situated in the curricle.

Charlotte sat up beside him, resting the basket upon her lap, while Jenny nestled between them. To Kit's utter delight, he was elevated to the position of tiger and rode at the back of the vehicle.

Charlotte found herself wishing that the village was not so close, so that she could be near Maximilian and watch him handle the reins forever. The hat shaded her eyes a little, so she found herself able to leisurely peruse his wide shoulders, his broad chest and his muscular thighs without seeming too bold. He was not a big man, like Alf, but tall and perfectly proportioned, Charlotte decided, her heart leaping like an acrobat.

All too quickly, Wycliffe maneuvered the curricle in front of Alf and Sarah's shop. He removed his driving gloves and jumped down easily, displaying the grace that Charlotte so admired. Then he lifted his arms to help her down.

For a moment, Charlotte could do naught but stare at his outstretched hands, strong and lean, with long, slender fingers. They dazzled her. When she finally remembered to stand, Charlotte completely forgot about the basket in her lap until it tipped forward, drawing her attention. She squeaked out a warning even as she watched the entire container of fresh eggs head toward Wycliffe. He grabbed for it and caught it in his competent hands, but not before an egg launched itself at his shoulder and broke along the seam of his chest.

Arrogant disdain oozing from every pore, the Earl of Wycliffe glared at the pieces of shell while yellow yoke dripped down his well-cut coat of blue superfine.

"Oh!" Scrambling down, Charlotte pulled the napkin from the basket and wiped at the mess on Wycliffe's shoulder. He was so tall that she had to lift her hand high to reach his broad shoulder. It was well-muscled, for no telltale lumps of padding bunched beneath the taut material under her fingers. Leaning closer, she absently rested her other hand upon his chest to steady herself. She was unaware of the gesture until a change in his breathing made her glance at his face.

"Thank you, Charlotte. That is quite enough," Wycliffe said, releasing a slow smile that somehow spoke volumes to her body. Every fiber in her being jumped to attention, as if being called into service, and she stepped back hurriedly, lifting her fingers from his embroidered waistcoat. Deliberately, she looked away from his features to the stain on his shoulder. It did not seem too noticeable, but the smell soon would not be pleasant.

"We shall see if Sarah can wash it out for you at the shop," Charlotte said.

"No, Charlotte. We most assuredly will not," Wycliffe said, the ghost of that smile lingering to wreak havoc among her senses.

"But, my lord, I fear that as the day wears on, you will...ripen," Charlotte protested. She peeked up at him and caught the startled look on his face before he laughed, a sound deep and rich and pleasing to the ear.

"Then you will be forced to endure my malodorous company as your punishment for pelting me with eggs," Wycliffe said, his eyes and mouth teasing. "Are you naturally clumsy, Charlotte, or is it only me you have targeted?"

"It is only you," she said carelessly, reaching up to help Jenny. As she set the child down, Charlotte caught herself. "I mean, it is just that you seem to have a particular...an affect... You discompose me, my lord. We are not used to such elegant gentlemen here in Upper Bidwell," Charlotte explained, not daring to even turn toward him.

"Do I have to get off now?" Kit called, and Charlotte loosed a low sigh of relief at being saved from further embarrassment by his complaint.

"Yes! Be careful, and stay with us, please," she said as her brother darted past.

Maximilian cocked his head, eyeing Charlotte as she spoke to Kit. Deuced if she was not the most interesting creature. Of course, his question had not been fair or proper, but he had never expected her to answer him truthfully. He was accustomed to simpering, flirting females who used the language of subterfuge, not Charlotte's fresh openness. He discomposed her, did he? The notion pleased him immensely.

Flushed a delightful pink, she sent him a swift smile and headed toward the shop owned by her sister's husband. They stepped inside the dim, crowded building, which appeared to contain nearly everything a villager could want, from a paper of pins to a side of bacon. Coming face-to-face with a cured ham, Maximilian stepped back, neatly side-stepping Charlotte. "Sort of puts one off one's taste for pork, doesn't it?" he asked.

"Oh, do not say so," Charlotte admonished. "This is why we have one of the best laid tables in the village," she whispered, leaning close. "Papa has often said that Sarah did us all a great service by marrying Alf."

As soon as the words left her mouth, Charlotte blinked at him and then looked away, her brow furrowed, her frown pensive. Before Maximilian had a chance to reflect on her shift in mood, Kit mumbled something and raced off behind the counter, and Sarah came toward them. Although her smile was friendly enough, she eyed him a bit warily. Did she think he would soil her beautiful sister? Stupid chit. It was more the other way around, Wycliffe decided. Charlotte was always dousing him with foodstuffs.

"Hello, Sarah! Wasn't it good of his lordship to drive us in?" Charlotte asked, smiling in his direction. Sarah nodded, although she obviously was not enthused. The feeling is mutual, Maximilian thought uncharitably, for he was not enthused to be standing in a village shop holding a basket of eggs like some plowboy from his fields.

"Here are the day's eggs," Charlotte said, taking the basket from Maximilian. "Minus one. Would you please wash out a spot in his lordship's coat?"

Maximilian's fingers twitched imperceptibly. Ignoring Sarah's questioning look, he took Charlotte's arm gently but firmly and pulled her aside. He gazed into her upturned face, sweet and dismayed, his features set. "I am not removing my coat."

Charlotte blinked at him in surprise. "Botheration!" she said. His lordship obviously was stubborn. "A wet cloth then, Sarah, please," she called to her sister.

When Sarah handed her the towel, Charlotte wiped his shoulder again. "You need not stand upon such strict propriety with me, my lord," she scolded as she worked at the stain.

Wycliffe's fingers wrapped around her wrist like steel bands, and so quickly that she had no time to react. She looked up, startled, into his handsome face. His thick, nearly black brows lowered over his eyes as if he were angry. "Yes, I do. And I expect everyone else to do the same," he said in an oddly threatening tone. His voice was low, his features harsh. "Perhaps you are accustomed to such behavior in Upper Bidwell, but I do not want to hear of anyone in London removing his coat in your presence. Do you understand me?" he asked.

Charlotte stared into his great brown eyes, dark with some nameless emotion, and swallowed. "Yes, my lord," she answered meekly. She dropped her hand from his shoulder, and he released her wrist. "Is it so very scandalous?" she asked, wide-eyed.

"Maybe not here, but in town, yes," Wycliffe said. "Young girls like yourself must behave within rigid boundaries, or you may find your reputation blackened beyond repair and all your father's investment gone to naught," he said roughly as he stepped back.

Charlotte hid the smile that tugged at her mouth while she ducked her head and turned. Wycliffe's proprietary air sent a surge of hope trilling through her blood. Perhaps Sarah was wrong, and the deity before her might take a simple mortal such as herself to wife.

"Ah, Mr. Green," Sarah said. "Nice to see you out and about again. Is your leg still paining you?"

"Yes, but thank you for asking," said the rotund villager. He turned to smile at Charlotte and Jenny and gazed curiously at Wycliffe. "Now who is that you have with you, Charlotte?" he asked.

"My lord, this is Mr. Green, our haberdasher. Mr. Green, this is Lord Wycliffe, the new owner of the Great House," Charlotte said.

"My lord!" Green said heartily. "It is a pleasure to meet you. I have heard nothing but good about you, and that is a fact. I have a cousin in London, and as soon as he became aware of the sale, he wrote to me. You could not have yourself a better neighbor, he said, and that is a fact. Lord

Wycliffe is a fine young man, a solid, dependable sort, he said.''

With a slow smile, Charlotte looked straight at Sarah, who pursed her lips and frowned a warning. Charlotte ignored it. Her heart was bouncing about the ceiling. If Mr. Green said Wycliffe was solid and dependable, what possible objection could Sarah have to him? That he was too rich? Too aristocratic? Charlotte grinned happily.

''Thank you, Mr. Green. I am sure my association with Upper Bidwell will be a long and profitable one for us both,'' Wycliffe said.

''Very good, very good,'' Mr. Green said, beaming. ''Hope to see you again, my lord. Stop in my business at any time. I will give you a good price on any of my merchandise. See if I don't!''

Kit chose that moment to emerge at top speed from somewhere in the back of the shop, his mouth full of candy, and they all bid their farewells. Outside in the pale spring sunlight, Charlotte looked at her lord with adoration. ''See how happy everyone is to meet you! We should introduce you to the rest of the residents.''

''Entirely unnecessary, I assure you,'' Wycliffe said dryly. ''Besides,'' he added, leaning close, ''I cannot have them saying that I smell like rotten eggs.''

''*My* lord, *my* lord.'' Jenny was tugging at Wycliffe's hand, and when she gained his attention, she pointed a stubby finger across the street to the pastry shop. Charlotte watched in amusement, waiting for Wycliffe's reaction.

''Aha! You want to go there, do you?'' he asked, leaning over to address the little girl. Jenny nodded solemnly. ''Since I can deny a beautiful lady nothing, you shall have your wish.'' Charlotte made a scoffing noise as he took Jenny's hand, and he glanced at her sharply. ''Are you maligning me, my dear girl?'' he asked.

Charlotte did not demur, but began walking toward the shop. Had he really called her ''his dear''? Struggling to maintain the light, bantering air, she rolled her eyes heavenward. "What fiddle-faddle!" she said. "To spout such nonsense when you cannot even remove your coat for me."

"My dear Charlotte, I vow you have me blushing!" Wycliffe teased. "But if you are truly that insistent upon seeing me in my shirtsleeves, perhaps we can arrange something."

Charlotte felt a rush of warmth. Although she knew he was only joking, the suggestion conjured up a variety of visions from Wycliffe without his coat to Wycliffe without even his shirt. What would his chest look like? Feel like? Blushing furiously, Charlotte was thankful they had reached the shop.

"Hello, Charlotte, Kit, Jenny," called a red-faced man, wiping his hands upon his apron.

"Hello!" Charlotte answered. "My lord, this is Mr. MacGregor. Mr. MacGregor, this is Lord Wycliffe, the new owner of the Great House."

"My lord, a pleasure!" Mr. MacGregor said. "I hear that you are doing up the place proper. It is a shame that old Mr. Hesby let it go so long, but now it will be better than ever, or so I have heard."

Wycliffe smiled and nodded. "It is a fine house."

"*My* lord, *my* lord," Jenny said, tugging at his arm.

"Oh, is he now, little Jenny?" asked Mr. MacGregor, leaning over to speak to the girl. "A bit old for you, I would say, but not for your lovely sister, eh?" Much to Charlotte's dismay, Mr. MacGregor winked at her before he picked out a tiny cake for Jenny. "Your favorite, miss, and what will you have today, Kit?"

"You are really going to have to control that tendency to blush, if you are ever to become a success in town," Wycliffe whispered. Charlotte darted a startled glance at him and ordered a sugared biscuit while he laughed softly. She felt like pummeling his chest with her fists for teasing her so, but decided that such antics might be frowned upon by a member of the nobility.

Instead, she stuck her tongue out at him when Mr. MacGregor was not looking. She was unprepared for the intense look she received in return. Wycliffe stared at her, the strangest expression on his face, and then looked away. "Why do you always refer to the manor as the Great House?" he asked when she had finished eating. "Its name, I believe, is Casterleigh."

"No one ever calls it that," Charlotte said, dusting off her fingers. "Casters haven't lived there for years upon years, and besides, no one ever liked them, anyway. The village held a grudge against them and never called the manor by name."

She bent down to wipe cake from Jenny's face. "Perhaps you can give it a new name," she suggested. Glancing up, she smiled at him only to be startled by his intent regard. His big, dark eyes were focused on her straining bodice. Charlotte stood up quickly, and he moved to the door, holding it open for them.

"I think not," Wycliffe said, "for I shall probably not be in residence very often." Charlotte turned sharply, searching his face. Was he jesting? "It is very nice here, to be sure, but Casterleigh is one of many small holdings of mine. I am most often in London or at my seat," he explained.

"But all your plans for the Great House..." Charlotte protested.

"Naturally, I like to make it comfortable for those times that I do visit, but I have many small manors like it," Wycliffe said. Jenny was lagging behind, and he stooped to pick her up.

Charlotte felt a sudden pang of envy for her sister. Watching Wycliffe smooth the child's blond curls, she wondered, dizzily, what it would be like to feel those fingers threading through her own hair. She swallowed hard and tore her gaze away. The Great House...small? "Your seat, Wycliffe Place, is much larger?" she asked, with no little skepticism.

"Yes," Wycliffe answered absently. "My great-grandfather built the original, but, of course, there have been many additions over the years. *Balanced* additions," he noted, slanting a look at her. "Not a hodgepodge like some of these country places. It is quite beautiful, actually, thirty-two bedrooms and lots of modern baths. Father had water piped upstairs."

Charlotte was not even listening, but following along blindly beside him. She had seen drawings of the palaces and such, but *thirty-two* bedrooms! It was beyond anything she had ever imagined. It was...monstrous. For the first time since having her talk with Sarah, Charlotte suspected her elder sister might have a point. Wycliffe was above her touch, above all their touches.

Charlotte knew herself to be dreadfully stubborn. Strong-willed, her father, bless him, called it. All too often, she seized an idea and stuck with it, resolved to see it through, not always with the best of consequences. This time, Charlotte decided, she might do better to change her course.

Although she could easily picture herself in Wycliffe's arms, she could not envision herself as the mistress of Wycliffe Place. It was intimidating to a girl who had never been intimidated by anything.

Sarah was right, Charlotte acknowledged. She was nothing more than a wet goose to consider herself a fitting wife for Wycliffe. Charlotte felt her throat clog up with tears, and she sniffed when they reached his curricle. The bright, shiny vehicle, with its prime horses champing at their bits, seemed to mock her.

Wycliffe was handsome and wonderful and beyond anything, but he was not for her. All a poor country miss could hope for from the Earl of Wycliffe was friendship, a pale imitation of what she had desired, but better than nothing. With grim determination, Charlotte abandoned the dozens of half-formed plans she had made.

They would be friends only.

Chapter Four

Maximilian lingered over coffee as he went over his lists in the dining hall of Casterleigh. He was scheduled to depart at noon, a half hour away yet, but his attention kept wandering from his trip to his surroundings. Dark walls were hung with hunting portraits and heavy draperies covered the windows, making the room a dreary place. Maximilian found that he craved light and made a note to remind his architect that the windows of the old house were to be used to their best advantage.

"My lord." His thoughts were interrupted by the appearance of the butler, one of the staff members he had retained. "Yes, what is it, Richardson?"

"Miss Trowbridge is here to see you," the butler said, a slight twitch of his lips giving away his amusement. Impudent rascal! Maximilian did not like the man above half. He preferred his butlers to be staid, silent and unsmiling. "Shall I show her in?"

Show her in? Charlotte? Here, alone? Maximilian was momentarily at a loss. He frowned and drummed his fingers upon the table. He did not like surprises, nor did he favor unexpected guests, especially at his breakfast table. However, a flash of pink behind Richardson forced his decision. "Of course," Maximilian said. Compelled by courtesy, he rose from his chair, vowing that he would deal with the butler later. Guests were to be shown into the drawing room, not trotted about the house....

Charlotte walked into the room with a fluid grace, easily diverting his mind from his troublesome servant. Her hair was up again, tucked under a small straw chip with a pink ribbon that matched the pretty but rather childish gown she wore. Obviously, she had outgrown it, for it strained across her breasts, and Maximilian felt an answering tightening of his breeches. She held out his walking stick.

"Hello! You left this at the house," she said, smiling. Despite his disdain for unexpected callers, Maximilian felt himself returning her salute. Suddenly, the gloomy dining hall seemed bright with life and sunshine. Did Charlotte have her own supply that she flung about her like a May Queen?

"Thank you," Maximilian said smoothly, taking the stick from her hands. "You need not have bothered. I have several." He put the "affectation" aside, uncertain whether he would ever carry one of them again, and contemplated Charlotte.

She was tall for a woman, the top of her head reaching above his shoulder. Young, sweet and alluring, she stood before him with her hands together and her angelic face turned up in a serene pose, as if she had not the slightest notion of her effect upon him. He frowned. "You should not have come alone, Charlotte. It is quite improper."

"Oh, Kit and Jenny and Carrie came with me, but they ran off to chase the geese by the pond. I expect they will be in shortly," she said, carelessly waving a hand toward the door.

Maximilian stared. This was a way of life to which he was wholly unaccustomed. He was used to schedules and discipline and strict rules of behavior that forbade a lady of quality from breezing into a gentleman's home unescorted. Maximilian told himself that although such conduct might be acceptable in Sussex, he ought to persuade Charlotte to leave, for her own sake.

If she were any other woman, he might suspect that she had planned this visit to ensnare him into marriage, but not

Charlotte. She was all guileless innocence as she glanced wide-eyed around the dining hall.

"A bit gloomy, isn't it?" she asked.

"I am having it done over," Maximilian answered tersely, annoyed that her views so echoed his own. He ought to toss her out on her delicate ear for waltzing in here alone. How would the poor child ever get on in town? She had no notion of... Abruptly, Maximilian was assailed by a startling vision of her blithely visiting some gentleman in London, and his fingers twitched. He decided to enlighten her as to society's strictures. "Won't you sit down?" he asked.

"Yes, thank you," she answered happily. She positively beamed at him, and Maximilian felt himself responding to her genuine pleasure. He relaxed into his own chair, and then caught himself as he realized the girl radiated a warmth and gentleness that drew him in an alarming way. He tamped down his attraction.

"I'll ring for another place," Maximilian said.

Fortunately, the footman who answered his summons saw nothing out of the ordinary in the sudden appearance of a young lady at his breakfast table. "Some coffee or tea perhaps?" he asked Charlotte. When she agreed to tea, Maximilian pushed his papers aside a bit impatiently and settled down to broach his topic.

"My dear girl, I feel it is my duty to prepare you in some small way for your life in London," Maximilian began. He pressed his fingers together into a steeple, pleased to note that he had her complete attention. "I am afraid that things here in the country are a bit more... informal, and it might be acceptable for you to call upon those whom you have known all your life. However, in town, a young lady must never be seen without a chaperone, or at the very least, a respectable lady's maid."

Maximilian paused while the footman set a place before her and departed. He drew a breath to continue, but halted when his gaze was caught by Charlotte's ample breasts, which strained against the material of her gown as she reached for a piece of toast. Fascinated, he watched while she spread marmalade on the edge and lifted it to her mouth, his train of thought completely lost.

Charlotte was just beginning to take a bite when noise erupted from the kitchens. What the devil? Maximilian half rose from his seat in expectation of some mishap. Then the doors to the kitchens flew open and Kit raced in, followed by a giggling Carrie and a solemn Jenny.

Kit had his mouth full of something, but waved merrily before seating himself comfortably at the table without even pausing for an invitation. "Do you ever walk?" Maximilian asked.

Kit swallowed a great lump of food and grinned toothlessly. "No fun in that," he said.

Maximilian firmly quelled the smile that tugged at the corner of his mouth. "Nevertheless, in my home you shall walk, young man," he said.

"Yes, sir...uh, my lord," Kit said, looking noticeably chagrined.

"*My* lord, *my* lord," Jenny chanted. Coming around to Maximilian's chair, she crawled onto his lap without preamble and rested her back against his chest. Maximilian felt his irritation at this morning's interruption disappear in a rush of warm feelings. The child's devotion to him was something that touched him deeply, and he had to admit there was something to be said for the easy familiarity of the Trowbridges, so different from his own upbringing.

He was glad they were not at Wycliffe, however, for his servants there would faint dead away to see him surrounded at table by small children, including one who was comfortably ensconced upon his lap. "What treats has this scamp been stealing from the kitchen?" Maximilian asked, inclining his head toward Kit.

The footman grinned. "I believe cook gave him a bit of cinnamon bun, my lord. Shall I bring in some more?"

"Most definitely. And more toast and...milk," he said. He looked in question at Charlotte, and she nodded.

"Very good, my lord," the servant said, bowing and disappearing into the kitchens.

The children were soon sitting down to a lively feast, Cook having also thrown in some tarts for good measure. "Kit, please try to chew your food," Maximilian said, eyeing the boy askance. "I imagine without teeth that is a difficult task, but a gentleman does not gulp."

"Humph," Kit grunted, nodding his agreement. Charlotte muffled a giggle behind a slim hand, and Maximilian shot her an admonishing glance, but the sparkle in her green eyes made him chuckle. He leaned back in his chair. Deuced if he did not feel good.

Maximilian looked around him, noting the astonishing change in the hall's atmosphere. Just a short while ago, the room had been silent and forbidding, but now it was filled with noise and high spirits and a companionableness that he had known only at the vicarage.

Amazing as it seemed, he enjoyed the low mumble of youthful voices, and he was content to hold Jenny on his lap, even though she had a tendency to wipe her jellied fingers upon his expensive sleeve instead of her napkin. He realized that he had never quite finished explaining the appropriate rules of behavior to Charlotte, but when he glanced at her, his eyes focused on her bright curls, which threatened to escape from their pins at any moment. How he wished he could be the one to release the soft cloud of her hair....

"My lord!" Maximilian heard a gasp and swung his head around. His valet, Levering, who was accustomed to check with him before their trips commenced, stood staring aghast at the assemblage.

"Yes, Levering?" Maximilian asked mildly.

"My lord, I..." It took the valet a good minute or so to recover. "I...I just wished to report that all is in readiness for your departure."

"You're leaving?" Kit's outraged question rose above the sounds of the others, and Maximilian sent him a silencing look.

"Very good, Levering," Maximilian said. "You may go." The poor man turned and walked from the room as if in a daze. In all his years of service, he had never seen Maximilian or his father upbraided by a boy of six, of that Maximilian was certain.

Before Maximilian could reprimand Kit for interrupting, the cook, a large, burly woman with a white mobcap, opened the kitchen door. "Charlotte, the boys are here. Shall I send them in?"

Charlotte had the good grace to glance at him. "My lord?"

Maximilian's fingers twitched. "My good woman," he said to the cook, "in the future, please be so kind as to address your questions to me."

"Yes, my lord," she said, but she did not looked chastened, only extremely harried.

Maximilian sighed. "Send them in."

Even before they entered, the arguing voices told him that James and Thomas were on their way. "Hello, my lord!" they chimed, pulling out chairs and glaring daggers at Charlotte.

"You could have waited for us!" Thomas said.

"Why didn't you tell us you were coming to the Great House?" James asked.

"I did not think his lordship would appreciate the whole family accompanying me, and now I am certain that he does not," Charlotte explained, her face pink.

All heads at the table, with the exception of Jenny, swiveled toward Maximilian, and ten pairs of eyes focused on his in the dead silence. Although he understood her embarrassment at her family's foibles, Maximilian thought it an awkward time for Charlotte to finally exert her authority. She was giving him an opportunity to shoo them out, he realized, but to do so would brand him an ogre in their eyes forever. And despite the disruption to his household, Maximilian had to admit that he was enjoying himself. "Where's Jane?" he asked gruffly.

The tension in the air immediately dissolved, and chattering voices rose up around him. The beleaguered footman brought in more plates, and James and Thomas each tore into huge helpings of eggs and ham as if they had never eaten a thing in their lives.

"Is that why you are leaving, my lord? So we won't bother you anymore?" Kit asked suddenly.

"Of course not," Maximilian answered. "I have a tight schedule, and business calls me back to London." Their faces drooped, and Maximilian was struck by the strangest feeling. Had anyone ever been upset at his departure before? He had friends in London, to be sure, friends who protested when he left, but the sadness here was palatable and sincere. It touched him somewhere deep inside.

And Charlotte? She seemed to be the least affected by the news, for she was studying a ghastly hunting scene above Kit's head with intense regard. Maximilian found himself slightly irked that she did not share her siblings' disappointment.

"I wish we could go to London," James said.

"You will never get to go," Thomas said.

"Yes, I will!" James argued.

"Never," taunted Thomas.

"When do you go, Charlotte?" Carrie asked.

"I shall be leaving in another month, I expect," Charlotte said, her smile a bit dimmed. Did she not want to go, Maximilian wondered, or would she, indeed, feel his loss?

"Will you see Charlotte there, my lord?" Kit asked, his cheeks stuffed with sticky bun.

"Do not talk with your mouth full," Maximilian said instinctively.

"Of course he will see her there, won't you, my lord?" Carrie asked. "You will be going to wonderful parties and grand balls together, will you not? And dancing! Think of it, Charlotte!" She sighed dreamily.

Maximilian let his eyes travel slowly over Charlotte, and he felt a pang. This innocent young thing in her too-small dresses could never move in the society in which he traveled. "Yes, you must give me your cousin's direction," he said aloud, "so I can look in on you."

Charlotte turned her green gaze upon him, and she lifted her chin, as if sensing his reluctance. Somehow, he got the impression that this honest country girl saw through lies very clearly. "That is really not necessary, my lord."

"I insist," Maximilian said, trying to hide his annoyance. He was not accustomed to argument.

"I am sure I do not know it off the top of my head, my lord," Charlotte replied, dismissing him with a slight smile.

"See that you send it to me then," Maximilian said. "I shall give you the direction of my town house." He reached for a piece of paper and wrote it out for her in bold, swift strokes, rather than his normal careful script.

Why was he so annoyed with her? Undoubtedly, it would be best if they had no further contact, for he did not want some poor country girl hanging on to his coats, especially in London. Better to cut off their association now, Maximilian thought firmly.

Then he pictured Charlotte in town, among nasty, gossiping ladies and worldly, unscrupulous men, and he wanted nothing more than to protect her. A natural response, Maximilian told himself. She was, after all, the daughter of the vicar whose living was provided by Casterleigh. And Maximilian had promised her father that he would look in on her. "Send it to me," he ordered, more harshly than he intended. When she blinked at him in surprise, Maximilian attempted a smile. "Send it to me...please," he added.

"Have you no further correspondence for me?" Wycliffe asked impatiently.

"No, my lord," his secretary, Peter Wilkes, replied. "Perhaps if you told me what you were expecting, my lord." The earl had been in London but a month, and each day he became increasingly surly, especially when presented with his post. Peter found the behavior most unusual, for Wycliffe was known to be a patient and fair, if distant, employer.

"Nothing from Sussex?" Wycliffe asked.

"No, my lord," Peter answered. What had happened in Sussex? His lordship had just returned from there, where he had looked over a new property. Was it not to his satisfaction?

"Peter," Wycliffe snapped. "I have a job for you."

"Yes, my lord?" Peter braced himself. He did not want to go to Sussex. That was the venue of a steward, not a secretary, and he prided himself on his excellent work. Since entering his lordship's employ five years ago, Peter had made himself invaluable. The earl's household, business ventures, correspondence...his very *life* ran like clockwork. And Peter counted himself responsible for much of that smooth operation.

"I wish you to find out all you can about a woman of quality named Augusta Thurgoode," Wycliffe said. "Be discreet, and discover her residence, please. I may wish to pay a call."

Peter nearly gaped. A *woman?* Was the earl's ill mood brought on by a woman? Peter knew a moment's trepidation at that distressing thought. He was aware that the earl had already broken things off with his current mistress, because the lady's allotted time had been inked from the schedule. Surely, Wycliffe had not become entangled in an affair of the heart.

Shaking his head, Peter scoffed at the ridiculous notion of the unemotional Wycliffe displaying a tendresse for anyone. This Thurgoode probably was going to be the earl's new mistress, Peter decided, forgiving his employer for being a bit testy during the transition. He made a mental note to leave space in the weekly itinerary for visits to the lady.

Peter smiled, pleased with his foresight. He prided himself on anticipating the earl's needs, for in his mind, it was the sign of a superior employee. Although he dared not ask Wycliffe for confirmation, Peter felt sure of his deduction. The lady could hardly be anything but a mistress, Peter told himself, for he knew that Wycliffe did not intend to take a wife until his thirtieth year. And Wycliffe was nothing if not punctual.

* * *

"The Earl of Wycliffe! What is he doing here?" Augusta Thurgoode sat back among her perfumed pillows and stared at the card her manservant had presented to her, half expecting it to change before her eyes. She blinked and looked again, but the elaborate gold lettering remained the same. Lord Wycliffe, the handsome, wealthy young earl, was waiting in her drawing room.

She had seen him before, at a distance, of course, and then only rarely. He did not frequent the engagements of her social set, or any social set, for that matter. Supposedly, he disdained frivolous pursuits such as dancing and gaming, focusing instead on the businesses that made him so very rich and a fashionable interest in the ancient world or some such nonsense. What he was doing here, she had no idea.

"Tell him we shall be down directly, Milo. And send my niece to me immediately!" Augusta bounced out of bed as well as she could, considering her generous figure, while her abigail pulled out one of her best day dresses. The door had barely closed upon Milo when Charlotte appeared.

"Oh, Charlotte! Consider this! The Earl of Wycliffe is here," Augusta said, as she was helped into her clothing. She stared at her cousin then, as if seeing the girl for the first time. "Look at that gown you are wearing. It is hopeless, hopeless, I tell you! If only the ones we ordered were ready! That you should be here only two days and receive a visitor like this one," Augusta wailed.

She gazed at Charlotte critically. "Perhaps I should not even introduce you... but to forgo this opportunity! Well, it must do. It simply must do," she muttered. "Wycliffe! I cannot think what he wants. I have never met him." Holding out her arms, while the abigail adjusted her sleeves, she finally noticed that Charlotte was flushed pink. "What is it, girl? Speak up. Are you unwell?"

"I suspect he is here to see me, cousin," Charlotte said.

"You! Don't be silly," said Augusta. She tossed the black curls, which Charlotte suspected somehow must be colored. She hated to imagine what the vicar would think of such a practice, but during her brief stay, she had discovered more than a few things about Cousin Augusta that her papa would certainly not countenance. "What could he possibly want with you?"

"He is a particular friend of mine," Charlotte said.

"What?" Augusta screeched so loud that Charlotte stepped back, watching in some alarm as her cousin's unusually pale face became even whiter. "You have never been to London. What would you know of Wycliffe?"

"He owns the Great House near the vicarage," Charlotte explained. The horrified look on Augusta's dainty features told her that she had better make light of her acquaintance with the earl. Charlotte was learning to take cues from her cousin's behavior and adjust her own accordingly, but there were so many silly rules here in town that she was rapidly becoming exasperated. One could only wear certain things and be seen in certain places at certain times with certain people. Somehow, it was not at all what she had expected. "He promised Papa that he would look in on me in town," Charlotte said.

Augusta heaved a small sigh of relief. "I see. And Wycliffe is a man who honors his obligations. Shrewd and dependable, he is, for all that he seems a bit stodgy." Charlotte wanted to deny that her elegant, handsome earl was stodgy, but she held her tongue while Augusta took on a look of concentrated calculation.

"Well, this is beyond my expectations. If he should make an effort..." Augusta's words trailed off as she stood still, allowing Jeanette to pin a cap upon her head. "With a nod from him, you could be launched, my girl, beyond our wildest expectations!"

Charlotte patiently let Jeanette straighten her gown, while both her cousin and the abigail clucked critically. She tried to listen as Augusta filled her head with last-minute instructions, but they all blurred together when she walked down the steps to the drawing room. *Walk slowly. On no account be forward. Dainty, demure, fragile, that is what makes a girl a success!*

Charlotte had never felt dainty or fragile in her life. She towered over her tiny cousin like a great, gawky giant. But she did not tower over Wycliffe. He stood waiting for them, and Charlotte forgot all else when she saw him.

Had it been only a month since they had parted? Surely, he had grown more handsome in the interim. His claret coat was superbly cut to his tall frame, as usual, and his buff breeches fit him to perfection. Her gaze seem to linger on his thighs, which she remembered as hard with muscle beneath her fingers. Quickly, she forced her attention to his face, but not before she caught his brown eyes widen at her perusal. She blushed.

Augusta was babbling introductions, and Charlotte stepped forward. Wycliffe took her hand. She stared at the lean, long fingers, encased in impeccable gloves, and when he brushed his lips to her hand, she felt his touch deep down inside her. His long hair was pulled back with a ribbon today, and she was struck with the most improper desire to... brush it.

At one time or another, she had groomed everyone's hair in her family, even her papa's, but Wycliffe... That would be different. She imagined him sitting before her in his shirtsleeves while she loosed the ribbon to let the dark locks fall straight down his back, then standing behind him while she brushed through it with long, clean strokes....

"Miss Trowbridge," he said, dropping her hand. "It is a pleasure to see you again. I hope you are well?"

Miss Trowbridge? Charlotte blinked at him in surprise, but he seemed distant, cool, not at all the man who had hugged Jenny to him or teased her with his eyes and his full mouth.

"Yes, I am fine," Charlotte answered, sitting automatically. "And you?"

"I, too, am well, thank you," he said. "And your journey? It was not too taxing?"

"No," Charlotte said, feeling as though she were conversing with a stranger. "It was delightful, actually. I have never traveled by coach before—"

Her words were cut off by Augusta. "Of course, so much is new to my dear young cousin, but we will endeavor to make her visit here most enjoyable. So much to see and do," Augusta said, fanning herself vigorously. "I vow I will enjoy it all as much as she will, for it will be like seeing the town through new eyes."

"Have you vouchers for Almack's?" Wycliffe asked.

Augusta fanned herself with even more agitation. "Not yet, my lord. La! My niece has been here but two days. We have not even been out, as yet."

"I will speak to Lady Jersey," Wycliffe said. "In the meantime, I expect you shall present her at one of the early season galas?"

Augusta practically squirmed on her chair, and Charlotte suspected her cousin was not used to dealing with such directness. Wycliffe could be a bit formidable, especially today. He seemed so grim and unhappy. Did he hate making this call? If so, why had he come? She knew he felt obliged to Papa, but she purposely had never sent him Augusta's direction, so that he would not be forced to see her. Yet, somehow, he had discovered the residence himself— and a scant two days after her arrival. The realization both pleased and confused her.

More than anything, Charlotte wanted to get him alone, away from her cousin, to regain their warm familiarity. Perhaps then she could discover his motives and coax him from his sour mood. But how could she arrange an assignation? She could hardly suggest a walk or an outing. *Above all, do not be forward.* Charlotte remembered that much. And from what her cousin had told her, she was not ever to be alone with a man, anyway, for whatever reason. It all seemed a bit silly.

"La, my lord! I fear I am not as organized as you. We have several invitations," Augusta said. "I shall sift through them and choose something suitable, you may be sure."

"The Coxbury affair?" Wycliffe asked.

"Ah, I am not at all certain we have received an invitation," Augusta said. "My correspondence has been piling up most dreadfully. With Charlotte visiting, I have let it go," she said, darting a nervous glance at her cousin.

"I am sure you will be most welcome. I look forward to seeing you there, Miss Thurgoode, Miss Trowbridge." He rose, checked his watch and nodded to them both. Charlotte longed to say something, but she felt intimidated by this London version of her lord, so stiff and formal, his immaculate clothes free of stains from tarts or eggs or Jenny's jellied fingers.

"Thank you, my lord. You are most gracious," Augusta said, bobbing her head. "Most gracious, indeed."

Her simpering smile disappeared as soon as Wycliffe did. "That man!" she exclaimed. "One would think that *he* was your sponsor from that awful tone he took with me. And checking his watch! La, it is just as they all say. He lives by the clock. Take his watch from him, and he would surely expire."

Augusta snapped her fan together sharply and set it aside. "And he as good as told me where I was to present you," she complained. "I have a notion not to appear just to spite him...but to get us entrée to the Coxbury affair! That is truly something, my girl."

She smiled, her lined face becoming even more wrinkled. "I will say this for the high-handed creature, he is definitely doing his best by your father. We shall see what happens at the Coxbury gala, shall we? I suspect that you are going to be splendidly launched in society."

Augusta leaned back in her seat and chuckled. "Milo, my sherry! This calls for a celebration!"

Chapter Five

Where was she? Trying to rein in his temper, Maximilian sent his gaze sweeping around the Coxburys' reception room again. He was not accustomed to his plans being thwarted. He had obtained Charlotte and her relative an invitation, and, by God, he expected them to use it. He allotted himself an hour, at most, at these dreadful affairs, and he had already been here an hour and a half. It was insufferable.

If they did not appear within fifteen minutes, he was leaving, Maximilian decided, and Charlotte could be left to the mercy of that shabby-genteel cousin of hers. As if the woman could do her any good! He cringed at the thought of his poor beauty, dressed in country clothes and moving on the very fringes of society during a season sponsored by that woman.

Having stopped by to check on her, to make sure she had arrived in London, as he had promised her father, Maximilian had been horrified to discover her circumstances. The girl would never find a decent husband under that old crone's tutelage! Immediately, he had decided to take a hand in the business. He felt it his duty, to prevent the vicar's investment from going to waste and Charlotte from ending up leg shackled to some half-starved shopkeeper.

"My lord! My lord!" Maximilian stifled a groan. He had spent the evening fighting off the attentions of marriageable ladies, and now some other female was beckoning him. He pretended not to hear. "My lord Wycliffe!" The voice, soft, but with its hint of boldness, sounded oddly familiar, so he relented and turned to see a tall young woman in a lovely pink gown. It set off the girl's fair coloring and was extremely fashionable, although it was not cut low like most of the others here tonight. In fact, it reached to her slender neck, ending in a gentle ruffle that made her appear delightfully feminine despite her height. Did he know this girl? She was stunning, really, with pale pink lips and the loveliest green eyes . . .

Maximilian felt a jolt down to his toes. "Charlotte?" Her given name escaped his lips before he could catch it. Surely, this elegant woman could not be the vicar's daughter?

She smiled, her eyes sparkling delightedly at his surprise, and Maximilian realized that she could have passed in front of him a dozen times this evening without him recognizing her. His country goose had turned into a peacock before his eyes, and he was not the first one to notice her plumage. With a stab of annoyance, Maximilian noticed that she already had a small entourage of admirers, vying for her attention like a gaggle of honking geese.

From the looks of them, the young cubs trailing in her wake were not worthy of a second glance, and Maximilian felt a rather smug satisfaction. Despite her transformation, Charlotte would never draw the attention of the ton's elite, without a nod from him.

Of course, she would never be a great success, Maximilian admitted. Although there was no denying her beauty, most men preferred the practiced flirting of women of their class over the green simplicity of a girl barely out of the schoolroom and fresh from the country, too. And, naturally, the greatest impediment was her lineage. She was, after all, only a vicar's daughter.

The odds were against her, but with his help she would have a sporting chance. He felt magnanimous. "Miss Trowbridge," Maximilian said smoothly, bending over her hand. "It is truly a pleasure to see you again, and looking so lovely."

"You are looking well, too," she said, blushing pink. He gripped her fingers a little too tightly before dropping them, surprised by the sudden heat she inspired. Why this girl should continue to have such an effect on him was infinitely puzzling. He was normally attracted to older women, not young chits of indifferent parentage. Maximilian released a tense sigh as he realized that the sooner she was married off, the better he would feel.

His gaze lifted to her own, and he noticed that she was staring at him in a free manner that would be frowned upon by the town matrons. It was on his lips to warn her, but, mindful of their audience, he bit back the comment. Sliding an impatient glance over the rabble that traveled in her wake, Maximilian dismissed them out of hand. "You will excuse us, gentlemen?" he asked pointedly. One of the pups tried to protest, but Maximilian gave him a long, hard look, and the fellow slunk away.

"If you would be so kind, Miss Trowbridge, there are some people I would like you to meet," he said, smiling at her. Her new gown fit her quite well, Maximilian noted with approval, although he missed the way her tight clothing had hugged her breasts. She had covered up her lush bosom with an excessive amount of fabric when most women would have bared it fashionably. Maximilian smiled. His country goose still had a little to learn about London ways, he thought as he tucked her fingers into the curve of his arm.

Maximilian introduced her to several of the patronesses of Almack's, subtly making known his desire to see her in those elite assembly rooms. She would need vouchers from one of these ladies before she could even purchase tickets, and Maximilian was determined to gain her entry. What better place to contract a suitable marriage?

Next, he planned to dance with her and, finally, to acquaint her with a few eligible gentlemen of whom he approved before he considered his task completed. He was already leading her onto the dance floor before he was abruptly struck with a twinge of foreboding. "You do dance, do you not?" he asked, staring at her intently.

"Do you expect me to trod upon your toes, my lord?" Charlotte asked, her eyes twinkling.

"Well..." Maximilian hesitated, imagining an embarrassing turn about the floor with his young charge. "I was not sure if your cousin had seen to your instruction."

Charlotte laughed as he took her in his arms for the waltz. "I see no tarts or egg baskets here, my lord, so you may feel secure in your impeccable costume," she said. "I assure you that I am not as clumsy as you may think."

Maximilian smiled, feeling some of his tenseness slip away. The disruption of his evening's schedule had put him in a sour mood, but Charlotte seemed to be able to alleviate his distress. Again, he had the sense that his beauty shone like the sun, brightening this corner of the candlelit ballroom with her glow. "Am I to gather that I no longer discompose you?" he asked.

She blinked at him, her long silky lashes fluttering like butterfly wings over her springtime eyes. Then she made a show of glancing about and grinned at him wickedly. "I must say, there are a lot of other elegant gentlemen here tonight."

"Meaning I have lost my luster?" he teased.

"Never that, my lord," Charlotte said softly. Although her bold gaze never left his, her mouth drooped, and Maximilian felt a tug at his heart. Deuced if she did not have the strangest effect upon him.

"Charlotte..." Her name escaped again. Maximilian was not sure what to say, and yet he felt compelled to warn her not to— But it was not necessary. She was already looking away, her attention upon the other dancers. Perhaps he had just imagined that hint of bitterness in her voice. "Are you enjoying yourself?" he asked.

"Oh, vastly," she answered lightly. Why did he get the impression that she did not mean it? Her careless tone reminded him of the pampered, perfumed ninnies around him, not of Charlotte, and Maximilian did not like it. His goose may have turned into a peacock, but he did not want her to imitate the London birds too closely, especially with *him*.

"I have a small library at my town house. Shall I send you over some volumes from my collection?" he asked, suddenly anxious to see the honest, intelligent girl that had so intrigued him in Sussex.

Her expression changed instantly, to his pleasure. "Oh, would you?" she asked, her upturned face a picture of delight. "I am still studying the royal house of Thebes." She frowned suddenly. "On second thought, you had better not. Cousin Augusta does not approve of reading. She would surely take me to task if she found me with scholarly works."

Stupid hag, Maximilian thought uncharitably of the cousin. The old crone probably did not even know her letters. "Perhaps if I delivered them myself?" he asked, certain that Augusta Thurgoode would not dare to raise an objection then.

"Perhaps," Charlotte said, although she appeared unconvinced. "I am not to be a bluestocking, you see, my lord. That would not do at all."

"In your efforts to snare a husband?" Maximilian heard himself say caustically.

"Yes," Charlotte answered, still frowning. "Cousin Augusta says men do not at all care for a woman who reads or thinks or even voices her own opinion."

"And you would want to marry such a one?" Maximilian asked, annoyance making him grip her fingers tightly.

"Truly, I do not know, my lord," Charlotte replied as if mulling over a great puzzle. "It is all so different here, and there is so much to learn. Cousin Augusta is doing her best..."

Her best to change you into a brainless decoration, Maximilian thought angrily. Before he could comment, however, the music came to an end, and he could see several gentlemen waiting for a turn with his partner. "You may dance once with the others. Then I will be back to claim my second waltz with you," he ordered roughly.

"Doing your duty to launch me into society?" Charlotte asked, her mouth quirking up at one corner.

"Yes," Maxmilian answered. "I always take a turn with the girls in their first season, but only one. A second dance will show the room that I have taken special note of you, while any more dances would be unseemly."

"It is quite complex, is it not? All these minute rules of behavior..." This time there was no mistaking the bitterness in Charlotte's voice, and when she glanced at him, her eyes no longer sparkled.

Maximilian could do nothing about it, though, for a handsome young buck claimed her, and he was left staring after them. Instead of squiring another lady onto the floor, he stood, watching Charlotte and her partner move off together, and felt an urge to depart the Coxburys' gala now. He had already been here an inordinate amount of time. He pulled out his watch and checked it to confirm the worst. He would be very late for his club.

Struggling with his irritation, Maximilian told himself that he could not leave yet. He had promised Charlotte another dance, which would assure her of a place among the ton's most desirable young ladies. But instead of filling him with satisfaction, that prospect dropped like a leaden weight into his belly.

It had all seemed so simple. Once properly gowned and instructed in the rudiments of gracious society, Charlotte would find a good match and depart his life forever, ridding him of this gnawing interest in her. Now, however, seeing the results of Augusta Thurgoode's handiwork, Maximilian was not so pleased with this course.

Properly gowned, Charlotte had turned out to be enough to tempt a saint, and he was already casting suspicious glances at the men who were watching her avidly. When he caught Montgomery, a notorious rake, eyeing her, Maximilian felt the fingers of his hands twitch, itching to close upon the man's throat. This was definitely not the sort of attention he wanted for her!

Worse yet were the other changes. Although he had wanted Charlotte to behave in a fashion befitting her new venue, instead of in the uninhibited manner of a Sussex villager, Maximilian found, perversely, that he did not like her new behavior. He realized, rather suddenly, that her open manner and bright mind were part of what drew him to her. London was altering Charlotte, dimming her brilliant glow, and it disturbed him.

Maximilian did not like grays. He liked everything in black and white, as easy to evaluate as a sheet of accounts. Confusion was not something he normally struggled with, and he shunted it aside irritably. He told himself firmly that his ill mood stemmed from the disruption of his schedule and closed his mind against any other possibilities.

Watching Charlotte twirl around the floor with one fellow and then another did little to improve Maximilian's disposition. He looked at his timepiece again. His scowl deepened. When he approached Charlotte for the second dance, it was with little enthusiasm. She did not look eager to see him, either, which blackened his temper further.

For awhile, they moved through the steps silently, Charlotte staring at his neck cloth while he glared at the ridiculous hat upon her head, a lacy, pale pink confection. How long had it been since he had seen her hair down? He pictured it the way he had first viewed it, loose and frothy as spun gold.

"I must thank you, my lord, for your kindness in making such an effort for me," she said in a sarcastic manner. He looked down, taken slightly aback by her tone, into green eyes glinting with...anger? What reason did she have to be piqued? He was the one who had totally forsaken his evening's itinerary in order to introduce her into society. He was the one who had seen her whirl about happily with slavishly attentive young pups who sickened him. And probably not a one of them could be trusted....

Maximilian felt an alien surge of rage. Drat the vicar's daughter! He wished that he had never met her. He was tempted to give her a good set-down, but his innate courtesy held him in check. He was doing this for her father, Maximilian told himself.

"You are quite welcome, I am sure," he said stiffly. He wanted to finish this dance, get to his club and have a drink. Although he had made no special arrangements, everyone knew he spent Thursday nights at White's. Lord Raleigh and Crenshaw were probably there waiting for him, wondering why he was so late. He was never late.

"I will be sure to write my father that you have fulfilled your obligation," Charlotte said as the music ended. Her smile was forced, and she stepped away from him hurriedly. "Please do not bother about the books, my lord," she added. "You have done more than enough."

Why did he feel as though her words held not gratitude but scorn? The audacity of the girl! This was the last time he went out of his way for her, Maximilian decided as he headed toward the door. He had singled her out for attention, introduced her to the patronesses of Almack's and danced with her twice, the ungrateful chit. He had done more than his duty by her. What else could he do to see her married off as soon as possible?

It was not until he was settled in his coach that Maximilian realized he had not presented her to one eligible bachelor. He decided to ignore that lapse. He had done enough for the vicar's daughter; he would be damned if he was going to handpick her future husband.

With a sigh of frustration, Maximilian decided it was too late to go on to his club. Instead, he went straight home to bed, but he found that he could not sleep as easily as he normally did. Gossamer-soft hair and eyes the color of mist-laden spring shoots invaded his thoughts, making it difficult to relax. Finally, with an oath of annoyance, Maximilian rose and went to the library, pulled out a book and sat down to read about the royal house of Thebes.

Maximilian was not exactly sure why he was standing in the gallery at Bradley House. The rout had not been on his schedule, and his secretary had been most put out when he changed his plans at the last minute. It was not like him to veer from his routine, but he knew Charlotte would be here because he had heard Lady Bradley invite her the other night at the Coxbury gala.

Maximilian wanted to see how she was getting on.

Although he had not forgotten her rather shabby behavior toward him, Maximilian's irritation with her had dimmed over the past few days, overcome by his curiosity as to her progress in society—and an uncanny desire to see her again.

Maximilian admitted that he liked the vicar. Deuced but he liked the whole family! Although his recurring interest in Charlotte made him a bit uncomfortable, Maximilian explained it away under the guise of duty. He felt a sense of obligation to her father to see her suitably married, and since he had done his best to launch her, he could not help taking some responsibility for the girl. And everyone knew Maximilian never shirked his responsibilities.

"Wycliffe! Missed you at the club Thursday!" Maximilian smiled to see Viscount Raleigh. Although his taste in clothes leaned toward the dandy, Raleigh was a good fellow. He had a good seat, a good set of hands on the reins, a good head for his liquor and, for the most part, good luck at the tables. Although Raleigh did not care for literature, Maximilian did not hold that against him. Few people shared his passion for the classics.

"I could have used your clear head," Raleigh said, stepping up beside him. Shorter than Maximilian, he sported light brown hair and a friendly face above his ridiculously high shirt points. With a studied gesture of indolence, Raleigh raised his quizzing glass and surveyed the room.

Maximilian wondered briefly what Kit, who had called his walking stick an affectation, would think of that piece of work. Then he frowned; the Trowbridge family was entirely too much on his mind of late.

"Afraid I imbibed a bit too much and lost my allowance for the month," Raleigh complained as he peered through his glass.

"Sorry," Maximilian said. "I stayed at the Coxbury affair longer than usual."

"I say!" Raleigh said. "Is it true, then?"

"What?"

"That you are enamored of some young thing in her first season," Raleigh said, dropping his glass to stare at his friend. "I say, Wycliffe, the whole town's buzzing with the gossip."

Maximilian slid Raleigh a skeptical glance. "Have you ever seen me enamored of anyone?" he asked coolly.

"Good lord, no!" Raleigh answered immediately. "Oh? So you ain't now, either? All a hum, I suppose," Raleigh said, looking a bit disappointed.

"The lady in question is the daughter of a vicar who ministers on one of my new holdings. I promised him I would look out for her, to see that she makes a good match," Maximilian explained.

"Lud, is that it?" Raleigh asked, frowning in distaste. "How can you take your duty so seriously, Wycliffe? I wish you were not such a paragon, you know. Makes it hard on the rest of us. My own father was extolling your virtues yesterday. 'Why can't you be more like Wycliffe?' he asked me. As if anyone could!" Raleigh shook his head as best he could within the confines of his high starched collar.

"Gad, I would be hard-pressed to recognize my own vicar, let alone his daughter! You should get a medal for pretending interest in the chit. Probably a fat country cow, too," Raleigh said, shuddering.

Maximilian felt himself tense. "Charlotte is not a cow," he said, as evenly as he could.

"Of course not. Slip of the tongue, that," Raleigh said. "Still and all, I do admire you. Would not make the effort myself, even if the girl were the least bit comely." He lifted his quizzing glass again and swept his gaze down the room. "Suppose I should take a look at the new crop of ladies myself. My father keeps telling me to wed. Thinks that will settle me down."

Maximilian grinned. Raleigh was not deep, but he was kind and he put up with Maximilian's rigid schedule, which not everyone could stomach. "Are you here for your obligatory hour?" Raleigh asked, as if divining his thoughts. Maximilian nodded as he pulled out his watch and glanced at it.

"I'll meet you when it is up then, and we can go off together. Tonight is Brooks, is it not?" Raleigh said, referring to Maximilian's weekly itinerary.

"Yes," Maximilian answered, but Raleigh was already moving off, apparently to view the fresh flesh pressed onto the marriage market this season. Although Maximilian thought Raleigh's father might be right, he could not imagine the young viscount shackled to any of the giggling misses that crowded the room. He ran his eye over them critically, dismissing them all in favor of one particular lady.

Maximilian found her at the end of the gallery, surrounded by admirers, none of whom, he decided, was worthy of her attention. He scattered them with a few cold looks. When she noticed that her entourage was fleeing, he stepped forward, and she turned to him easily, a bright smile on her lips.

Whatever mood had struck her at the Coxburys', she seemed to be over it now, for her face lighted with pleasure at the sight of him, and Maximilian felt an answering surge within himself. She was radiant, a vision in a Pomona green gown that reflected the color of her eyes.

"My lord!" she said. "What a delightful surprise! And thank you for ridding me of those fellows. They are sweet, but..." She trailed off. "It all gets to be a bit much, does it not?" she asked, her eyes twinkling.

"I suppose so," Maximilian answered, "although I cannot say I have ever had a problem with too many suitors." Charlotte laughed delightfully. She had been fanning herself when he approached, but now she snapped the fan shut and let it dangle from her wrist. His gaze strayed there and traveled up her slim hands while he remembered how they looked without gloves. "You are especially beautiful tonight," he said. He suspected that she would look good in anything, but better in nothing at all....

"Oh! I thought you came to rescue me from all that," Charlotte complained with a teasing grin.

"Very well then. I am most happy to rescue you. What do you expect of me, if not compliments?" Maximilian asked, bantering easily.

"Honesty, my lord," Charlotte answered softly. She fixed him with a clear gaze that told him she was absolutely serious. It struck a chord deep within him, and Maximilian stilled. For a heartbeat, silence stretched between them, fraught with significance, charged with some hidden meaning.

Maximilian drew in a slow breath. Unwilling to let the strange mood continue, he purposefully spoke lightly. "Well, then, I shall be brutally honest. You look very fetching in your new gowns, but I do not care for the hats. Must you hide your hair from view?"

Charlotte giggled at his audacity, but her lips drooped apologetically. "I am afraid so, my lord, for Cousin Augusta says my hair is most unfashionable. She keeps telling me to cut it—"

"Cut it?" Maximilian nearly shouted the words. "Charlotte, you are not to let that woman trim one lock of your hair!" Instead of nodding meekly, Charlotte laughed at his blustering, annoying him further. Although Maximilian sensed he ought to drop the subject, he could not. He was outraged. How dare that old crone try to snip away at his beauty?

"Augusta says it is too unmanageable to dress atop my head, and so it must be clipped short to curl about my face," Charlotte explained, demonstrating with one of her slender hands. "Even then, she says I will have to use some sort of device to curl it exactly right, which I confess I have no interest in. I daresay Papa would not approve of frivolous beauty enhancers."

"Good for him. You tell your cousin that your papa will not allow you to cut it, either," Maximilian said. He imagined that lovely cloud shorn and twisted into an unrecognizable form, and he felt his stomach clench.

"Well..." Charlotte appeared hesitant to tell an outright falsehood.

"Charlotte, promise me you will not cut your hair," Maximilian ordered firmly.

One corner of her luscious mouth twitched. "All right, but if Cousin Augusta becomes too much for me, I shall send her to you, my lord, and you may explain to her your reasoning in the matter."

"I shall," Maximilian said, amazed at the relief that swept over him. "But I cannot imagine anyone becoming too much for you."

Charlotte laughed again, the husky sound familiar, yet fresh to his ears. It was a pleasure to listen to, he decided. His country beauty was acquiring town polish, but retaining herself. If only that old crone stayed away from her with the shears.

"Cousin Augusta is a...challenge, shall we say?" Charlotte said. She spoke softly, as if sharing a secret with him, and Maximilian felt again that strange sense of intimacy between them. He grinned.

"I shall give the woman this, she has good taste in clothing," he said, his eyes roving over the smooth lines of her dress. Although quite flattering, it covered her as thoroughly as her others, ending in a bit of trimming at her neck that made it look more like a day dress than evening wear. He leaned his head to one side to assess her more closely. "I heartily approve of your new gowns, but they are a little high in the neckline, are they not?"

Charlotte turned a luscious pink and looked at her fan. "I...well..."

"I am sorry. That was rude of me. I took your request for honesty too far," Maximilian said, immediately regretting his words. What had possessed him to speak so boldly?

"No! Oh, no," Charlotte said, placing a gloved hand on his arm. Maximilian looked at it, a soft, comforting caress upon the fabric of his coat, and he felt as if she was touching his skin. He lifted his gaze to her face, flushed with embarrassment and concern, and attempted a brotherly smile. Having appointed himself her protector, he did not want any unsuitable stirrings, but her fingers burned into him, and he seemed powerless to alter his response.

Charlotte leaned close, and Maximilian's attention drifted to her mouth, soft and ripe, as she whispered to him. "I am too large in the chest," she confided, her face crimson. "Although Sarah never really said much about it, I know she thought it was a bit . . . unseemly, especially for a vicar's daughter."

Maximilian's efforts to maintain a brotherly attitude deserted him abruptly. In fact, he had no idea that a few simple words could affect him so profoundly. Her innocent confession was provocative in the extreme, sending Maximilian's blood rushing to his extremities. By great strength of will, he prevented himself from glancing at the area in question while he searched his brain for a reply to her confidence.

"Charlotte," he finally choked out. "A woman can never be too wide in the chest. My advice is take advantage of your blessings. Wear what the other young ladies are wearing, within reason, of course."

He tried not to imagine the results of his suggestions, for the gentle curve of those silken-draped mounds suddenly seemed more stimulating than any other woman's bare breasts. Maximilian stepped back and told himself that he was her sponsor and, as such, he had better turn his attention to a more innocuous subject.

"Wycliffe!" Luckily, their tête-à-tête was interrupted by Raleigh, who sauntered toward them, eyeing Charlotte through his quizzing glass. A quick surge of possessiveness made Maximilian sway closer to her.

"Wycliffe, I thought you were supposed to be doing your duty by the vicar's daughter, and here I find you thicker than thieves with the most beautiful girl in the room!" Raleigh accused.

Maximilian's fingers twitched as he glared daggers at his friend, but Raleigh was oblivious. He was too busy ogling Charlotte. "Raleigh, may I present Miss Trowbridge. Miss Trowbridge, this fool, for some reason, is a friend of mine. Viscount Raleigh."

"Wycliffe! She is an angel, a goddess!" Raleigh said dramatically. He bent low over her hand. "How do you do, my dear?"

"I am fine, although I must admit that I am no angel nor goddess," Charlotte said. "I am simply the vicar's daughter."

Raleigh halted, clutching her fingers and staring at her in stupefied amazement. As much as Maximilian appreciated the scene, he did not like the way Raleigh lingered over Charlotte's person. He nudged his friend.

"A thousand pardons, Miss Trowbridge. A hundred thousand pardons! But this is all Wycliffe's fault, for he failed to mention that you were the loveliest creature ever to make her London debut!" Raleigh said. He pressed a lengthy kiss to her hand before finally dropping it.

Maximilian scowled while Charlotte laughed merrily. "Perhaps because my lord Wycliffe does not think me the loveliest creature ever to make her London debut!" she said.

Raleigh sent Maximilian a horrified glance. "The man is truly a monster, then, but I have known that for some time. He is too busy making his schedule and keeping time to notice the beauty around him."

Maximilian restrained an urge to check his watch.

"Let me take you away from the cruel fellow," Raleigh urged. "Can I persuade you to dance with me, goddess?"

Although Maximilian was accustomed to Raleigh's antics, he felt a twinge of annoyance at his friend's manner. Charlotte, who he was sure had more sense than to fall for such nonsense, was stifling a giggle.

"How can I refuse?" she asked.

Raleigh smiled in triumph, undoubtedly because he so rarely bested his friend. "You will pardon us, Wycliffe?" he asked airily.

"Which one am I?" Charlotte asked.

"Which what, goddess?"

"Which goddess?" Charlotte supplied, laughing.

"Why, the most beautiful one, of course!" Raleigh replied as he led her away. Maximilian felt his fingers twitch. He knew full well that Raleigh did not know Aphrodite from Agamemnon, and the foolish banter annoyed him. He gritted his teeth, disgusted with his fawning friend and with Charlotte.

If she thought to snare Raleigh, she would be sorely disappointed, Maximilian thought with grim satisfaction, for he knew the viscount's father, an earl, would never allow his son to marry a vicar's daughter. Despite her beauty and charm, Charlotte was strictly mortal.

Chapter Six

"I saw you with Wycliffe again tonight," Augusta said, pulling off her gloves and dropping into her favorite chair in the drawing room.

"Yes," Charlotte replied, simply because her cousin seemed to expect a response. Tired, she stifled a yawn behind her hand. She wanted nothing more than to seek her rest, but Cousin Augusta always insisted on reviewing the evening while it was still fresh in her mind. Any missteps of Charlotte's were duly noted, as were her triumphs and Augusta's suggestions for future behavior.

"He has put forth quite an effort for you, girl, so we must not disappoint him," Augusta noted, looking sharply at Charlotte.

Charlotte said nothing, but eyed her cousin attentively. After only a week, she was growing accustomed to these lectures, although where this one was leading, she was not sure.

"Neither would we wish to be rude to him, for he has been a most kind benefactor, and he remains in a position to help us throughout the season. However..." Cousin Augusta paused dramatically, as if preparing to make a pronouncement. "We do not want him to take up too much of your time—time that should be spent with legitimate suitors."

Charlotte blinked in surprise. Was she to avoid Wycliffe? She would have thought it prudent to cultivate him, considering his wealth and influence. "You do not want me to see him?" she asked in confusion.

"I did not say that, child," Augusta answered. "I am simply advising you that you must pick and choose your companions to best further your goal—of marriage."

Charlotte frowned as Augusta's words became all too clear. She was to evade Wycliffe in favor of other, less interesting men who were within her reach. *Sorry, my lord, but only those considering matrimony are worth my while.* Undoubtedly, there was some cryptic way to convey this message through the use of one's fan or the tilt of one's head. Whatever the means, Charlotte could just imagine Wycliffe's reaction to her defection; it would not be pretty.

"That is not all, dear," Augusta said. She waved Charlotte to the adjacent chair. Then she made a great show of smoothing her gown over her lap. "Some rumors have been troubling me. Naturally, whenever a man shows marked attention to a girl, some people get the wrong impression." She eyed Charlotte keenly. "Gossip has it that Wycliffe is taken with you."

Charlotte could not contain the snort of disbelief—a pale imitation of the type used by James and Thomas—that erupted, unladylike, from her lips. She had given up any hopes she had once held on that score, for she had too often seen the condescending look in the earl's eye. It told her that, despite his kindness toward her, he would never consider a lowly miss such as herself to be his proper consort.

"Yes, well, I am glad you have some good sense, child. I knew you did," Augusta said, nodding her approval. "The fact of the matter is that titled lords like Wycliffe do not marry country girls straight from the schoolroom. Obviously, you are clever enough to see that, but I wish to make it clear that you are to remain cordial to his lordship—and nothing more. He will not have you, girl, and there is no sense in wasting your precious time upon him when you must cast about for a husband."

Charlotte bridled at her cousin's turn of a phrase. She knew that Wycliffe did not care for her *in that way,* and she had tried to take pleasure only in his friendship, but Augusta's blunt words were grating. Charlotte felt her stubborn pride, beaten down by London, rise to the fore. "What of the Gunning sisters?" she asked abruptly.

Augusta sent her a quelling look. "The Gunning sisters made their conquests decades ago, child. Men today are not so easily gulled by a lovely face." Augusta frowned, making even more wrinkles appear in her lined face. "I do not know how marriages are arranged in the country, but among the nobility, they are made for money, property and bloodlines. That, my dear child, leaves you out."

"You are saying that I *cannot* possibly have Wycliffe?" Charlotte asked, lifting her chin in challenge.

"I am indeed," Augusta confirmed. Apparently unmoved by the determined set of Charlotte's mouth, she picked up her closed fan and pointed it at her young charge. "And what is more, you had better not fritter away your clever brain power on thoughts of trying to snare him, for it is quite hopeless. Now, off with you. All this activity is making me weary. I vow, you shall be the death of me yet."

Charlotte felt a stab of guilt. Reminded of all that the elderly lady was doing for her, she fought back the rebellious urge that had plagued her all her life. None of her siblings seemed burdened with it, especially dear, dutiful Sarah, who always did the right thing. Only Charlotte struggled with the devil's prompting in moments like this— when she wanted nothing more than to try to prove her cousin wrong.

Grimly, Charlotte remembered her purpose. Her papa was spending a lot of money, money he could ill afford, upon her season, and she had a responsibility toward her family. She had only a few short months in which to find a spouse who would return that investment.

Augusta was right, Charlotte told herself. She had no business mooning over his lordship. If only her cousin had not used the word *cannot*...

* * *

Charlotte looked at the three men surrounding her and tried her best to see one of them as her husband. It was not an easy task.

To her left stood Roddy Black, a smooth-faced boy who seemed even younger than her own seventeen years. According to Augusta, he was a prime candidate because his merchant father had amassed a substantial fortune.

Roddy was sweet and rather handsome, with his light brown hair and blue eyes, but he seemed so...silly. He was always at her elbow, spouting ridiculous compliments and gazing at her worshipfully. How could she take him seriously? It was all Charlotte could do to contain her laughter when he told her she was the fairest creature ever to walk the earth or that she possessed the grace and poise of a queen.

Gently deflecting some of his prose, Charlotte turned her attention next to Sir Burgess. Augusta said he owned a small estate in Suffolk, which seemed in good order, and that he had come to London specifically to find a new wife, his first one having passed away last year. Sir Burgess had a rather distinguished air about him, for his black hair was streaked with white, and he was rather appealing-looking in a craggy sort of way, Charlotte reflected. He said little and seemed rather listless, but he made her uncomfortable in an undefinable way.

Then there was Captain Stollings. He was very handsome, rather dashing, in fact, with his thick blond hair and flashing blue eyes, but Charlotte had the feeling that the captain saw little farther than his own white smile. She knew full well that he paid her court only because of her beauty. She suspected they all did, and that made her feel... unsettled. All her life, she had been told that her face was her fortune, but now that the time had come to bargain, Charlotte found she did not care for the process.

She sighed softly, hoping that her choice would not come down to these three fellows. She had more suitors, of course. More men evinced interest in her daily, but Augusta approved only of those who were most likely to come up to the scratch. The titled gentlemen would not, Augusta informed her often enough. Others who had no money or few prospects were not to be considered, nor were the dandies and rakes who circled around her simply because she had been proclaimed a toast of the new season.

Augusta pointed out those with the blackest names, like Lord Worthington, and Charlotte had been astounded to learn that some of the elegantly dressed men who moved in society could not be trusted with a girl's honor. Although they flirted with Charlotte quite outrageously, she gave them no encouragement. In truth, not one of them caught her fancy, for it had already been seized.

It was all a far cry from the vicarage and the loving family and neighbors who liked her for what she was inside. They had doted on her beauty, but not to the exclusion of all else. Here she felt increasingly like an ornament to be admired and placed upon a mantelpiece.

Struggling with a wave of homesickness, Charlotte longed to escape from the stifling company of the men around her. She glanced about for a female acquaintance who might give her comfort, but she knew that many of the girls and their mamas were envious of her success. Still, her eyes raked the crowd before halting abruptly.

Wycliffe. Charlotte saw him standing near the doorway, looking so very tall and elegant and handsome that she could not understand why every woman in the room did not mob him. Her heart did its customary flip-flops at the sight of him, dressed in raven black. Unlike herself, he looked wholly at ease in this glittering world, and Charlotte was acutely conscious that, despite the celebrity he had thrust upon her, she was only a visitor here.

She wanted to go to him immediately, although she knew Cousin Augusta would not approve. Remembering her duty and her purpose, Charlotte thought to ignore him, but the pleasure that seeped into her at his presence would not be denied. "Please excuse me, gentlemen," she said, nodding and smiling. Her suitors protested, especially Roddy and the

captain, but Charlotte shook her head firmly and was fi
nally rid of them.

Having acquired some sense of discretion, she did not go
directly to Wycliffe, but walked through the crowd, working toward him gradually. She edged around a large group
only to find herself hemmed in near the wall, behind a cou
ple of very expensively dressed women. About to beg their
pardon, Charlotte hesitated when she heard a familiar name
on their lips.

"Ah, there's Wycliffe," said one of the ladies, her back
to Charlotte. "A fine specimen, that. And rumor has it he
has broken with his latest mistress."

"Lud, you can have him for all he is devilishly handsome," said the second one, a dark brunette whose thin
gown did nothing to conceal the curves of her figure.

"And you should know whereof you speak," the first one
said slyly. "But tell me, is he not a wonderful lover?"

Charlotte caught back a gasp and thrust her fan in front
of her reddening face, while the brunette chuckled softly
unaware of an audience. "Well…" She sighed. "He is very
skillful. Painstaking, I would say."

"I knew he was not the cold fish he is painted," said the
first, a tall and slender lady with a husky voice that dropped
even lower with her apparent interest in the topic.

"No, he is not cold, not by any means. It is just that you
feel as though you are allotted a certain amount of time, and
despite your attractions, that is all that you will get. Rather
like coming on cue," the brunette said with a laugh.

"Coming at all would be a change for me, what with that
ancient fool I married," the slender one said. "I would take
my cue from Wycliffe any time."

The brunette laughed again. "I am afraid that for all your
charms, Isabelle, you just would not do for his lordship. He
likes his ladies well-endowed. Besides, rumor has it that he
has fixed an interest on some country chit. Perhaps he shall
marry. Knowing Wycliffe, that will be the end of his dalli
ances."

"La!" the slender lady said, her voice heavy with scorn. "The chit is a poor relation or something. Wycliffe's only interest is his obligation to the family. I had that straight from Raleigh," she added.

Charlotte's cheeks flamed anew at the realization that the two women were discussing her. "Lucky girl," the brunette said. "I, for one, will heartily pity the poor creature Wycliffe marries. He will order her life by the minute, a boring, stifling existence that no woman in her right mind would want. I tell you, no one can exist by his clock."

"Perhaps," the slender one admitted with a sniff. "But I have heard no complaints about his prowess in the boudoir, even from you. Oh, look, there is Ophelia with that monstrously handsome cousin of hers. He is looking particularly splendid tonight."

With relief, Charlotte decided that the ladies were through talking about her, and she moved off, away from their gossiping tongues. She told herself she ought to be ashamed of eavesdropping; dear Papa would never approve! But he would never have approved of the conversation, either. Some of it Charlotte had not understood, but one thing was clear. The brunette had been Wycliffe's lover! How Charlotte wished she could have gotten a good look at the lady's face, but she did not want to lose sight of Wycliffe, who was walking across the reception room.

Charlotte stepped toward him, her cheeks still warm. Although she had no idea what made a man a wonderful lover, the thought of Wycliffe described in such glowing terms made her insides turn to jelly. She put a hand to her throat and, as her fingers touched the decorative lace of her gown, she remembered something else the ladies had said. Wycliffe, it seemed, liked buxom females.

With sudden interest, Charlotte glanced down at the bosom that had annoyed her since her youth, when it had blossomed far beyond her expectations. Was it only coincidence that Wycliffe had suggested she wear more revealing clothes? Charlotte tugged at one of her fingers thoughtfully.

And what of his rough order not to cut her hair? With an intent expression, she pulled at a second finger. And the way he glowered at her admirers, chasing them all away with his scowls? Charlotte flicked at a third digit, her stubborn streak surfacing. If she did not know better, she might think it possible, despite Cousin Augusta's opinion, to fix Lord Wycliffe's interest.

Hope, wicked and delicious, burgeoned in her chest, but then she thought of Sarah's sensible advice and of Papa, patiently waiting for her to do her duty. And the boys, who would have few prospects if she did not marry soon. And Jane and Carrie and Jenny, who could be launched in seasons of their own, if only she made a successful match.

Charlotte frowned bitterly, feeling the heavy weight of her responsibility to the family as never before. Abruptly, the gay colors and careless chatter of those around her appeared grim, the sparkle of the chandeliers and the glitter of the room's fabulous gilt furnishings worthless.

Standing there, alone amidst the crowd, Charlotte caught a glimpse of herself in one of the huge, elaborately framed mirrors that lined one wall, and the woman who stared back at her appeared a stranger. Tall and elegantly gowned, she was a creature of her surroundings, as empty and hollow as all else in this fancy world.

For the first time in her life, Charlotte cursed the beauty that had brought her to this impasse. With grim resolution, she turned and walked away from the only man she wanted.

The chit was avoiding him. Maximilian could not believe it, but every time he neared Charlotte, she managed to evade him just as though he were an unwanted interloper. Him! And all the while, she smiled and laughed and fluttered her fan for her motley group of admirers. It made his blood boil. With a fiery determination not in keeping with his usual calm demeanor, Maximilian longed to teach her a lesson, although he was not at all sure what form it should take.

Rarely inclined toward precipitous behavior—or violence—he nonetheless felt like turning the girl over his knee...or something. Maximilian hesitated to pursue those thoughts too far, but decided to let his rage simmer until he found a way to maneuver himself behind Charlotte.

When he did, he could not help but notice the smooth-cheeked boy who seemed to be fairly drooling at her feet. Good God, was the infant even weaned yet? And the fellow with the streaks in his black hair had a decidedly menacing air about him. Who was he?

Maximilian frowned. His eyes next traveled over a rakish blond officer, whom he dismissed as just the sort of character who would appeal to empty-headed females. Was Charlotte so shallow as to find the man appealing? The thought grated on him, as did the suspicion that she preferred the company of these louts to his own.

"Miss Trowbridge." Maximilian spoke her name softly. What would she do now, when he was so close, he wondered, knowing that she could hardly escape his presence. He steeled himself for her dismay, and then she whirled, blinking in surprise to see him. Before he could prepare himself for repulsion or duplicity, her beautiful face lighted with delight.

"My lord," she said in that husky voice of hers. The greeting was like a caress, low but bold in the expression of her pleasure. Maximilian felt as if she had touched him, and his anger was transformed into a heat of another kind.

"Excuse us, will you?" he asked of her entourage, his implacable gaze brooking no resistance. Then he turned to Charlotte. "Shall we dance, Miss Trowbridge?" He waited, watching her. Still a bit dazed by her response, he half expected her to refuse, but she did not. In fact, she smiled at him so eagerly that he stared. If he did not know better, he would have thought he had imagined her earlier behavior. She had been avoiding him, had she not?

"I say, Wycliffe, I resent you spiriting this lovely lady away when I have just arrived." Raleigh's voice interrupted his musings, and Maximilian glanced at his friend in annoyance. Didn't the man have anything better to do?

"Then you should have arrived earlier," Maximilian said in a less than gracious tone.

"While those two squabble, let us dance, Miss Trowbridge," said a deeper voice. Forming an angry retort, Maximilian shifted his gaze to the newcomer, only to choke back his reply. The man who spoke was not some whey-faced youth, but Lord Wroth, one of Maximilian's peers.

Startled to see the famous marquis bending low over Charlotte's hand, Maximilian hesitated a moment, and that was his downfall, for Charlotte sent him an apologetic glance and walked off with Wroth before he could utter another word. In the blink of an eye, Maximilian saw only her tall, straight back as she moved with easy grace away from him.

Maximilian was livid. How dare she treat him so shabbily after all he had done for her? Wroth would never have deigned to notice her if it had not been for him! When he realized that he was standing there like a dolt with four of Charlotte's admirers, he felt like slamming his fist into something.

"Really, Wycliffe, you must learn to concede graciously if you are to move in Miss Trowbridge's circle," Raleigh said, eyeing Maximilian with a comical expression on his face.

Maximilian's fingers twitched. The other men moved away, and he turned upon his friend, his unaccustomed rage barely leashed. "I was not aware that she had a circle," he said through gritted teeth.

"But of course, man. Where have you been? Miss Trowbridge has been proclaimed a Toast of the new season." A dazed expression on his face, Raleigh rhapsodized about Charlotte's charms in the most nauseating manner. "She is a goddess, a nonpareil, as you should well know, since you were acquainted with her."

"She is a beauty, yes, but hardly a goddess," Maximilian said, scoffing, "so spare me your insipid prose. It is the same every year. A group of seemingly intelligent men make cakes out of themselves over a pretty face—until the next one comes along. My God, Raleigh, I thought better of you."

Instead of taking offense, Raleigh cocked an eyebrow and looked at his friend intently. "I say, you *are* smitten," he marveled.

"I am *not* smitten," Maximilian snapped. "I simply wish to speak with the chit, and I find it extremely inconvenient to have to fight my way through a pack of drooling puppies."

Raleigh chuckled, apparently enjoying himself. "I would hardly call Wroth a drooling puppy. I think his mother birthed him full-grown with a pair of dice in one hand and the reins of that huge fortune of his in the other."

Maximilian's eyes narrowed. "He is a rake and an unsuitable companion for Ch—Miss Trowbridge."

Raleigh laughed. "I say, Wycliffe, quit humming me! How many times have I heard you say you admired Wroth for having one of the few clear heads among the ton?"

"That may be," Maximilian acknowledged, "but he has no business hanging about Charlotte."

"Lud, man, why do you say that?" Raleigh asked. "He is one of the most sought-after bachelors in London. Only think of it! Your vicar as the papa-in-law to one of the most powerful men in the country!"

Maximilian cursed softly and pierced Raleigh with his gaze. "Wroth has no intention of offering for her, and you know it. The girl will never gain a title."

Raleigh looked at him with bland surprise. "Why ever not?"

"Because she is a deuced vicar's daughter," Maximilian answered sharply.

"So? Do you think anyone would dare to shun Wroth for marrying beneath him?" Raleigh asked. He paused, as if considering the action, and shuddered. "I suspect that Wroth could marry his kitchen maid and no one would dare gainsay him. Dash it all, Wycliffe, when the lady is as beautiful as Miss Trowbridge, matters of birth are forgotten."

"Well, he cannot have her," Maximilian said firmly.

"What?" Raleigh turned blue eyes wide with astonishment on his friend.

"Wroth is a coldhearted devil who would never make her happy," Maximilian muttered.

Raleigh looked too stunned to reply for a moment, then shot his friend an assessing glance. "I suppose you would approve of the gallant young captain or the lad barely out of the cradle, as opposed to a wealthy and powerful marquis."

Maximilian snorted. "If you are referring to the rabble that surrounded her earlier, I would have to say no. Not one of them is worth a farthing."

Raleigh stared at him solemnly. "So, you are saying that those fellows are all unworthy of our goddess, as is, of course, the marquis," he mused. "Who, then, do you think a fitting husband for Miss Trowbridge?" He lifted his chin to preen wickedly, and Maximilian suddenly knew where this discussion was leading.

"Not you!" Maximilian answered, sending Raleigh into gales of laughter so uproarious that heads turned to stare at him. "And what is so funny?"

"Nothing. Not one blessed thing," Raleigh answered between gulps for air. "I say, Wycliffe, this season promises to be the most entertaining one I have seen in many a year. Tell me this, are *you* perchance the only man fit to marry our goddess?"

Maximilian eyed him dispassionately. "Do not be ridiculous." Then, suddenly, he remembered his schedule. He pulled out his watch and cursed softly, unable to believe that with all his attempts to seek out Charlotte, he had wasted more than an hour at this idiotic function.

At the sight of the timepiece, Raleigh seemed to be seized with another fit of laughter, and Maximilian glanced at him irritably. "Good God, Raleigh, get yourself under control. You sound like a deuced hyena." When his glares seemed to do naught but aggravate Raleigh's condition, Maximilian smiled tersely. "I am leaving. You may tell your *goddess* that I could not wait upon her leisure."

"Tell her yourself," Raleigh said, with a nod to his right, and suddenly there was Charlotte, beautiful and fashionable, despite the high-necked gown.

For a moment, all Maximilian could do was stare at her in admiration, though why she insisted on swathing herself in all that material was a mystery to him. Abruptly, Maximilian pictured her throat bare but for a rope of rubies—the Wycliffe rubies—wrapped several times around her pale skin. He shook away the thought, along with the temptation to linger.

"You will excuse me, Miss Trowbridge, but I must be going," he said harshly.

He expected Charlotte to greet this news without reaction, considering the way she had been avoiding him all night. Instead, she surprised him by putting a slim hand on his arm and leaning toward him in a rather intimate gesture. Surely, she would not pretend that she wanted him to stay? Maximilian scowled in disgust, for he was not one of her fawning admirers to be led about by the nose.

But Charlotte did not urge him to remain. She lifted her green eyes to his in rather anxious entreaty. "Can you come by tomorrow afternoon around three o'clock?" she asked.

For a moment, Maximilian was at a loss for words. Was something the matter? Her invitation was hardly a normal one. Her clear gaze fixed upon him, waiting for answer. "Certainly," he said roughly. She gave him a grateful smile while her hand dropped from his sleeve in a gentle movement. It was all he could do not to catch it back, to feel her touch, a warm caress, upon his arm again. Gad, he was going around the bend!

"Good night," Maximilian said with a stiff nod. He stalked off, eager to be away. Not only had he disrupted this night's itinerary and stayed longer than he had intended, but now he had committed himself to visiting Charlotte tomorrow. He swore softly.

The vicar's daughter was wreaking havoc with his schedule.

Chapter Seven

Maximilian stood on the threshold of Augusta Thurgoode's set of rooms and wondered what had possessed him to agree to come here. His secretary had gaped in amazement when told to reschedule Maximilian's meeting with the banker. Faced with Wilkes's astonishment, Maximilian did not have the heart to inform the man of the reason behind the appointment shuffling. Or perhaps he did not want to admit to his own folly. *Sorry, but I have an important engagement with the vicar's daughter...*

Of course, he could have sent round a note to Charlotte, claiming a prior commitment, but he had promised her. And, in truth, he was curious as to the reason for her rather secretive invitation. Was something amiss in Miss Thurgoode's household or at home? Was the vicar calling her back from London?

Maximilian tried not to gloat over that notion, with which he heartily concurred. As far as he was concerned, Charlotte had no business being a Toast and should be sent on to Sussex where she belonged. There he certainly would not have to fight through a pack of males to see her. She could retain her sweet innocence, marry one of the locals and depart from his thoughts.

After waiting for what seemed an interminable length of time, Maximilian was informed by the rather seedy-looking manservant that Miss Thurgoode was out. Good, Maximilian thought, because he did not care to visit the woman. "I am here to see Miss Trowbridge," he said.

When the servant had the gall to look him over, Maximilian did his best to glare the fellow into the next county. Apparently, it had some effect, for the gangly gawker swallowed hard and eyed him nervously. "Sorry, my lord, but I have been instructed to turn away all of Miss Trowbridge's suitors until such time as my mistress returns," he said.

Maximilian felt himself go livid, but he kept his voice even. "My good man, although I hardly deem it any of your business what my relationship is to the young lady, suffice to say that I am *not* a suitor of Miss Trowbridge's."

The servant hesitated, as if wavering, and then shrugged his shoulders and held open the door. Impudent rascal! Maximilian strode into the drawing room, where he began to pace back and forth restlessly. It was bad enough that he had disrupted his routine for this visit, but he was deuced if he would be barred from the door like some tradesman.

The sound of footsteps made Maximilian turn, and he saw Charlotte on the threshold. The first thing he noticed was that her hair was down. It was swirling about her shoulders like a yellow cloud, beckoning him more powerfully than Circe ever could. It would be fragrant, he knew, smelling of lilacs and fresh country Charlotte...

"My lord! I am so glad you could come, my lord!" she said, stepping toward him. The movement made Maximilian notice her dress. A far cry from the ill-fitting, childish garments she had worn as a simple vicar's daughter, it was also different from the fashionable clothing he had seen her wear in London, for this pale green confection did not cover Charlotte up to her neck. It was cut low over her lush bosom, revealing for the first time the swelling curves of her breasts, pale and creamy and so very full....

"I decided to take your advice about my gowns, my lord," she said. Was he staring? Maximilian tried to shift his gaze, but he could not. The high waist of her gown pushed her breasts upward, where they gleamed, flawless and silky, the dark cleft between them a well of secrets.

Suddenly, Maximilian wanted nothing more than to hold them in his hands, and his groin sprang to life. He tried to form a reply, but his mouth felt dry and unworkable. *Was he staring?* With an effort, he dragged his gaze to her face, where her cheeks were flushed a lovely, becoming pink. "Very fashionable," he choked.

"I knew you would be pleased, my lord," Charlotte said. The corner of her mouth twitched upward, making him wonder if she were teasing him. But, no. His country goose was far too unsophisticated for such repartee, wasn't she? She had better be. Maximilian did not care to see her practice the wiles of the jaded London ladies. He sent her an assessing gaze, but she had turned.

"Now that you have seen my new gown, I would have you judge my new walk, my lord," she said. Then she proceeded to mince away from him in small steps that were nothing at all like Charlotte's graceful strides. "How do you like it, my lord?" she asked.

"I hate it," Maximilian answered mildly.

Charlotte whirled and laughed softly. "But I have been working so hard to perfect it, my lord. Cousin Augusta says—"

"Spare me!" Maximilian said, holding up his hand. He had no intention of listening to whatever drivel the old woman was passing off as gospel. "What in God's name is she doing to you?"

"My lord!" Charlotte said. Although she spoke in shocked tones, her admonishment was spoiled by the twinkle in her eye, and this time there was no mistaking the twitch of her lips. She looked exactly as she did when she tried to scold one of her younger siblings. "You should not take the Lord's name in vain. Papa would be most put out, my lord."

"My lord, my lord!" Maximilian snapped. "Enough of the my lords! It is supposed to be a sign of respect, not a litany."

Charlotte's ebullience seemed undimmed by his churlish words. "But I do not know what else to call you, my lord," she protested.

"You know my name," Maximilian replied tersely. "You may call me Wycliffe."

"Wycliffe?" Charlotte said, blinking. "But that is not your name. That is your title."

"And so I am known by it," Maximilian answered.

"You have always called me Charlotte," she said simply, her clear gaze holding his own. Why did she make him feel ... pretentious? He scowled.

"No one calls me Maximilian but my mother!" he snapped.

"Maximilian," Charlotte repeated in a rush of warm breath that made all his senses sharpen. "It is beautiful! Oh, thank you, Max!" To Maximilian's complete and utter surprise, she threw both her arms around him and hugged him, just as she might Kit or Thomas.

For one moment, he savored the feel of her slender arms around him, her heavy breasts pushed into his chest and the scent of her hair.... His breeches, snug since she entered the room, tightened further. With a grunt, he disengaged her. "For what?" he asked.

"For allowing me the liberty of your name! Oh, Max, I am so glad that I may count you my friend," she said. Apparently determined to continue her familiarities, Charlotte took both his hands in hers and looked at him, her features a picture of innocent delight. "We are the best of friends, are we not?"

Startled, Maximilian could only nod. Looking at her now, her thrusting, white breasts only inches from him, her fingers warm over his own, he hardly thought of her in such an innocent light, but what else could she be? He had appointed himself her protector, and she obviously saw him as such. Why did he find that irritating?

"Oh, thank you!" she said, squeezing his hands gently before letting them go. Maximilian stepped back, away from her warmth. "I knew it! But I must tell you that my cousin frowns upon our companionship."

"Why?" Maximilian asked, bristling. Did that harridan question his honor? Did she not trust him with a young lady?

Charlotte sighed. "I find it difficult to say," she admitted, her eyes downcast.

"Tell me," Maximilian urged between gritted teeth. He steeled himself to expect the worst, but he swore that if Miss Thurgoode had soiled Charlotte's innocent young mind, he would have the woman's hide!

"Very well," Charlotte said, folding her hands before her in a pose so reminiscent of the country maid she had been that he wanted to take her by the arms and kiss her soundly. "She wants me only to cultivate those men whom she thinks will offer for me, so she has forbidden me to spend time with you! There you have the awful truth," she said, her head bent.

Maximilian didn't know whether to laugh or strangle the cousin. Although Miss Thurgoode had a point, he thought it the height of ill manners to cut him when he had made Charlotte a success. "I will talk to her," Maximilian said firmly.

"Oh, no! You must not," Charlotte said, putting a slim hand on his arm. "Then she will know that I spoke with you about it, and she would surely be angry. She does not understand our special friendship," Charlotte added with a sweet smile.

That makes two of us, Maximilian thought bitterly, for he was not sure he understood it, either. He knew, for certain, that he did not care for the way Charlotte said *special friendship*. It made him appear to be an ancient guardian, a grandfatherly figure doted upon by a young girl.

"And I do not wish to lose our fellowship, for I can talk to you as I can no one else, dear Max."

Max? No one in his life had ever called him Max. And what was this about fellowship? It sounded like some sort of religious communion.

"Can we speak...openly?" Charlotte asked, turning to hide her face from his.

"Are we not already?" Maximilian asked, a bit testily. He did not like being a confidant. Was that not a woman's role? First he had felt like an elderly uncle, then a spiritual adviser, and now she had reduced him to a eunuch.

"Yes, we are. You are right, of course," Charlotte said, flashing him a quick smile over her shoulder. "So I shall feel no qualms about broaching my subject. Max," she said, whirling to turn her clear, green gaze upon him, "if you were pursuing a female with marriage in mind," she asked, her eyes sparkling mischievously, "would you want to kiss her?"

For a moment, Maximilian was taken aback, so thoroughly was he surprised by the question. Then a black suspicion planted itself in his brain. "Who has been trying to kiss you?"

"Oh, nearly everyone," Charlotte answered blithely.

Maximilian felt his fingers twitch. "Give me their names and I shall take care of the matter," he said, red rage coursing through his blood.

Charlotte waved a hand carelessly. "Oh, I cannot even remember all their names," she said. Before Maximilian could assess that startling statement, she was moving on. "What I wish to know is this. Would you want a girl you are thinking of marrying to kiss you?" she asked.

"Certainly not!" Maximilian replied. "A true gentleman would not ask such a thing," he added, stretching the truth for the sake of protecting her. "And any man who would press you in that fashion is not at all the sort you should consider for a husband."

"But I am curious," Charlotte said. "Surely, you have kissed many women. Is it the same every time, or is each experience unique?"

"That, young lady, is none of your affair," he answered brusquely. The impudent chit! Why was she dragging him into this?

"Botheration! How am I ever to know what it is like if I cannot try it?" Charlotte asked. Although her eyes were twinkling, her lush lips were frowning in annoyance.

"You may try it with your husband, once you are wed, and not before," Maximilian said firmly. The vicar's daughter obviously had a devilish streak buried under that angelic exterior, for she was sorely trying his patience with this nonsense.

"I know!" Charlotte said suddenly. She lifted her head, which sent her hair swirling about her face in a luxurious mass, while her bright gaze sought his expectantly. "You!"

"What?" Maximilian asked, glaring at her with some annoyance. He was heartily sick of this ridiculous conversation.

"*You* may kiss me," Charlotte suggested, "and then my curiosity will be satisfied."

Maximilian stared at her, astounded by her audacity. Then he laughed harshly. "I will not kiss you, you little minx! What would your papa say?"

Charlotte frowned briefly, as if considering this argument and rejecting it. She stepped closer to him, her spring eyes holding a tantalizing glow. "Please?"

"No!" Maximilian said sharply, turning away from the soft entreaty in her gaze. Deuced, but the girl had no idea what she was asking! Temptation warred with his better self. "I shall not kiss you."

"Botheration, but you are a stubborn man. Well, I guess I will just have to let one of my suitors do it," Charlotte said with a sigh.

"No, you will not," Maximilian replied, his temper flaring. By God, he felt like taking her over his knee. How dare she defy him? Alarmed at the rush of anger that swept him, he took a couple of deep breaths and spoke more softly. "Or you will ruin your reputation and your chances of making a successful match."

"Oh," Charlotte said. She appeared momentarily deflated before brightening again and sliding a glance at him under silken lashes. "But if you do it, Max, no one will know."

"I am not *Max*, and I am not going to kiss you," Maximilian replied. "My God, child, although I may seem like a stodgy ancient to you, I remain very much a man, and kissing can lead to... other things."

"What other things?" she asked pertly.

Her innocence was a tangible thing, apparent in her every movement, no matter how bold she might make with her questions. Maximilian glared at her, determined to jar her from her reckless attitude. "Lovemaking," he said through gritted teeth. "Pregnancy."

She blinked at him, her eyes wide, and then laughed. "You do not trust yourself to kiss me?" she asked.

Damn it! She seemed to know just how to push him to the limits of his patience. "Very well," Maximilian vowed. In one swift motion, he took her by the arms, pulled her forcefully against his chest and pressed a hard, closed-mouth kiss upon her lips. Then he thrust her away quickly. Although disinclined to admit that she might be right, Maximilian could still feel the firm thrust of those luscious breasts against him. Maybe he did not trust himself with her, after all.

He had hoped his rough treatment would scare the curiosity from her or startle her, at the very least, but one glance at her told him differently. Charlotte looked... disappointed. "Is that it?" she asked.

Sorely tempted to show her the consequences of meddling in things beyond her experience, Maximilian nonetheless held on to his control. "That is it," he answered. "And I do not want to hear anything more about kissing. Is that clear?"

She nodded, a bit reluctantly, and hung her head.

"Now," Maximilian said, pulling out his watch. "I have other engagements today, so I must be going. If your suitors press you further, inform me at once, and I shall take care of the matter," he ordered. "Although a Toast of the new season, you are in a very delicate position. One misstep and you shall find yourself shunned and without prospects to take home to Papa."

Charlotte nodded, her head drooping, and Maximilian felt partially mollified by her docility. "If your cousin should give you any trouble, about me or anything else, let me know. You may get a message through Raleigh. Although he can be a bit much, he can be trusted, and you know my direction."

She nodded again, silently, and he tilted her chin up with his fingers to look her in the eye. "You must call me Wycliffe in public, do you understand?" he asked. "It is not at all the thing for a young lady to be so familiar."

She flashed a sad smile at him that tore at his heart. "Good girl," he said. Then he couldn't resist. He stroked the curve of her jaw with his thumb. Her skin was deliciously smooth, her scent floating around him, her hair drifting over his knuckles. He stepped back. "Good day, Charlotte," he said with a tight smile.

"Goodbye, Max," she said. He was out the door before he realized that, despite her cowed demeanor, the sparkle had never left her eyes.

Maximilian did not seek her out, nor did he accept social engagements where he might see her. Still, he could not seem to avoid thoughts of Charlotte. Her name was on everyone's lips, especially Raleigh's, who seemed to take great pleasure in telling him about the girl's latest conquest.

From all of Raleigh's chattering, Maximilian would not be surprised if the vicar's daughter had half the nobles in England eating from her hand. For himself, he heard nothing from her, no notes or messages through his enthusiastic friend. After a week spent keeping to his schedule, Maximilian felt restless. He told himself he really ought to look in on her; it was his duty to her father.

Someone would have to sort through all the proposals that Raleigh swore were in the offing, and her cousin was certainly not up to the task. Feeling magnanimous, Maximilian decided to take the responsibility upon himself, so he penned a letter to the vicar. In it, Maximilian apprised Charlotte's father of her success and assured the man that he could be counted upon to weed out any unsuitable prospects.

That done, he went to a party where he knew, from Raleigh's indefatigable apprisals, that Charlotte would be in attendance. Upon entering, he looked pointedly at his watch. *One hour,* he told himself, and this time he was not going to let the vicar's daughter upset his schedule.

Maximilian glanced around the reception room, but Charlotte was not among those dancing or talking. However, he soon spotted Raleigh, who was languidly standing at the edge of a group, quizzing everyone with his glass. It was obvious that Raleigh was still awaiting his next allowance, for he appeared heartily bored.

Maximilian made his way to his friend after a few brief nods and acknowledgments to other guests. "Well? Where is she?" he asked without preamble. Raleigh's smile of amusement told Maximilian that they both knew exactly whom he was talking about.

"If you are referring to the popular provincial, I hesitate to say," Raleigh answered slyly.

Maximilian's brows lowered. "Why?" he asked.

Raleigh affected an air of innocence. "You know, my dear friend, that I am not the sort to tell tales," he said. "Nor do I wish to get the lovely lady in dutch with her guardian. That is the role you have assumed with her, is it not?"

Maximilian's fingers twitched. "What are you babbling about, Raleigh?" he asked. Suddenly, he longed to take his careless friend by the high collar of his stiff shirt. "Where is she?"

Raleigh's only response to Maximilian's hostility was a show of surprised delight. He did have the sense to step back, however. "My, my, Wycliffe. Do not get yourself in a state!" he admonished with a grin. "I saw your vicar's daughter go into the garden some time ago...with Roddy Black."

Maximilian barely heard Raleigh's soft chuckles; he was too busy making his way to the doors leading outside. For the first time in many years, his temper was close to snapping. He stalked outside and glared ferociously at a couple whispering in the evening air, but the dark-haired lady was definitely not Charlotte.

He moved on to some decorative Grecian columns, paused when he heard soft voices and then stepped boldly around the pillars to find his quarry. The slender outline of her form was unmistakable, as was the fact that she was not alone. Charlotte, his fresh, innocent young country beauty, was locked in young Roddy's embrace.

Maximilian seethed—red-hot anger bubbling to the surface like molten lava. "You forget yourself, Black," he hissed through gritted teeth.

The young man fell back from Charlotte with a start, staring at Maximilian as if he feared for his life. Maximilian felt a slow, seeping satisfaction at the reaction. "I would have a word with you," he said, nodding toward the fellow. "Charlotte, please stay where you are."

For a moment, Maximilian wondered if the boy would hide behind Charlotte's skirts, but Roddy finally stepped forward, nearly shaking with fright. As well the boy should, Maximilian noted with contempt. It crossed Maximilian's mind to call him out, not to fatally shoot him, but to teach him a lesson. Perhaps a shoulder wound would stifle his amorous tendencies for a time.

"Please, sir," Roddy said. "I...I beg your pardon. I became carried away and—"

Maximilian stopped him with a scowl. The boy was obviously quaking in his boots, fearful of a challenge, for Maximilian had a reputation as a crack shot. Although he had fought only one duel and that a long time ago, he had killed his opponent. The incident had proved to all and sundry that despite his quiet demeanor, Maximilian did not intend to be provoked. Nor did he intend to let this young pup soil the reputation of the ton's latest Toast.

"You will withdraw your attentions from Miss Trowbridge immediately," Maximilian said. The boy's eyes grew wide, and he opened his mouth to argue, but Maximilian did not give him the chance. "If you do not, you will find yourself stricken from the list of society's desirable guests. And your father's small cache of funds will not be able to change that. Do you understand?"

Roddy nodded mutely, his desire for Charlotte apparently warring with the threat to his way of life. "Well?" Maximilian asked.

"Yes, my lord. I will do as you say, much as it—"

Maximilian cut him off. "Spare me your lovesick prattle," he snapped. "Now go in to the party before everyone there marks your absence." With one last, frantic look at Charlotte, Roddy fled, fairly racing back to the safety of the crowd inside. Maximilian watched his exit and then turned, crossed his arms upon his chest and looked, for the first time, at the vicar's daughter.

Unlike her swain, Charlotte did not appear the least bit frightened—or even chagrined—by Maximilian's presence. His anger flared again. "What the hell do you think you were doing?" he asked.

"I was kissing him," Charlotte answered. She stood very still, moonlight playing upon her flawless features...and the curves of her generous breasts exposed to view by the cut of her new gown. Suddenly, it seemed indecently revealing. Had young Roddy drooled over the sight? The very thought outraged Maximilian. His fingers twitched.

"Kissing him? Are you mad?" he asked.

"No. Just curious. I wanted to compare the...experience," she said. Although she clasped her hands together demurely in front of her, Maximilian was not fooled by the innocent pose. He had the distinct, unsavory impression that she was laughing at him. His sorely tested temper cracked like a twig.

Maximilian's brown eyes narrowed, and Charlotte could see just how enraged he was. It was all she could do to keep her tone and her posture careless. Although she had pushed him to this, she had a fleeting misgiving as to the wisdom of her actions.

"You think that slobbering young pup is a better kisser than I? Is that it? Is that what you are telling me?" Maximilian asked, his features harsh in the shadows.

Before Charlotte had a chance to reply, he was moving. He grabbed both her arms and pulled her to him abruptly, his mouth swooping down upon hers in a bruising, punishing communion that was not at all like Roddy's kiss—that was unlike anything she had ever experienced.

He was not gentle, but he was Max, and she slipped her arms around his neck, clinging to him, glorying in the feel of him. And when his tongue sought entrance she opened her mouth willingly, soaring with the electrifying new sensations it invoked. Her blood raced, her heart pounded, and her head swam dizzily while every inch of her body sprang to life, just as though his mouth breathed vitality into her own.

The pressure of his lips lessened as his tongue swept inside, running over her teeth and exploring the hidden recesses, and as the kiss changed, so did his hold on her. His hands left her arms to stroke her back and lower until one of them was playing upon her buttocks.

The layers of cloth separating their flesh suddenly seemed painfully thin and yet much too heavy, for even though his touch was shocking, it was so pleasurable that Charlotte had a brief, outrageous wish that it was her bare skin he caressed. He moved in widening circles, in a maddening rhythm that made her lean into his body.

Sighing against his mouth, Charlotte slid her fingers into his hair, stroking the sleek strands that were pulled back by a ribbon, and with one quick tug, she boldly loosened the tie, so that the smooth, black locks fell toward her. She thrust her hands into its thickness, reveling in the feel of it even as she pulled his head down closer.

In response, Maximilian plunged deep, sucking her tongue and taking her breath away. Charlotte whimpered low in her throat. *This* was kissing. This was what she wanted from this man—and only this man. She gulped for air as he pressed his moist, hot lips along her jawline and down her throat and his hand moved over her buttocks, cupping her curves with greater intimacy. Charlotte's head fell back while the lower part of her body sank closer, more fully into his, jolting her with exhilaration.

He was raining her with kisses, bringing each tiny, previously unimportant bit of her skin to life, pulsing at his touch along her neck, her shoulder... When Charlotte felt his mouth move lower, toward her breasts, she shivered. This was beyond anything. This was heaven!

Suddenly, Maximilian stilled, his head bent over her low neckline, his breath warm upon her. Whether it was the tremors of her body or a sound in the garden that halted him, Charlotte did not know, but she ached for his return. *Don't stop now!* She tried to form the words to tell him, to whisper them—even to shout them in his ear. Instead, her overwhelmed senses refused to respond, and she watched helplessly as he lifted his head a fraction.

For one long moment, she saw him stare intensely at the expanse of bosom revealed by her gown. Then he whispered an expletive and stepped back abruptly, his hands falling from her body. Charlotte felt a loss so keen that she nearly wept with it.

He gazed at her, his eyes narrowed, his features tense. "I want you to compose yourself and go back in there immediately, before you are missed," Maximilian ordered. Then he loosed a low, shaky breath that sounded louder than his words in the quiet of the gardens. "That was a kiss, and I do not want you to experiment with any more of them until you are married."

Charlotte looked at him, half-formed protests dying before they escaped her lips. She could tell by his expression that it would do no good to throw herself into his arms.

Maximilian, the responsible gentleman, had remembered himself.

Fool! She could almost hear Augusta's outrage. *Wasting your time on Wycliffe!* And Sarah...poor, staid Sarah would be so shocked if she knew that Charlotte was up to her old tricks, kissing the boys again, and worse...much, much worse. She had tried to snare the earl, attempting against everyone's advice to gain his interest.

It was that rebellious streak of hers—that and the tiny little things that hinted to her that he was not indifferent to her. Oh, yes. Charlotte was sure as of this night that he was not indifferent, but was he not indifferent enough to make a difference? One glance at him now told her that Max had withdrawn from her totally.

He looked cold and stern and respectable, Charlotte noted with a heavy heart, making the passion that had flared so abruptly between them seem but a dream. Like a restless sleeper, she sought for some evidence of its reality, but all that remained was his hair, which still hung about his face like a dark, seductive shadow. "Wait! Your hair," she whispered.

Maximilian swore under his breath and glanced at the ground, a black void in the night. "Where is the deuced ribbon?"

"Here, take this one," Charlotte said, lifting her fingers to her bodice where a dark blue ribbon was threaded. For a moment Maximilian stared at the offering as if it might bite him, then he slowly untied the bow and tugged until it came loose from the fabric. Although he said nothing, Charlotte noticed with a certain grim satisfaction that Maximilian's eyes never left the ribbon, and when he reached to pull the last of it from her bodice, his hands were shaking.

Chapter Eight

Maximilian made an effort to attend more social functions so that he could keep an eye on Charlotte, for he intended to make sure she did not kiss any more of her suitors. Of his own wretched lack of control, Maximilian preferred not to think. She had goaded him into it, he decided, and the fact that holding her in his arms had been beyond anything in his experience simply did not signify. She was not for him.

He had a responsibility to the vicar, Maximilian told himself, and that was the sole reason for his continuing interest in the man's daughter. Although he accepted invitations he previously would have ignored and all but gave up visiting his clubs, there were still many times when he could not watch over Charlotte. In these instances, Maximilian was forced to rely on reports from Raleigh, who seemed to take a perverse pleasure in telling him just where Charlotte had gone and with whom.

Although Roddy no longer dangled at her skirts, other men stepped forward to take his place. They called upon Charlotte and took her out on every conceivable excursion—nights at the opera, evenings at Vauxhall and rides in the park. With increasing regularity, these engagements propelled her out of Maximilian's reach, and he found himself unreasonably irritated by the turn of events.

Despite his annoyance, Maximilian could hardly adjust his calendar more than he already had. Already this afternoon he had been bickering with his secretary, and he was in a foul humor. "Why do all my stewards expect me to review every detail of their work?'' he snapped, throwing a sheaf of papers down upon his massive desk in disgust.

Ignoring Wilkes's stunned expression, Maximilian rose and walked to the windows of his study. They were covered with heavy, deep blue velvet, which gave the room a rather dark ambiance he had always thought conducive to work, but which now seemed stifling and gloomy. With an impatient gesture, Maximilian pulled one of the hangings aside and looked out onto the sunlit garden.

"Have Mrs. Mulhaney tie back these drapes," he said over his shoulder. "It is infernally dim in here." His words were met by a strangled noise emanating from the general direction of his secretary, and Maximilian turned to look at the man curiously.

"Yes, my lord," Wilkes said. He swallowed hard, his throat bobbing up and down with the effort. "But you have always demanded a strict accounting from them—from your stewards. You have always looked over all their reports most minutely."

"Have Egremont look over their correspondence and bring any problems to me," Maximilian ordered. Then he swiveled again toward the window. He felt oddly restless, his body curiously alive with some undefined longing, and the sunshine seemed to call to him. Perhaps he should go out, he thought, wavering in his resolve to spend the afternoon in conference with his secretary, as scheduled.

"Yes, my lord," Wilkes answered unsteadily. "Then, the only other letter you may wish to see is from your vicar in Suffolk."

Maximilian whirled from the window. "I shall read it myself," he said, nearly snatching the paper from Wilkes's hand. He ignored his secretary's startled expression to lean back against the casement and open the missive. The light shone upon the pages as if to bring the green Sussex countryside to life beneath his fingers.

My dear Lord Wycliffe,
   I pray that this letter finds you in good health. As you

can imagine, I was most reassured to receive your message. I am greatly indebted to you for taking the time to inform me of the events transpiring in London Town and for your continued interest in our small family.

We were all thrilled to hear of our Charlotte's great success. I trust that her sensible nature will not allow her head to be turned by such attentions, but should she fall prey to vanity, I know that you will set her to rights.

Maximilian grinned at that. He could not picture Charlotte becoming enamored of herself, nor could he envision himself setting her to rights on any subject, for the vicar's daughter had a mind of her own. His smile lingered as he glanced at the spindly writing.

The boys were pestering me with so many questions to include, concerning Tattersalls and boxing matches and other interests of that nature, that I finally persuaded them to write to you themselves, so please do not be dismayed to find they have posted you on their own. Although we know it is best for Charlotte to have you there watching over her, we must admit to longing for your return.

Jenny misses you dreadfully and will demand her lord whenever you are mentioned. Kit has taken to helping your new groundskeeper, which, he explained to me, could not be viewed as pestering the fellow, but as keeping an eye out for your interests.

Jane sometimes joins him, and, as a consequence, has taken an interest in gardening this year. She plans to reclaim our sorry plot beside the house, so perhaps it will look entirely improved when next you see it.

Carrie nearly swoons over each of her sister's letters, determined that she, too, will have a season someday. She is sure that all is wonderful in London, but Sarah worries about Charlotte, as is her way. I assured her that you had the situation well in hand.

As to your questions concerning any offers she receives, I trust to your good judgment, my lord. Naturally, you may pick and choose as you see fit, as long as Charlotte is in agreement, for I have no wish for her to be unhappy.

Maximilian scanned the rest of the page, where the vicar filled him in on the latest doings in the village and ended with a heartfelt wish for his own well-being, and he felt oddly affected. Had anyone ever missed him? Although he shared correspondence with friends throughout the country and employees at his various properties, he had never received a letter such as this, filled with humble but sincere greetings.

For the first time in his life, Maximilian had the sensation of belonging wholly to something, as though he were a member of this warm, loving family. It was a strange but not unpleasant feeling.

With sudden surprise, Maximilian realized that he would not mind seeing them all again; sweet little Jenny, Carrie, Jane, Kit—even the squabbling older boys. He shook his head firmly. He was becoming dotty. The ties that bound him to the vicarage were strictly a matter of duty—and nothing more.

Maximilian folded the letter, tucked it in his pocket and noticed Wilkes's expectant visage. He had almost forgot the man was there. His secretary cleared his throat. "Now, as for today's schedule..." he began. "You were to check the sale at Tattersalls for some new stock."

At the mention of the horse auction, Maximilian smiled. What was little more than a mildly diverting errand for him would thrill the boys beyond anything. Perhaps someday he would take them along. Idly considering the idea, Maximilian noticed that Wilkes was evidencing alarm at his wandering attention. He nodded for his secretary to continue.

"Then the dinner party given by Lord and Lady Shacklesby—"

Maximilian cut off Wilkes's words with a careless wave of his fingers. "Send my regrets and have someone go round to Augusta Thurgoode's to discover what invitations she has accepted for this evening. I shall adjust my itinerary accordingly."

Wilkes looked as if he might faint dead away. "You wish to go wherever they go, my lord?" he asked, his brows crawling up his forehead.

"Yes," Maximilian answered with determination. His mood had been lightened by the vicar's letter, and he had a desire to share the small bits of news with Charlotte.

"But you do not wish to go with them?" Wilkes asked.

"No." Maximilian never escorted Charlotte anywhere, for he did not wish the gossips to get the wrong impression. He was, after all, only doing his duty by her father.

Feeling a sense of renewed vigor, Maximilian strode away from the window. "I think I shall take a turn around the garden before I leave," he said. Then walked right by his secretary, whose jaw was hanging open, without even checking his watch.

Charlotte hid a yawn behind her fan. She had finally mastered the art of this particular fashion accessory to her cousin's satisfaction. Now she was able to convey subtle messages with a mere flick of the bone and fabric, but tonight she used it only to mask her weariness. They had been out until nearly dawn every evening this week, and the pace was telling upon her. Although Charlotte could have protested, she did not, for at each new function she hoped for a glimpse of Max.

He had been showing up more frequently, usually staying in the background, a presence across the room that drew her as a bee to the hive. Sometimes he sought her and spoke with her, but ever since that night in the gardens, he had kept his distance.

Charlotte tried to rein in her disappointment. She had failed in her attempt to win him, and now she must accept her defeat with good grace and turn her attention to the admirers from whom she must choose a husband. With firm resolve, Charlotte told herself to enjoy the evenings that had sounded so magical when she had dreamed of them in her bed at the vicarage, but which, in reality, were not that wonderful. Unfortunately, once the pomp and glitter of London began to lose its shiny, bright newness, the nature of her predicament became all too apparent.

What she had always seen as a lighthearted romp, a pursuit of wealth and affection, now seemed a grim matter indeed, for none of her suitors captured her feelings. Forced to pretend to delight in men she did not want to marry, Charlotte was miserable. The attention and the success beyond her wildest imaginings were no longer savored, and with each passing day, she became more aware of her dilemma. She had only a few short months to make a match, while indecision and the rebellion of her heart plagued her. In truth, she only wanted Max.

"I am simply being perverse," Charlotte mumbled aloud.

"What is that?" asked Phillipa Stollings, who was seated beside her. Although Phillipa very much resembled her brother, the dashing captain, the likeness worked to her detriment, for what was pleasing on his male countenance did not suit her female one. She was tall and big-boned, with a nose too long and a chin too square to be beautiful. What's more, her failings seemed to have soured her disposition, making it difficult to like her.

Lately, she always appeared to be at hand, perhaps in the hope that one of Charlotte's suitors might take an interest in her. Although Charlotte tried her best to be accommodating, she often sensed jealous looks directed toward her, which did not bode well for a future relationship by marriage.

Marriage. Charlotte was well aware that the good captain was growing impatient for her, although Augusta had not spoken of an offer as yet. Stollings's increased attentions and the constant presence of his sister made Charlotte feel as if she were backed into a corner with no way to gracefully exit.

"Oh, I was just thinking aloud," Charlotte answered. "Why is it that we always want that which we cannot have? The classics are full of such tales!" she said, frowning. "Can we not learn from them?"

Phillipa giggled, a rather horsey sound, which she made whenever Charlotte's conversation drifted over her head. Sensing the girl's dismay, Charlotte turned the track of her thoughts from the lessons of the Greeks to more earthly advice. "Papa is forever sermonizing that we should be happy with our lot," she said, "but it is easier said than done."

Phillipa giggled again, and Charlotte gave up her attempt at conversation. She had long since decided that none could share her distress, for those girls who were not so jealous of her popularity that they avoided her did not understand her anxiety. Why, Miss Singleton had actually admitted that she fully intended to marry for money and seek affection elsewhere! Charlotte had been too shocked to respond. Despite the loose morals of the ton, her upbringing would never allow her to contemplate such a thing as taking a lover.

"Shall we stroll through the conservatory?" Phillipa asked with a rather sly look. "I believe that it is quite lovely."

"As you wish," Charlotte answered. Perhaps it would do her good to walk through one of the indoor gardens she had heard so much about. She had certainly been feeling sorry for herself lately, and guilty over it. She tried to remember Papa's teachings and apply them to herself. Then she rose and forced a smile for Phillipa. It was unusual for the homely girl to take the initiative, and Charlotte wanted to encourage her to pursue her own interests.

The conservatory was quiet and rather dimly lit, some of the larger specimens casting shadows as great as trees, and Charlotte could not help but think that in the daylight, it would be easier to view the vegetation. But Phillipa seemed determined, in a rather nervous way, to explore. Stollings's sister was even more giggly than usual, although Charlotte failed to see the humor in the lovely flowers blooming under the glass.

"Oh, look!" Charlotte said, stepping toward a delicate orchid in full blossom. "Isn't it beautiful?" she whispered.

"Not as beautiful as you are, Charlotte," a man whispered back. Starting in surprise, Charlotte felt strong arms enclose her, sliding down her own with an easy familiarity.

"Captain!" Charlotte said with some alarm as she placed the voice. Although she was a bit freer in manner than other young ladies, she knew her suitor should not be here, touching her in the relative privacy of this shadowed bower.

"Phillipa?" she asked. Her distress increased when Stollings's sister did not answer.

"My sister knew I wanted to speak to you alone, dear Charlotte," the captain said smoothly. He pulled her so close that her back touched the long length of his tall body, shocking Charlotte with his boldness. It was one thing to play at kisses with Roddy Black, for she had been totally in control then. Now she was dismayed to discover that the worldly captain had planned this assault on her person with his sister's cooperation.

Charlotte felt a trickle of panic ease up her spine. It was not Stollings that she feared, but the possible consequences of his behavior. If someone saw them here together, she could be ruined...or forced to marry him! Was that his plan? Charlotte's heart quickened its pace considerably at the thought.

She whirled around and realized her mistake immediately, for now she was pressed against his broad chest as he enclosed her in an unwanted embrace. He smelled of some strong cologne, which seemed to rouse her from her stunned state, and Charlotte wrinkled her nose at the effeminate scent. "Unhand me this moment!"

The captain only smiled lazily, in what Charlotte suspected was a practiced flirtation. "Now, Charlotte, we are come to a reckoning, are we not?" he asked, his long lashes lowering.

"We have come to no such thing," she said, vainly pushing her hands against his chest. She could feel her hair, never too solidly anchored, coming loose with her excursions.

The captain laughed softly. "Oh, you are a lovely maid, and will make me a lovely wife," he whispered. He lowered his head, and then his mouth was on hers. He was not rough, nor was he unskilled, but Charlotte found his kiss distasteful, the intimacy an invasion of her person. She shoved again at his chest to little avail, for the captain was not budging.

Perhaps he thought her resistance feigned or the result of an innocence that he would gladly tutor. Whatever his reasoning, the good captain obviously thought so much of himself that he could not imagine a woman disliking his attentions, and he had no intention of letting her go. Realizing that, Charlotte ceased her struggling and stiffened instead, clamping her jaw shut tight and dropping her hands to the sides of her rigidly unyielding body.

"You forget yourself, Stollings," a man said, and Charlotte knew a giddy relief as she recognized the voice. Stollings stopped kissing her, and although he did not release her, he loosened his hold upon her. Charlotte took the opportunity to step out of his embrace and draw in a deep breath. She wanted nothing more than to throw herself into Max's arms, and for some absurd reason, she felt tears threatening.

"Wycliffe? This is none of your affair," Stollings said. Obviously, he was not as easily cowed as Roddy had been. Charlotte glanced at Max. His face was composed, his breathing even, but the slight twitching of the long fingers in his right hand gave away his anger.

"I believe it is the duty of gentlemen everywhere to protect innocent young women from the unwanted attentions of upstart cits," Max said smoothly, a wealth of insults in that one sentence.

"Now, see here, my lord," Stollings protested. "For your information, this woman is to become my wife!"

Charlotte watched Max's fingers move again, almost imperceptibly. His jaw clenched, and his great brown eyes narrowed as his gaze traveled over her. Dismayed to have that anger turned upon her, she nearly trembled.

"Is that true, Miss Trowbridge?" he asked.

Frantically avoiding that intense regard, Charlotte looked from Max to the man at her side, who was smiling smugly at her, and she was at a loss for words. Despite his forward actions this evening, Stollings had been one of her foremost suitors. Well-favored and even-tempered, he had seemed less objectionable than the rest, and if she refused him now, she would have even fewer choices. The weight of her responsibilities pressed down upon her, threatening to choke the life from her while she struggled for an answer.

"Well, Miss Trowbridge?"

Charlotte's eyes flew to Max. Darkly handsome and elegant in his understated attire, he was far more attractive than the younger man at her side. And tonight he was revealing a glimpse of a fiery spirit at odds with his usual placid demeanor. Charlotte wondered what else he hid beneath that quiet exterior. If only she could discover all his secrets...

She forced her attention to the captain. Flashing her a careless grin, he was obviously well aware of his charms. Too well aware of them, Charlotte noted. So many of his movements were studied—designed to show off his dashing profile or his white teeth to their best advantage—that it was hard to see beyond them to the man inside. Yet, somehow, Charlotte suspected that there was very little of substance under the captain's dazzling surface.

He certainly had no interest in literature and would be appalled to hear of her studies. He was what he was—brave and handsome, and very proud of both. Charlotte wondered briefly if he would continue his flirtations after they wed, and she tried to shake the image of a philandering husband from her head.

After all, the captain offered her his name and a comfortable living for her and her family, and she simply must consider those advantages. How could she weigh them against the man himself and find him wanting? She would have a lifetime to probe his depths, admire his much-vaunted looks…and grow accustomed to kisses that left her cold and miserable.

"No," Charlotte managed to squeak. "It is not true."

Charlotte felt, rather than saw, Max relax. She turned to Stollings, who was staring at her in utter disbelief, and put a hand on his arm. "It was very kind of you to offer, sir, but at this time I am afraid—"

Max cut off her pretty speech. "All proposals should be presented to your papa, Miss Trowbridge, as Captain Stollings is well aware, I am sure. And you can rest assured that he will be informed of the liberties you have taken with his daughter," Max warned.

"Now, see here, Wycliffe," Stollings sputtered. He looked as though he was going to grab her arm, and Charlotte moved swiftly away from him even as Max stepped forward to intercede, his dark brows drawn over narrowed eyes. "This is none of your affair, and I would appreciate it if you would take yourself off, so that we may discuss this in private."

"And I would suggest that you take *yourself* off, so that the lady is not accused of any impropriety," Max said. "I am sure your devotion to her includes holding her reputation in the highest regard."

Stollings drew himself up to his full height, although he was still much shorter than Max, and took an aggressive stance. "By what right do you interfere?" he asked. "I warn you, my lord, that I find *your* interest in Miss Trowbridge rather suspect."

Charlotte had to stifle a gasp, for Max looked more murderous than she had ever imagined he could. His normally quiet-looking countenance was black with fury. "I certainly hope you are not trying to sully the lady's good name, for then I would have to call you out," he said slowly. Even as Charlotte reeled in shock at the threat, she realized that Max had given the captain the opportunity to demur.

Stollings had no intention of forgoing the challenge, however. "Name your seconds," he hissed.

"Lords Raleigh and Wolverton will call upon you to make the arrangements," Max replied. He appeared to have regained control of himself, and was smiling grimly.

She glanced at the captain, who sent her an accusatory look, as if she were the author of all his troubles. Then he tossed his blond head and strode from the room with as much dash as he could muster under the circumstances.

Charlotte bristled. Stollings had a lot of nerve to blame her when he was the one who had schemed with his sister to pounce upon her. It was not her fault that Max appeared to rescue her, nor was it her fault if the captain got himself embroiled in a challenge.

A duel! Charlotte felt a momentary qualm, for she certainly did not care to see anyone hurt, especially dearest Max, who had rushed to her rescue. She resisted an urge to fly into his strong arms and rain kisses on that handsome visage. Instead, she stood still, not nearly close enough to him. "Thank you, Max," she said softly.

She was unprepared for his response. He whirled on her, his fine mouth drawn tightly, his dark brows heavy over turbulent eyes.

"You are a fine piece of work!" he snapped. "Your appalling lack of self-control astounds me! Have you no sense of honor, your own or your father's? Did you truly come to London for a husband or to spread your thighs for every snot-nosed gallant in town?"

Charlotte drew back in horror, his words piercing her to the bone. Then she reacted instinctively. She kicked him as hard as she could in the shin.

"Ow!" Max yelped and reached toward his injury while Charlotte watched with pleasure.

"That is for your filthy talk, my lord Wycliffe!" she said. Then she kicked him just as hard in the other leg with all the force of her righteous indignation. She heard the low curse he uttered and saw his face flame with fury, but she ignored his response. "And that is for thinking such things about me!"

As angry as she was, Charlotte was hurt, too, stung that he could believe the worst of her, and she felt the misery that had been building up in her all evening press behind her eyelids. She had to get away before it broke loose, embarrassing her further, and she turned to flee.

She did not get far. "Damn it, Charlotte!" Maximilian said. He grabbed both her arms and spun her around to face him.

"Let go of me! And...and stop that dreadful cursing!" Charlotte scolded as the tears threatened to spill.

Maximilian looked at her in stunned confusion. Was this the same woman who had calmly admitted to kissing Roddy Black for the sake of "experience"? Caught in the same situation with Stollings, she was striking out at him, and now... Now she looked likely to weep at any moment. Maximilian was bewildered, and he did not like it. Women were such strange, illogical creatures. Of course, he had always known that, for his mother was a perfect example of the species.

"Are you trying to tell me that you were not expanding your horizons again?" Maximilian asked, skepticism heavy in his voice. Charlotte did not answer, but just looked up at him helplessly, her green eyes awash, her luscious mouth drooping. She looked miserable. "Do you deny kissing that overweening coxcomb?" he asked, giving her a little shake.

"I do not have to answer to you, my lord. And what is more, it makes no matter to me what you believe!" she said. "Let go of me! I hate you and I hate London and I want to go home."

Maximilian seized upon the suggestion. "Then go home," he said. "I will take you myself," he added magnanimously, while he mentally played out his schedule in his head. Could he take off a few weeks to safely deposit Charlotte back at the vicarage?

She struck him in the chest with her fist. "I cannot go home until I have a husband, and now what am I to do? Oh, I wish I had been born ugly as a post!" she wailed.

"Hush," Maximilian said. Wrapping his arms around her, he drew her close. Although giving comfort was foreign to his nature, he found the embrace oddly affecting. "I am certain that your papa will not mind if you return home. He loves you very much.''

"I cannot," Charlotte mumbled into his chest. "They are all depending on me. Papa, and the boys, and Jane, bless her, who is no great beauty. Carrie might have Mama's looks, but it will be years before she is old enough, and by then it will be too late! I must..." She sobbed into his waistcoat as if the world were at an end.

Maximilian felt a wrench in his gut. He would much rather see the feisty wench who kicked him in the shins than this melancholy creature. "I will take you home, and I will work out something with your papa," he said softly.

Charlotte shook her head. "I will not have you un-happy," Maximilian said firmly, and he meant it. The words drew a lopsided smile from her, and he felt encouraged. "And stop calling me 'my lord.' I thought I was Max."

"Max," she whispered. The word weaved itself around him like a breath of smoke, sweet and heady, drawing him to her like some siren's song. She had lifted her face, and the tracks of her tears glistened on her pale skin like starlight in the darkened conservatory.

Something inside him moved, and without a thought for caution or aught else, Maximilian took her face in his hands and kissed her wet cheeks. He tasted the salt on her lashes, pressed his mouth to the springy curls that escaped along her hairline and met her lips, luscious, warm and innocent, de-spite all her foibles. His thumbs stroked her jaw, his fingers wrapping around her neck where her hair brushed against his knuckles. He did not care where they were; he did not care about anything but the woman in his arms.

Her lips moved against his tentatively, like a child taking its first steps, before parting. His tongue accepted the invi-tation and slid inside. He could feel her hands clutching the lapels of his coat for dear life, then the first gentle forays of her tongue, imitating his own. Dear God... They met, en-twined in a primeval union, and Maximilian felt a great, swelling surge of desire. He wanted her—all of her. Now. Here on the floor of the conservatory, among the hot, ex-otic blooms.

Her breasts, creamy and white, glinted in the lamplight, begging for his touch, for his mouth. Maximilian moved a hand to her shoulder and felt skin like the finest silk under his touch. It would be so easy to push down her sleeve, to slip his fingers inside her bodice. She was his for the taking, soft, sweet and light, as fresh as springtime, as earthy as the lush buds that surrounded them.... He was losing his mind.

With rigid discipline, Maximilian withdrew his lips from hers. For a long moment, he simply held her hard against him, then he pressed a fierce kiss to her forehead. Was he trembling like a schoolboy? "I beg your pardon, Charlotte," he whispered hoarsely. "Forgive me."

Forgive him? There was naught to forgive except his defection. "Max..." She was losing him, she could feel it. And it would always be this way. He would always retreat because of what he was, honorable and fine, and she would have him no other way. He released her.

"I did not kiss Stollings," she said, wanting him to know that truth, at least. "His sister led me in here on a pretext and then left me, and he was trying to persuade me to, but..."

"And I am no better than he, am I?" Max asked, his face taut.

"No! Do not compare yourself to him," Charlotte protested. "You were comforting me."

"Is that what it was?" Max asked. He laughed humorlessly. "Very well, then. I believe you are sufficiently comforted. Now, tuck up your hair and try to appear composed. I will leave by the other door." She turned to go, but he stopped her with a clearing of his throat.

"And, Charlotte..." She turned. His brown eyes were wide and mocking. "Try to keep yourself out of any man's arms, including mine—" Maximilian paused, looking both apologetic and rather rueful "—*especially* mine, for any reason."

Chapter Nine

Charlotte was tempted to throw herself upon Max's mercy and beg him not to go through with the appointment at dawn, but she knew him well enough to spare both Maximilian and herself the indignity of such pleas. All she could do was stand in the copse facing the empty field where the duel was to take place.

It had been easy to discover the time and place of the meeting. Her other suitors were prevailed upon to tell her what they knew, but even they were not certain what would happen. Although the prevailing attitude was that Maximilian would shoot Stollings dead, some thought the captain's military experience would serve him well. He, they believed, would kill his lordship.

Charlotte gripped fingers white with strain and prayed that neither one would be hurt. Although it was chilly, she felt sweat dampening her chemise under her gown and cloak. It contrasted sharply with the chill of the dew that seeped through her slippers.

The sound of horses and the rattle of a carriage made her duck farther behind the trees, and when she peeked out again, she could see both Maximilian and Captain Stollings separated by a span of cropped grass. Each spoke quietly to the men she knew to be their seconds, and each appeared to be maddeningly calm.

Charlotte knew a moment of outrage. How could these men be so stupid as to try to put bullets in each other and not feel a qualm about it, while she was quaking with agitation? Not wanting either one to be hurt, her anxious gaze flew back and forth between them, but her eyes kept lingering on the taller figure closest to her. Max.

She stared at him. Tall, straight, and elegant, he moved with cool grace, as unruffled as if this were how he spent every morning. Charlotte was not so unaffected, and she choked back a cry as he took his position. She heard a voice, and then, as if in a dream, she saw Max turn, aim and fire. The blast of his pistol, deafening in the dawn silence, was followed quickly by another.

It all happened so fast that the scene took on an air of unreality. Charlotte raised a hand to her mouth fearfully as she waited for some sign that Maximilian had been hit, but he did not move or flinch, and the breath she had been holding released itself in a rush.

Her eyes flew to the captain. He was still standing, valiantly clutching his shoulder while he shouted something that was lost on the wind. Then his seconds closed in about him. He must have been hurt, but not badly, Charlotte realized.

Relief that neither man had been killed made her dizzy, and Charlotte closed her eyes. When she opened them again, she recognized Lord Raleigh striding to Maximilian along the line of trees that hid her from sight. "A flesh wound only!" he said. "Deuced good aim you have, Wycliffe, as always."

Charlotte must have made a noise, some strangled sound of gladness, because Raleigh and Maximilian immediately looked toward the spot where she was standing. She stepped out.

"Charlotte!" Maximilian said, frowning with disapproval.

"Miss Trowbridge!" Raleigh said, grinning with pleasure. "Come along, and we shall take you home. Best not dawdle here, dueling being against the law and all that," he added, motioning her to them.

Charlotte moved briskly to Max's side and stole a glance at him. The set of his dark brows told her he was not happy to see her, but he walked along with her to the waiting carriage. Although her presence at the dawn meeting was, she knew, the height of impropriety, Charlotte did not care. She could not have waited at home, worrying herself sick and wondering if he was hurt. Let him scold her all he wished about society's rules; there were some that she simply could not follow.

The Wycliffe coach was waiting, stationed near the copse, and Charlotte was only too glad for the opportunity to return to her cousin's home in comfort. When Maximilian helped her inside and slid his tall frame in beside her, she sighed, letting her tense limbs relax into the luxurious cushions.

Instead of taking the opposite seat, Raleigh remained on the ground, holding the door. "I say, Wycliffe, you will see Miss Trowbridge home, won't you?" he asked, grinning. "I really must get some rest. Much too early to be up and about, you know." Without waiting for an answer, Raleigh slammed the door, leaving them alone in the carriage.

Maximilian's spacious vehicle suddenly seemed very small, and Charlotte could feel the heat emanating from the tall masculine form stretched out alongside her. He was close enough to rub against her shoulder, and his thigh could easily brush her leg. She drew in a deep breath and looked away. Her prayers had been answered, and he was here, alive and whole and well. She should be thankful.

She was. Charlotte felt heartily grateful to her maker that Maximilian was unharmed, and yet... Fresh on the heels of her relief came anger at the entire episode. That he should sit here, so calm and collected, after the scare he had put her through! And Stollings—bloody and bowed, for what? Charlotte felt like cuffing them both about the ears, for, though grown, they had no more sense than James and Thomas.

"Although I know you felt compelled to engage in this ridiculous duel, I am not at all happy about it, my lord," she said as evenly as she could.

Maximilian grimaced. He had not failed to notice his demotion. Whenever Charlotte was displeased with him, he went from being "dear Max" to "my lord." He tilted his head to the side to study her perfect profile.

"And the poor captain! What is to become of him now—a soldier injured in his sword arm?" she asked.

"Excuse me, but I tried to disrupt his aim, just in case he planned to put a bullet through my chest!" Maximilian snapped. Surely she did not care for that overblown popinjay? "I had no idea that you would rather I take his fire!"

"I would rather no one was hurt at all!" Charlotte retorted. "Really, Max, you can have no idea how I feel to know that blood was shed because of me. And the man's only crime was asking me to marry him!" Turning to him, she displayed a pair of eyes flashing with green fire.

Maximilian felt his temper rise as he thought of the captain's foibles, especially the man's last bit of bravado. Stollings had sneered at his wound and at Maximilian. "You are welcome to her, my lord, for she kisses with all the passion of a fence post!" he managed to say before his seconds, obviously not anxious for a repeat of the morning's proceedings, hushed him.

Maximilian had been furious. He wished he had shot the bastard between the legs, so that the captain's amorous bent would be curtailed for good.

Struggling out of his dark thoughts, Maximilian found Charlotte glaring at him, her face pink with annoyance, and he was struck by the memory of kissing her himself. She had been flushed then, too—not with anger but with exquisite desire for him. She had never treated *him* like a fence post.

His lips curving at the recollection, Maximilian realized that Stollings had, at least, confirmed Charlotte's story. She had not joined the captain in the conservatory to test her amatory skills. If she had, he would hardly claim her to be unresponsive.

For a moment, Maximilian enjoyed the notion of Charlotte's innocent passion reserved strictly for himself—her tender lips opening only for him, her sweet, hot sighs called up only by his touch. Then he mentally shook himself, annoyed at such ridiculous thoughts.

"Stollings's crime was behaving atrociously," Maximilian snapped. "Have you so swiftly forgotten how he enlisted his sister to lure you into an inappropriate position and then forced himself upon you? What would have happened if I had not come along? Would he have stopped at kisses?" Maximilian saw Charlotte's startled glance and knew his words were penetrating her pique.

"What if someone else had arrived? You would have found yourself married to the man, whether you wished it or no," Maximilian added. By the alarmed look that crossed her features, he judged that the possibility gave her pause.

"All these rules between men and women," she grumbled, waving a gloved hand in dismissal. "A fellow unable to remove his coat.... Two friends unable to be alone for a moment.... It is all too silly."

Maximilian felt disinclined to point out that those guidelines existed for her own protection, for he had ignored them too often in his dealings with her. As it was, Charlotte appeared indisposed to debate the issue, too, for when she spoke, she uttered a new complaint.

"When Papa gets wind of this duel of yours, he is not going to be happy," she noted sullenly.

Maximilian frowned. What did he care for the disapprobation of a country vicar? Still, he felt a bit chagrined by the distress he knew Charlotte's father would feel, just as if he had let the man down somehow. Maximilian shook off the ludicrous idea.

"I will post a letter to your father, explaining the situation," he said gruffly. A jolt of the coach brought him closer to Charlotte, and he saw her attention shift to the dark hair that slid across his shoulder.

With an effort, Maximilian fought the attraction that seemed suddenly to flare between them. He had never thought of his hair as particularly stimulating, but the way she looked at it made all his muscles tighten. He could imagine Charlotte's slim, capable hands enmeshed deeply in the heavy locks, clutching them ...

"Why do you wear your hair long?" she asked.

"I like it that way," he answered curtly.

Charlotte smiled, her eyes twinkling. "Max, I know that you do not do anything without some underlying reason. Now, let me think," she said, pausing mischievously. She tugged at one of her long fingers. "Because you cannot fit a trim into your busy schedule?"

Maximilian shook his head, his lips twitching.

Charlotte pulled at another digit. "Because you are too miserly to pay a barber?"

Maximilian tried to frown at her, but could not.

"Is the reason a deep, dark secret?" she asked. Her green eyes were fairly dancing, her full mouth parted in question, and Maximilian had to stifle the urge to kiss her. He shook his head again. "Then, why? Tell me. On my honor I will not reveal the truth to a soul," she added, placing a hand over her heart.

Maximilian's gaze strayed past her fingers to the swelling of her breasts revealed beneath the open folds of her cloak. They rose out of the bodice of her far too low-cut gown like pale mounds. He had difficulty dissembling. "To annoy my mother," he said hoarsely.

Tearing his gaze away from her creamy curves, Maximilian watched her blink at him wide-eyed for a moment. Then she started laughing, a lovely, joyous whoop that lit her face. Maximilian grinned at her mirth before he added, more soberly, "Quite a bit of what I do is calculated to annoy her."

"Surely not! You can only be a dutiful son!" Charlotte replied. Maximilian laughed with a tinge of bitterness, but further discussion was cut off by their arrival at Augusta's lodgings. Eager to escape the path the conversation was taking, he stepped out and handed her down.

"Shall I see you in?" he asked, mentally reviewing his day's schedule. Would a visit delay him?

"No," Charlotte answered. She smiled so wickedly that for a moment he could swear she had read his mind. "There is no need." She stepped away from him, but then turned to eye him levelly. "I sincerely hope that this morning's duel is the last such bit of nonsense that I will have to view while I am in London."

Maximilian thought of all the males vying for her hand, and he felt a sense of foreboding totally at odds with his normally clear thinking. "My dear Charlotte," he said, smiling grimly, "I certainly hope that you are correct."

The obnoxious manservant met them on the steps.

"Miss Trowbridge! Miss Trowbridge!" he whined, showing far more agitation than Maximilian had thought possible. "Your cousin has been worried sick!"

Charlotte felt a pang of guilt, for she knew the elderly lady would be horrified to learn of her whereabouts. In truth, she had never expected her absence to be discovered, for Augusta rarely rose before noon. Frowning, Charlotte hurried to the door. She did not spare a glance at Maximilian and was surprised when a movement behind her told her he was coming with her.

"There is really no need," she repeated, but the look on his face brooked no argument. Charlotte knew that when Maximilian took his protective stance, there was no reasoning with him. She would have smiled had not the situation been so serious.

They found Augusta ensconced on the settee in a state of dishabille. She was wrapped in several blankets, although the room was near stifling, and Charlotte felt a new surge of remorse for causing her cousin distress.

"Charlotte!" Augusta's face was pale, and she waved a lace handkerchief in a dramatic gesture that reminded Charlotte her cousin was no longer a young woman. Moving into Augusta's arms, she received a weak hug while nearly being overcome by the heavily scented perfume rising from the lady's prodigious bosom.

"Where have you been?" Augusta demanded in stronger accents. Before Charlotte could answer, the elderly woman turned her attention to Max.

"Wycliffe! I would never have suspected your complicity in this little escapade! Have you been alone with my niece? Do not tell me that you dragged her from my house to watch your shameful bout with pistols this morning!"

"I most certainly did not drag Charlotte anywhere, Miss Thurgoode," Maximilian said. He stepped toward the prostrate woman, who reluctantly extended her hand. He bent over it. "I trust you are not seriously ill?"

"Humph," she said with a heave of her chest. Charlotte could see that although Augusta's awe of the earl prevented her from insulting him in any way, she was definitely not pleased with him. "As if you would care when you are the cause of my decline! Dueling over my niece! She will be ruined! Ruined!" Augusta said before letting her head fall back upon the pillows.

"Nonsense," Maximilian said smoothly. "I assure you I was protecting her good name, not besmirching it, and if anything, the episode should only add more luster to her exalted position as the season's most coveted lady," he added, his lip curling in what Charlotte suspected was very close to a sneer.

"Perhaps," Augusta acknowledged with a sigh, "but I am too ill to brave the gossips and too old for such excitement. This latest incident has exhausted me." Suddenly she lifted her head as if remembering that her question had gone unanswered. "If not with you, where was Charlotte this morning?" Augusta asked, her chins jiggling with the force of her dismay.

"Although I did not invite her," Maximilian said, sending Charlotte a black look, "she somehow discovered the location of our meeting and hid herself among the trees."

"Oh!" Augusta fell back again with a such a cry of alarm that Charlotte stepped forward. "She will be ruined! Ruined!"

"I assure you, Miss Thurgoode," Maximilian said in a tone that brooked no resistance, "that she shall not be ruined. No one knows of her presence except myself and one of my seconds, who can be trusted not to speak of it."

Although Augusta appeared uncertain, she was not bold enough to dispute his words. "Charlotte, you must write your father at once. This is too much for me in my advanced years. Perhaps later in the season, after I have rested, or next year..."

The gnawing guilt that had kept Charlotte quiet was overshadowed by panic. Did her cousin intend to send her home? She thought of the fabulous sums spent on clothing and foolish fripperies Augusta insisted were necessary for a season. Had Papa's money gone for naught?

If she went back to Sussex now, Charlotte knew she would let them down—Papa, Sarah, all of them. Her eyes flew to Max's in horror, silently pleading for him to help her somehow. And he did. With a simple shake of his head, he checked her growing alarm. It was just a brief movement, unseen by her cousin, but Charlotte felt hope rise again with the certainty that Max, dear Max, was in control.

Unfortunately, Maximilian did not feel in control. His usual, easy assurance had deserted him, as it so often did in Charlotte's presence. Although he could not bear to see his beauty in such distress, he was sorely tempted.... It would be so easy to accede to the old lady's wishes and send Charlotte home. Then she would be gone, far away from London's more unsavory types and no longer his responsibility.

Of course, her father's money was undoubtedly spent, and to no avail, since Charlotte was sure to find no great marital prize in Upper Bidwell. However, Maximilian told himself that he could step in to help the family, to see the boys off into careers, at least. And Charlotte? What would she do? Marry a farmer, a baker, a shopkeeper like Alf? She deserved better....

She was staring at him, her startling green eyes wide and awash with unshed tears. Despite the misgivings she had expressed to him about husband-hunting, Maximilian knew that she would be devastated by the move back home. *The toast retires in disgrace...* He could imagine the titters of the ton, and something wrenched deep down in his gut. As much as he would like to send her away, he could not, in good conscience, ruin her only season.

"Let us not be hasty," he urged Augusta in a tone that suggested he was unaccustomed to argument. "This morning's work will no doubt be forgotten within the week, when some new on-dit claims society's attention. As I told Charlotte, I will convey to the vicar my deepest regrets for the unfortunate incident.

"However..." Maximilian looked meaningfully at Augusta. "Charlotte is not at fault. Stollings is to blame and no one else. And I fear that such things are inevitable when one is the most sought-after young lady of the new season." He forced a smile and turned to Charlotte. "Your cousin is overset. Perhaps a few days of rest will improve her health. In the meanwhile, I am sure she can persuade upon one of her female friends to escort you about.

"If your health does not improve," Maximilian said, glancing back to Augusta, "then, naturally, we must make other arrangements." Taking the elderly lady's hand again, he bent over it and looked directly into her pale blue eyes, a device he used to quell any inclinations to protest his authority. "Good day, Miss Thurgoode."

"My lord," she answered meekly. Stepping away from her, Maximilian motioned to Charlotte with a tilt of his head.

"I will see his lordship out," Charlotte said to her cousin as she followed him into the hall. When they were alone in the comparative privacy of the entry, Maximilian turned toward her in a businesslike manner.

"Is she truly ill?" he asked.

"I do not know," Charlotte answered.

Although he tried to ignore it, Maximilian was stricken by the distress on her lovely features.

"My cousin is not young..."

Maximilian cut her off with a sharp look. He did not want her wallowing in guilt over the old lady's condition. "We shall see. I shall stop by in a few days' time. Meanwhile, I wish you to continue as you normally would. Your disappearance, coming on the heels of the duel, would be marked."

Charlotte nodded, her eyes wide. "But if she is truly ill, then I cannot impose upon her any longer," she protested.

"Certainly not," Maximilian said.

"Oh, Max! I cannot go home in disgrace!" she moaned, twisting her hands in front of her. Her face was pale, her full lips atremble, and Maximilian wanted nothing more than to take her in his arms and comfort her—in the manner he had used but a few nights ago.

One step toward her, and he knew she would be pressed against him, soft and warm and delectable. His eyes moved down the slim column of her throat to the curves of her breasts, and his hands itched to touch her. Just one step and she would be in his arms, responding to him and only him...

But that would not do. Maximilian knew she was his responsibility and that he must behave accordingly. He steeled himself against the desires of his body. "Hush," he said, more sharply than he intended. "If she remains unwell, you shall simply stay with someone else."

"Who?" Charlotte asked, appearing truly baffled. "There is no one in London I know well—except you," she said, with an uneasy laugh.

Maximilian gave her a crooked grin. "I will write my mother."

Maximilian sat staring at the page before him, the fingers of his right hand drumming absently on the table. Despite his promise to Charlotte, he was wavering. Unleashing his mother into his life would be like opening Pandora's box. He could not be entirely sure what she might do, and once she was here, she might prove difficult to restrain.

He must be cracked in the head. Why else would he suggest such lunacy? Shifting uncomfortably in his chair,

Maximilian knew why. He had but to look into those great, spring-colored eyes of Charlotte's and his good sense deserted him. He sighed, staring at the empty sheet until the rhythmic sound of his fingers finally penetrated his brain and he picked up the quill. Telling himself the vicar was counting on him, he wrote, "My dear Madam."

Although Maximilian was tempted to address her as *Mother,* he knew that would only annoy her, and then she might not answer his summons. Sibylle disdained the title of Mother, which reminded her much too forcibly of her age, and Maximilian had always called her by her given name.

His father had been a stiff, stodgy man whose one impulsive act had been to marry Sibylle Mollineaux, and Maximilian had often wished the earl had not succumbed to that bit of uncharacteristic impetuousness. Releasing a low sigh at the follies of men, Maximilian wrote a brief message under the greeting.

"I find myself in need of your services. Please attend to me at once." Without a thought to the imperiousness of the words, Maximilian signed his name and put his seal to it. Then he frowned, staring at the paper, while his fingers resumed their thrumming upon the polished surface of his desk.

He assumed that the message would serve its purpose and bring his mother to London. But once here, just what would she do?

Chapter Ten

Miss Thurgoode was not recovering. Maximilian had to
face that fact, along with the realization that Charlotte was
blaming herself for the woman's illness, whether real or
feigned. Although his beauty went out nearly as often, her
quips to her beaux were less spirited, her smiles more forced,
her eyes dull and lifeless. He noticed it all whenever he saw
her. Didn't the others see as well as he?

Although he told himself it was not his concern, Maximilian wished he could ease her distress. This selfless desire
struck him at the oddest moments. In the middle of business discussions, over a hand of cards, even when he was in
the company of some beautiful woman, suddenly he would
wonder how he could make Charlotte happy.

He justified these strange thoughts by telling himself he
was attached to Charlotte in the same manner that he was
to her little sister Jenny. He had, in a sense, adopted the
whole Trowbridge family and was receiving letters from
nearly all of its members. The writings of James and
Thomas were a hodgepodge of questions about horseflesh,
boxing and driving, while Jane's were very serious and well-
informed. Carrie wrote silly, endearing messages, and Kit
struggled valiantly with his name, but Maximilian's favorite piece to date was a picture of himself drawn by Jenny.

No one had ever seen fit to give him such a touching gift.
His staff members were chosen for their quiet efficiency, not
their friendship, and they endeavored to keep children from

his path. His mistresses knew he did not care for affectionate displays or sentimental tokens, and they would have been hard-pressed to provide any. His tenants had always treated him with formality, out of deference to his rigid schedule, perhaps. In truth, everyone kept a certain distance from the Earl of Wycliffe—except the vicar and his family.

Although the very uniqueness of Jenny's present made it precious, it was the message implicit in the drawing that meant more. *I am thinking of you. I miss you.* Who had ever longed for his company as the Trowbridges did? Their sincere affection for him moved him in places he had not known existed.

The picture itself was an outrageous thing that showed him with a huge, lumpy head and appendages that were no more than scribbles. Yet Maximilian treasured it. Still, he was embarrassed to place it in his study where it might readily be seen, so he stuck it in the edge of a frame that graced his bedroom, effectively covering up most of a priceless painting of Prometheus.

Prometheus! Suddenly, Maximilian had the answer to Charlotte's blue devils. He knew she had neglected her passion while in London for fear of being labeled a bluestocking. Although he could not blame her, Maximilian frowned at the thought of his brilliant beauty married to some barely literate squire.... He shook aside the idea. The vicar had given him carte blanche where Charlotte's proposals were concerned, he reminded himself, and he would make sure she did not end up with such a man.

Without pondering the difficult subject of exactly whom Charlotte would wed, Maximilian grinned as his plan took shape. He would send over a few books. No, he would take the classical texts to her himself and thereby enjoy the look of surprise on her lovely features. Still grinning foolishly, he abruptly excused himself right in the middle of a conversation with his head groom and, with a total disregard for his schedule, Maximilian headed for his library.

He chose several volumes that he thought Charlotte might enjoy, keeping in mind her interest in Thebes. Then his fingers brushed against a book of sketches of Greece and lingered there. Naturally, he had visited the most famous sites on his tour of the Continent, but that was many years ago. Now he was struck with a vision of showing them to Charlotte, of viewing the world with someone who shared his enthusiasm.

With uncanny clarity, Maximilian pictured Charlotte at his side, climbing the ancient hills, seeing gods among the ruins and standing amid the soaring columns of Athena's famous temple . . . before he discarded such thoughts as ridiculous. The only way he could travel to Greece with Charlotte was if he took the entire Trowbridge family, and knowing Carrie's and the older boys' disdain for such things, such a trip would be utter misery.

Maximilian scowled at the book of sketches and moved on, but then he returned to pull it from the shelf and place it with the others. Suppressing the strange disquiet he felt at the thought that Charlotte would never see her favorite sights, he decided that at least she should be able to gaze at the drawings to her heart's content.

"Miss Trowbridge is out, my lord." It took a moment for the servant's words to sink into Maximilian's brain. Out? Maximilian frowned. Had he set aside his afternoon's schedule only to find her out? "Where is she?" he asked.

Miss Thurgoode's servant gave him an assessing glance that made him want to box the man's ears and then shrugged insolently. "Riding in the park with one of the gentlemen," he answered. Then he prepared to shut the door.

"One of the gentlemen?" Maximilian's voice boomed out, forestalling any plans the servant had to escape his presence. "What gentleman?"

"I am sure I do not know," the servant answered slyly. "You would have to ask Miss Thurgoode."

"That I will," Maximilian said. He tried to quell the anger that was seeping into his veins at the thought of Charlotte out alone with some unknown person. The memory of

Stollings's unconscionable behavior was still fresh in his mind, and he forced away an image of her in some cad's embrace, unwilling—as responsive as a fence post.

"I am sorry, my lord," the servant said with a triumphant smile. "Miss Thurgoode is indisposed." He ducked his head in a brief bow and shut the door.

Maximilian stood on the doorstep, enraged. By God, he wanted Charlotte home when he came to call, not dallying with one of her ridiculous suitors. And by God, he would know with whom she was dallying! Did no one but himself give a damn about the vicar's daughter?

He released the hands that had tightened into fists at his side and drew a deep breath. He had never been the vengeful sort, never been prone to violence of any kind, but at this moment, he would gladly have tossed that audacious servant down the stairs and into the street without a qualm.

All thoughts of leaving a message were abandoned in the face of the ignominy of knocking again on the door. With a scowl that frightened his driver, Maximilian turned on his heel and returned to his waiting carriage. He vowed that this was the last time he would be ill-treated by that household, its impertinent servant or the mistress who had all but abandoned her cousin to the perils of London.

From now on, he wanted Charlotte where he could keep an eye on her. Deuce it all, where was his mother?

A pensive expression on his face, Peter Wilkes stepped out of the earl's town house to avail himself of one of his lordship's coaches.

"Leaving a bit early, are you?" asked a voice, and Peter turned to see Wycliffe's head groom, Harry, loping toward him. Harry was a grizzled old fellow with a slight limp acquired after a fall many years ago, but he was still an excellent man with horses.

"Yes, it appears his lordship is... out for the afternoon," Peter said. He was unable to hide the slight frown that indicated his opinion of the disruption in his routine.

He had once thought Wycliffe and himself were kindred spirits, but the way the man was behaving lately...

"Aye. I saw him take off," Harry said. Something in his voice made Peter look closer at the head groom. He was clutching his cap before him and moving it from one hand to the other in a nervous gesture.

"What is it, Harry?" Peter asked.

"Well, if you must know," Harry said, looking relieved to be asked, "it's his lordship. I'm worried about him. Earlier today he was in the midst of talking with me, it being our usual time to look over the horses, and all of a sudden he gets this odd look on his face—"

"What kind of look?" Peter asked, with no little alarm. He had an uncle who was struck down just as suddenly by a case of indigestion and who never lived to see the morning.

"Well, now, it is kind of hard to describe," Harry said. He lifted a gnarled hand to scratch the top of his head, where tufts of gray grew out in all directions. "It was kind of... wistful, like," he said finally. "And then, as quick as you please, he took himself off right in the middle of our meeting, which is not at all like him, you see."

Peter felt relieved that his lordship's expression had not been one of pain, but he agreed, with a sense of foreboding, that Wycliffe's actions were highly unusual. Harry paused to shift the cap in his hands. He looked a bit uncomfortable, as well he should, for it was not the head groom's place to question his master's actions. However, knowing that the old man truly cared for his lordship, Peter nodded for him to continue.

"Then, just a bit ago, his lordship came hurrying into the stable, yelling for his horse and rushing off as if the very devil were after him," Harry said, his face creased with concern.

"His lordship never rushes," Peter said. He stated the fact dully, dazed by Harry's information. Wycliffe never forgot his appointments, was always punctual and always moved at the same steady pace. The only time he ever wanted speed was when he drove his curricle in a race. "Surely you exaggerate."

Harry shook his head firmly. "I wish I did, Mr. Wilkes. Took off like a shot, he did," he said, demonstrating with a swoop of his hand. "Why, in all my years with his lordship, I've never seen the like."

Peter stared off into the distance where the walls of the town house garden marched away in an even line. The grass had recently been trimmed and ran neatly up to the stones. Everything about Wycliffe's life—his homes, his possessions, his business, his travel—were all arranged to the smallest detail. What the devil was throwing things awry?

With a sinking feeling, Peter thought he knew the answer. He also knew he had no business gossiping with the earl's servants as if he were a low-bred stable boy. With a sigh, he decided to dismiss Harry's queries, but something in the old man's eyes stopped him. Instead, he threw his usual closemouthed attitude to the winds. "You had better get used to it, Harry, for I suspect it will grow worse before better."

"Is he sick, sir?" Harry asked, his head bowed.

"That is a matter of opinion," Peter answered.

"What is it then? Do you know?"

"I am not sure, Harry," Peter replied tiredly, "but I suspect it is a female."

Harry's small black eyes widened in surprise and then he burst into low, garrulous laughter. "So that's it!" he said, catching his breath.

"I see no cause for amusement," Peter said stiffly.

"You don't?" Harry chortled. "I do! That I do! Things will be changing around here, rightly enough. You wait and see! Nothing like a lady to change a man's habits!"

Although Peter gave Harry a frosty glance, it did little to stifle the man's mirth. With a few more mumbled prophetic announcements, Harry took off, limping to the stables, slapping his cap against his leg and laughing all the while.

Peter watched him with a frown. Wait and see, indeed! He drew himself up and walked toward the waiting carriage. If things got much worse, he would no longer be around to see it. He had received other offers of employment that he had never considered before, but now might be the time to rethink his career—before the female totally ruined his lordship.

Maximilian was well aware that by the time he got his mount and reached Hyde Park, he might miss Charlotte entirely, but he had no desire to go gawking after her in his carriage like an old woman. As he spurred his horse on, he realized that he had not even been aware Charlotte could ride. The knowledge that some idiot suitor was more cognizant of her skills than he was irked him somehow. Where had she learned? Maximilian could swear that the vicarage boasted no horseflesh.

He had the foresight to send a boy round to her lodgings with instructions to inform him at once of her arrival, so that he might not waste hours searching for her after she had gone. With any luck, Maximilian told himself, this fool's errand would be over before it had begun.

If it was a fool's errand, Maximilian counted himself the fool. He hated traveling in anything other than a sedate manner. He detested feeling harried. And he despised throwing his schedule to the winds to run off after the vicar's daughter.

He had half a mind to ignore the whole situation, but every time he considered turning around, he pictured Charlotte hounded by some blackguard anxious for a taste of the season's reigning Toast. Whom was she with? Although Roddy Black and Stollings had vanished from the scene, their places had been eagerly taken by other young bucks, mostly smooth-faced lads who made Maximilian feel ancient. Cavely and Merton immediately sprang to mind. Worthless pups, both of them, and fully capable of trying to steal a maid's virtue in the course of their flirtations.

There was still Raleigh, of course, but Maximilian thought his friend was simply amusing himself. And Raleigh, at least, could be trusted. Maximilian did not feel the same about all the members of Charlotte's entourage. She had been seeing a lot of a squire in from the country, Bottom by name, and Clemson's youngest boy, who was destined for a clerical career. Although they seemed harmless enough, Maximilian knew that Charlotte could tempt a saint to indecorous behavior. Lord knows, she had tempted him often enough....

Maximilian pushed aside memories of his own folly and tried to concentrate on Charlotte's admirers. That fellow Burgess, who had doted on her from the first, was still pursuing her. Maximilian did not care for the man, although he could not quite put his finger on what it was about the baron that bothered him. He grimaced. And those were only her most serious suitors. Others, including older, more hardened rakes, flitted about her like bees to honey. Maximilian spurred his horse.

Although it was past the fashionable hour of five o'clock, Hyde Park was still crowded with the pink of the ton ogling one another. Maximilian thought the ritual ridiculous, but he condescended to participate once a week on Thursdays, per his calendar. Since today was Tuesday, his appearance produced sufficient comment to hinder his search.

Unfortunately, it seemed as if everyone of his acquaintance felt compelled to stop and exchange words with him, and he was forced to abandon his most polished style. A smile and a nod were the best he could do, if he were to find Charlotte among the throng.

"I say, Wycliffe! Have you changed your schedule?" The sight of Raleigh, perched atop a phaeton with a woman beside him, made Maximilian urge his mount closer. Although he had been told Charlotte was riding, that insolent manservant of Miss Thurgoode's might be wrong.

Maximilian tilted his head to the side to get a better view of the lady beside Raleigh. She wore a large hat that shaded her face, but brown hair peeped from below the brim, and

Maximilian easily recognized Raleigh's sister. He nodded a swift greeting to her, then glanced back to Raleigh. "Have you seen Charlotte?"

Raleigh grinned widely. "Why, no. Are you looking for her?" Maximilian nodded and rode away without so much as a farewell. "I shall tell her if I see her," Raleigh called to his back.

"Mercy! What is the matter with Wycliffe?" a decidedly annoyed feminine voice asked. Raleigh turned to his sister, who was fanning herself furiously, an outraged expression on her face. "I thought he was the only one of your friends possessed of good manners, but I see that I was wrong."

"Pay him no mind, Lisbeth," Raleigh advised, chortling. "Wycliffe's in love, and it has rattled his brain."

"Wycliffe in *love?* You are humming me," his sister accused, making a face.

"No! It is true, I swear it! But Wycliffe doesn't know it yet, so you must not tell him."

Lisbeth sat back in her seat, her prim mouth set with disapproval at his foolishness. "What drivel! I should have known better than to try to talk to you! Why I ever consented to drive with you, I will never know."

When Maximilian finally found Charlotte, sweet relief banished the specters that had been pushing him on, and he halted to stare at her. Although some distance from her, he knew at once the unmistakable curves of the lush figure in the carmine riding habit was Charlotte.

From the looks of her docile mount, Maximilian suspected that she was a middling rider, but she did not seem uncomfortable. Nor did she appear to be in any imminent danger from her companion. In fact, as far as Maximilian could judge, she was enjoying herself immensely, laughing brightly at some quip from the man beside her. He maneuvered himself so as to get a better look at the fellow and nearly groaned aloud.

Wroth! Maximilian had thought the marquis out of town, and now here he was—returned and at Charlotte's side.

Maximilian's grip tightened on the reins as he felt unreasoning, hot anger at the sight of the man bending his head near to Charlotte's. With an effort, he relaxed his fingers, for he had the sense to realize his response was not at all in keeping with the innocuous situation.

Still, he had been in seemingly innocuous situations with Charlotte several times, and things had happened that he could not control. With a grimace, Maximilian suspected he had far more reason for controlling himself than Wroth did. Would Charlotte kiss the good marquis like a fence post— or melt in his arms? Maximilian urged his horse closer.

"Good day, Miss Trowbridge. Wroth," he said, finding it absurdly difficult to speak the man's name.

"M—my lord!" Charlotte said, blushing delightfully. Was it with pleasure at the sight of him? Or had she been testing her amorous talents again? Maximilian felt his fingers clench at the thought of her honing her skills with such an experienced partner.

"Wycliffe." Wroth raised one dark brow in amused question at Maximilian's barely restrained displeasure, and Maximilian tried to regain his composure.

"Miss Trowbridge, I am so glad that I happened across you here." Although Maximilian spoke as smoothly as he could, the words sounded forced, even to himself. "I have a package for you. May I call this evening?"

"Well, I..." Charlotte appeared momentarily at a loss, and Maximilian cocked his head. Surely, she did not intend to refuse him? She glanced swiftly to her companion and then back at Maximilian. "I am not normally receiving callers because of my cousin's indisposition. However, I am sure, since you are such a good friend of the family, it would be permissible."

She smiled a little nervously, and Maximilian struggled to interpret her odd mood. Well aware that he would discover nothing while Wroth looked on, Maximilian wished the marquis to perdition. The constraints of polite company exacerbated his already heated temper. He wanted Charlotte to himself, damn it!

"Very well," Maximilian said with a grim nod. "Around seven o'clock?"

Charlotte blinked in surprise. What was Max about? She would barely have time to get home and dress! She opened her mouth to protest, but something in the set of his lips made her change her mind. "That would be fine."

"Good day, then, Miss Trowbridge, Wroth." As quickly as he had appeared, Maximilian rode off, and Charlotte stared after him. He was upset, but what about? And what package could he have for her? Something from the vicarage?

"I hope there is no difficulty at home," she murmured.

"I very much doubt it," Wroth said dryly.

Charlotte glanced over at him with no little surprise, for she had nearly forgotten his presence. Max had a nasty habit of overwhelming her senses. "Oh, my lord, I must apologize for cutting our ride short. You will forgive me, won't you?"

"You leave me with no choice, Miss Trowbridge," the marquis said evenly. Although his mouth was curved in amusement, Charlotte had the feeling that Wroth was not used to having his plans thwarted. In that case, she decided, the experience would do him good. He was doted upon entirely too much by the females of his acquaintance.

Men were such troublesome creatures! Charlotte would never have suspected, but dealing with them had become extremely tiresome. Sometimes they acted more childish than Kit or Jane. And the titled ones, like Wroth and Wycliffe, were the most spoiled of the lot—always expecting the world to stop and wait upon them!

In truth, she had been a little stunned to see Maximilian. Unlike her suitors, he usually disdained seeking her out and simply sent round a note with one of his innumerable servants. If he had not been riding in the park, he probably would have dispatched a messenger, Charlotte thought ungraciously, for she knew that nothing irritated him more than altering his schedule. The thought gave her pause.

"My lord?" Charlotte asked abruptly.

"Yes?" Wroth attended her easily.

"What day is it today?"

"It is Tuesday." His answer made Charlotte duck her head in an effort to hide the smile that tugged at her lips. No wonder Max had been out of sorts! He was off his calendar. But why?

Charlotte firmly quelled the hope that cavorted in her breast and told herself, as she always did, that Max's actions changed nothing. He was the Earl of Wycliffe, and she was only a country vicar's daughter. And he would never see her as anything else.

Max was still angry. Charlotte faced those dark brows, lowered menacingly, and those eyes bright with something indefinable, and she felt her heart beat frantically in response. She was unafraid, regretfully; fear would have been easier to endure. It was excitement that made her breath catch. There was something about seeing him this way—viewing the fiery, passionate side of him he usually hid from the world—that set her pulse to racing. Charlotte summoned all her will to appear serene as she rose to greet him.

"Max! It is—"

He cut her off. "Please do not see him again," he said tersely.

"Who?" Charlotte asked, genuinely mystified.

"Wroth! That is who, or have you so quickly forgotten the man you were with this afternoon?" His smooth voice was grating, his generous mouth unyielding.

"No, I have not forgotten, but—"

Her protest was again halted. "Although I am sure your cousin is fairly drooling over the prospect of Wroth coming up to scratch, let me advise you that he will not. He has been one of the ton's most eligible bachelors for years now and has shown no sign of changing his ways. By all accounts, he has ice water running through his veins and has no intention of ever setting up his nursery. His dalliance with you can lead to nothing. You are not to see him again," Maximilian ordered.

Charlotte seethed, anger rushing forth at his peremptory behavior. Did he think he was her father? God forbid! Papa was a doting, gentle, reasonable man, not a spoiled, rigid, overbearing aristocrat.

"Do not take that tone with me, my lord! I am not one of your lackeys! I do not know what has caused your foul mood, but until it improves, I do not care to speak to you! Now, if you will excuse me?" She turned on her heel to leave the room, but Max caught her arm.

Charlotte felt as if her heart would leave her chest, for it pounded against her ribs so forcefully as to break through them. If she turned, would he pull her against his hard body and kiss her, as he had on occasion before?

Very slowly, her breath held tightly and her breasts heaving with the force of her agitation, Charlotte faced him. With the same careful movement, she lifted her faltering eyes to his. They were dark, so murky and deep that she shivered, anticipation sliding up her spine. Her gaze fell to his lips in a subtle plea. *Kiss me, Max...*

With an oath, Max released his hold on her arm and stepped back as if she had burned him. Charlotte remained standing, separate from him now and trembling foolishly while she stared at him. Max returned her steady regard, and the air between them seemed to shimmer with heat as real and sudden as a furnace blast. They remained there for endless moments, struggling with desires that threatened to ignite until the smoldering, heavy silence was broken by a rustle in the doorway.

"Will you be wanting tea, miss?" asked a soft voice. Charlotte tore her gaze away from Max to notice the young serving girl Augusta had recently hired.

"Yes, please," Charlotte managed to say. She stared after the girl then glanced at Max. Apparently totally unruffled by their exchange, he was now holding a parcel wrapped in paper. The strange mood obviously had passed, but Charlotte did not know whether to be relieved or disappointed. She moved to the settee and sat down, cursing the man for his ability to overwhelm her senses.

Max stepped toward her, holding out the parcel. "I brought something for you," he said, and Charlotte's irritation vanished. A gift from Max... Her heart soared as she lifted her eyes to his.

"I had them done up because I was not sure whether your aunt would be here, and I knew you would not care for her to see," he explained. He leaned against the wall and grinned as Charlotte ripped the paper with as much as enthusiasm as Jenny opening a birthday present.

Books. She could tell by the weight of them, and she could think of nothing better. How quickly she had forgotten their shared scholarship in the frivolous atmosphere of London's elite. Charlotte lifted the volumes one by one, running her fingers over the titles, her hands smoothing the bindings in a reverent gesture. Long after the silly season was over, she would have these to treasure, to stimulate her mind...

"Oh, Max!" Charlotte smiled at him. "How wonderful! I have heard that these are excellent translations. If only I have the time to read them," she added wistfully. "And what is this? A picture book! How very thoughtful of you."

"I thought you might enjoy glancing through it," Max muttered. "Pittenger does justice to the most famous spots."

"Oh, Max! Do not tell me you have been there yourself?" Charlotte asked, looking at him with new eyes.

Max tugged on his collar as if it suddenly choked him, and straightened. "Yes, I took the grand tour after school."

Awed and excited, Charlotte let her worries about Augusta and her obligations to her family fade for the moment as she was caught up in the wonder of ancient Greece. "Do sit down, Max, and tell me about all these wonderful places," she urged, patting absently at the place beside her.

"I do not wish to keep you, if you are going out this evening," Max said a bit gruffly.

"I am not going anywhere," Charlotte assured him. "Aunt Augusta is not well, and her friends are tired of squiring me about, I am afraid." Seeing the look of annoyance on Max's face, she gestured again for him to sit next to her. "Oh, please, Max," she asked in a plaintive tone. "Can we not stay home one night?"

Chapter Eleven

With an undisguised relief that made Charlotte hide a smile, Max agreed that they need not go out. Sitting down cozily beside her, he began to tell fascinating stories about the drawings in Pittenger's book. But, to her surprise, Charlotte found that concentrating on ancient mythology was not as easy as it once had been. The nearness of the elegant earl posed the difficulty, for whenever her arm brushed his or he leaned close to point out some hidden detail, Charlotte felt her heart race and her breath catch.

The serving girl provided a welcome diversion when she brought in the tea tray. "Thank you, Anna," Charlotte said. "Perhaps you could fetch us some of those little cakes and the fruit tarts." Charlotte tried to maintain an affected pose as she poured, but, with Anna's departure, she was suddenly aware of how alone they were, seated together on the same settee. As usual, she had no idea how Max felt, but in her opinion, he was creating static more powerful than that of an electrical machine right here in Miss Thurgoode's drawing room.

Her hands trembling, Charlotte turned to present Max with his teacup, but somehow she lost her hold and dropped it into his lap. "Oh!" she gasped instantly. She saw his widened eyes, knew the liquid was scalding hot and reached for the napkin. Retrieving the cup, she pressed the cloth against his inner thigh, and he emitted a strangled noise, making Charlotte certain that he was truly hurt. Nervously, she dabbed at his leg. "Oh, Max!"

His fingers flew to her wrist, closing around it tightly and effectively halting her ministrations. Bent toward him, Charlotte lifted her gaze to his as he cleared his throat to speak. "Tell me that you have never, ever done this to anyone else," he said. His voice was strained, his mouth tight and his eyes wide and intent upon her.

Charlotte was not sure whether he was talking of the spills or the mopping up, but she could answer honestly on both counts. "I have never, ever done this to anyone else," she echoed. It came out rather breathlessly, as if it were not a simple confession, but something more secretive and vaguely illicit.

Although Charlotte was not sure why, the room spun itself into a dizzying inferno again, so hot that she could hardly draw a breath. It affected her thinking, making her realize that if she leaned forward slightly, she could touch his lips with her own. She noted suddenly that her hand was still pressed against his pantaloons; his grip held her there.

Staring into his great brown eyes, murky with some unnamed emotion, Charlotte swiftly vaulted past concern for his clothing toward unresolved longing. With a boldness she was certain bordered on wickedness, she closed her fingers upon his thigh, gripping his leg intimately. It felt wonderful. Max's muscles tightened beneath her touch, and his long, thick lashes drifted shut as he breathed her name. "Charlotte..."

Her body swelled and tingled, especially her breasts, which seemed suddenly ready to burst from her low-cut gown. Only inches from him, they ached, as if even the flimsy covering was too constricting. She was close enough to catch his clean scent, which sent its own heady shock waves through her, making her want to lean toward him when she knew she should move back.

She should move back. She told herself so, and yet, when Charlotte looked at Max—elegant, fastidious Max—vulnerable before her, she felt some kind of giddy, undefined power. His head was tilted back slightly, his eyes were closed, his lips parted, and Charlotte wanted nothing more than to take his mouth with her own.

Without thinking, she stretched upward slowly and pressed small, moist kisses along his jawline. "Charlotte..." He whispered her name like a low moan that sent a fission of excitement through her. Emboldened, she reached for his shoulders, as if to hold him to her will, and put her lips to his.

His reaction was instantaneous. His tongue burst into her mouth as if it had only been awaiting her invitation, and his hands closed upon her waist to pull her nearer. Suddenly, he was bending over her, pushing her back against the pillows of the settee, his body a delicious weight on top of her.

His chest was hard, crushing her breasts and abrading them through the thin material of her gown. Everywhere they touched her skin seemed to burn, and all the while his kisses plundered her, stealing her breath and her senses. Her cool, composed Max was acting like a starving man at his last meal. It was as if she had opened the gates to unleash a tempest, and Charlotte never wanted it to stop. *Never.*

She ran her hands down the smooth fabric of his finely cut coat, frustrated by all the layers that separated his body from hers. Finally, she found his buttocks, encased in tight pantaloons, and she stroked the taut muscles that leapt under her attention. He moved against her roughly in response, making her aware of the rigid press of his desire, and his eyes flew open.

Dark with passion, yet bright with a kind of startled, agonized look, they met her gaze and then dropped to the breasts that were so close to his face. "Do not move," he whispered, his hands dropping to his sides. His voice broke, as though he were in pain, and Charlotte knew a restless ache herself, a need that began where they met, male to female.

Was this sin? She noticed a bead of sweat break out on his forehead as silence, hot and tense, reigned between them. Max continued to stare at the curve of her bosom like a man struggling with some inner demon, and Charlotte knew, suddenly, that she wanted him to lose his vaunted control, to let the tempest rage no matter what the cost.

She moved, thrusting her chest upward and pushing against his erection. "Charlotte!" He gave out a low, heated cry, of exultation or surrender, she did not know which, before he reached for her bodice. His fingertips brushed against the exposed curve of her bosom, making her lean into his touch, but did not stop there. He tugged at her gown as if to pull it down, and then, with a soft, impatient sound, he slipped his hand inside.

His fingers closed around her, gliding over her naked flesh, stroking her skin and rubbing her nipples until Charlotte thought she would surely die from the pleasure of it. For one glorious instant, she found heaven in his passionate groan, in watching Max as he lay hot and heavy upon her, his eyes closed and his hand buried in her bodice.

But a gasp and the clatter of a tray brought them both up short, and Max's wonderful heat was gone in a flurry of clothes adjusting, twisting and straightening. When Charlotte was finally seated properly again, she saw Anna, still standing the doorway, staring at them as if she had just seen a ghost. The entire tray of cakes and tarts lay at her feet, obviously dropped by the startled serving maid, who had a hand to her mouth and a flush that went to the roots of her hair.

"Beg pardon, miss, my lord! Beg pardon!" she stuttered.

Charlotte heard Max take control of the situation, coolly contriving some excuse for what had to have looked like a lover's embrace. With the easy authority of an aristocrat, he would both calm down Anna and make sure Aunt Augusta never heard a word of gossip about the incident.

Darting a glance toward the red-faced maid, Charlotte wondered just how much the girl had seen. Although Max's form must have hid the worst of her indiscretion, there was no doubt that the Earl of Wycliffe had been lying atop an unmarried miss—and she a vicar's daughter.

At the memory, Charlotte had the grace to blush herself.

Maximilian was going over the household accounts. Once a month he met with his London steward and made sure that all was in order. If his staff was suddenly spending thrice the amount on wine, he would know why—or find the culprit who was swilling it without his knowledge. He prided himself on keeping abreast of the latest prices. There were no spendthrifts among his servants.

Immersed in a column of figures, Maximilian did not even look up when a knock sounded on the door. He frowned irritably, for he always left strict instructions not be disturbed when he was in conference. "Enter," he called.

Maximilian finished his calculations before lifting his eyes to the door where his butler stood. Staid, morally upright and loyal, Hoskins had been serving Maximilian since he first established his own household. And with just one glance at him, Maximilian knew at once that something out of the ordinary had occurred to ruffle Hoskins's feathers.

"She is here, my lord," the butler said, giving Maximilian a baleful stare.

"Who is here?" Maximilian snapped, his brows lowering.

"Lady Wycliffe, your mo—"

"Do not put that hated moniker to me, you old fustian!" called a high but strong feminine voice that wafted into the room from behind Hoskins.

Maximilian flinched as he recognized the unmistakable tones of his mother. His steward and butler, true to their training, did not bat an eye at the woman's words, and he took a moment to admire the caliber of his staff. Then he stood. "We shall resume later, Egremont," he said.

Sibylle was in the gallery, moving with her typical boundless energy and grace. Maximilian had often wondered how someone so tiny could be so lively. She was dressed in what he was certain was the newest of French fashions, the bottle-green silk cut so low over her small bosom as to be practically indecent. And he wanted her to sponsor Charlotte? He felt a moment's misgiving before stepping toward her.

"Madame." She flitted to him like a butterfly and brushed her lips against his cheeks. As long as he could remember, Maximilian had presented his face to her in this parody of affection. "You are here."

"Naturally, I am here. How could I not respond to such a summons?" Her mouth curving into a soft pout, she pulled his letter from her reticule and waved it about. "The great Earl of Wycliffe sends for me, like a servant," she complained. "What can I do but rush to do his bidding?"

Maximilian vowed not to let her bother him.

"If I were not so intrigued by your note, I would have stayed in Paris. La, Maximilian," she breathed. "I had the most wonderful hotel in the Rue de Clichy. And the food! How I shall miss the Beauvilliers! How can I eat this English slop after I have dined on the finest? How could you drag me away, you cruel boy, when I only just settled in?"

"You have been in Paris for more than a year," Maximilian noted dryly.

"La! I cannot measure my life by the tick of the clock as you do," she said, waving airily in dismissal. His mother spoke volubly with her hands, a trait that Maximilian despised. He thought of Charlotte, clasping her fingers together before her, and hoped that she would acquire none of Sibylle's habits.

"But, I am here," she said with a shrug. "Now, tell me what these services are that you desire."

Maximilian seated himself in one of the carved and gilt Adam chairs lining the walls. "I wish you to sponsor a young lady, the daughter of a vicar who ministers to one of my holdings," he said. He had the immediate gratification of watching outrage steal onto his mother's face while he smiled at her pleasantly.

"What? You drag me away from my friends to play companion to a horse-faced nobody? It is too much! You have gone too far this time, Maximilian. You insult me!"

Maximilian waited patiently while she paced around the room, flouncing this way and that, a dainty flash of green. "I shall not! You cannot compel me! This is what I think of your request!" He sat back in his chair, watching dispassionately as Sibylle tore his missive to bits and tossed them into the air.

Then she stood back, waiting for his reaction, but she would have a long wait, Maximilian thought mildly. He was not one of her hot-blooded French lovers, but her only son. He had spent years perfecting ways to deal with his mother. Leaning his elbows on the arms of the chair, he touched his fingers together.

"Perhaps I should have mentioned that Miss Trowbridge has already been launched and is the season's most sought-after female, an Incomparable, the newest Toast..." He let his words trail off purposely, giving her just enough information to pique her interest before he gazed out of the tall windows that looked over the garden.

"So! I am not impressed," Sibylle protested. "A mealy-mouthed female has captured the attention of the ton. I cannot play hostess to her. I would expire from boredom in a day."

"Of course, she would need lavish entertainments thrown in her honor and someone to sort through all her invitations and the suitors..." Maximilian paused significantly. "But perhaps you are right. You are not as young as you once were. It was wrong of me to ask you to perform such a taxing duty."

"Hmm." Sibylle sent him an assessing glance under her long lashes. When he returned her regard blandly, she tossed the dusky curls that framed her face. "I shall have a look at her. I can promise no more."

"As you wish, madame," Maximilian said, inclining his head.

"I would need funds, an increase in the paltry amounts that you give me," she said. "Why your father put everything in your hands I cannot know... He can have cared nothing for me!"

Maximilian bit back a retort. "But of course you would have to have money, lots of money," he said baldly. She smiled at him coquettishly then. He felt like telling her she was too old to play the part of the French kitten any longer, but decided against it. She would sponsor Charlotte. That was all that mattered.

"She will be at Hamilton House tonight, if you would care to accompany me," Maximilian said.

"La! I have no wish to go with you and forever watch the seconds tick by on your timepiece," Sibylle replied. "But I shall attend this party and see your Toast for myself. Then I will decide."

She was already partway down the gallery when she stopped and turned toward him. "What is her coloring?" she asked.

Maximilian smiled. "She is fair, a buxom blonde," he said, knowing full well why Sibylle posed the question. She would be far more disposed to host a girl whose beauty would not be compared to her own dark loveliness.

"Very good," she said, brightening. "We shall contrast then. A blonde will be... Buxom, did you say? You have no interest in the girl, do you?" she asked. Her eyes took on a shrewd glint as they searched his face.

Maximilian felt the blood run to this cheeks, followed by a surge of annoyance that his mother still had the power to embarrass him. "Me?" he scoffed. "Certainly not."

"But of course not!" Sibylle said. "How stupid of me. The great Earl of Wycliffe and a vicar's daughter? Impossible!" She laughed airily as she walked away.

Maximilian looked after her, a brooding expression on his face. He failed to see the humor.

"Where is she?" Maximilian asked irritably. His fingers tapped restlessly against his leg before he lifted them to pull out his watch and check the time.

"Good Lord, Wycliffe," Raleigh said, raising his quizzing glass to scan the Hamilton's reception room. "Your mother is always late."

Although Maximilian had to acknowledge the truth of that statement, he fumed anyway. Tonight his mother was hopelessly late, and if she did not arrive soon, she might miss Charlotte entirely. He drew in a deep breath and fought against the gripe in his belly, which recalled to him all too readily why he never had dealings with his mother.

Maximilian had remembered her frivolousness, her insincerity and the grasping greed that disgusted him, but he had forgotten how she affected his digestion. It annoyed him that she could still set his gut to churning when he was a grown man, but his irritation only intensified his stomach distress. "Damn." He breathed the word softly.

"Already regretting your scheme?" Raleigh said with a sympathetic smile.

"Yes. No. Deuced if I know," Maximilian admitted, ignoring Raleigh's astonishment at his uncharacteristic indecision. "What else could I do? That cousin of Charlotte's has obviously deserted her post, and I have no other female relatives to take her in."

"Too bad we couldn't install her with one of mine," Raleigh said wistfully. "Unfortunately, I have a surplus of the creatures, always picking at me. Don't like my clothes or my manners. Never satisfied. Don't think they would take Miss Trowbridge in, though. Father would not like it, for one. He wants me to marry an heiress. Claims we need the money," Raleigh said with a frown.

"It would not be proper since you are one of her suitors," Maximilian said with a slight frown.

"What's that?" Raleigh asked, dropping his glass. "Then how is it proper for *your* mother to sponsor her?"

"That is different," Maximilian snapped. "I have connections with her family."

"Ho!" Raleigh laughed out loud.

Irked at his friend's amusement, Maximilian snapped at him. "What would you have me do, then? Send her home?"

"Only if I might have her direction," Raleigh quipped between chuckles. Maximilian slanted him a black look. "Oh, for God's sake, Wycliffe! Of course I don't want the girl sent home. I'd be struck with the Lombard Fever straightaway. Lud, but she has enlivened a deuced dull season. And installing her with your mother should prove vastly entertaining."

Raleigh laughed again, apparently in delighted anticipation of what was to come, while Maximilian scowled. "Of course, you know that this move will only increase the talk about you both," Raleigh said, a wicked gleam in his eye.

"I have never heeded gossip," Maximilian said curtly. "People will always talk, especially about Mother."

Raleigh stepped back, the better to observe his friend. "I am not referring to Sibylle, but Miss Trowbridge. They are laying odds that you will wed her yourself," Raleigh announced. He knew he had Wycliffe's attention when he saw the dark brows lower.

"Rubbish," Maximilian said.

"Some claim this is all an elaborate way to introduce her to society before your marriage," Raleigh added. He watched his friend closely, waiting for a hint that those rumors might be true, but Maximilian's only response was a snort of derision.

Raleigh choked back a gasp of surprise and amusement. He could not believe that Wycliffe was so stubborn as to ignore what was, to him, woefully apparent. It was obvious that Miss Trowbridge had lost her heart to her gallant protector, and Wycliffe was not only too blind to see it, but too thick-witted to acknowledge his own affection for the girl. "Do not try to tell me that the thought has not crossed your mind!" Raleigh protested.

Maximilian eyed him with maddening innocence, his lips curved a bit contemptuously. "My dear Raleigh, you really cannot expect me to marry my vicar's daughter."

Raleigh swore softly, for his friend was deadly serious, a fact that did not bode well for the romance. "I would like to know why not!" he demanded.

Maximilian looked stupefied. "I would think the answer is obvious," he replied, all too smoothly. "The girl is too young, too unsophisticated, and hardly has the bloodlines

I would consider necessary for a bride, if I were considering marriage, which I am not. As I have explained to you before, unlike some rudderless unfortunates, I have a life plan, which I have adhered to since I was old enough to write it down."

"And that life plan does not include a wife?" Raleigh asked, gaping at his friend.

"Naturally, it includes a wife," Maximilian answered. "I am well aware of my responsibility to produce an heir. However, I see no need to rush into a youthful alliance. I plan to wed when I am thirty. Therefore, I need not begin looking for a suitable female for a couple of years."

With a desperate effort, Raleigh tried to contain his astonishment. Knowing Wycliffe's penchant for timetables, the man would probably follow this one to the letter. He had already succeeded in meeting his own rigid calendar for school, business and a seat in the House of Lords.

With a rather horrified fascination, Raleigh could well imagine Wycliffe selecting his bride with all the passion attendant on viewing the departure notices for the daily mail. "And just how will you go about choosing this female?"

Maximilian paused as if actually considering the question for the first time, much to Raleigh's dismay. "She must come of good family, of course—a daughter of the peerage, at least, for I am well aware of my duties to my title and my name. Money will not be a consideration, since I am well satisfied with my income."

He tilted his head. "Although she need not be a diamond of the first water, she must be pleasant to look upon. And she must have a mind. She cannot be too frivolous, but must possess some good sense. Most of all, she must be able to fit into my life and arrange her own schedule accordingly.

"Ch— Miss Trowbridge would never do. However appealing she might be," he said, cocking an eyebrow at Raleigh, "she is much too impulsive. My wife must accede to my authority. Miss Trowbridge rarely, if ever, heeds my advice. She has a tendency to be impulsive, headstrong, argumentative..."

Raleigh unobtrusively shifted his eyes to Wycliffe's fingers, which were drumming against his leg in a ceaseless rhythm that gave away his agitation. "As you well know, Raleigh, I desire a peaceful existence, not constant upheaval. I do not expect, nor do I want, any emotional bonds. Mutual respect is all that is necessary for a sensible union.

"In truth, I suspect my life will change little after marriage, for I expect to keep to my usual schedule, with subtle alterations for those events which require my wife's presence. Naturally, I shall not even consider anyone who is not punctual."

Raleigh cleared his throat, his eyes on Maximilian's hand, which had now relaxed against his thigh, and tried not to laugh. He pictured some poor female receiving a calendar in which "production of future heir" was scheduled for eleven o'clock to eleven-thirty every Friday night in the earl's bedroom. He lifted his gaze to Maximilian's face. "And just where do you expect to find this woman?"

Maximilian eyed him mildly. "I assume I shall find her among the ranks of the daughters of my peers when the time comes. However, since I have no intention of wedding as yet, it would be foolish to fix my choice at this early date."

"Certainly," Raleigh whispered. He glanced surreptitiously across the room at Charlotte, surrounded by her beaux and laughing gaily, and wondered if the poor child had any inkling of what she was getting herself into.

Charlotte stared at the tiny woman who walked around her and tried to ignore the odd feeling that she was being assessed—just as if she were a piece of merchandise—and found wanting. This bold little thing was Maximilian's mother?

"She is...so very tall," the lady said, a hint of disapproval tinging her accented English. Charlotte's gaze flew swiftly to Maximilian's.

"Sibylle," he said in a low, warning tone. He called his mother by her Christian name? Charlotte was confused. When he had first introduced her as Lady Wycliffe she had been certain for one breathless, horrible moment that he was married, even though no one had ever mentioned his wife. God bless Lord Raleigh who had silently mouthed "his mother" from his position behind them both.

Charlotte silently watched the woman's eyes flicker darkly over her bosom and she felt a familiar rush of dismay. Automatically, she lifted a hand to cover the bared expanse. Lady Wycliffe's gown was cut far lower, so low that her nipples practically peeped out, but she had small, inconspicuous breasts.

Charlotte flooded crimson at the size of her own. Embarrassed, she lifted her faltering eyes to Maximilian, only to find his attention focused on the area in question. But Max did not look one bit disgusted. He looked . . . hot.

Suddenly, Charlotte felt all warm and weak in the knees. She lifted her chin, for, despite Sibylle's censure, she liked her own body—simply because Max did. She forgot his mother's appraisal, forgot everything but the man whose eyes were fixed on her bosom. Then very slowly and very deliberately, she moved her hand away, exposing her curves further to his admiration. Their gazes caught and held. Was he blushing? Charlotte felt as if he had reached out across the space between them to touch her.

He looked away all too quickly and snapped at his mother. "Really, Sibylle, cease inspecting the girl as if she were a porcelain figure to add to your collection."

At his words, Maximilian's mother stopped circling like a vulture and paused reflectively. "I wish she would not be so tall, but she is very beautiful. Such eyes . . ." She turned to address Charlotte for the first time.

"You are charming, my dear. Maximilian says your cousin is unwell. I am sorry to hear it, but it is truly fortunate, for now I can invite you to come stay with me. I have a town house here that Maximilian bought me. It is not as spacious as his own," she said, throwing an accusatory glance at her son, "but it is adequate. Will you come?"

Charlotte looked at Max. His face was impassive, giving away nothing, as usual. She wondered what he would do if she refused. She knew she really ought to refuse, really should avoid getting herself further entangled with the Earl of Wycliffe. The same heart that leapt in her breast at the sight of him would surely lie broken and bleeding by the time the season was over.

But the family was counting on her to succeed in London, and how could she do so without a place to stay and a sponsor? Poor Augusta was so obviously overwhelmed she was making herself ill, and no one else had offered to take Charlotte in. Despite argument from her better judgment, Charlotte knew she had no choice. And, besides . . . she had never been the sensible one.

"Yes. Thank you so much," she said softly. "That would be delightful."

Maximilian smiled cheerfully as he approached his mother's town house. He was feeling much better since he had installed Charlotte with her. His schedule had returned to some semblance of normalcy, for he did not have to keep such a close eye on the vicar's daughter. Sibylle might appear to be totally frivolous, but he knew her to be, in some ways, very shrewd. She could be counted upon to watch over Charlotte, to know at all times who was with the girl and to sort through the suitors, carefully cutting the rakes and disreputables.

He felt quite good, in charity with himself for the magnanimous offer of his mother's sponsorship, which seemed to suit everyone. Charlotte's cousin was on the road to recovery, for, as he suspected, her ailment stemmed from the discovery that she did not care for the responsibility and effort of squiring about a young girl. Maximilian had sent off a slew of letters to the Trowbridge clan and was confident that he would soon receive replies thanking him heartily for his generous support of Charlotte.

His mood was a little dampened by the sight of Chevalier, his mother's manservant, at the door. Maximilian thought the man far too impertinent and eccentric to make a decent servant, which, he supposed, was precisely why his mother kept the man on.

"My lord! What an unexpected pleasure!" A tall, slender reed of a fellow with black hair and laughing blue eyes, Chevalier greeted Maximilian with more warmth than was appropriate. "It is always wonderful to see you, of course."

Maximilian slanted the man a quelling glance and disputed his words. "I believe I am expected," he said. He knew full well that his secretary had sent round a note advising his mother of the exact date and time of his proposed visit.

"Oh, really? My lady did not mention it. Shall I show you into the library?"

Maximilian frowned. His mother knew he detested being kept waiting. "Where is Miss Trowbridge?" he asked.

"She is in the morning room, my lord," Chevalier replied with a sly look.

"Then I shall see myself there," Maximilian said. He dismissed the servant from his thoughts as easily as from his presence. Although he refused to admit it, Maximilian was looking forward to seeing Charlotte. He had stayed away nearly a week to allow her to become settled, and, well... He put down his vague, restless longing for her as the natural desire to see a family friend.

The tall doors to the morning room stood open, and Maximilian slowed his pace, eager for a glimpse of her. He ignored the subtle changes in his body, the quickened intake of his breath and the sharper beating of his heart. Would she be reading one of his books?

In his mind's eye, Maximilian could see her curled in a chair, outdoing the sunshine with her bright presence, her glorious hair down, her feet bare. Although he had never seen her without shoes, Maximilian was suddenly struck by the vision of well-formed toes and well-turned ankles tucked beneath a simple gown, and he was astonished at how the thought of feet could be so...stimulating.

Shrugging away such foolishness, Maximilian stepped in front of the doorway and looked in. Charlotte was seated in a chair, but there any resemblance to his homey imaginings ended, for she was not alone.

Sir Burgess, an expression of rapt adoration on his face, was kneeling on the floor before her with one of her slim hands pressed to his lips.

Chapter Twelve

"*What the hell is going on here?*"

The bellow from the doorway made Charlotte jump in her seat. Her eyes flew to the male figure there, and she was even more stunned to recognize Max as the author of the uncivilized shout. Never having heard him raise his voice before, she stared at him wide-eyed.

"*Well?*" A genuine roar rose from the normally unruffled earl, and Charlotte found her tongue leached to the top of her mouth in astonishment. She glanced down at Sir Burgess for help, but he was in the process of rising and moving away from her, his eyes darting anxiously around the room as if he were looking for a hiding place.

Charlotte was on the verge of suggesting he try for one of the long windows when the baron seemed to recover himself. He drew himself up and fixed his eyes upon Max. "I was making Miss Trowbridge an offer of marriage," he said through tightly set lips. Although she did not know him well, Charlotte judged Burgess to be the proud, restrained sort who would not take well to Max's outrageous interrogation.

For his part, Max did not appear to be mollified by Burgess's explanation. His dark brows were drawn down over his eyes like thunderclouds, and he was scowling in a positively ferocious manner. Charlotte did not know whether to applaud his efforts to protect her or laugh at his misplaced

fury, for, in truth, Burgess had never done anything untoward.

"If you wish to offer for Miss Trowbridge, you may submit your proposal to me, and I will forward it to her father," Max said. The words grated, as if the poor man could
hardly get them past his gritted teeth. "He has put the matter entirely in my hands," Max added in a threatening tone
that seemed to challenge Burgess to dispute his claims.

That Burgess would do anything of the sort appeared
highly unlikely, for the baron's gaze dropped away from
Max to flit about the room nervously. Charlotte suspected
Burgess wished to avoid a confrontation of any kind, and
she could hardly blame him. He had certainly done nothing to merit Max's outlandish behavior.

Although she had to admit that Max's possessive manner was rather wonderful, Charlotte knew that no marriage
proposal would come from that direction. Meanwhile, the
man was scaring away a prospective groom, and Charlotte
deemed it appropriate to soothe Burgess's ruffled feathers.
"There now, since that is all settled, shall we all sit down and
have some tea? Claret, gentlemen?" she offered, rising from
her seat.

Burgess turned to her, his face hard as stone except for a
little muscle in his cheek that twitched. Botheration, Charlotte thought with some annoyance. He was really angry.
She sent a reproachful glance at Max, but the earl was still
glaring daggers at the baron. "Perhaps some...brandy?"
she asked, grasping at straws.

"No, thank you," Burgess said. Then he swiveled to face
Max. "I would formally submit my proposal to you now,"
he ground out.

"Contact my secretary for an appointment," Max answered.

Burgess turned pale, and for a moment Charlotte thought
the normally listless baron was going to launch himself at
Max. All she needed was a brawl right here in the countess's morning room. Or, worse yet, another duel fought on
her behalf! In a thrice, she maneuvered her way between the

two men, just as she often came between James and Thomas.

"Where is your dear mama, my lord?" she asked pointedly as she stepped toward Max. Distraction usually worked well with the boys. "I am sure she would love to join us for refreshments. Run and find her, will you?"

Maximilian gaped at her. Did she think to shoo him off like an unwanted pest? Did she *want* to be alone with this second-rate pretender to a nobleman? Well, he was not going to oblige her. "I will ring for her servant," he said tersely.

Charlotte's eyes widened at his tacit refusal to leave. "Do that, will you?" she asked. The look she sent him made him pause. Was she angry? Before Maximilian could sort out the message she was sending, she moved to Burgess, and he felt unreasoning rage wipe out all his better judgment. Suddenly, he wanted nothing more than to punch his fist into the baron's pasty white face.

"Please excuse me, Miss Trowbridge, but I must take my leave," Burgess said as Charlotte drew close. Obviously, the man had an instinct for self-preservation, Maximilian thought with some satisfaction.

Although he had never made use of the lessons learned in Jackson's Rooms from the boxing master himself, Maximilian figured now was as good a time as any to demonstrate his skills. When Burgess moved as if to take Charlotte's hand, Maximilian's expression told him in no uncertain terms that he had better not.

"Oh, must you?" Charlotte asked. Maximilian's eyes narrowed. Was she disappointed that the baron was going? At Burgess's stiff nod, she urged him to call again. She was smiling at the man, sending him the gift of her sunshine, and Maximilian seethed.

Remaining where he was, Maximilian forced Burgess to step past him, with the half-formed hope that the man would give him some excuse to challenge him. The baron gave Maximilian a wide berth, however, just as if he expected some sort of snarling attack from the normally sedate earl. The idea, which should have been humorous, was not. Maximilian *did* feel like attacking.

Pausing just out of reach, Burgess said, "You shall hear from me, Wycliffe." When Maximilian inclined his head in a parody of polite farewell, the baron turned two shades paler and stalked off. Maximilian allowed himself a few moments of grim satisfaction before he strode into the salon, ready to take Charlotte to task for entertaining gentleman callers unchaperoned.

He did not have a chance to open his mouth.

"What did you think you were doing? How could you be so rude? Whatever has possessed you?" Charlotte said, flinging up her hands in despair.

"What has possessed *me?*" Maximilian replied. "I could ask the same of you! I install you with my mother to prevent any more of these ... incidents, and upon my first visit I find you here, locked in some man's embrace again."

Charlotte whirled, her eyes wide and flashing, her springy hair escaping from its pins. "I was not in Burgess's embrace, and you know it! How dare you insult me so?" Her voice rose angrily.

"Humph!" Maximilian snorted. "Perhaps not at the exact moment that I entered, but how do I know what you were doing before—or what form his devoted affection might take when you gave your answer! And just what answer were you going to give?" he asked, his voice loud, too.

"That, my lord, is none of your business!" Charlotte shouted. Her hands on her hips and her face scarlet, she glared at him as if she were scolding one of her brothers. The thought annoyed him.

"You are not to see Burgess again. Do you understand?" He tossed out the order while keeping a wary eye on the legs that might suddenly kick him in the shins.

Instead of using her feet this time, however, Charlotte put both hands against his chest and shoved him with all her might. Since he was in the process of stepping away from her at the time, Maximilian was thrown off balance. He stumbled backward just as he heard Chevalier say, "Refreshments, anyone?"

With an uncharacteristic lack of grace, Maximilian knocked into the servant and his tray. He heard the clink and crash of crystal and china and the splash of liquids as everything flew into the air. Struggling for his footing in the midst of this chaos, Maximilian was upright for a moment until his boot slipped on something and he went down onto the floor in an ignominious tumble.

Never in his entire life had he appeared so grossly undignified. Sitting there upon the waxed wooden surface of the morning room floor while something wet seeped into his coat, Maximilian was so enraged that he actually saw red. The entire scene disappeared into a blazing flash of crimson before he regained his vision. Then he heard Chevalier mumbling something under his breath and bustling about behind him, but Charlotte was, for once, conspicuously absent from the cleanup operation. Maximilian refused to look at her.

"Charlotte, my dear! What have you done to poor Monsieur Burgess?" The sounds of his mother's faintly amused accents simply heaped more fuel upon the fire of his temper, and with a soft oath, Maximilian lifted a hand to his head—only to find it plastered with some sort of gooey substance.

"I heard the most dreadful shouting. Is this the way you behave in my home, sir?" Sibylle demanded. Maximilian watched the swirl of her skirts as she moved in front of him, but he stubbornly refused to look up at her.

"Maximilian!" She shrieked out his name in horror, and unable to avoid it any longer, he raised his eyes slowly to his mother. She had one dainty hand clasped to her throat as if she were going to faint from shock, but he felt no sympathy. "Maximilian, is that you? It cannot be! Whatever are you doing down there? And why have you cake in your hair?"

Without waiting for answers, Sibylle turned to Charlotte. "Surely, that was not Maximilian shouting, for he never raises his voice. Maximilian is always in control of himself. How could he not be?'' His mother looked genuinely stupefied.

Charlotte did not. Nor, he noted, did she look the least bit regretful of the mess she had precipitated. ''My Lady, I hesitate to inform you of this, since you have been nothing but kindness itself to me, but I do believe your son is quite mad!'' Charlotte explained, her magnificent breasts heaving with her agitation.

Far from taking offense, Sibylle laughed merrily, while Maximilian attempted to rise with some semblance of aplomb. ''My dear child, Maximilian is many things—most of them aggravating—but I would hardly call him mad.''

Maximilian took note of the feeble tenor of her defense, but said nothing as Chevalier held out a clean cloth. Was it his imagination, or were the man's lips twitching? Maximilian knew that if Chevalier laughed, he would cheerfully plant a facer upon those smirking features.

Charlotte appeared nonplussed by Sibylle's argument. ''Well, then, I do not know how to explain his behavior. He says he wants to help me make an advantageous match, and yet he chases away every serious suitor who tries to approach me!'' Although in the midst of wiping cream and cake from his fingers, Maximilian's head shot up at Charlotte's words. What the devil was she saying?

She glanced at him, colored and looked back at his mother as if she wanted to say more, but snapped her mouth shut at Sibylle's astonished expression. ''Forgive me, please, my lady,'' she said. ''I forget myself.'' Head bent, she hurried from the room.

Maximilian snorted. He was not fooled by Charlotte's downcast eyes as she swept past him. He wanted to grab her by the arm and shake some sense into her—or something equally violent but more intimate...

''Is this true?'' Sibylle asked. With effort, Maximilian turned his attention to his mother, who was staring at him as if he were a stranger.

"No, it is not true," Maximilian answered. "Damn it, make yourself useful, Chevalier, and help me with my coat," he snapped, slipping out of the sopping mess. When he glanced at Sibylle, she was pressing her fingers to her lips thoughtfully, her bright, dark eyes boring holes into him.

"What is it?" he barked. "Have you never seen a man covered in food before? God knows I should be well used to it by now."

"Very becoming," Sibylle said, her lips curving into a smile. "Poor, poor Maximilian." She lifted a finger to his forehead and returned with a dollop of cream, which she promptly tasted. Although Maximilian suspected her of goading him, he frowned in disapproval nonetheless. As usual, Sibylle was not behaving the slightest bit like a mother.

Laughing gaily, she swept past him, but paused for a moment on the threshold to point the errant finger at him. "Beware, Maximilian, that you do not fall, like your papa, for someone unsuitable."

Ignoring Chevalier's low giggle, a coatless Maximilian stormed past the servant and his mother, intent upon leaving the household immediately. As far as he was concerned, everyone in it was all about in the head.

Charlotte threw herself onto her bed. For a moment, she felt like giving in to the misery that choked her, but she would not. Instead, she rolled onto her back and stared at the elaborate bed that she now called her own. Her eyes followed the slim, spiral-turned posts up to the canopy, where the pale pink silk hangings were drawn together in a swirl.

It was beautiful. It was also a far cry from the narrow truckle she used at home, and as much as she tried to remember her father's warnings against coveting material things too dearly, Charlotte admired it excessively. She wished she could stay here forever, but time was slipping away so quickly....

Charlotte closed her eyes against the recognition, denying it. She could feel the restraints on her hair, precarious at best, give up all pretense and release the awful, puffy curls. Her hair was her worst feature, she noted with contempt. That and her oversize bosom, although Max...

Thoughts of the earl made her pull one of the pins from her hair and toss it across the room in a burst of pique. After days of neglecting her, he had suddenly appeared, as was his wont, to wreak havoc upon her life. As far as Charlotte was concerned, his behavior today meant only one thing.

Although Max did not want her for his wife, he did not want anyone else to have her, either. Charlotte bit back a cry of outrage. She would spend no tears on the elegant earl's account! He could strangle on one of his own schedules, for all that she cared.

But what was she to do? Each time one of her suitors tendered an offer, Max found some way to intimidate the man. She could see herself returning home penniless and husbandless, thanks to the generous guardianship of his lordship. Her anger was so great she realized she was shaking with the force of it, or was she sobbing?

A knock on the door made her sit up and wipe her face hurriedly. For one brief, horrified moment, she suspected it to be Max himself. She would not put it past him to come strolling into her private bedchamber without a qualm, to lecture her in a fatherly fashion, although there were times when she swore his interest in her was far from avuncular. "Yes?" she breathed.

But it was his mother, not Max, who came through the door. Sibylle did not appear the least bit concerned or offended about what had transpired in her morning room. "Do not fret, my child," she said, waving her hand in that dramatic way of hers. "We will not let stuffy old Maximilian drive away all your beaux. If it is the baron you want, it is the baron you shall have."

Sibylle stepped closer, smiling slyly. "In fact, I am certain, my dear child, that with a little scheming, you may have anyone you desire."

* * *

Maximilian downed his second brandy and called for another, but since he was at White's, and he invariably only partook of two glasses during his evenings at the club, he had difficulty obtaining a third. The waiter stared at him, gape-mouthed, for a long moment before responding with a hurried nod and a shake of his head.

The incident soured Maximilian's already foul mood, which had been tried by an afternoon of unexpected fury, culminating in an ignominious fall into a tea tray. Never, in all his life, would he have predicted the mishaps that had befallen him since his acquaintance with a certain green-eyed beauty.

And Charlotte, he told himself as he gulped his brandy, was an ungracious, ungrateful chit who, left to her own devices, would sully her reputation with every man in town. Maximilian was inclined to abandon her, but he felt a niggling responsibility for her fate and to her father, who had no idea that his daughter was hell-bent on disaster.

Although he had effectively curtailed Burgess, Maximilian was well aware that there were others, too many for him to even keep straight. Why, by last count, she had under her dubious spell Raleigh, Cavely, Merton, that backward squire whose fitting name was Bottom, Clemson's youngest boy and perhaps even . . . Wroth!

As if his thoughts had conjured the man, the Marquis of Wroth suddenly appeared before him, looking cool and composed, as always. The marquis' lips curved in a hint of haughty amusement, and Maximilian felt a rush of outraged annoyance, for Wroth's famous disdain had never been turned upon him.

"Just what I detest seeing, a normally intelligent man making a cake out of himself over some female," the marquis said. He looked down from his great height, as if gazing upon an insect, and Maximilian squirmed under the stare. The words sounded awfully familiar. Was he himself the author?

"What are you talking about?" Maximilian demanded churlishly.

"I am talking about you being besotted by the Trowbridge chit," Wroth said easily, taking a seat.

Maximilian felt himself flush with anger and embarrassment, a decidedly unusual and revolting combination. "Have you been listening to Raleigh?" he asked.

Worth just looked at him in that maddening way, as if his protests were both amusing and an insult to the man's intelligence. "My dear Wycliffe, I consider myself a superb judge of human foibles. I hardly need Raleigh to advise me."

Maximilian ignored the insult implicit in Wroth's reply and glared at the peer he had heretofore admired. "Well, you are mistaken," he said.

Wroth simply shrugged negligently. "Then I would advise you to stop acting like the girl is your personal property." The words were spoken lightly, but Maximilian caught the steel in their inflection, and it aggravated his already sorely used temper.

"You stay away from her, too," Maximilian snapped. "God knows you don't intend to marry her!"

Wroth stared at him. His cold gray eyes turned silvery, but he did not lose his composure. He never did—something Maximilian realized could have been remarked about himself until recently. When the marquis spoke again, his lips curled into a smile that hinted of contempt. "I have no idea what our maker knows of the subject, but what leads you to believe that I do not intend to marry the girl?"

Maximilian snorted. The answer to that was easy. "She's a vicar's daughter."

To Maximilian's surprise, Wroth laughed in that cool way of his, as if genuinely amused. "My dear boy, if I wish to marry the pig sticker's daughter, I will. And I dare anyone in this town to gainsay me," he said, his cold eyes boring into Maximilian's warm ones. "If I wish to marry my sweep's harridan grandmother, I will. That, I suspect, is the difference between us. I am wholly comfortable with who I am. Are you?''

The question struck so close to the bone that Maximilian nearly flinched under that chill gray gaze.

"I will excuse you, due to your youth," said the man who was only a few years older than Maximilian. "But let me leave you with this bit of information. I like Miss Trowbridge. I find her uniquely refreshing, and I would be extremely...displeased...if anyone, including you, were to bring her unhappiness."

Maximilian felt a hot rush of panic at the implication that the marquis held Charlotte deeply in his affections. "Just what are your intentions?" he demanded roughly.

Wroth laughed softly and rose from his chair. "My intentions, my dear fellow, are to find better company this night. But, if you are truly concerned about Miss Trowbridge, I suggest you investigate a certain baron who has been paying her court."

"Burgess?" If the advice had come from anyone but Wroth, Maximilian would have scoffed, for he thought he had effectively maneuvered the baron and his proposal into a corner.

Wroth smiled coolly. "My sources tell me that he has always been a bit, shall we say, wrong in the upper story, and now he has developed a taste for a particularly obnoxious substance, which further distances him from reality. He appears to have become obsessed with Charlotte—and Charlotte alone—because of some past grievance against her family."

"Burgess?" Maximilian asked again, unable to believe that the same mild-mannered gentleman he had practically tossed from his mother's town house could be an opium addict and some sort of raving lunatic, to boot.

For a moment, Maximilian thought that Wroth would not deign to reply, but he slapped his gloves against his palm and spoke softly. "Some are not what they seem, Wycliffe. You would be wise to put your energies into studying people, not time clocks, for true power lies in the ability to control others."

With a formal nod, the marquis took his leave, weaving easily among the men who crowded the club. Staring after him, his emotions stretched by now to the limit, sat Maximilian, feeling for the first time in his life overwhelmed and at a loss as to his own direction.

"A picnic! How delightful for you, my dear. You simply must go," Sibylle said. She was finishing what Charlotte viewed as her interminable daily toilet, twirling around and showing off yet another new gown. Although Charlotte could not approve of the frivolous nature of so many of Sibylle's concerns, the woman's buoyant nature was infectious. One could not help liking her.

"Are you certain?" Charlotte asked again, turning her attention to the invitation from Sir Burgess. She could not share Sibylle's careless attitude. The idea of defying Maximilian's wishes so blatantly—even if his wishes were unreasonable—made her uneasy.

"I am never certain," Sibylle answered airily. "Certainty is for people like Maximilian. But this will be an excellent occasion for you to acquaint yourself further with Sir Burgess. He seems to be the best prospect at this time, for I suspect Raleigh is but amusing himself, and I hold out no hopes for Wroth. Now that would be a coup!" Sibylle said wistfully.

"We shall wait and see," the countess added, tapping her finger to her lips. "There is no hurry, after all. We can keep Burgess happy while Maximilian puts the man off indefinitely. Then, if Wroth comes up to the scratch, you shall be free to accept him."

Charlotte looked askance at her sponsor, for she could not share Sibylle's enthusiasm for the plan. Although she knew she must find a husband, it hardly seemed right to keep Burgess dangling on the line while she sought bigger fish. "Is that fair?" she asked.

"Fair?" Sibylle looked puzzled and then laughed. "What is fair in love, my dear?" She dismissed Charlotte's reservations with an amused smile before turning to the mirror to admire her appearance.

Love. What did love have to do with it? Charlotte wondered. Here in London, marriage was a business proposition and far less romantic than she had ever dreamed possible. Love was something she dared not even consider.

"How do I look, my dear?"

Sibylle's words brought Charlotte out of her dark thoughts. "Beautiful, as always," she answered, forcing a smile.

"You are a sweet girl," Sibylle said, reaching up to pat her on the cheek. "Now, let us see what horrible foods have been laid out upon our table. A French chef! La! That is what we need. Why have I not thought of it before! Chevalier!"

"The picnic, my lady. Will you join us?" Charlotte asked, trying to keep Sibylle's errant thoughts on the matter under discussion. It was often a difficult task.

Maximilian's mother laughed merrily. "Such simple, rustic entertainments are not for me, my dear," she said, waving her hand in dismissal.

Invitation in hand, Charlotte blinked at the tiny woman who swept past her, and she felt, not for the first time, the unintentional bite of Sibylle's tongue. After two weeks in the household, she had begun to recognize why Max was at odds with his mother.

Lady Wycliffe was hardly the maternal type. She could be kind, yes, and witty, but she was also vain and selfish. Charlotte thought of her own loving papa, her precious siblings and their mother—gone but not forgotten—and she felt sorry for the earl. He might have fancy homes and horseflesh and money to burn, but he did not have a loving family, and Charlotte would not trade hers for wealth any day.

"But what of a chaperone? Max—the earl said—" Charlotte protested.

His mother cut her off with a wave of her pale white hand. "Maximilian! La! As if anyone pays attention to what that stuffy old fustian says. What does he know of courtship? He lives and breathes by rules! The man is mad, as you said."

Charlotte sighed. Although she did not like to be reminded of her outburst, Sibylle thought the accusation quite amusing and dredged it up constantly. No wonder Max was not devoted to his mother. Did he know she called him such names? Charlotte tried to picture her dear papa saying anything bad about his children, even in teasing, and she could not. The vicar could barely manage to discipline the boys at their worst.

Although Charlotte told herself she was still angry with Max over his high-handed treatment of her, sympathy for the earl was rapidly diluting her lingering ill feelings. And worse yet, she found herself aching to defend him—to his own mother.

Despite Sibylle's assurances, Charlotte did not feel quite comfortable leaving unchaperoned with Sir Burgess. Traveling some distance was not like driving in the park, and although there would be others there when they arrived, Charlotte still was uneasy. Max had told her often enough that a misstep could result in her immediate expulsion from polite society, and she had no desire to court trouble.

She certainly didn't expect any from Sir Burgess. He had always behaved in gentlemanly fashion. He was quiet, and a bit intense maybe, but not at all the sort, like Stollings, to presume upon her. Charlotte knew she would be safe enough with him, yet she did not want to draw anyone's censure. And she was more and more aware that Sibylle, with her flamboyant French ways, might not be the best judge in these cases. And when Max found out...

Charlotte tried not to think of that, for, in truth, she did not know if Max would even care. He had studiously avoided her in the week since their argument, and for all she knew, had abandoned her entirely to her own devices. She stifled the ache in her chest that such an assumption engendered and tried to smile politely at Sir Burgess as he assisted her into the carriage. Adjusting the perky straw hat that was perched atop her tightly knotted hair, she settled back to enjoy the drive.

They made polite conversation, but the warmth of the carriage and the late nights that Sibylle insisted upon keeping lulled Charlotte into a state of lethargy. Repeatedly, she adjusted her skirts and blurted out some question to keep from drifting off impolitely. She had the silly notion that if it were Max sitting across from her, she could simply sleep where she was without compunction. Better yet, she could join him and rest her head against one of his massive shoulders, taking in the familiar scent of him....

Charlotte looked up at the ceiling, vaguely disoriented. She blinked at Sir Burgess and then looked out the window. Had she been resting? They were in the country now, and the sun was moving across the sky. Surely, they had traveled past the picnic site. "Why have we not arrived?" Charlotte asked, her voice rough with the lingering edges of drowsiness.

Instead of answering her, Sir Burgess slipped from his seat and awkwardly dropped to the floor between them. He reached for her gloved hand and pulled it toward him gently. "My dearest, dearest Miss Trowbridge," he said softly. "Forgive me for being so bold, but I had hoped to alter our destination."

Charlotte sat up straighter in her seat and stared at the man before her. The white streaks at his temples abruptly took on a sinister look, and his gray eyes glinted strangely. She could see the marks of age in his forehead, but, unlike her father, he had no laugh lines about his eyes. He was too serious, but in a different way than Max, Charlotte decided. A grim way. She shifted uncomfortably. "Whatever do you mean, sir?"

Burgess looked at her hand reverently. "You must have some notion of my regard for you, my dear Miss Trowbridge. The other day when I spoke with you, I was given to hope that you looked favorably upon my suit." He paused as if the depth of his emotion made it difficult to go on.

"I have no patience for delays that would keep us apart, so I have taken matters into my own hands," he said, his eyes rising to hers again, with bold intent.

"Miss Trowbridge, we are on our way to Gretna Green."

Chapter Thirteen

"Gretna Green!" Charlotte was aware that the Scottish town was a haven for lovers who wanted to elope, but she never would have dreamed that the quiet baron would come up with such a wild scheme. Raleigh, perhaps...Roddy, if he had possessed enough courage, but Sir Burgess? What was she to think?

For one tiny moment, Charlotte was tempted to go along with Burgess's plan and be done with her husband hunting. She would have a good name, a nice country manor and enough money to assist her family, if she but let the carriage follow its present course. It was something that many other young ladies would not dare turn their backs on.

But Gretna Green! The very name reverberated with censure, and Charlotte knew that her dear papa would not really approve of such a hasty wedding. Neither would Sarah—or Max...

Unwanted, the image of the overbearing earl appeared in her mind, and Charlotte felt a piercing pang of longing. Suddenly, it did not matter that she knew she could never have him. She simply knew she could not settle for anyone else.

Charlotte's fingers tangled in the fine material of her gown, crushing it heedlessly while she trembled with the force of the revelation. *She loved Max.* No matter how irritating and arrogant and bossy he was, she loved him with a potency that overpowered all else in her life.

Blinking into the pale face staring so intently at her, Charlotte realized she could not give her consent to this man, not now...nor ever. However rich and willing he was, however polite and kind, Charlotte could not imagine herself living with Burgess, day after day, night after night...when her heart belonged to another.

She envisioned his cold, thin lips upon hers and his hands upon her body, and she shivered. Although she was not well informed about the marriage bed, she comprehended the basics of reproduction, and the thought of sharing such intimacies with the man before her made her recoil.

The simple task of finding a husband to provide for her family had seemed so clear and easy most of her life, but now it took on a deeper significance. Charlotte knew, abruptly and irrevocably, that she could not do it if it meant giving herself over to someone like Sir Burgess.

Marriage, she decided, had to be founded on more than money and comfort and advancement. She thought of her own parents, who had filled a house with love, if not material goods. They had always gotten by, somehow....

Charlotte felt her heart thumping loudly in her breast as the consequences of her decision became clear. The children would have to fend for themselves, but was not that the way of the world? Sarah had done well enough right there in Upper Bidwell. And, as for the boys, something might turn up. Something always did....

Charlotte lowered her eyes, trying to disguise her growing agitation with a nervous flutter. "Sir! I am most flattered, most flattered, indeed, but my papa, the vicar, would not approve of such a wedding. He would want to preside at the ceremony himself. You understand," she said, sincerely hoping that Burgess did. "If you are truly interested in making a formal request for my hand, you must speak to Lord Wycliffe—"

"Wycliffe!" Burgess surged to his feet and threw himself back down upon the cushions, his black eyes hard, his mouth pulled into an angry line. "The man will never approve of my suit. He wants you for himself! Everyone knows it."

In spite of herself, Charlotte laughed. "Wycliffe does *not* want me for himself, I assure you," she said, a bit brittlely. "However, if you do not want to speak with him upon the manner, you may present your offer directly to my papa."

"I think not."

Charlotte's head flew up at his answer, and she looked at Burgess with a new wariness. His gaze was hooded and his lips were drawn almost into a smirk. As he crossed his arms upon his chest, she was cognizant of a subtle change in him, as if he exuded a hint of danger that had never clung to him before.

Charlotte was stunned. She realized with belated insight how very little she knew about her suitors. The ridiculous rules that governed courtship among the ton did not allow for much familiarity, and perhaps there was more than one reason for that. A delicate young lady might not be so eager to marry if she knew more about her husband-to-be! Burgess, curse him, had pressed his suit as a quiet, gentle, self-possessed older man, when, in fact, he might turn out to be some kind of vicious wife beater.

"My dear sir," Charlotte said as steadily as she could. "Please turn this carriage around instantly and return me to Lady Wycliffe's town house."

"I cannot," Burgess said smugly.

"I must insist."

"And I must refuse, my dear Miss Trowbridge. I apologize if my haste has unnerved you." The near smirk was replaced by an ingratiating smile, which did not reach his eyes, and Charlotte stared at him, amazed at his subterfuge. "Perhaps the wedding will not be all that you might wish, but we cannot go back. We have been gone, alone together and traveling far, for a long time. Your reputation has been compromised."

Burgess dropped his gaze as if he could barely contemplate the shameful issue, but Charlotte was not fooled. He had planned this! So much for Sibylle's idea that they keep the man dangling. Drat Wycliffe's mother! Charlotte knew she should have been chaperoned. If only Sibylle had listened to her, she would not be in this dreadful coil.

"No one need know," Charlotte replied sensibly. "If you turn around now, some excuse can be made. Lady Wycliffe can easily concoct a tale to explain my absence."

"I could not in good conscience allow you to face such disgrace," Burgess protested.

Conscience, my eye, Charlotte thought, assessing him under her lashes. Obviously, he was not going to consider her wishes in the matter. So adamant was he that Charlotte almost suspected him of harboring an ulterior motive for this abduction. Heiresses were regularly rushed off to Gretna Green, but not vicars' daughters.

Was the baron so enamored of her? He certainly did not look it, nor did he act as if he were in the throes of some wild passion. Thank heaven for that much, Charlotte thought. After that last business with Stollings, she could not imagine being trapped for hours in a coach with an amorous admirer...unless it was Max. Max! Perhaps a threat might work where pleading and demanding had failed.

"My lord Wycliffe will be most...distressed," Charlotte said, in what she imagined was an understatement. She folded her hands in her lap neatly and gazed down at them. "He is quite close to Papa, you know." She sighed. "And he does have a temper. There was that nasty business with Captain Stollings—"

Burgess cut her off with a hissing sound. "Wycliffe can do nothing!" Startled, Charlotte glanced up to see him positively glaring at her. "We shall be legally wed, and he will have no power to interfere."

Trying not to let his anger unsettle her, Charlotte gave Burgess a look that said she was unconvinced. Although she hesitated to say so in the face of her companion's fury, she would not be surprised if Maximilian came upon them at any moment. He had, after all, extricated her from all the other scrapes in which she had become embroiled since coming to London.

Instead of raging at her disbelief, Burgess relaxed and smiled slyly, which disconcerted her even more. "If you are expecting him to appear before the ceremony, let me assure you that he will not. Wycliffe spends the third Friday of every month engaged with members of his driving club. Baring extremely foul weather, of course."

Smirking openly now, Burgess pointedly glanced out the window to confirm that snow and hail were not in the forecast. Then he paused to make his final words most effective. "Wycliffe has never, ever missed a meeting in the two years since the club was formed."

Charlotte leaned back against the seat, dismayed by that piece of news. She had no doubt that Burgess was, in this case, speaking the truth. She realized she had just assumed that Maximilian would come to her rescue as he always did, an elegant knight who took his duty to her papa very seriously.

There was, of course, no reason to believe that he would appear whenever she needed him, and yet... Notwithstanding Burgess's words, Charlotte still expected Maximilian to come for her. It did not matter that he was engaged elsewhere. He had broken appointments for her before; she was sure of it. It did not matter that she had not seen him for a week, or that they had parted on less than amicable terms. Despite all, Charlotte felt, deep in her heart, that he was coming for her. And Burgess, with all his planning and scheming, could do nothing to prevent it.

Stilling the smile that threatened to emerge, Charlotte looked out of the window, watched the scenery... and waited.

She did not have long to wait. Perhaps she had sensed his closeness or felt the force of the uncharacteristic hot rage that drove him behind them, ever closer. Or perhaps she just knew that Max, dear, insufferably responsible Max, could not let anything untoward happen to her. Whatever the source of her knowledge, when Charlotte heard the horse draw alongside them and the shout from outside, she was not surprised.

Sir Burgess was. Charlotte saw the flash of fear in his eyes. "Highwaymen?" he croaked. Before he had time to say anything else, the carriage stopped and the door was yanked open.

Charlotte blinked as the sun dipped behind the tall, elegant Earl of Wycliffe, framed in the doorway like a loving portrait. Even though he was scowling ferociously, her heart took to its customary leaping when she saw his handsome face. His black brows were drawn down heavily over his eyes in a familiar pose that was fast becoming so dear to her that the sight made her throat thicken and fill with emotion. She cleared it.

"You certainly took your time!" she said as briskly as she could manage. She rose from her seat and stepped toward him, but Burgess shot out an arm in front of her, effectively halting her progress.

"What is the meaning of this, Burgess?" Max roared. Without waiting for an answer, he grabbed hold of Burgess's arm with one hand and the man's collar with the other, and dragged the baron out of the vehicle before Charlotte could even draw a breath. She thrust her head out of the doorway only to see the two brawling in the dirt of the roadway like farm boys.

Lifting her skirts carefully, Charlotte nimbly jumped down just in time to watch Max plant Burgess a bruising facer that should have knocked him out. Unfortunately, she suspected that the baron had an awfully hard jaw, for he did not fall, but tried to strike back at his opponent.

So immersed was Charlotte in the contest that she did not see the coachman until he was upon the earl. To her horror, the driver grabbed Max from behind, holding him fast while Burgess rammed a fist into his stomach. Max doubled over and groaned.

"Stop that this instant, you!" Charlotte shouted as she rushed forward. Without a pause, she gave the coachman a vicious kick behind his legs. He stumbled and obviously oosened his hold, for Max broke away and lunged at Burgess.

The coachman, apparently distressed at her treatment of him, swung round toward her, but Charlotte hiked her skirts and thrust her foot right between his legs as forcefully as she could. He gave a great gasp and bent over, one arm flailing in a vain effort to reach her. After a few hefty breaths, he came hobbling after her again, but he stumbled and fell against Wycliffe's horse, which managed to kick him in the leg before it took off across the field at the side of the road.

With a few hoarsely mumbled oaths, the coachman obviously decided that Burgess was not paying him enough for this kind of abuse and struggled to his perch. Charlotte let him go without a qualm, but the sound of snapping reins produced a different reaction from Burgess.

"Stop! Wait! Damn it!" the baron shouted. Although he looked not too steady, he managed to pull away from her avenging earl, reach for the flapping, open door of the coach and fall inside as the vehicle began to move away.

"Coward," Charlotte shouted after him. Then she turned to her gallant rescuer. He did not look well, either. He was filthy dirty, and his hair fell loose about his face in sweaty, matted strings. His coat was torn, his mouth was bleeding, and he swayed as if he could barely stand. In short, she had never seen Max look so utterly dreadful. "Are you all right?" she asked.

Charlotte stared into the depths of those gorgeous brown eyes for one long moment before they closed and the Earl of Wycliffe collapsed in a heap at her feet.

She managed to drag him to the edge of the road, to avoid possible traffic, and to rest his head upon her lap. Sitting there with the fading rays of sunlight caressing his dazzling, albeit dirty, features, Charlotte was conscious of several things, the most overwhelming being just how much she loved him.

It was true. No matter how hard she had fought against it, no matter how much she had tried to like other men, no matter how foolish and painful it was, she, the vicar's pretty daughter, had fallen helplessly, hopelessly in love with the Earl of Wycliffe.

Charlotte put a hand to his face and pushed a lock of hair off his forehead. Beneath the dust sprinkling it, it shone with life, a long, nearly black strand. Charlotte moved it between her fingers. So silky...

She dropped the lock guiltily. Instead of caressing him, she ought to be trying to revive him, but how? She had no smelling salts for him to breathe or water to dash upon his face, and he looked so battered from the fight that she did not want to slap him awake. Burgess was but a speck in the distance, and Maximilian's horse was nowhere to be seen. She was left with nothing but her reticule... and Max.

Pulling out her handkerchief, Charlotte leaned over him to gently wipe the blood from his mouth. She let her eyes move tenderly over his face, taking her time, enjoying the chance to peruse him closely. She had not realized that his lashes were so long or his nose so well-formed. Running a trembling finger down his cheek, Charlotte felt the rough hint of stubble. Warmth, sweet and heady, spread through her, engendered by the simple act of touching him.

Emboldened by the heat that drove away the evening's chill, she traced his full bottom lip and shivered with the thrill of its form and texture. So smooth... Reverently, she began again, lightly outlining the edges of his mouth, but when he stirred, she jerked her hand away. The flutter of his lashes made Charlotte straighten, for he might not welcome her kiss. She knew he would not welcome her love.

His eyes, those wonderful, chocolate eyes, opened at last and he looked at her dazedly, as if he were confused. For one long moment, he stared up at her dreamily, and Charlotte stared back, enthralled by those deep, dark depths. Finally, she opened her mouth to explain, wetting her dry lips with her tongue, but when she did, Maximilian sat up so abruptly that she nearly fell back into the grass.

"Good God!" he grunted. Then he groaned, grimaced and put a hand to his forehead.

"Are you all right?" Charlotte asked.

She was rewarded with the blackest look she had ever seen slanted from under his long lashes. "No, I am not all right," he answered through gritted teeth.

Charlotte searched his face and noticed that under the dirt, he was beginning to bruise. One eye had started to swell, as had his lip, but she certainly was not going to tell him that. Happily, she had no mirror with her.

"My head is splitting, and I ache all over. Do I look all right?" he asked, his voice heavy with sarcasm. He stood up, glanced down at himself and groaned anew. "Look at me. Just look at me!" he demanded.

Charlotte's gaze swept up and down his tall frame, taking in his muscular thighs, his trim waist, his broad shoulders, his handsome if rather bedraggled features, and her heart hammered irregularly. There was something rakish about his torn clothing and his less than perfect appearance that made him seem more desirable, more accessible... "I think you are even more attractive than usual," Charlotte said softly.

Max ignored her. "I cannot believe this! I have never in my life been involved in a brawl in the dirt like some...some country chaw-bacon!" He was raging now. "Where is my horse?" he asked suddenly, dropping the hand from his temple. "Do not tell me my horse is gone," he warned her in a low, decidedly menacing voice.

Charlotte stood up and shook out her skirts, but wisely said nothing.

"My horse is gone! Damn it, Charlotte! My horse is gone, and I am a bloody mess!" Maximilian put a finger gingerly to his red lip, made a face and glared at her. "No more, Charlotte. No more. Ever since I met you I have been dragged from one tangle to another, each more wretched than the last, but this is it. I have had enough. I refuse to—"

He broke off to lift a hand to his head, and Charlotte realized that it must be hurting him dreadfully. Still, his sharp disgust with her, coming as it did on the heels of her discovery that she loved him, was rather painful. She met his dark eyes, and they bored into her with the furthest thing from affection. "Something will have to be done to remedy the situation," he warned softly.

Charlotte felt her heart lurch. What would he do? Send her home? She blinked at him, feeling the pressure of tears behind her eyes, and told herself it did not matter. Whether she was in London or Sussex or on the moon, nothing would change the way she felt about him, and nothing, obviously, was going to change the way he felt about her. She dropped her gaze, unable to look any further into the dark depths for what was not there.

"Something must be done, and I intend to do it." Max was muttering to himself now, in between wincing and groaning and touching his face. He really was acting childishly, Charlotte decided. She would have laughed, if her heart had not been breaking.

Maximilian stopped mumbling and cursing long enough to stand and glare down the roadway. Where was his mother? Although he had known he could catch up with Charlotte and that perfidious Burgess on horseback, he had ordered Sibylle to follow in the coach. So where the hell was she? He glanced up at the lowering sun, the empty roadway... and Charlotte.

This was just the situation he had hoped to avoid. If Charlotte's reputation was to be salvaged, she needed a chaperone quickly. She should not be here, at sunset, alone with anyone, including him. Especially him...

Although his head throbbed, his lip and his eye stung, and his whole body ached, Maximilian could still summon up desire for the woman standing beside him. He imagined that if he were totally incapacitated, she would still tempt him. From the moment he had opened his eyes to find her luscious, full breasts above him and her lips only inches from his own, he had known he was in trouble.

With an oath, Maximilian kicked at a stone and stared into the distance, willing his mother's vehicle to appear. He admitted to himself that his attraction to Charlotte, powerful from the first, was becoming an obsession that he struggled with all too frequently.

Something had to be done. And this annoying interest in her was not all that troubled him about the vicar's daughter. Because of her, his life had become a mess of canceled appointments, disrupted schedules, duels and the like, culminating in his headlong rush to rescue her tonight, and topped by fisticuffs in the roadway. "Attacked by a common coachman!" he said aloud, his breast filled with disgust. "The mind positively rebels."

Something had to be done. Maximilian refused to look at her, but gazed resolutely down the highway while he examined his alternatives. Several possibilities presented themselves as permanent solutions. He could send her home; he could go away himself; or he could see her wed. He scowled into the sunset.

With grim finality, Maximilian vowed that before this night was over, he would write her papa.

Viscount Raleigh sat kicking his heels in Wycliffe's drawing room and wondering where on earth his friend was. When the predictably punctual earl had failed to attend the quarterly meeting of his driving club, Raleigh had been compelled by curiosity to find out why. Sniffing about, he had been able to discover nothing except that the earl had ridden like a wild man from his mother's town house this afternoon.

It was now well past dark, and Raleigh was no closer to solving the mystery, although he had treated himself to his absent host's best Bordeaux. He glanced up at the clock, trying to decide whether to go on to White's or crack open another bottle, when the door burst open and a large, foul-looking fellow rushed in.

"Here, now!" Raleigh mumbled, straightening up in his chair. Momentarily in fear of his life, or, at the very least, his friend's valuables, he had no idea how he was going to fend off the knave.

"What are you doing here?" the creature demanded.

"I would ask the same of you!" Raleigh protested before something in the man's face made him practically swallow his tongue. He gaped, he stared and he stammered, dumbfounded at the sight of the always perfectly groomed Earl of Wycliffe standing before him in filthy, torn and stained clothing, his eye nearly swollen shut and his lip bruised and bloody. "Good God, Wycliffe! What happened to you?" Raleigh half rose from his seat in astonishment.

With a heedlessness wholly unlike himself, the fastidious earl sprawled in a nearby chair and frowned grimly. "The vicar's daughter. That is what happened to me."

Raleigh nearly dropped his teeth. "You mean...Miss Trowbridge did this to you?" He was still gawking at Wycliffe's wounds when a pale-faced Hoskins appeared.

"Your brandy, my lord, and your...ice," said the unflappable butler before withdrawing silently.

Wycliffe took a huge gulp of liquor, wrapped the ice in a cloth and put it to his eye, emitting a low, and heretofore unprecedented, groan.

"I rue the day that I met her, Raleigh," the earl replied, a glazed look in his good eye. "If I had known what awaited me, I would never have entered the vicarage. I would have turned tail and run in the opposite direction with all speed!"

Raleigh wondered just what kind of head injuries his friend had suffered. He knew that no female, let alone the lovely Miss Trowbridge, could have so damaged the earl. "But who assaulted you?" he asked.

"Burgess. I am going to kill him," Wycliffe replied, setting down his glass.

Raleigh was too astounded by the name to remark on his friend's unnatural vehemence. "Sir Burgess? The old baron?"

"He is not *that* old," Wycliffe said.

"Well, obviously, he is not too old to throw a punch!" Raleigh agreed.

Wycliffe lifted the ice to glare at him with both eyes. "I was doing fine, thank you, until the damned driver took me from behind. Blasted coward!"

"Good God, Wycliffe, you do not mean to tell me that you actually brawled with a coachman!" This was too much. Raleigh reached for the second bottle and poured himself a liberal portion. "Dueling is one thing, but fisticuffs... Not your style at all, Wycliffe! Too messy, for one thing..." He glanced at the earl's torn clothing and shuddered.

Wycliffe gave him a pained expression. "What could I do? The man tried to steal Charlotte off to Gretna Green."

Raleigh tossed off his drink in one swallow, although his head already felt none too clear. "Burgess? The quiet, polite gentleman farmer?"

Wycliffe nodded grimly. "He is not what he seems. The fellow is as queer as Dick's hatband, and I have it on good authority that he is obsessed with Charlotte. Something to do with a family connection."

Raleigh tried not to seem too skeptical. "What ties would a barony have to a country vicar?"

"I do not know," Wycliffe said, flinching and shifting the ice to his lip and back again. "I am still trying to gather information, which is woefully slim, about the man. From the accounts I have received, he was much attached to his mother, who died suddenly when he was a young man, leaving him in the hands of a strict and demanding father. The father arranged Burgess's marriage to a homely but rich tradesman's daughter, and Burgess came into the title when his father died a few years ago. His wife was killed in some sort of suspicious accident shortly afterward, and somewhere along the line, our wealthy widower took up opium smoking."

"And became enamored of Miss Trowbridge," Raleigh supplied.

Wycliffe nodded, grimacing. "And now he has run to ground, his tail between his legs, but I shall find him."

"But surely you cannot mean to kill the man in cold blood?" Raleigh protested.

"I do! The bastard abducted Charlotte against her will and attacked me. He blackened my eye, bruised my body and ruined my clothes, not to mention my dignity!"

"Be reasonable, man," Raleigh said, nearly choking on the irony of his plea. Wycliffe always *was* the reasonable one. "You simply cannot do it. Think of Miss Trowbridge! You have already fought one duel over her. She cannot afford any more scandal. Your mother may face it out, but no matter how you hush it up, something is bound to get out about this day's escapade. If you go chasing after Burgess, it will simply confirm all manner of rumors. And if, as you say, the man fancies himself in love with her, then losing his bid for her will be punishment enough. He will certainly never get close to her again."

Wycliffe still looked alarmingly prone to violence, so Raleigh desperately tried another tack. "And, speaking of Miss Trowbridge, dare you leave her here alone? She appears to attract an inordinate amount of trouble. While you are away, who knows what else will happen to your vicar's daughter?" He was taken aback by the sharp glint in Wycliffe's eye.

"Yes," the earl said softly, staring off into space. "Perhaps you are right, Raleigh. I will stay here, at least until I have matters well in hand." He straightened, dropping his icy cloth in a shallow dish left by Hoskins, and picked up his unfinished brandy.

"But, make no mistake about it, this day's piece of work is the last I intend to suffer for the vicar's daughter," Wycliffe said before emptying his glass in one swallow. "I am going to put an end to Charlotte's adventuring, once and for all."

Chapter Fourteen

Charlotte blinked down at the printed words, trying to make some sense of them, but it was futile. No matter how hard she tried to concentrate on *The Suppliants*, her thoughts always returned to the owner of the book before her. With a loving finger, she traced the binding, imagining his dark eyes intent upon the pages, his well-groomed hands cradling the text...

"Drat the man!" Charlotte snapped to the empty room. Putting the volume aside, she walked to the window and peeked out, hoping to see his coach or his figure striding gracefully toward the town house, but all was quiet below.

Cursing her longings, she turned away. It had been a long, difficult week since her aborted elopement. Charlotte had spent much of her time in introspection, a habit in which she rarely indulged, but which was called for now.

She faced her failure head-on. As the season approached its end, she realized that it had all been for naught. Her father's money had been wasted as surely as if he had tossed it to the wind, for she was in love with the one man who would not have her and she could not bear to marry another. How she would make it up to her dear papa and the siblings who depended upon her, Charlotte did not know.

They would not scold her. Charlotte knew that as surely as she knew her own heart, and it made her dread facing them all the more. They would be happy to see her return, and only the oldest among them would even be aware that she had squandered the family's future. Papa would brush aside her apologies, and even Sarah, dear, sensible Sarah, would probably say nothing except that they must watch Papa's spending and put a patch of garden...

Charlotte blinked back the tears. Their kindness would make it worse. She would rather they bluster and blast her like Max, for then she could fight back. Their sweet smiles would only make her berate herself enough for all of them.

She sighed, aware that she had sunk into the first case of blue devils she had known since the death of her mama, but she seemed unable to drag herself out of them. Even Augusta's recovery could not seem to cheer her. If only she could see Max.... Charlotte knew instinctively that he would lighten her mood, if only for a little while, but Max stayed resolutely away.

Charlotte had seen nothing of him after that strained evening on the road and the tense ride back in Sibylle's coach. His mother, laughing merrily, said that he was ashamed to show his injuries in public, but Charlotte was not amused. She was worried about him. Had his eye swollen shut? Was his beautiful lip black and blue? She wanted to stroke his brow and prepare a poultice and pamper him, but she could not. She cursed the restraints of town life that prevented her from visiting him as she surely would if he were at Casterleigh.

Charlotte was tempted to go to him anyway, flouting convention entirely, but she knew that Max would not be pleased to see her. Unlike her, he did not approve of breaking the rules or endangering her reputation, which had been tarnished by the Gretna Green debacle.

Sometimes Charlotte had the cowardly wish that her reputation had been destroyed. Then she could return home without admitting her failure and without taking the blame for her lack of a husband. Much to her disappointment, however, her good name remained intact. There were whispers, of course, but Sibylle put it about that the baron had been called home suddenly. Quite suddenly, Charlotte thought with a bitter smile.

It was ludicrous, but no one cut her. She received invitations just as before and went out, although only to smaller functions and always with both Sibylle and another trusted escort, usually Raleigh, to watch over her. The sumptuous surroundings, rich foods and glorious costumes that once bedazzled her went unnoticed, however. She was too miserable.

Admirers still crowded around her, fetching her refreshments, begging her to dance and trying to coax a smile from her, but Charlotte wanted to see only one face, be it bruised and battered. And she did not. Max, she suspected, was avoiding her.

Earlier in the week, he had summoned Sibylle to his town house, where he lectured her unmercifully over her dereliction of duty and threatened to cut off her funds if she did not keep a closer watch upon her guest.

Charlotte had been horrified at both the warning and the fact that Sibylle would tell her of it, but the lady laughed off the shameful episode as entirely amusing and typical of Maximilian. She claimed she had even managed to sit still through part of his scolding because he was in such a muddle that she enjoyed watching him.

That airily presented explanation, like so much of Sibylle's chatter, was unintelligible, so Charlotte gave it no heed. She did pay attention, however, when Sibylle mentioned that Max should appear tonight at their small fete.

The party had been hastily planned to present a good face after the Burgess scandal, though Charlotte suspected that Sibylle hardly needed an excuse to plan lavish entertainments. She thrived on such things. Charlotte did not, and yet she was looking forward to this evening.

She hoped to get one final look at the man she loved, one last conversation, one more dance.... What she really wanted was one last kiss, but Charlotte knew she could hardly count upon it. Although she vividly remembered the few times Max had treated her as a desirable woman, she was far more likely to receive a scolding than a heated embrace.

Charlotte frowned. She did not want to part on those terms; she wanted to take a glorious memory home with her, a memory of Max's dark eyes filled with the wanting of her. She knew that she would never have more than that from him, but that might just be enough to sustain her until her heart healed itself.

And tonight might be her last chance to make that memory. Although Sibylle had not mentioned it as yet, others were already making preparations for the move to their country homes. Summer, for the ton, would be played out at house parties at grand estates or in visits to the famous watering spots like Bath. Charlotte had already received invitations to join them, but she had declined politely. Such entertainments held no allure for her.

What she wanted was Max, and this evening promised to be the last time she would see him, the last time she would feel that fission in the air between them, and the last time her heart would gallop in her breast—for a lifetime.

Charlotte planned to savor every moment.

Maximilian glanced at his reflection in the tall gilt mirror that graced the entryway and frowned. He could still see a hint of color around his eye and mouth, a reminder of his recent injuries, which served to sour his mood. Noticing Chevalier's attention upon him, Maximilian turned slowly, pinning the Frenchman with a look that dared him to speak. For once, the servant wisely kept quiet, though his eyes fairly danced.

"Your mother has not yet come down, but I believe I saw Miss Trowbridge looking over the refreshment tables in the dining room," he said.

Maximilian gave him a curt nod of thanks and a hard gaze, but Chevalier was already turning away. With a grimace, Maximilian decided he was seeing affronts to his dignity everywhere, even in places they might not exist. His experiences with Charlotte had made him permanently apprehensive, he suspected. The thought made him reflect, a bit uneasily, that his dignity might be lost to him forever.

He pulled himself up straighter in an attempt to retrieve it and made his way to the dining hall and the woman who had become a thorn in his side more aggravating than any split lip or blackened eye could ever be. Remembering all too well the last time he had come upon her unannounced in the Wycliffe town house, Maximilian took a deep breath before peering in.

He realized, belatedly, that he was actually expecting to find her in the arms of yet another overzealous suitor, and the surge of relief he felt when he saw her alone was nearly physical in its intensity. She was addling his brain; he was certain of it. Would he ever be right in the head again? Silently, Maximilian picked up one of the glasses of champagne that were standing ready on the table and took a sip, trying to steady nerves that had never needed steadying before.

She looked more beautiful than ever in a fantastic Corbeau satin gown that would, no doubt, heighten the effect of her luminous eyes. Lush and expensive, the material dipped over her breasts in a manner calculated to make every man in the room take notice and added sophistication and allure to her already luscious form. With a groan of dismay, Maximilian immediately recognized his mother's fine hand in the garment, for it was certainly not something Augusta Thurgoode would choose.

"Charlotte!" He roared. He had not meant to shout. Good Lord, he never shouted! But some sort of sound erupted from his lips in protest against a dress that would have all the males fighting each other to rid her of it. Unfortunately, the noise startled Charlotte, who whirled around so abruptly that the contents of her glass flew onto his waistcoat.

"Damn it, Charlotte!" In his later years, Maximilian would claim he did not know what possessed him, but suddenly he was so heartily sick of being doused with foodstuffs by the vicar's daughter that something inside of him snapped. He did not stop to think. He did not even hesitate. He simply dashed the champagne he was holding all over the front of her far too provocative gown.

"Max!" Charlotte shrieked his name softly and blinked at him, while he stood frozen in horror, unable to believe that he had committed such a dreadful act, such a grotesque breach of etiquette. With an air of confusion, Maximilian lifted the glass in his hand and stared at it suspiciously, as if it had acted of its own accord. Only when he had assured himself that the vessel could not be blamed did he look back at Charlotte.

He expected her to be aghast, to be near fainting or weeping, or perhaps, knowing Charlotte, to be so furious she might lash out at him with a swift kick. To Maximilian's infinite relief and utter amazement, she was none of those. She was, instead, doubled over with amusement. Maximilian stared at her golden head, bobbing up and down, and he was as stunned by her reaction as by his own behavior. Then, before he could speak a word of apology, she grabbed up another glass from the table and aimed the liquid at him. It splashed all over the shoulder of his black Weston coat.

"Damn it, Charlotte. Have you lost your mind?" Maximilian asked as disbelief and outrage warred within him. Charlotte did not immediately respond, but ran around the end of the table, giggling like a girl, and flung more champagne at him. It soaked his hair and dripped into his eyes.

With a low oath, Maximilian grabbed the nearest glass and tossed off another portion at her. She ducked and came up laughing to send another shot of liquid at his head. This volley wet his fáce, and he sputtered furiously before tossing two at a time across the table at her.

They hit her throat and her bodice, and Maximilian noticed the way the thin, dampened material clung to her breasts, revealing the hard tips of her nipples to his fascinated gaze. He stopped and stared, his eyes fastened to her ripe curves as she picked up two more glasses, feinted superbly and sent the contents toward the burgeoning bulge in his pantaloons.

It was her last real effort. She was laughing so hard that she had to pause for breath, and Maximilian took the opportunity to pick up a nearby bottle and shake it soundly. Charlotte saw his intent, but could do nothing but back away, her slim hands held up before her while he descended upon her.

"No, Max, no!" she shrieked between gasps. Unheeding, he grinned wickedly and unleashed a stream of liquid that sprayed all over her. She fell onto the floor in a sodden heap, giggling and spluttering, while Maximilian stood over her feeling ridiculously victorious.

He was enjoying himself.

The absurd thought made Maximilian feel light-headed—weak and strong altogether—and when he looked down on the vicar's daughter, her bright hair escaping its bounds, her gown plastered to her like a second skin and those breasts, those wonderful breasts... They were wet. He wanted nothing more in that moment than to lie on top of her and taste them.

Temptation made his head throb and his body grow heavy with desire. Even the thought of the servants who might walk in at any moment or the guests whose arrival was imminent did nothing to stop the thrumming of his blood. Slowly, he set down the bottle he held and took a step forward. Charlotte lifted a hand up to him...in invitation?

Maximilian sucked in his breath and took it, allowing her to pull him down beside her. Once there, however, he discovered that Charlotte was oblivious to his need, for instead of coming into his arms, she grabbed the bottle and dribbled the last of its brew upon his head. What might have easily turned into something else became, once again, a subject of humor, and when his mother arrived, they were still on the floor, soaking wet and laughing like loons.

"Charlotte!" they heard Sibylle call from the doorway. "Who have you got there with you? Get up, the both of you! Maximilian will blame me for any fun you are having.

And he will have a fit when he sees what you have done to his carpet! Do you hear me?''

Sibylle was actually stomping one of her dainty feet. Charlotte sat up abruptly, obviously chastened, but Maximilian stayed where he was, one arm flung over his face as he choked back his mirth. "You, sir!" Sibylle called. "Get up this instant, or I will send Maximilian after you! Then you will find yourself facing pistols at dawn.''

With a groan, Maximilian lifted his head slowly, and the look on his mother's face was well worth the price of a new rug. "My God! Maximilian, is that you? No! It cannot be,'' she protested, teetering on her feet as though she might collapse. "It is not you!''

Maximilian rose as gracefully as he could under the circumstances and helped Charlotte up to stand beside him. "It is me, madame,'' he said calmly. "And I hate to disappoint you, but I have no intention of calling myself out.''

As a romantic evening, it did not rate highly, but it had been memorable, Charlotte reflected as she gazed dreamily at the delicate silk hangings on her bed. She had not gotten her kiss, but she had a final waltz with Max, when both of them had changed into dry clothes, and during that all-too-brief dance, he had watched her with something other than his usual detachment.

Coupled with the previous events of the night, it was enough. Smiling, Charlotte recalled with vivid clarity the moment Maximilian had let himself go, cavorting like a boy with her among the splash of expensive wine. Drowning in champagne... It was a luxury she would never know again, and that thought tempered her guilt over the expense.

Of course, Sibylle had not cared. The carpet had been rolled up and the floor mopped before any of the guests arrived. The only lingering effects of the whole episode had been the odd looks Maximilian's mother had sent her way, as if Charlotte had turned out to be much more of a puzzle than she had anticipated.

Sibylle obviously had been surprised to catch her son in such play, so much so that Charlotte suspected poor Max had never been a boy. And yet, the child was still there in him somewhere, with its lighthearted love of life intact, just waiting to be released.

Charlotte shut her eyes against a vision of Max with Jenny, bemused but happy to hold her, and Max sharing a quip with Kit as a smile tugged at the corners of his mouth. When she pictured the earl running and laughing with his own children, she felt tears wet her cheeks. She sat up abruptly. Oh, Max, I hope your wife, whoever she may be, can unlock that secret part of you, Charlotte wished silently. A knock on the door made her wipe her face guiltily.

"Come in," she called. Her maid, Annette, brought in a morning tray and set it neatly in front of her. Breakfast in bed! How her brothers would scoff and her sisters would swoon, if they only knew, but Charlotte had decided to pamper herself in the little time she had left. She would surely never know such delights again, and besides, she told herself, she was always up long before Sibylle. The dining room was vast and lonely at this hour, so it was much cozier to eat in her room.

"Good morning, Annette," Charlotte said. "Thank you," she added as the maid plopped up her pillows.

"You have a letter, which must have been missed in yesterday's excitement. I put it on your tray," Annette noted with a smile.

"Oh, thank you!" It was from her papa, and Charlotte felt a sudden homesickness coupled with an eagerness to hear news of those who loved her for herself, be she only a poor vicar's daughter. Pushing the tray aside impatiently, Charlotte broke open the wafer and unfolded the sheets. Her food remained untouched, and Annette's quiet retreat went unheeded as Charlotte read and reread the page until finally she stared at it in disbelief.

My dearest Charlotte,
We are all rejoicing at the welcome news from Lord

Wycliffe. Although he says many gentlemen have been pressing offers for your hand upon him, he has forwarded to me only the most welcome one, from Viscount Linley. Wycliffe assures me that the viscount has an impeccable reputation as well as great wealth, and, indeed, he has presented an astounding settlement for my approval.

We are so proud of your success, my dear, and the girls are all agog that you are to gain an unexpected title. They are already calling you Viscountess Linley, as you can well imagine. The boys are not as impressed, but are begging for details about the viscount's stables, and etc. One hopes that he is not put off by children, for I suspect they are counting the days until they can ask to visit.

Since Wycliffe said you were anxious to be wed, I have told his lordship to accept on my behalf. I hope this is welcome news to you, my dear, and that you have not been kept chafing at the bit, so to speak, while all was under consideration....

The letter went on with news from home and more felicitations upon her betrothal, and no matter how many times Charlotte read it, the words never altered. She would have thought it all an elaborate hoax but for the fact that Max was involved, and Max was nothing if not reliable and responsible.

Finally, after her fourth look at the pages, she began to accept the bizarre news. To her dismay, it appeared she was suddenly to marry Viscount Linley—a man she could not recall for the life of her.

Vainly, Charlotte searched her memory, but there were so many gentlemen who flitted in and out of her orbit, teasing and talking with her, fetching her this treat and that refreshment or begging her for a dance, that Charlotte could never have recalled them all. The name tugged at her mind, just out of reach, for although she knew she had heard it before, she could put no face to it.

The mysterious viscount was not one of her more persistent suitors, of that she was certain, or she could have recalled him easily. Roddy Black, Captain Stollings, Sir Burgess, Viscount Raleigh... Charlotte blinked and looked down again at her father's scrawled lines, but there was no mistaking the name. It was not Raleigh. And although a dozen other admirers came quickly to her mind, none of them were Linley.

Charlotte was betrothed to a man she did not know. The irony of it made a bubble of laughter choke her. A year ago, perhaps even a month ago, she might have accepted the offer of a man with an impeccable reputation and a hefty income, knowing that she was doing her duty for her family. And she might have managed to find some happiness with her faceless swain.

But not now. Not when she was in love with another man. It would be unfair to this Linley and utter torment for herself. Maybe someday she would be able to gift herself to another, but at this moment, her love was too new, too hot, too bright to imagine anyone but Max in her life... and in her bed.

Max. Charlotte stared down at the page, a sob of denial escaping her throat, as the recognition of his betrayal knifed through her. *Since Wycliffe said you were anxious to wed.* The phrase made her dizzy. All along, she had known he would never step so far beneath himself as to marry a vicar's daughter, but she had suspected that neither did he want her to belong to another.

Charlotte remembered what she had come to view as his jealous rages, how he had lost his temper whenever he found her with another man, and she wondered, suddenly, if she had imbued him with her own motives. With a sickening twist to her stomach, she recalled how she had accused him of driving away her suitors, when in fact he was just waiting for the most advantageous offer.

Embarrassment and pain shot through her at the realization that she had been reading into Max's gestures some sort of affection that simply was not there. His interest had been, and always would be, strictly that of a peer toward one of his lowly tenants.

And his kisses? Those Charlotte had a more difficult time explaining until she remembered what Sarah had told her years ago. Men had urges they could not always control, and that is why a girl should not beg them to kiss her. Hadn't Max warned her of the same thing? Those few times he had lost his vaunted self-restraint and touched her, he was simply giving in to such impulses.

Charlotte threw back the covers and leapt out of bed, as if the very air agitated her. Her skin prickling, she wrapped her arms around herself as a wave of nausea hit, turning her lovely memories of the evening before into nothing but a bad taste in her mouth.

Last night. Charlotte could not fathom it. She could not reconcile the man who had joined her yesterday in the dining room, tossing away his dignity as easily as he did the champagne, with the cold-blooded character who had accepted a proposal without even consulting her. And he had known! Max had known last evening when he had stood over her, sporting with her like a friend.

Shivering, Charlotte remembered lying on the floor, looking up at him and seeing something in his eyes, hot and glinting, that made her feel strange all over. The wet tangle of her clothes had suddenly become exciting, the sheen of champagne on her skin exotic and demanding of something... She did not know what.

Nor would she ever know, unless the mysterious Lord Linley had a penchant for bathing in champagne. The thought made her cringe. Had the viscount been at the party last night, too? Charlotte did not know. Her eyes had been only for Max. Although she had never had another chance to see him alone, they had danced together and talked briefly of their mutual interest in mythology, and all the while he had known of her betrothal—and said nothing. How could he?

I plan to do something. Max's threat came back to her abruptly, making her stiffen. That day on the roadway, bedraggled and sore and furious, he had vowed to put an end to her escapades. Charlotte's eyes slid to the letter lying on her bed, and bitter anger bubbled up through her pain.

It appeared that the earl had found a most expedient way of ridding himself of her forever.

Maximilian was in the process of dressing when Hoskins knocked on his bedroom door. "My lord," Hoskins said, his face showing a strain of some sort. "A young woman has arrived who is most adamant about seeing you—"

"Max!" At the sound of Charlotte's voice, Maximilian hurriedly tucked his loose shirt into his breeches, gazed down at his stockinged feet and grimaced. It would have to do. If she insisted on bounding into his private apartments, what did she expect but to find him in his shirtsleeves—or worse? Heaving the sigh of the eternally burdened, he nonetheless smiled a greeting.

"Max!" she repeated. Although Hoskins placed himself in the center of the doorway, apparently with the hope of detaining her, Charlotte handily evaded him and rushed into the room.

"My dear girl!" Hoskins spluttered. Obviously appalled by her lack of convention, he looked like he was going to have a stroke.

"It is all right. Hoskins, Levering, you may go," Maximilian said. Levering, his valet, went with a curious glance toward Charlotte, but Hoskins seemed reluctant. "You may go, Hoskins," Maximilian said more firmly. When the butler still did not move, Maximilian shut the door in his face.

"Good God, Charlotte, you practically gave my butler a coronary," Maximilian complained in a surprisingly even tone. "What the deuce are you doing here—in my bed-chamber—at this hour of the morning?"

"As if you did not know!" Charlotte responded, glaring daggers at him. Her eyes were flashing green fire, and her hands were on her hips in her most martial stance. She appeared fierce enough to carve out his liver. He wondered idly if she were armed. "Oh, Max, how could you?"

"What?"

"Marry me off to a...stranger!" The fury that Charlotte wore so valiantly and so well seemed to waver before his gaze. As he watched, her lovely pink mouth drooped, and he felt a pang of guilt for upsetting her. He opened his mouth to speak, but she thrust a paper at his chest.

"Oh, Max, how could you? To write Papa, without even discussing it with me, and get all their hopes up!" She shook her head, freeing some curls that had obviously been pinned up in haste, and Maximilian took a moment to admire the soft tendrils that sprang about her face.

"But isn't that why you came to London, to find a husband?" he asked evenly.

"Yes, but...I do not even know this man!" Charlotte protested.

Maximilian shrugged. "I imagine you will quickly enough."

"I will not." The certainty in her voice made him pause, and he slanted a look at her.

"Oh, Max," she whispered miserably. The anger that she had worn before her like a shield dipped and fell, revealing a trembling lip and lashes that blinked back some kind of emotion. "I cannot. I tried, I really tried, but I cannot marry without...affection, and I have none for this Viscount Linley."

"Are you so sure?" Max asked softly, taking a step toward her.

She nodded, her head bent, the coils of her hair bobbing like soft down upon her crown. "I hate to fail my family, but I cannot, will not, wed any of my suitors. That is my final word, and you may break it to his lordship." Her voice broke at the end of her speech.

Maximilian cleared his throat. "You feel nothing for any of them?" he asked, stepping closer again.

Charlotte tugged anxiously on a finger. "Well, I suppose I like Raleigh well enough, but it is not the same as..." Her voice trailed off and she deliberately looked away.

"The same as what?" He was near enough to speak in a hush, and taking her by the shoulders, he gently turned her to face him.

"The same as...as giving one's heart," she concluded softly, staring down at her yellow skirts. At her words, Maximilian felt a convoluted sense of victory that she felt nothing toward all the others, coupled with a bitter defeat that he must needs be included in the throng.

With some effort, he reined in his raging emotions. "There is an alternative," he suggested softly. He could smell the fresh fragrance that clung to her, reminding him in some lunatic way of sunshine and green meadows and great, shading trees. The logic of equating this spontaneous creature with a peaceful setting escaped him, but what about this entire affair made any sense?

"What alternative?" Charlotte asked quietly.

He spoke as lightly as he could manage. "Me."

Her eyes darted to his immediately. He felt them searching his while she choked back a laugh. "Do not tease me, Max."

"I am not teasing you," he answered. His hands were still on her shoulders, his thumbs methodically, absently stroking her skin. "I believe we have been in the most compromising of situations many times, culminating with this early morning visit to my bedroom."

Charlotte appeared truly horrified. "Oh, Max, I did not come here to...to compromise you. That was truly not what I intended," she protested. He believed her. She was too guileless to plan such a trap. She probably viewed this charge into his bedchamber as no more dangerous than visiting her grandpa's sickroom. Maximilian scowled at the thought.

"I know," he said a bit bitterly. He tried to imagine what it would be like to be seduced by Charlotte, her slim hands on his body, her breasts pressing against him.... His breathing quickened, and his groin tightened. He focused on her face. "I realize that you see me as a fatherly figure—"

Charlotte's bright burst of laughter surprised him. "You can hardly believe that after...when..." She seemed unable to complete her thought. Lowering her lashes against flushed cheeks, she placed one palm against his chest, and he felt the heat of it through his shirt.

His heart began hammering with a painful, hopeful beat. He chose his words carefully. "You do hold me in some regard?" he asked, cursing the stiff and formal sound of the question. He gripped her arms tighter, a flutter of panic gnawing at him.

"Of course," Charlotte answered softly. "Surely you cannot doubt it?" She lifted her eyes, wide and glittering, with what he dared not name, to his.

"Then I see no obstacle to our marriage."

"Oh, Max," she protested with a trembling frown. "You do not want me."

"Don't I?" he asked hoarsely.

Chapter Fifteen

Slowly, so very slowly, Maximilian slid his hands along her shoulder to her throat and up the curve of her neck to her nape. His body was humming, all hot need, the blood thrumming through his veins in some primitive beat. Just one taste, he promised himself, to prove to her just how very much he wanted her.

Her lips were soft and yielding as he touched them with his own, shaping and slanting across them before sliding his tongue inside. She was as fresh and sweet as her fragrance, and he pulled her closer as he thrust deeper into her mouth. She made a soft sound before slipping her arms around his neck.

So good. He had never felt so good as when she clutched him, pressing her soft body into his own. He ran his hands down her back to cup her buttocks and pull her up against his hardness. *Did he want her?* Dear God, he had never throbbed and ached this way for any woman.

Charlotte sighed into his mouth, her delicate tongue making tentative forays against his, and he gripped her bottom. Its round, lovely contours made him think of her other curves, and he abruptly tore his lips away from hers. Pressing a hot kiss against her throat, Maximilian tried to catch his breath while he thought of her bosom, her lush, tempting bosom... He should not. He knew he should not, but ...

Good God, his hands were trembling. For a moment, they fumbled with her gown and then they were pushing it down, off her shoulders to her waist. He barely glanced at the thin wisp of material that was her chemise before dragging it down, too, while his heart thudded madly against his ribs.

Then Maximilian released them, full, milky breasts with wide rosy nipples made for suckling by an infant—or a man, he thought. He took them in his hands, cupping them, letting his fingers learn their texture, smooth and silky and so heavy... And all the desire he had ever felt for her, submerged to duty and honor, surged to the fore, driving away all that should have held him back.

With a groan, he buried his face between the soft mounds. His mouth roved over her creamy skin, licking and tasting until he found his goal. Then his lips closed over her nipple and he rolled it against his tongue, teasing and pulling, while Charlotte threw her head back and whimpered.

She arched against him, her thighs straining at his, and he eased her back onto the bed, stroking her bottom as he pulled it to him. Charlotte had such a luscious, round rump; he could feel its firmness even underneath her clothes. Before he could muse further on that delightful part of her body, her hands were in his hair, forcing his head to her breast, and he sucked harder, first one ripe globe and then the other until she was rocking against him, rubbing herself on his groin in an action that pushed him even further toward the edge of what would surely be madness.

Lifting the hem of her gown, Maximilian slid one hand up her leg, over her dainty ankle and her smooth stockings to the silky skin above. He caressed her bare buttocks, making wide circles and cupping her curves eagerly beneath her chemise. She was so incredibly soft, so sumptuous... He continued to feast upon her breasts while she murmured beneath him, urging him on with her whimpers and the thrust of her hips against his.

Finally, Maximilian moved his hand to the juncture of her thighs. Just one touch, he told himself, but he met a hot, slick wetness that was his undoing. He groaned. Unable to stop himself, he slipped a finger into her tight sheath. Oh, to be inside her himself...

He worked her flesh gently, stroking her throbbing core and slowly sliding his fingers in and out until she was writhing beneath him. Sweet, innocent Charlotte—she was like a wild thing, her head thrashing back and forth against the bed covers as she made indistinct sounds of pleasure.

Maximilian's hair had come loose to fall down about his face, washing over her chest, and Charlotte grabbed it in great handfuls, clutching him to her full breasts while she pushed herself against his hand. Together they created a rhythm that made sweat bead upon Maximilian's brow. Then suddenly she tensed beneath him, and he felt contractions take her body. "Max!" she cried out in hushed pleasure.

Maximilian couldn't think. He was beyond thought, mired in desire such as he had never known. He fumbled with the fall of his breeches and released his sex, hot, hard and eager. If he could just...

Pushing up her skirts to her waist, he spread her legs wider and settled between her thighs, guiding himself to her opening. She greeted his head with moist heat, and he glided inside, the pleasure of his entrance so sharp that he bit back a cry.

Maximilian had enough sense left to force himself to go slowly, although he wanted nothing more than to bury himself to the hilt in her welcoming tightness. He moved carefully, his fingers gripping her pale thigh as he struggled for the very last semblance of control. Just a little more... He met her maidenhead at the same moment that a knock sounded on the door.

Maximilian froze, then swore underneath his breath. He looked down at Charlotte. Her face was flushed, her lips were parted, and her green eyes were wide and awash with sated desire. Her hair had come loose and was flowing about her like a cloud. Never in his life had he wanted anything more than to pound into her until he spent himself.

He withdrew.

"Charlotte," he whispered painfully. His whole body trembling with need, he pulled her gown over her legs. Then he fell onto his back, unable to do more. The knocking, loud now, did not seem to penetrate his senses, for he was still rock hard and throbbing. "Charlotte... Oh, God, I'm going to burst."

Then her face was above him, her beautiful features so familiar, but so changed by her passion. She blinked, surprise and concern in her gaze. "Oh, Max," she whispered. "Tell me what to do."

Maximilian moaned, hesitating for an instant before the last vestiges of his legendary control deserted him. Then he told her. "Touch me," he begged. She reached out, and he took her hand, guiding it to him and closing her fingers around his shaft.

With a groan, he dropped his hand and watched her. Her hair was awhirl about her, drifting down to her glorious, milky breasts, still bared to his view, while her pale, slim fingers gripped the arousal that thrust upward from the open fall of his breeches. That sight alone was nearly enough...

"Stroke me," he whispered, his mouth dry with need. "Up and down. That way, Charlotte. Yes!" he cried. He jerked against her hand, once, twice, and then release—blessed, endless release—came, and he spewed his seed across the covers even as Hoskins shouted at the door.

Charlotte moved back with a little cry, as if startled by the response from his body, but then she leaned over him and pressed a quick, warm kiss to his mouth before moving from the bed. While he fumbled with his breeches, she stood and arranged her gown as best she could.

"My lord! Are you in there?" Hoskins's voice rang out. Now that he was satiated, Maximilian turned his energy toward becoming wholly enraged at his butler's behavior, beginning with a violent urge to strangle the man. Giving Charlotte a cursory glance to make sure she was dressed, he leapt from the bed, strode to the door and swung it wide.

"What is it?" Maximilian asked through clenched teeth. His fingers twitched, itching to strike the man who had served him so long and so well—until today.

If Hoskins sensed the enormity of his folly, he did not show it, for his features were as impassive as usual. "I have taken the liberty of readying a carriage for your visitor," he said stonily.

"Hoskins," Maximilian said, hardly daring himself to speak.

"Yes, my lord?"

"You are dismissed."

"Max, no!" Charlotte protested. She came to his side and laid her fingers on his arm as if to restrain him. Maximilian looked down at the capable, pale hand, the same that had brought him to orgasm, and he felt dizzy. "He was only trying to..."

"Trying to protect you from me?" Maximilian supplied coolly. She dropped her gaze, and her cheeks, already flushed with their loving, now turned crimson. "Unfortunately, that is not his job."

"Very well, my lord," Hoskins said, his expression grim.

"Max," Charlotte chided, digging her fingers into the sleeve of his shirt. He gazed into her face, floating amid a cloud of blond hair, and he realized that he had not even touched her hair, the hair that he had longed so often to caress. It was billowing about her, soft and inviting, while his own hung down his back in disarray.

Had he even noticed her tresses? Maximilian could not recall, for the recent episode in his bed bore no resemblance to his usual thorough, gentle lovemaking. Mindless, uncontrollable passion such as he had never known before had driven him to behavior he could hardly condone. The truth came to him bitterly.

Were it not for Hoskins, he would have deflowered Charlotte. And not during a long, luxurious night of wedded bliss, but in a hurried moment of lust while both of them were fully dressed. Disgusted with himself, Maximilian nodded at Hoskins.

"Very well," he said. "As the lady wishes. You may remain in your current position in my household. And, Hoskins?"

"Yes, my lord?"

Maximilian glared at his butler, as if daring him to react. "We would have your felicitations, for Miss Trowbridge and I are getting married as soon as possible."

"Very good, my lord," Hoskins answered, and to his relief, Maximilian saw no hint of censure in the butler's eyes.

"Good," Maximilian muttered. "Then let us understand each other. *I* will escort Miss Trowbridge back to my mother's town house."

Maximilian watched the butler's gaze flick to his stockinged feet, and he cursed under his breath. Although certainly not a dandy, Maximilian prided himself on his impeccable appearance. And yet he had nearly left the room in nothing but his shirt and breeches. Maximilian suspicioned that he might as well toss that pride out the window, along with his dignity, now that Charlotte was to be a permanent fixture in his life.

Although galling, somehow he could not mourn the loss of such things when he looked at Charlotte's mouth, ripe and red from kissing, curving into a tender smile. With uncharacteristic spontaneity, Maximilian reached out to push a swirl of springy hair away from her face. It felt soft and delightful under his palm. "What wonderful hair," he whispered.

Maximilian saw the quicksilver shadow of surprise cross her lovely features. "You cannot mean it."

"Of course, I do," Maximilian answered. "When we are married, I shall expect you to wear it down for me." He squeezed a thick mass of it between his fingers and drew in a deep breath at the realization that desire was throbbing through him again.

"When we are married," Charlotte said in a husky whisper, her green eyes glittering darkly on his own locks, "I shall expect you to wear yours down for me."

Maximilian stepped back, the air between them much too ripe with promise for his peace of mind. "I shall be just a moment," he said, a bit too heartily. Then he sat down and grabbed one of the boots that Levering had laid out so neatly. He pulled it on with something less than his usual aplomb, while attempting to ignore the ache in his groin.

Hoskins cleared his throat. "Perhaps Miss Trowbridge would care to wait for you to join her in the drawing room," he suggested.

"No, thank you." Charlotte's careless answer made Maximilian grin, and he glanced up to see her walking around his bedroom as though it were the most natural and comfortable of environments. She seemed very much at home among his personal effects, Maximilian noted as he tugged on his second boot. The thought warmed him somewhere deep inside.

"Oh, Max! This looks like..." Charlotte's words trailed off as she held up the drawing that Jenny had sent him.

"Me?" he asked ruefully.

Charlotte burst into that wonderful laughter of hers while he stood up and searched for a neckcloth. All his life, he had been dressed or assisted by a valet, but now he was beginning to see some advantages in doing for himself. He liked Charlotte's company. When she was near he felt... loved? Cherished?

Maximilian grimaced at his own foolishness and told himself to be sensible. Charlotte had admitted that she held him in some regard; she had not declared her undying devotion. Nor did he expect her to voice such sentiments. Such delusions were better left to those in need of romantic fancies.

Love? What rubbish! He had never seen any evidence that the emotion existed. With a vicious yank, he pulled off the neckcloth, which refused to tie properly, tossed it to the floor and drew out another. He was startled to see Charlotte, out of the corner of his eye, reach down to retrieve the errant piece of material. Something about the gesture tugged at his heart.

She placed the white linen on his dresser and came to stand next to him while he looked into the mirror. No wonder he could not tie his usual mathematical! Charlotte was holding up the drawing beside him and smiling wickedly. "Yes, I do see a resemblance."

Maximilian choked back a laugh and tried once more to finish his toilet.

"I think the large head is especially telling," Charlotte noted.

Maximilian let the neckcloth drop from his fingers and turned his startled gaze upon her. "Are you saying that I think too highly of myself?"

Charlotte laughed again and put a steadying hand upon his chest. "Oh, Max!"

"Well?" He demanded an answer. He had always considered himself the most modest of men. He neither preened in dandyish clothing nor lorded his wealth and title over others, so her playful accusation stunned him.

"I admit that you are sometimes a trifle too proud, but I have great hopes for your improvement," she teased. Her eyes were brimming with affection that took the sting from her words. "Oh, Max!" To his surprise, she threw her arms around his neck and hugged him tightly, crushing his second attempt to tie a decent knot.

Hoskins cleared his throat again, and they both turned to look at the butler, who stood in the doorway like a solemn male duenna, eyeing their display with disapproval. Muttering imprecations too low for Charlotte to hear, Maximilian disentangled himself from her embrace and swiftly redid his wrinkled neckcloth in the simplest of arrangements.

"After your less than flattering comments, I suspect that you had a hand in your sister's completion of my portrait," Maximilian said over his shoulder. He strode toward the bed, where his waistcoat had been laid, only to find it crumpled beyond redemption. Refusing to let his thoughts drift to the reason for its condition, he rifled through his wardrobe for another and thrust it on hurriedly.

"Then it *is* Jenny's drawing!" Charlotte said. "I thought it seemed familiar. Jenny sent you a picture?" The odd note in her voice made him glance at her. She was looking at him with a wondrous expression on her lovely features and a gaze that seemed to pierce his innermost self. Maximilian grunted and slipped into his coat.

Finally, he was dressed. It was, of course, well past his scheduled appearance for breakfast, and he felt the distinctly unusual sensation of impatience nagging at him. The ritual of his toilet seemed far too lengthy when Charlotte was waiting for him. He walked to her side, took the paper from her fingers, stuck it back in the frame and held out his arm for her to take.

"Let us be off, then, before Sibylle raises the alarm about your absence," Maximilian said, giving her a crooked smile. They passed their self-appointed chaperon, Hoskins, and headed down the stairs.

They had not even reached the bottom when Maximilian noticed the approach of his secretary, carrying a sheaf of papers with a harried air. Wilkes stopped dead and gaped at the sight of Charlotte descending with his master. The slip in his employee's manners irked Maximilian, but he ignored it, pressing on as if young female visitors were a commonplace feature of his household.

"Good morning, Wilkes. We will have to postpone our meeting until later," Maximilian said, as he moved past his secretary. "I am going to escort Miss Trowbridge back to my mother's, and upon my return, I plan to leave for Castereigh immediately. Please notify the staff and have Levering begin packing at once. Cancel all my engagements in town indefinitely and—"

"No!"

Maximilian, with Charlotte on his arm, was nearly to the door when he heard his secretary's shout. He turned in amazement.

Wilkes, white-faced and wild-eyed, was rooted to his position at the foot of the stairs, clutching the sheaf of papers to his chest in a death grip, while Hoskins looked on with an astonished expression.

"I beg your pardon?" Maximilian asked.

"No! I will rearrange your schedule no longer, my lord," Wilkes said, his voice trembling with the force of his emotion. "When you took me on, I thought we were of like minds, methodical, punctual and orderly beings, but I can see that we are no longer in accord. In the past few weeks, a change has come over you, and not for the good! You have missed appointments, ignored reports and tossed my carefully composed schedule to the winds! Look at you. You have begun to rush about, always in a hurry, in a manner wholly beneath your station."

"Now, Wilkes," Maximilian began. He decided to placate the man. Despite his outburst, Wilkes was a good secretary, and Maximilian did not care to lose him. "I admit there has been some upheaval of late—"

"Upheaval!" Wilkes laughed in a high, strained voice. "It is pure anarchy, my lord. Anarchy brought about by that... that female!" He pointed a bony finger at Charlotte.

Maximilian felt his hand twitch as anger surged to the fore. Anarchy, was it? With a great effort of will, he stilled his fingers and swept the room with an assessing glance. The footman who stood attendance at the door was gaping like a schoolboy in the most amusing fashion, and Hoskins, poor beleaguered Hoskins, appeared apoplectic. It was certainly not business as usual. Maximilian felt his lips quiver.

Charlotte, her green eyes huge at the charges, was nevertheless patting his arm as if to calm him, and he lightly slipped his palm over her hand in acknowledgment. The signs of change were all about him, but they were for the good because, for the first time, his household was humming with life, laughter and... warmth.

Turning his attention to the principal actor in the melodrama, Maximilian saw a skinny, bespectacled fellow possessing more studiousness than humanity. And he was extremely glad that the man no longer reflected himself.

Throwing back his head, Maximilian laughed at his secretary's words. "If this is anarchy, then so be it, Wilkes. Good luck to you in your new position. May you find an employer as humorless and orderly as yourself!"

Maximilian turned with an elegant flourish and looked at his butler. "Hoskins, please see to readying for my departure. And then sit down, man. You don't look well, by half."

As Charlotte had anticipated, no one had raised the alarm over her absence. In fact, Sibylle, who was just coming down from her toilet, obviously had no idea that Charlotte had left the town house unescorted to pay a call upon a gentleman.

"Maximilian! How nice to see you." Sibylle fluttered toward him and pressed her cheek against his in what Charlotte imagined was supposed to be a kiss, although she had seen Kit buss the dog with more enthusiasm.

"How can you be out and about at this wretched hour? You are positively inhuman, and you, too, dear," Sibylle said, eyeing Charlotte. "Our country girl is always up early and looking so fresh-faced, too, odious creature. Have you breakfasted? Come, join me." The dainty woman indicated with an airy wave that they should follow her to the dining room.

Charlotte saw the telling movement of Max's fingers and put a restraining hand upon his arm. It was just as well, for his brows were lowered over dark eyes that glittered with the urge to take his mother to task. "I apologize, Charlotte, for entrusting you to such negligent care," he said stiffly.

"Now, Max," Charlotte said, squeezing his arm. "No harm was done."

For a moment, he just stared at her. Then his lips moved crookedly, and Charlotte knew he was remembering the extraordinary events that had occurred this morning in his bed. "That, my dear, is a matter of opinion."

Charlotte flushed crimson and dropped her gaze, suddenly embarrassed by what had happened. It had all seemed so exciting, so glorious—the things Max had done to her and the way he had made her feel—that she had never wanted it to end. The look on his face when she had touched him there, when he begged her to... The recollection was enough to set her heart pounding at a furious pace.

She wanted to see him like that again, to hear the groan that rose from deep in his chest as he spilled his seed—and she wanted him to be inside her at that moment. Charlotte realized that she would have gladly given herself up to that final, irrevocable passion with no thought to the consequences, but at the same time, she recognized that Max might not appreciate her wanton desires. She clasped her hands together before her. The palms were moist. "Do you regret...it?" she asked, her voice low and unsteady.

She had barely spoken when she felt his fingers under her chin, forcing her to meet a gaze that was soft and glowing. "Never," he whispered huskily. "I regret only my own appalling lack of self-restraint." A rueful smile tugged at the corners of his mouth at the words with which he had once accused her.

Then he nodded toward Sibylle's figure, disappearing blithely into the dining room, and his mouth tightened. "But what if you had gotten it into your stubborn head to go to some other man's home? Who would have stopped you? Who, indeed, would have noticed you gone?" he asked scornfully, his grip on her chin tightening.

Charlotte was dismayed by his anger, even though she knew it was prompted by concern for her. She put a palm to the side of his dear face, willing him to understand. "I would never go to any other man's home! Tell me you know that, Max."

"I do not know it," he said, turning away with a sulky grimace. "First there was Roddy Black, then Stollings, then Burgess and God knows who else! One of the best reasons I can think of for this marriage is so that I may be relieved of the burden of protecting you from every besotted gallant in London."

He looked so much like one of the boys grumbling about his chores that Charlotte nearly laughed. "I am sorry about Roddy. I only kissed him out of curiosity—and to tease you, you know," she admitted. "The other mishaps were not my doing, however, and I do not care for your intimation that I got myself attacked by the captain and abducted by the baron simply to cause you inconvenience."

Max appeared unconvinced by her disclaimers, and Charlotte took a deep breath before speaking again. "I swear that, although I have often wanted to visit you, it has never crossed my mind to go to any other man's residence. And I would certainly never let any other man touch me. Tell me you know that, at least," she said, indignant that he could possibly think otherwise.

His gaze slid over her, openly assessing, before he spoke. "I know it." He answered so solemnly that Charlotte felt relieved. She was not anxious to wed a man who did not trust her. Nor did she want him to believe that her easy capitulation in his bed was the result of anything but her special feelings for him—and him alone. Charlotte stared at him, trying to tell him with her eyes what she hesitated to voice.

He returned her look with such warmth that she felt giddy. "I knew it the minute Stollings complained about your kisses, but I have never understood why. Why, Charlotte?"

Charlotte shook her head, unable to say the words that he might scorn. "It has always been you, only you, since I set my eyes upon you at the vicarage," she whispered. Her admission seemed to spark something in the brown eyes that traveled over her, and suddenly the very air seemed to fission with unexplained heat.

Only the appearance of Chevalier stopped them from coming together and kindling the blaze between them right here in the hall. Charlotte was dismayed to notice that her hand was trembling when she took Max's arm, and she hoped, as thoughts of the morning's events flashed through her mind, that Max did not plan on a long engagement. Then she turned to him suddenly.

"What do you mean Stollings complained about my kisses?"

Chapter Sixteen

When they entered the dining room, Sibylle was being served eggs and barely glanced up at them. "Sit down, Maximilian. I stand on no ceremony at my breakfast table, as Charlotte well knows." She flashed a pretty smile that Charlotte acknowledged with a gracious nod.

Then Sybille paused to frown slightly at her son. "I hope you have no intention of tossing eggs at one another, however, for I do not care for the mess. Personally, I cannot see the enjoyment in such endeavors, but la! I have never understood you, Maximilian. I want you to know," she added, sending him a pointed glance, "that I am ordering a new carpet today and sending the bill to you."

Charlotte choked back a laugh before she was struck dumb by the prospect of endless nights ahead with the man who took a seat across from her. She pictured his mouth on her skin, licking the champagne from her body, and she wondered if Maximilian was thinking of the same thing.

He was. Charlotte saw it in the heated gaze that settled upon her and, thrilled and mortified at the same time, she could not hold his eyes but looked at her plate.

"You will undoubtedly be pleased to know that your rather haphazard duty as a sponsor is now over," Maximilian said, accepting some toast from a servant. "I plan to take Miss Trowbridge back, at once, to Sussex, where we will be married as soon as arrangements can be made."

If he was trying to rattle his mother, he succeeded, although Charlotte noted that the woman was not quite as shocked by the precipitate announcement as she had been to find her son cavorting in a champagne bath the night before.

Sibylle's eyes grew wide, and her dainty hand dropped the utensil in her hand. "You do not mean it?" she asked, glancing from one to the other. Charlotte smiled, although Max did not. "But of course you mean it! You never jest. But this is wonderful news!"

Charlotte released the breath she had been holding unawares, glad that Max's mother was happy for them. The woman often seemed so heedlessly thoughtless that Charlotte had not known what to expect. Charlotte's relief was short-lived, however, for Sibylle soon revealed the reason for her excitement.

"I can return to Paris immediately!" the dowager said, clapping her hands together in delight. The breath that had so recently left Charlotte's lungs was drawn back in, making a low gasping sound. She darted a glance at Max to see if he had noticed, but he was smiling in a most disconcerting manner at his mother.

"Yes, *Mother,*" he said. Charlotte realized that she had never heard him call Sybille by that name, and the reason was soon evident. The lady flinched at the word and glared daggers at her son, who ignored her reaction and continued speaking in his usual smooth tones. "Do not feel that you must tarry on our account."

Charlotte thought he was teasing, but from the look on Sibylle's face, she could tell that Maximilian was absolutely serious. Obviously, he knew his mother well enough to guess that she would rather go to France than stay with her son and his bride-to-be. Charlotte blinked in confusion, unable to believe it. "But surely you wish to attend the...wedding?" she asked.

"What? Some provincial affair?" Sibylle waved a hand in dismissal, then her eyes brightened. "But if you would have the ceremony in London, I might—"

"No, Mother." Maximilian seemed to take pleasure in denying Sibylle's wish for an elaborate event, and Charlotte might have taken him to task if she, too, did not long for a small ceremony among her family.

"Stop calling me that! I do not feel old enough to be mother to a grown man," Sibylle said, her eyes snapping. Throwing down her napkin, she rose from her chair, tossing her dark curls in a pretty pout. "I am going back to Paris where I am young again!"

Alarmed at Sibylle's attitude, Charlotte rose from her chair. "My lady, wait," she called. Ignoring Max's advice to let Sibylle go, Charlotte hurried after her, catching up with her in the hallway. No matter what Max might wish, she did not want to part on such terrible terms with his mother.

"I wanted to...to thank you for opening your home to me. You have been more than gracious and generous and—" Charlotte began.

"Hush, child!" Sibylle said with a laugh. "Do not make me out to be a paragon. That role is for Maximilian, and he is welcome to it. But you! You have the spark of life in you. Are you sure he is what you want? He is an earl, yes, but you could still hold out for the Marquess. Wroth is far wealthier and, I must say, monstrously intriguing."

Aware that her mouth had dropped open, Charlotte closed it as quickly as she could while trying to form a reply to Sibylle's speech. "But I love him...Max, I mean," she stammered.

"Do you?" Sibylle asked. She sighed lightly. "I suspected as much, but... Ah, well. I wish you happiness. I think you will be good for him," she added, as if that was some sort of consolation for the cruelty of her previous words. "Write to me in Paris, won't you?" the lady asked, and suddenly Charlotte was engulfed in a cloud of expensive perfume as Sibylle leaned close and brushed a soft cheek against her own.

Charlotte stood back, watching in bafflement as Sibylle gracefully moved away in a swirl of silk, more intent upon the social whirl of Paris than the happenings within her family. With no little wonder, Charlotte realized that she had just received a kiss from the woman who was to become her mother.

The thought made Charlotte long for her own home, where meals were lively, affectionate affairs that did not seethe with dark undercurrents. Despite the inevitable quarreling, her relatives truly loved one another, and kisses were frequent and genuine, especially the great smacks on the lips that Jenny so ingenuously delivered. Charlotte realized that she wanted one right now. And she wouldn't even care if the child was sticky with sweets.

They journeyed home immediately, spending much of their time alone together in the elegant Wycliffe coach. Although Charlotte's new maid was ostensibly acting as chaperone in Sybille's absence, the good woman was usually shunted to one of the other vehicles that made up Max's retinue.

Charlotte approved of the arrangements wholeheartedly, for she enjoyed the opportunity to spend so much time with the busy earl. Max often propped his feet up on the opposite seat as they discussed some salient point of Euripides, or sometimes Charlotte curled up against his shoulder, resting as comfortably as she had expected she would against his tall, hard frame.

Max, she discovered, was the most wonderful of traveling companions. Intelligent, well spoken and wryly amusing, he kept her entertained even during the long silences, for then she would simply gaze at him, admiring his handsome features to her heart's content. He was invariably polite and, for one usually so focused upon himself, he surprised her with his thoughtfulness.

He did not, however, touch her.

Not since the amazing morning in his bed had the man so much as kissed her, and Charlotte was a bit dismayed by this display of restraint. She suspected that his rigid set of rules about honor held him in check, but she was disappointed to find he could return so easily to the guise of the dutiful earl.

She wondered if he would take his *husbandly* duties as seriously as he did all others, and the thought made her tremble with anticipation. Of course, she could have pressed the issue. Sometimes Charlotte imagined what he would do should she put her arms around him or slide her hands over his elegantly dressed body, but she knew Max enough to respect his wishes—just as long as he did not plan a lengthy engagement.

Charlotte still found it hard to believe that he was to marry her, and since it all had come about so quickly, she was a bit bewildered as to his reasons. He had offered for her before their passionate interlude, so she knew he had not spoken out of guilt. However, she was just as sure that he did not love her.

In truth, Charlotte feared that he had proposed simply because he knew she did not want Viscount Linley, and the thought tugged at her happiness. She did not want to be married out of pity or expedience or any other altruistic motive.

She wanted Max's affection, and she prayed that he had some feeling for her that had precipitated his actions. Obviously, something had swayed him strongly enough to override his objections to her background, for Charlotte knew that he held her lineage in contempt. A vicar's daughter good enough for the Earl of Wycliffe? Never! And yet, he was marrying her.

It all was a bit baffling, but Charlotte was loath to question her good fortune. She would love him enough for both of them, she swore to herself, though she had said nothing of her feelings so far. A man like Max was sure to scoff at such tender emotions. Romance, being not readily identifiable nor easily set to a schedule, was, she suspected, beyond his ken.

Their arrival in Sussex was met with a deal more interest than their departure from London. The moment the elaborate Wycliffe coach with its gilt coat of arms approached Upper Bidwell, they were hailed, everyone apparently agog with the news of the vicar's daughter's triumphant return. Heads stuck out of windows, hands were waved, and neighbors came to stand outside their doors just to have a look.

Charlotte wanted to stick her head out the carriage window and wave back, but she could see from Max's face that it would be an affront to his dignity. Since she had caused him to lose his composure often enough already, she restrained herself and gave him a warm smile instead. When he appeared to visibly relax, she had to look down and bite her lip to avoid laughing.

Their reception at the vicarage was quite another thing entirely. The vehicle had not even stopped before Charlotte could hear youthful shouts emitting from the building. She glanced at Max to gauge his reaction, but he seemed pleased by the excitement. She could see the corners of his mouth twitching, and then, with heart-stopping suddenness, she realized that he was glad to be home.

Oh, Max, I love you, Charlotte thought. She wanted to shout it and throw herself into his arms, but he was helping her down to stand before her old home, and greetings were erupting from the doorway.

"Charlotte! Charlotte!"

"Lord Wycliffe!"

The sounds of the girls' more restrained feminine voices mixed with the boys' whoops as they all tumbled out of the house. Carrie and Jane rushed up to hug and kiss their sister, while the boys chattered at Max, interrupting each other in an unintelligible babble of questions and comments.

Ignoring the defection of the older boys, Charlotte grabbed Kit, who was deftly weaving among the others, and gave him a kiss on the cheek. He looked a bit put out by such a loving gesture, but he positively preened when Max reached down to tousle his hair in a friendly manner. Charlotte noted the byplay with approval, for she did not begrudge Max his popularity. He seemed so much

ore...human among the children than he had in the glit-
ring world of London that she wished they could stay here
orever.

"My lord! My lord!" They all turned to watch as Jenny
ame running down the walk, her face shining as brightly as
er yellow curls. Without a moment's hesitation, the littlest
rowbridge threw herself at the Earl of Wycliffe, and he
vung her up in his arms, suffering her to strangle him with
er tight grip about his neck. She gave him a loud kiss and
en turned to them all. "*My* lord," she announced.

The siblings laughed and all started talking at once while
harlotte caught Max's gaze over their heads. She felt an
naccountable pressure behind her eyes when she looked in
is fathomless brown ones. They were wide with chagrin
nd wonder and...a need that was buried so deeply that for
moment she did not even recognize it. When she did, she
linked at him in surprise and blamed herself. Why hadn't
e seen it before?

The Earl of Wycliffe, with his ordered, responsible life
nd his important meetings and schedules, desperately
aved affection.

The knowledge both stunned her and moved her to ac-
on. Although he glanced away to answer a question from
it, Charlotte kept her attention focused on him as she
ade her way through the group to his side. Then she placed
trembling hand on his arm and leaned up to whisper in his
r. "I love you, Max."

The startled look he sent her was followed by a smile such
s she had never seen from him. His full lips curved up in a
in of pure, unadulterated pleasure, with a bit of male
nugness thrown in.

"I love you, Charlotte," said a small voice. Jenny, not to
e outdone, was looking at her solemnly over Max's shoul-
er.

"I love you, too, pumpkin," Charlotte said, tweaking the
rl's nose and eliciting a shriek that made her wriggle in
Max's arms. Laughing gaily, Charlotte was pulled away by
ne to see her efforts in the garden. She was appropriately

impressed by the roses and honeysuckles and tall holly-hocks that were standing free of rambling weeds that had once choked the beds.

"It is truly wonderful, Jane. You have wrought a mira-cle!" she added, giving her sister another hug. Then she heard Max's voice ring out above the babble of the chil-dren.

"Thomas, James, cease your squabbling. I have a pres-ent for each of you," he said.

His words made Charlotte turn toward him. She stopped at the corner of the house to watch as he tried to impose some order on the mob that surrounded him.

"You may notice the two handsome animals that are fol-lowing the second coach—"

"A matched pair of bays!" Thomas interjected.

"For us? You cannot mean it!" James breathed, his face a study in awe and amazement.

"Yes, for you, but you shall have to keep them up at the Great House, since you have no stable here," Max said. Horses for the boys? He had said nothing to her. The thoughtful gesture made Charlotte's heart melt in its cav-ity. "Do not look so disappointed, Kit. I have brought presents for all of you, but you must wait your turn."

"Charlotte." The sound of her father's voice brought Charlotte out of the dreamy euphoria in which she was drifting. She blinked back the liquid that had somehow formed in her eyes and stepped into her papa's arms.

He hugged her close, and Charlotte felt the love that he gave so freely close around her like a welcoming cocoon. "Oh, Papa, it is so good to be home," she whispered. "I did not realize how much I would miss all of you."

The vicar smiled gently. "I am glad that you have re-turned to us unspoiled by the gaiety of London," he said. "And how can I complain about losing my second daugh-ter when you shall be so close to us?" he asked, glancing toward Casterleigh, whose chimneys could be seen over the crest of the hill. He entwined her arm with his and patted her hand. "God certainly works in wonderful ways."

Although he spoke not a word of rebuke, the children parted for him, enabling him to walk to Max. "Lord Wycliffe," he said, with a friendly smile. Max was more than gracious, as though he genuinely liked her papa—and all of them, Charlotte thought dizzily. The girls were already rushing inside, giggling under their burden of hatboxes and other parcels. Obviously, Max had chosen their gifts well.

"Papa! Papa!" Kit was fairly dancing around their feet. "Lord Wycliffe has a pony for me!"

"Oh, my lord, you shall spoil them," the vicar chided.

"Shall I?" Maximilian asked, a smile tugging at the corners of his mouth. "That was certainly my intent!"

They all laughed, and Papa turned his teasing eyes upon Charlotte. "See what kind of a father your betrothed will make, Charlotte," he warned. "Lord Wycliffe will be forever spoiling the children, while you shall have to mete out the discipline." The vicar gave Maximilian a broad wink, and Charlotte blushed. If her father only knew how close they had come to creating a child between them already, he would find no jest in the matter, she thought.

Then, suddenly, Charlotte realized that her father had spoken of Max as her future husband, but how had he known? She glanced sharply at the earl, deciding that he must have sent a messenger on ahead to apprise her father of the change in circumstances. If her father found the abrupt switch from Viscount Linley to the earl himself unusual, he did not let on. In fact, he seemed immensely pleased with her choice.

As if to confirm her thoughts, her papa turned around. "I would say congratulations are in order to our happy young couple!"

"Yes, Papa!" was followed by a chorus of well wishes, and soon the group was surrounding them again, dragging them inside for a celebration of sorts.

There her father toasted the betrothal with a glass of Sarah's homemade wine. Although Charlotte eyed him warily, Max, God bless him, did not bat an eye as he drank down the sweet brew. He was, she realized, making the transition from London to Sussex far more easily than she could ever have credited. Smiling happily, she found herself clinging to him and squeezing his arm tightly, as though he might evaporate like a figment of her girlish dreams.

The evening was a busy one, and Charlotte had no time to speak to her father alone. Sarah and Alf joined the party, and preparations for the wedding were launched. The date was set for two weeks' time, sending the ladies into a frenzy of activity, and somehow, something always prevented Charlotte from broaching the subject of Viscount Linley, a subject which, in any event, she really did not care to discuss. She assumed that Max had refused the Viscount's suit, but whenever she thought to ask him about it, she was diverted. And so the matter was forgotten.

The days until the wedding seemed to fly. Suddenly, the ceremony was but a night away, and Charlotte was tucking in the children, urging them to get their sleep before the morrow. Sarah, whispering gently in her low voice, blew out the lamp, and they filed down the narrow steps together, as they so often had in the past.

Papa and Alf were waiting in the parlor, but Sarah drew her toward the kitchen, where they sat companionably, each with a glass of cool milk from the cellar. Charlotte eyed the simple drink with a smile, for she imagined Max was probably being served a glass of brandy by one of the innumerable servants up at the Great House.

"Charlotte." The tone of Sarah's voice immediately dragged Charlotte from her thoughts. Sarah was seated across from her with a rather grim expression on her face, heralding what, Charlotte did not know. Surely Sarah did not intend to express misgivings about Max at this late date?

Sarah seemed to cling to her healthy suspicion for the nobility, as though they were a breed apart, of some derivation than other men. And the Great House with all its trappings was so remote from Sarah's expectations that she could not understand how her sister could plan to live there.

Charlotte did not have the heart to inform her that Max considered Casterleigh nothing more than a small holding.

"Please do not worry about me, Sarah. I know that Wycliffe's wealth is intimidating, but if you had seen the houses in London, enormous places full of glitter and pomp, gilt dishes and golden spoons and..." She stopped when she noticed Sarah was eyeing her with no little skepticism.

"Believe me, Sarah, all the fripperies there did not make the people any happier than our neighbors in Upper Bidwell. And, as strange as it would seem, I think the earl would much rather be here with us than dashing from one crush to another as his calendar dictated." Charlotte leaned closer and dropped her voice to a whisper. "Do not breath a word of this to anyone, but...I think Max was a very lonely man."

Sarah stared, as if stunned by her confidences, before finally smiling slowly. "I will not worry about you, Charlotte," she said. "I admit that I was wrong about the earl. There were so many differences between you two that I thought it was impossible, but I should have known that *impossible* is not a word you recognize!"

Love and admiration glowed in the glance Sarah sent her, taking the sting from what might have been a scold. "In the past two weeks, I have seen the earl watching you, and it is obvious that he loves you...very intensely." Sarah drew in a breath. "I know he will take fine care of you, but, in truth, that is not what I wished to discuss."

She paused to look down at her milk, and Charlotte realized that Sarah, dear, solid Sarah, was turning pink. Since nothing, but nothing, daunted the eldest Trowbridge, Charlotte sat up straighter and fixed her attention keenly upon her sister.

"Charlotte," Sarah began. Then she cleared her throat. "Mama is not here, so it falls to me to...speak with you regarding a wife's obligations to her husband."

Charlotte scoffed. "I am afraid you shall be wasting your time giving me advice, Sarah dear, for I am sure Max will have his own views on the subject. He likes to order his household just so, you know. I imagine that he shall have a schedule drawn up for me in no time, though he seems to have unbent a little with the loss of that wretched secretary of his.''

Sarah looked startled and then made a choking sound before continuing. ''I doubt that even his lordship would draw up a schedule...'' Sarah's words trailed off as she struggled with some strong emotion that Charlotte was astounded to realize was amusement. ''As that is neither here nor there...'' Sarah mumbled, recovering herself. ''What I am trying to discuss, Charlotte, is what happens in the marriage bed.''

''Oh, that!'' Charlotte smiled eagerly. Although her mind had been occupied with a seemingly endless number of details over the past week, it seemed that thoughts of such things could never be completely shunted aside. She remembered the morning in Max's London town house and she grew warm, her limbs heavy and aching for a return to that intimacy, which Max had refused her during their engagement.

''You have seen the animals here in the countryside, so I assume you know how it is done,'' Sarah said crisply. When Charlotte nodded, Sarah seemed relieved. ''I do not want to alarm you, but the first time... The first time is painful.'' Crimson now, Sarah was staring at the milk as if it were going to squirt her in the eye.

Painful? There had been nothing painful in what Max had done to her in his bed, married or no. ''Are you sure?'' Charlotte asked.

Sarah gave her an incredulous look. ''Of course, I am sure. I am a married woman!''

Charlotte tried to picture Sarah and Alf doing what she and Max had done and she dropped her eyes to her own glass of milk, wishing it contained something stronger. ''Is there any of your wine left?''

Sarah appeared to be momentarily confused by the question. ''Yes, I believe so,'' she said finally, and Charlotte immediately went to the cupboard. "I hope you are not developing a taste for spirits!"

Ignoring the scold, Charlotte pushed aside the glasses of milk and poured them each a measure of wine. Then she returned to her seat and lifted a glass, which glittered in the low light of the oil lamp. "To my wedding night, which sounds awful!"

"Charlotte!" Sarah's rebuke was swift as she refused the toast. "It is not awful. If you would but listen to me... Yes, the first time is... difficult, but after that, it actually is quite... pleasant."

Pleasant? Charlotte tried to equate the word with what had taken place in Max's bed. She took an unladylike gulp of wine and put down her glass with a shake of her head. "Painful? Pleasant?" she repeated. "Sarah, dear, does this sort of thing work the same for everyone?"

"Of course!" Sarah replied, taking a rather hefty swallow herself.

"But, but... pleasant!" Charlotte sputtered. "Is that *all* it is?"

"Well, no, I guess that is not really a strong enough word," Sarah admitted.

"I should say not!" Charlotte retorted. "Listen, Sarah, perhaps you had better go into further details about what happens, and we can examine the whole thing more fully."

Whether it was the wine or simply her own outspoken behavior, Charlotte did not know, but Sarah finally seemed to lose the embarrassment that was hampering their discussion. Her flush began to fade, and her eyes glittered with her usual self-possession. "Now, see here," she began. Then she stopped to gaze at Charlotte quizzically. "Charlotte! You have not... Do not tell me that... Charlotte, are you still a virgin?"

Charlotte recognized the familiar mixture of horror and reluctant admiration with which Sarah had always viewed her escapades. She smiled guilelessly. "In truth, sister, I am not quite sure..."

Chapter Seventeen

Once Sarah's initial embarrassment had disappeared, the sisters talked openly, laughing like the girls they had been not so long ago. Alf grew impatient, however, and came looking for his wife, ending the impromptu conference before the hour grew too late. Charlotte greeted Sarah's husband with a smile on her face, and it remained there until she waved them goodbye at the vicarage door, for she had acquired more knowledge about the marriage bed than she had ever dreamed possible.

"Are you nervous, my dear?" Her father's soft voice drew Charlotte from her lustful musings, and she flushed as she turned to face him.

"No, Papa, just happy," she said, truthfully.

"As I am, for you and for his lordship," he said, nodding.

Charlotte saw the tenderness on his face, and she went into his arms. "Oh, Papa, have I thanked you for making it all possible?"

"Humph," her father snorted. "I did little enough. It was your beauty and charm and wit that won your husband."

Charlotte shook her head. "You provided me with the money and the opportunity for my London season," she said. "Without it, I never could have become Wycliffe's wife."

"My dear," her father said, "no matter what our prosaic Sarah might think, I believe some things are meant to be. With or without your season, I suspect you would still be his countess."

Charlotte felt her throat tighten at his guileless faith. "I was so afraid I would disappoint you, Papa," she whispered in the warmth of his embrace.

"Never that, Charlotte. Never that." He released her to look at her, his spectacles tilting crookedly across his nose. "Even had you come back home without a husband, you could not have disappointed me. You are such a beautiful, graceful reminder of your mother." He paused to smile. "But you are your own woman, too, and I love you for it."

"I know, Papa," Charlotte answered. "But I would have been disappointed in myself, if I failed all of you. When I left for London, I thought it would be such a frolic, but I came to understand that marrying would be a serious business, indeed. That is why... When Sir Burgess asked me, I just could not say yes."

"Burgess. Burgess. Why does that name sound familiar?" Her father paused to consider the question, but made a wry face at his faltering memory. "Ah, well, it shall come to me, no doubt. What were you saying, child?"

Charlotte smiled at her sire's familiar habit of wandering away from the course of conversation. "I realized that I wanted the same happiness that you and Mama had, and that is why I could not wed Viscount Linley, although you wanted me to."

Her father sat back, a puzzled expression on his face, and straightened his eyeglasses. "Viscount Linley?"

"Yes, the man you wrote to me about," Charlotte said. "The man you gave your consent for me to wed!"

"Yes..." her father said. He nodded slowly, but appeared all the more baffled.

"Well, I just could not marry him," Charlotte repeated.

"What is this?" her father asked, his face showing a growing alarm. "The wedding is off?"

"With Linley, yes. I am marrying Wycliffe."

Her father shook his head, as if to clear it. "I am sorry, child, but I do not understand. You are marrying the Earl of Wycliffe, but not the Viscount Linley—"

"Of course!" Charlotte said. Her father's obtuse behavior was making her impatient, and she could only guess that he was tired and nervous over the impending nuptials.

The vicar shook his head again, then pushed his slipping spectacles up upon his nose once more. "But they are one and the same man, child."

"They are..." Charlotte blinked at her father as she echoed his words. "Whatever do you mean, Papa?"

"I am most confused," he answered with a sigh. "Wycliffe did write to me about Viscount Linley, but since I was aware of his various titles, I thought it was some jest between the two of you." He glanced at Charlotte, as if expecting her confirmation.

She tried to look noncommittal. Her father stood. "I have his full name here, of course, because I must use it in the ceremony tomorrow." He reached for his Bible, opened it and adjusted his spectacles. "Ah, yes, here it is...Maximilian Alistair Wentworth Fortescue, fifth Earl of Wycliffe, third Viscount Linley and Baron Haddlington." Her father looked up and smiled, obviously proud of himself. "I got it from the settlement papers."

"That rogue," Charlotte whispered to herself. "I never would have thought him capable of such a deceit. I think I shall have a little talk with the viscount." She grinned slowly.

"I'm afraid your speech will have to wait until morning, my dear," her father said. "Look at the clock. You must get some sleep, for tomorrow is your wedding day." He leaned over and kissed her cheek.

"Of course, Papa," Charlotte said. Wiping the wicked smile from her face, she nodded in acquiescence. Had Sarah been there, she would have recognized that look all too well as a harbinger of mischief. But, luckily for Charlotte, Sarah was gone, and her dear father would never suspect his lovely daughter of planning any misbehavior.

* * *

Although the hour was late, Maximilian lay awake in his bed at Casterleigh, staring at the hangings with their elaborate swags. He was thinking about his wedding day, which did little to make him drowsy. Actually, he was pondering, more specifically, his wedding night and wondering just how quickly he could spirit his bride away from her guests without engendering comment. Mumbling a low oath into the darkness, he finally decided to the devil with propriety! He wanted to bed his wife as soon as possible.

Ever since the fiasco at his town house when Hoskins had stood between him and disaster, Maximilian had kept his distance from the vicar's daughter who, alone among her sex, seemed able to rid him of his restraint. That, he decided ruefully, was putting it mildly. He thought of all his sexual encounters, from the lovely chambermaid who had ushered him into manhood until his last mistress, and he viewed them all as very pleasant experiences.

Charlotte, however, was a deal different.

With her, he lost his usual patient skills and became a raging, lustful beast. Maximilian knew he should have been disgusted with himself. He should have sworn to contain himself next time, but he had not. In truth, he was looking forward to the mindless, hot passion that flared between them, because nothing before had been so good.

And this time, there would be no butler banging on the door. Maximilian smiled and moved uncomfortably between the sheets. This time . . . he would take her virginity. He would take her and take her until he finally assuaged his wild yearning for her. . . . Only then could his life return to some semblance of order, he reasoned.

Maximilian was startled out of these pleasant thoughts by the sound of his door handle turning. Knowing that the servants would not be about at this hour, he immediately suspected an intruder and, feigning sleep, he looked out under lowered lashes toward the entrance to his room. Moonlight from the open windows cast a pale glow across the carpet, ending in shadows near the door, but he saw it swing open.

A young man dressed in baggy clothing and wearing a cap stepped in, and Maximilian was alarmed for an instant. Naked in bed, he had no arms at hand, but neither did the youth, apparently. In truth, the fellow did not appear menacing, but only a bit disoriented before he spoke.

"Oh, Max! Thank goodness I finally found you!"

With a sigh of incredulity, Maximilian recognized the voice of his bride-to-be, who, upon spying him, ran across the room and threw herself onto his bed. "Do you realize just how big this place is?" she asked breathlessly as she flung her arms around him.

Gently, Max lifted her away from his bare body. "Since I live here, the relative size of the residence has not escaped my notice," he said dryly. "What are you doing here?"

Having splayed one hand against his chest, Charlotte was sliding her fingers through the hairs there. She seemed so fascinated by the task that he wondered if she had even heard him, but finally she lifted her head. "I thought I would steal a moment with Viscount Linley," she said. Then she pulled a face at him.

Momentarily distracted from her touch, Maximilian laughed aloud. "What? Are you angry that I have used your own tactics against you?"

Charlotte drew back, giving a good impression of being aghast. "What methods? Are you insinuating that I used some sort of devious machinations to win you? How dare you?"

Maximilian laughed again. "Come now, Charlotte. Admit it! You have schemed once or twice to get my attentions." Maximilian thought of all their encounters, some of which might well have been caused by chance—or by design. "What about your sudden penchant for low-cut gowns?"

"You told me to wear them!"

Charlotte had him there, and he frowned. "What about your aunt's illness?"

She sat up straight and glared at him, as if truly incensed. "Are you saying it was feigned?"

"Was it?"

"Maximilian Alistair Wentworth Fortescue! It most certainly was not feigned! How could you think such a thing?" Charlotte was breathing heavily, and Maximilian noticed the thrust of her large breasts against her shirt. He swallowed.

"All right. All right. I concede your point," he said, a bit unsteadily. "What of the escapade with Roddy? Was that not staged for my benefit?"

Did she blush? Maximilian could not tell in the dimness of the room, but she had the good grace to look down and frown. "Aha!" he said, pouncing on her hesitancy. "I knew it!"

"Very well," Charlotte admitted with the loveliest scowl he had ever seen. "I admit that I might have tried to...gain your notice, but only on a few occasions, and only at first, before I realized that it would do me no good."

"Ah, but it did do you good. It wrung an offer from Viscount Linley," Maximilian said with a grin.

"Botheration! How could you, Max? When I received that wretched letter from Papa, it nearly killed me! Why, Max?" She was angry again and genuinely baffled, Maximilian realized.

He sighed heavily. He could see the glint in her eyes, and he felt a cad now that he was aware of her affection. She thought herself in love with him, and although he still had reservations about such nonsense, it pleased him to hear her say the words. At the time he proposed, however, he had not been sure if she cared for him at all.

"I was not certain of your feelings for me," he explained gruffly. "Although I was satisfied that the only way to put an end to your escapades was to marry you, I had no wish to wed a fortune-hunting miss."

Charlotte gasped. "So you invented a proposal from someone else?"

Maximilian nodded, rather shamefaced. "If you desired only wealth and position, then you would have accepted the offer, and I would have known that you did not hold me in regard." He felt rather silly mouthing such nonsense, but he had wanted affection from his wife. He stiffened at the thought of a life without it. "I did not want a marriage like my father's. He became infatuated with Sibylle, who wed him strictly for gain."

Charlotte was silent for a moment, looking down at the hand that still rested upon him. Her face, composed in the moonlight, was beautiful, despite the odd cap that covered her bright hair. "I understand," she said softly. "And I forgive your ruse." She smiled brightly then. "So..." She again entwined her fingers in the hair on his chest.

"So, now that all is clear, you must be on your way," Maximilian said, becoming acutely conscious of her attentions. To his surprise, she shook her head, a teasing smile tugging at the corners of her luscious mouth.

"But I am here for another reason, too," she said. Her voice was low, seductive, and Maximilian was suddenly aware of her fragrance, all heady spring, and how her body touched his hip, with just the thin sheet separating them.

He knew her well enough to be alert to her moods, and he suspected that Charlotte was up to something. "And what is that?" he asked as coolly as he could manage.

Her long lashes brushed against her cheeks. "I thought if I surprised you tonight that we could, uh, well, get this lovemaking business completed, and then you would not be so irritable tomorrow, or rather, so anxious to leave the party, which I know you will be."

"What?" The question came out louder than he intended, and he took a breath to calm himself. He did not want the servants to know he had a visitor at this hour, whether they were to be married or not.

"Oh, Max. Don't be angry with me. I just... I have been wanting you so much ever since that time in your town house, and you have been so standoffish and out of sorts lately... And then, when I heard that it was painful, I did not want to be dreading it, so I thought that the sooner, the better, if you know what I mean."

"What?" Was she talking about what he thought she was talking about?

"Botheration, Max! Are you deliberately trying to be obtuse? I came here to... do what we did before, in London, only more so..."

"You came here to seduce me?" he asked in disbelief.

"Well, I realize that I did not handle it all too well, but that was because I got lost, you see, in your home. I did not plan on that, and then I wanted to ask you about Viscount Linley, so I was diverted."

"What exactly was your plan?" Maximilian asked, crossing his arms behind his head. This ought to be good. The vicar's daughter, dressed as a boy, plotting seduction...

"Well, I was going to find your room easily, and then I was going to take off all my clothes and slip into bed with you." Maximilian drew in a breath, for her ingenuous recitation managed to make him hard. He tried not to picture the scene she painted. "I thought things would just progress naturally from there," she added.

"Which is quite possible," he noted dryly, "considering..."

"Your appalling lack of self-control." Charlotte finished the phrase for him and giggled. Before he could argue the point or put her out, she flung one leg over him so that she straddled his hips.

Maximilian attempted to ignore the pressure against his loins, but the moonlight picked up the curve of her nipples, straining at the man's shirt stretched across them. "Did you really think to masquerade as a boy, with that chest of yours?" he asked, when he could find his voice.

"I admit it used to be easier to fit into an old pair of trousers and a shirt when I snuck out," she said.

"When you snuck out," Maximilian repeated. He could not seem to take his gaze from those breasts, thrusting against their thin covering as if struggling to escape. "You will not sneak out when you are my wife."

"No, Max," she said. She rested both hands on his chest and began running them over his muscles. He sucked in a sharp breath.

"It is time for you to go home, Charlotte," he said firmly.

She shook her head. "No, I really think it better to do the deed now. Then I will not be nervous about it tomorrow, you see."

Maximilian raised his eyebrows. "You look about as nervous as a cat in heat."

Charlotte giggled. "But you know me, Max. I am at my most brazen when I am scared to death."

"All the more reason for you to go home to your own bed tonight. Now, get off of me," Maximilian said, recognizing in the same breath that he had never expected to say anything of the sort to his fiancé.

"No. I think not," Charlotte said, her mouth curving up wickedly. Then she lifted her cap and shook out her hair in one smooth movement. Golden curls poured out, glittering in the moonlight like soft cotton about her face.

Maximilian stifled the air that rushed into his lungs. How long had it been since he had seen her hair down, wafting about her face so sensually? "You seem awfully sure of yourself," he said roughly. Although he swelled against her, he maintained his casual pose.

Charlotte said nothing, her eyes meeting his and holding his gaze. Then before he knew what she was about, she raised her arms and lifted her shirt over her head, tossing it carelessly aside.

They were freed, her large and milky white breasts, and Maximilian jerked underneath her at the sight of them. What could he do? She offered herself to him, leaning toward him so that they swelled before him like so much ripe fruit, but a few inches from his face.

Maximilian made a noise in his throat, a feral sound, and lifted his hands. They fell into his large palms and spilled over, bounty too beauteous to be contained. He thumbed the wide nipples, and Charlotte arched back, sighing softly into the night air.

Oh, holy God, he thought dimly. Somewhere in the back of his mind, he knew he ought to toss her out of his bed. This was all wrong. He had a responsibility to his bride to not touch her until their wedding night... and he was nothing if not responsible.

With a groan, Maximilian dropped his hands to her thighs and tried to move her, but somehow, instead, he impatiently kicked away the sheet that covered him. She nestled against him once more, and he could feel the soft folds of her trousers against his hardness.

There was something wildly erotic about Charlotte, naked from the waist up and dressed in men's clothing below, and he rubbed against the material that separated them. If he could just... He pulled her down on top of him, taking her mouth in a hot, wet, fierce kiss hungrily, like a starving man, like a man wholly unlike himself as his hands molded her breasts, her luscious breasts...

She answered him, meeting his tongue with her own, moaning softly, her low sounds at odds with her sweet innocence. He slid his hands into that hair, crushing it between his fingers, so soft... He groaned. He made sounds he had never thought himself capable of making, and Charlotte joined him, whimpering as each desperate moan was torn from his throat.

He slid his hands over her shoulders and along her back, where the skin was fine and sleek, and then down. His fingers found the waistband of her trousers, and he slid a hand in to close over her naked buttocks, absurdly titillated by the pants, so alien and yet somehow seductive.

Someone was groaning again, and he suspected it was himself, but he could not stop. He kissed her throat and then eased her up so that her breasts fell toward him, the wide nipples bobbing like lodestars in the night. His mouth found one and he took it, sucking as if he could never get enough, first one then the other, while he pressed her against himself, grinding, gasping, until he had to take a breath and get his bearings.

He rolled her onto her back and looked down at her. Moonlight glistened on the golden sheen of her hair, tossed about her shoulders in wild disarray. It sparkled on the edges of her eyelashes, resting against her flushed cheeks, and on the moist curve of her lips, parted as she took in low, shallow breaths. It gleamed along the creamy curves of magnificent breasts, full and rich and glistening from his mouth.

With a hand that trembled in its eagerness, Maximilian unbuttoned the fall of her trousers and slid his hand inside. Wet. He shuddered and stroked her, his fingers finding the rhythm that made her gasp, made her whimper, made her move purposefully against him. Then, impatient, he pushed the trousers down to her knees and bent his head.

His tongue traced slowly at first, with the patience that had earned the praise of his mistresses, but she was too much of a feast. His command deserted him and he took her with his mouth, tasting and sucking. He heard her whimpers, felt her writhing in his hands, and he gripped her still and slid his tongue inside her. She jerked, taut beneath him, crying out his name.

He tugged off the trousers, spread her legs and positioned himself. Oh, God, finally... He tried to enter slowly, but she was so hot, so tight, that he could not help himself. With a groan, he drove himself in fully, and still he pushed, trying to reach farther. She was gasping, and when the sound penetrated his brain, he stilled. Trembling like a boy, he opened his eyes and realized, he was deeply embedded in the vicar's daughter. Dear God...

He must have made some sound, some look, because suddenly, Charlotte was whispering to him. "It is all right, Max. I am fine, really, I am. It had to be, and now it is over." She lifted her mouth to brush against his brow, his cheekbone, his jawline, and he realized that she was trying to comfort *him*.

"Charlotte..." He meant to say something, truly he did, but words failed him. He tried to concentrate, but he could feel the press of her breasts against his chest and her body tight around him. Was she lifting her legs to encircle him?

"Charlotte... Oh, yes, Charlotte, yes, do that..." Was that his voice murmuring approval? He was mindless, caught up in pleasure such as he had never known, as he lifted her luscious bottom, drawing her closer, nudging himself that much deeper. "Oh, yes, Charlotte... You are so hot, so tight, so..." He withdrew, nearly all the way out, and then plunged deep again.

She made a sound under him. And then he was lost, moving inside her, aware of nothing but the golden, wet heat of her. He tried to whisper his love against her shoulder, but all that came out was her name, a litany on his lips as he lifted her hips, taking her with him at each stroke. Hotter, deeper, harder, until he found surcease, shuddering in her arms, gripping her to him so that he was fully embedded in her warmth and then collapsing in a breathless heap upon her.

When he finally recovered enough to realize that he was lying heavy upon her, gasping against her hair like an oaf, Maxmilian lifted himself upon his arms. His voice did not seem to work properly. "Are you all right?" he croaked.

She nodded. Her lips were wet and swollen, and the curls around her face were tiny swirls, damp with exertion. "I love you, Max," she whispered. "I love to see you lose yourself in me."

The words made him swell again. "And I love...to do it," he said, giving her a crooked smile. He held himself perfectly still. Now was the time to end this. They were not yet wed, deuce it all! It was getting late, and she had sneaked from her home—a vicarage, yet!—to come to him. Tomorrow would be time enough...

"I spoke with Sarah," she said softly, a wicked smile teasing her mouth. She lifted her hands and speared her fingers through his hair, drawing his face closer to her. Sarah? For a moment his mind was blank before he recalled Charlotte's older sister. "She told me all sorts of interesting things,'' she added as her toes ran a sensuous path down his calf.

"Charlotte..."

"Let us do them all, Max," she urged. She brought a long lock of his hair to her lips, and it was a dark shadow against the moonlit planes of her face. "Show me..."

With a groan, he rolled onto his back and let the vicar's daughter straddle him again. Just one more time, he thought dimly. Then he would send her home. He would make certain that she was home sometime before sunrise, sometime before their wedding...

Chapter Eighteen

Maximilian watched his bride flit among her friends and family, happiness shining from her lovely features, and he felt an overwhelming sense of having come home at last. It was odd, to say the least, for the scene before him looked nothing at all like what he once would have considered normal.

Tables had been spread out upon the great lawns of Casterleigh, and mingling in the same rarefied air as Raleigh and his sister were Alf and the baker's boy. In truth, there were more people from the village than from the ton, and everywhere there were children, darting among the guests, laughing their musical laughs and shouting in their high-pitched voices.

Compared to your typical London wedding, it was bedlam.

And yet, just as he had begun to appreciate dinners en famille at the vicarage, so Maximilian found himself enjoying the antics of those about him. He had refused to join in a game of ninepins played by one group, but suffered one pretty little girl to sit upon his lap until she fell asleep and her mother, highly embarrassed, came to fetch her.

Despite the din, the atmosphere was warmer and friendlier than any he had known, and he found himself relaxing. He smiled as he saw Charlotte's great-aunt Augusta, looking as hale and hearty as a woman half her age, laughing with her nephew, the vicar. The nuptials had obviously done much to improve her health, Maximilian noted.

"Kit," he called out to the blur in brown that tried to slip past him.

"Yes, my lord?"

"Set down that piece of cake you have behind your back. You have had enough cake for one day, and no matter how much I would like to indulge you, I refuse to have you heave-ho at my wedding breakfast."

"Yes, my lord," Kit said. Looking disgruntled, he produced an enormous slice of the bride's cake tucked into one small hand.

"Put it on the table." Maximilian watched, approvingly, as Kit followed his direction, but before Maximilian had time to draw another breath, the boy wiped his fingers, white and sticky with icing, down the sides of his new coat.

Maximilian sighed. "Not quick enough, am I?" he asked rhetorically. "But I am learning. Run into the house and wash your hands, and have cook clean up your jacket. A gentleman does not wear his dessert upon his person. But before you dash off, tell me, who is that rather seedy-looking fellow who has been eyeing daggers at me all afternoon?" Maximilian cocked his head toward a young man who was lounging insolently against a tree.

"Oh, that's just Billy Hobson, the miller's boy," Kit said. "Sarah said he's a bad-tempered sort, but Papa said we must not speak ill of others."

"And what did Charlotte say?"

Kit paused as if dredging up the appropriate response from his memory. "She said she wanted nothing to do with him."

"Aha! A spurned suitor. That would certainly explain his black looks, if not his ill manners." Maximilian spoke his last words to the air as Kit shouted at another boy and raced off toward the house. Only years of good breeding prevented Maximilian from yelling a reminder to the boy about washing.

With an amused sigh, Maximilian turned his attention from the vicar's son to the vicar's daughter. He caught sight of her, deep in conversation with her sister, and he grinned lazily their way. Charlotte sent him a slow, heart-stopping smile that told him exactly what they were discussing, while Sarah, the prim elder sister, was actually blushing to be caught instructing her sister in some fine point of married life.

Maximilian lifted his brows in such a manner as to truly embarrass the girl. It served her right, he decided, since she had never treated him with any warmth. Still, he was grateful for the information she had been kind enough to pass on to her sibling. Was she adding to Charlotte's knowledge right now? Maximilian felt himself quickening at the thought.

As if Charlotte needed instruction... Maximilian was aware that his lovely young bride was gifted with instinctive skills that rivaled any courtesan's. He was also aware that her plan last night had failed miserably. She had seduced him so that he would not be so anxious to bed her today, but, unfortunately, their romps had only whetted his appetite. He suspected that he would have to spend a week in bed with his wife to get his fill. He would have to consider postponing the wedding trip to Greece...

Charlotte looked across the lawn at her new husband, saw his lips curved in that provocative manner and felt her heart knock against her ribs in a frantic beat. She could not take her eyes from him. He looked so very handsome and elegant, even more so than he had ever seemed in London, perhaps because he was more relaxed. It lent an ease to his features and grace to his body that had been lacking in town.

"Charlotte!" Sarah's voice made her finally stop staring at her husband. "Did you... Surely, you did not say anything to him about our conversation, did you?" Sarah's usually calm, low voice was high and strained, and Charlotte glanced over to find her sister turning crimson.

"Whatever is the matter, Sarah?"

"The matter! The matter is that your husband is looking at me in the oddest fashion."

"Oh, pay him no mind. He is probably anxious to be done with the party and on with the wedding night."

"Charlotte!" Sarah gasped. "Your plain speaking was not seemly alone with me in the vicarage's kitchen, so it is most assuredly out of place here, among your guests."

"Botheration! I suppose it is too early to retire..."

"Charlotte!"

"Oh, there is Billy, looking as if he would like to strangle Max. Who invited him?"

"Who? Oh, the miller's boy. Stay away from him, Charlotte. He grows wilder every year, and has harbored ill will for you ever since you refused his suit."

Charlotte made an inelegant sound. "As if I would want to go out walking with a boy as mean as Billy. He has always been a bully!" She paused to stare at the young man. "Botheration! I hope he does not plan some sort of disruption. Max has been heaving great sighs of relief all afternoon, thinking that he has at last brought me to heel and will have no more scrapes to enter on my behalf."

"Ha!" Sarah said callously. "He does not know you well enough yet, does he?"

Charlotte pulled a face, but was prevented from saying more by the crush of the Watkins family, who wanted to press kisses upon her and view her costly gown more closely. She let them, but her thoughts were racing toward the hour when she and Max could be alone again.

Afterward, Charlotte berated herself for not being more alert, but she was far too distracted. After all, it was her wedding day. She was surrounded by family and friends and not far from her husband, who, despite his elegance, could hold his own in everything from fisticuffs to duels. The vigilance that she had maintained in London slipped here in Sussex, making her easy prey.

It happened when she went into the house to wipe a spill from her gown and to pin up her hair yet again. The morning had fled and for once she was not surrounded by well-wishers. She felt a sense of relief to be alone in the quiet of her room and sighed, suddenly tired from her wild night and busy day.

Then she smelled an odd odor, and something came over her mouth, forcing her to breathe a strange smoke. Her brief sense of panic was overwhelmed by a strange lethargy before nothingness enveloped her like a cloud.

When Charlotte awoke, it was to a lingering sickening smell that churned her stomach. It was not until she regained all her senses that she realized she was on a boat. She closed her eyes again, thinking that her dream of a leisurely ride down the Thames had turned into a nightmare.

But this was no dream, and she was not upon the Thames. Although Charlotte had never been to sea, she realized that the choppy movement of the ship could only be due to the ocean waves. Memory was slow in returning. Were they already on their way to Greece?

She rose upon one elbow. "Max?"

Her quavering question was greeted with a low denial. "Put him out of your mind, Charlotte, dear. He can no longer control you. You are free of him at last. And we are together, just as we always should have been."

With the bile rising in her throat, Charlotte turned her head toward the voice. She took one look at Sir Burgess, reclining back upon the seat with what must be an opium pipe, and she vomited up her wedding breakfast.

Somehow Charlotte survived the Channel crossing, but she was too ill to even consider escaping from her captor. He solicitously tucked a blanket about her and whisked her away in the low light of dusk, and all she could do was lie back in the coach and long for the feel of the ground, unmoving, beneath her feet.

She did not even protest when he carried her into a château. Too quiet to be an inn, it presumably was a private residence, but, since they were beyond the niceties of propriety, she cared only that her bed was solidly anchored to an unmoving floor, and that the door had a stout lock. She locked it, lay down in her less than pristine wedding gown and slept like the dead.

When Charlotte awakened, she was served by a quiet, sour-looking French girl, who managed to prepare her a bath and help her into a new gown that fit reasonably well. The maid, however, refused all questions and conversations, announcing only that "monsieur" was in the morning room, awaiting her presence.

Charlotte thought briefly of escaping through the window, but since she was not sure where they were, and her French was not all that it should be, she decided to risk an interview with Burgess. Perhaps she could talk some sense into him. Perhaps he had abducted her in some opium-induced fit. Mayhap he did not realize that she was married, or that Max would surely kill him if anything happened to her...

"Hello, my dear." Burgess sat at a table near the window, obviously finishing some coffee. He looked more alert this morning, and the smell of his obnoxious habit was not in evidence, filling Charlotte with a swift surge of relief. "Will you join me?"

"Thank you, no," Charlotte answered stiffly. "I wish to be returned at once to my husband."

Burgess shook his head. "A sad event, that. I do apologize for not getting there earlier, but I did not discover your whereabouts soon enough. I did hope to arrive before the nuptials, but... Ah, well. An annulment shall be easy enough to obtain."

Charlotte stared at him. Had the man gone daft? "I do not want an annulment. I want to go home!"

"Come now, Charlotte." Burgess's lips twisted into a smirk. "We all know that Wycliffe only married you because of the compromising situations in which you two were discovered."

"That is not true," Charlotte replied. "Not long ago you claimed that he wanted me for himself. Obviously, you were right."

"Wanted you, perhaps, but he did not have you, did he?" Burgess asked. "I may have missed the ceremony, but I arrived before the wedding night. The marriage will be annulled quietly, and after things have died down, we will return to England."

Charlotte stared at him. *You are mad.* She thought the words, but dared not voice them. The baron had to be insane to think that talk of such a thing would ever die down and insane to kidnap anyone's bride, let alone Wycliffe's. The earl would be incensed. Charlotte thought of his carefully planned trip to Greece, and she wanted to weep. In marrying her, he had hoped to put an end these scrapes, and now she had somehow gotten herself immersed in another . . . the worst yet.

She felt a cold calm descend upon her as she decided that this man would not get the better of her. She had struggled through emotional turmoil to obtain her dream marriage; she did not intend to have it ruined by this interloper. "There will be no annulment," Charlotte said softly. "For you were indeed too late, Sir Burgess. You see, Max and I have been lovers for some time and married only to give the baby a name."

The smirk left Burgess's face to be replaced by a kind of mottled red fury as he half rose from his chair. He sputtered furiously, and Charlotte stepped back a pace. "So! He discovered it, did he? The bastard!"

"Discovered what?" Although Charlotte considered herself no shrinking wet goose, the wild look in Burgess's eyes was chilling. Her impression that he was mad was magnified tenfold.

"Do not play the fool with me, Miss Trowbridge," Burgess hissed. "Wycliffe knew all along! That explains his sudden bizarre interest in a vicar's daughter. He seduced you, got you with child and married you for one reason . . . to gain the Avundel earldom."

"The what?"

"The title, you fool!" he said. "It fell into abeyance when your grandmother's brother had no issue, as well you know."

"My grandmother?"

"It would have been my father's, was his by right until your mother threw him over for that pathetic cleric. All my life, I listened to him rant about his missed opportunity and blame my mother. Yes, it was all her fault for getting with child and forcing him to marry her. But now, it all comes full circle. What should have been his will be mine—not Wycliffe's. Baby or no, the marriage will be annulled, and you will be bound to me."

Astounded by his rambling, Charlotte searched her mind, trying to make sense of his words. She vaguely remembered her Grandmama Carew, but there had never been mention of an earldom in the family. The widowed lady had lived comfortably in a little house in Sussex, not far from Upper Bidwell, and had died when Charlotte was still a young girl.

"But . . . why you?" Charlotte sputtered. "If there truly is a title to be had, why would it not go to James or Thomas or Sarah's husband, since she is the oldest?" A picture of big, quiet Alf waiting on the villagers while they called him "my lord" nearly made her lose her composure.

Burgess snarled in disgust. "Pah! There is not but one drop of decent blood in the passel of the vicar's brats. They would not even know how to petition for the restoration of the title, and it would never be granted to a penniless vicar's boy, you stupid chit. I have the blood, and I have the money. I am already a baron, but deserve greater. You shall see. I shall win the title easily, and Wycliffe will have naught."

Charlotte hesitated to point out to Burgess, who was fairly foaming at the mouth now, that Wycliffe already was an earl and a viscount and a baron, and hardly needed an extra title to add to his lengthy name.

"But why me?" Charlotte persisted. "I am already wed. Why not wait until Jane is of marriageable age?" *And you, I hope, are rotting in jail.* Although she would as soon sever her arm as see one of her sisters married to Burgess, Charlotte's immediate thought was to extricate herself from his clutches. If she could just gain some time, she knew Max would make sure that the baron never bothered any of them again.

"Jane? Jane! Do not speak to me of homely children!" Burgess slammed his fist down upon the table in a fury. "I want no part of any of them. It is you I want, Charlotte, and you alone! You are the image of your mother. Did you know that?" His voice softened as he leaned back and studied her. "My father kept a portrait of her in his bedroom. It served to remind my mother that she could never live up to his standards. Of course, she never did, though she died trying..." Burgess's words trailed off as if he were talking to himself, and then suddenly his attention riveted upon her again like a cat that had sighted its prey. "I still have the painting, you know, though I never imagined that I would possess the original, as it were. You see, Charlotte, I had no idea you even existed until you appeared before me at Bradley House, like a vision. Like a vision," he whispered. "I have so many visions, sometimes I am not sure...but you...you are real. And you will be my wife."

Charlotte did not bother to argue, for it was obvious that Burgess was not rational. What surprised her was how easily he had hidden this strange side of himself in London. He had been smooth and silent and polite, giving the impression of a decidedly different man, and when she realized just how close she had come to marrying him of her own free will, she shuddered. Had it not been for Max, she might be spending the rest of her life with this lunatic.

She still might...

The thought made her ill. Reasoning with him was futile, that much was clear. She decided to placate him, instead. "Very well," Charlotte said. "You will have to manage everything, sir, for I am, at present, indisposed. I would like to go to my room, if you please."

Burgess stared at her, as if her sudden acquiescence confused—and disappointed—him. For a moment, she wondered if he would let her leave his presence. His wildness seemed to feed upon itself, like some dread disease, and she had the distinct impression that just as one cornered by some beast, if she showed the slightest hint of fear, she would be attacked. She stood very still, her hands folded before her as her mother had taught her.

Finally, his breathing slowed and the hungry light left his eyes. "Go, then. Get yourself settled, for we shall stay here for some time. I shall expect you at dinner."

Charlotte nodded. She realized why they were in France. No matter how brave Burgess might appear when in his rages, he still feared Wycliffe, and no matter how bizarre his actions, he had the sense to avoid pursuit.

The thought was not comforting.

Charlotte knew Max would come. She was as certain of it as of the sunrise and sunset. The problem lay in his timing. When would he arrive? How soon would it take him to discover her missing, to suspect Burgess and to take up the trail? The baron might have covered his tracks well, and Max, even now, might be harrying off to Burgess's estate, expecting her to be there.

In the meantime she would be here, on the Continent, housed with a man who was obviously unstable. Burgess's behavior downstairs had been frightening, and Charlotte did not trust him to retain his feeble hold upon his wits. What if he became violent, injured her or locked her away, destroying any chance for her to escape?

And although Charlotte hesitated to think of it, she wondered about the night to come. In truth, Burgess had never even tried to steal a kiss from her, as her other suitors had, and yet that very fact seemed to prey upon her anxiety. The crossing had left her too weak for his attentions, but what if he pressed his advantage now? There would be no one to hear her screams . . .

Grimly, Charlotte decided she could not risk waiting for Max; she would have to leave on her own.

With her decision came quick action, and she began to search the room for anything that might be useful, but Burgess's lucidity must have extended to her prison, too. The room was bare except for the furniture and a few gowns that hung in the wardrobe. A promising-looking trunk yielded nothing but more clothes, stored away.

Charlotte dug down deeply in the chest with the vague hope that some decorative sword or fine pistol might be buried beneath the fabrics, but she found nothing. Sitting back upon her heels, she stared at the worn buttons on some country gentleman's once fine coat, thinking...until she was struck by an idea.

Pulling out a pair of breeches, Charlotte held them up before her only to discard them for a smaller pair. These were overly long and large at the waist, but the best she could do. Heaving a sigh of disgust at the generous bosom that pleased Wycliffe so much, she wrapped it tightly in cloth and covered it with a shirt, a waistcoat and a coat. Taking a rueful look downward, she had to admit that the results were rather dubious. Barring the night before her wedding, it had been a long time since she had dressed as a boy, and her body had changed since those days.

She would not fool anyone.

Charlotte's eyes swept the room, looking for anything else that might aid in her masquerade, until they lighted upon the bed. Choking back an exclamation, she undid her outer clothing, grabbed up a pillow and stuffed it in her waistband. Covering all up again, she gave herself an assessing glance. Now, at least, she seemed less like a woman and more like a lumpy man.

She tucked up her hair as best she could under an old-fashioned wide-brimmed hat and made a mental note to let no one see her too closely. Then, with one last look about the room, Charlotte climbed out the window.

Years of sneaking out of the vicarage had prepared her for the swing into a nearby tree, and although her moves were a bit rusty, she landed among the branches without incident. Below her, the grounds were deserted. No doubt

Burgess did not want many witnesses to her imprisonment, but his caution could work to her advantage.

Despite the seeming quiet, Charlotte crept carefully down from her perch and flitted toward the stables, constantly alert for a sign of discovery from the château. She reached the outbuilding but kept up her guard, wary of surprising a groom. Luckily, she met no one, the only occupants being several horses, and she chose a friendly filly.

Hesitating briefly, Charlotte considered taking all the horses with her to release along the road, but the plan to eliminate that means of pursuit seemed too risky. It would be easier to lead one animal out of the stable, through the copse of trees and over the countryside.

In actuality, it was quite simple, and Charlotte realized that because of Max's self-assumed role of her guardian, everyone in London might think her incapable of taking care of herself. Burgess obviously expected her to cower in her room, waiting for a rescue that might not come, or he would have kept a closer guard upon her.

Perhaps most of the season's Toasts could be counted upon *not* to climb out their windows, she mused as she eased herself onto her mount. Finding themselves alone in a strange country, uncertain of their surroundings, they might be relied upon to swoon, but Sussex girls were made of sterner stuff and, as much as she enjoyed being rescued by her handsome earl, Charlotte could do very well on her own, thank you.

Once in the saddle, she hesitated a moment, for she knew Burgess would expect her to flee toward the coast, to England and her husband. With a grim smile, she decided against that course and urged her horse forward, heading inland.

Charlotte knew enough of the world to understand the location of Paris in relation to the Channel, but exactly how far away the château lay, she was not sure. All she could do was to travel in the general direction of the city and hope that she met no cutthroats along the way, for her destination—a destination Burgess would never dream of—was Paris.

She calculated that she had several hours before her escape would be discovered. If she was lucky, her captor would drift into an opium haze indefinitely, but Charlotte could not count upon that. Presumably, he would sulk until evening, when her absence at the dinner table would rouse him to a fury. However, his behavior was nothing if not erratic, and she was well aware that he might storm up to her room at any moment, demanding entry, only to find her gone.

She hoped he would not discover her escape. She hoped he would not be able to determine her route. She hoped.... Charlotte blinked, clinging to her hopes as she kicked her horse to speed, for she shivered at the thought of Burgess's reaction should he find her.

By nightfall, Charlotte was breathing easier. She found an old barn beside the burned-out relic of a house and curled up in the straw, trying to sleep, for she knew her brave filly needed rest. If not, she would have continued along the road, with only the moon and stars to light her way, for she was still consumed by too much agitation—and hunger—to doze.

Around midday she had found some wild berries, and later she had stolen a few carrots from someone's weedy garden, but she wished now that she had sat down to a good breakfast with Burgess before taking her leave. She was all too conscious that illness had driven everything from her stomach just the day before, and she had eaten nothing substantial since. The Trowbridges might not have had much at the vicarage, but they had never gone hungry, and the unfamiliar, gnawing emptiness threatened to keep her awake.

Finally, exhaustion overcame all else. Her last thought was of Max. Where was he? And then she slept.

Chapter Nineteen

The next day Charlotte came upon an English couple whose French was not sufficient to communicate successfully with some villagers. When she stepped in to help, they thanked her profusely, and nothing would do but that she join them for a healthy repast at the small inn where they were changing horses.

Although she had thus far avoided any dealings with people, Charlotte's stomach roared its assent, so she warily accepted the offer. If they thought her an odd young gentleman, with her funny hat and ill-fitting clothes, they said nothing of it, for they were a strange pair themselves.

Old Squire Titworthy was a rotund man who looked lumpier than Charlotte in an overly tight waistcoat and breeches, while his wife, a thin, tittering girl, appeared fairly silly and self-absorbed. It became obvious that the trip to France was her idea, and she had persuaded her husband to agree simply because it was the thing, not because of any great interest she had in the Continent.

The two were as out of place as a fish flopping upon land, and Charlotte often had to hide a smile at their arguments over the food, the roads, the language and all else that was French. For her part, Charlotte said little, but ate in perfect imitation of her brothers an amount that would have put them to shame.

After the meal, the Titworthys would not hear of parting with their newfound English friend. "Young man, you are the first sensible character we have met since our arrival in this godforsaken country.''

"Now, squire," said his wife, laying a restraining hand upon his arm. She tittered at Charlotte. "He is unaccustomed to foreigners."

"Foreigners! Harumph!" The squire seemed to use the sound, which gurgled deep from his throat, as an all-encompassing comment. "Our own countrymen are as ramshackle as the Frenchies here. Must be something in the water or the wine... Harumph! Fancy wines! They taste no better than a good cup of ale..."

Mrs. Titworthy tittered again. "I must say we did have a rather wretched encounter with an Englishman on the road yesterday."

"Harumph! Bloody cheeky devil!" the squire muttered with renewed outrage. "Demanded that we stop the coach and searched it. Looking for his wife! She probably ran off with some Frenchie. Certainly none of our affair."

"I told the squire that those nobs are different," Mrs. Titworthy whispered, as if to suggest that the possession of noble blood explained away a host of eccentricities. Charlotte wanted to smile until the gist of Mrs. Titworthy's statement became clear. Then her hand tightened so hard on her horse's reins that her knuckles turned white. A nob was looking for his wife! Max? Was Max here so soon, behind her?

"A nob, you say? Who was he?" Charlotte asked in a voice as low and steady as she could muster.

"Harumph! A baron, he said, though one wonders. The man ought to be setting an example, but instead he's harrying off over the countryside, chasing a runaway bride and bullying his fellows. Ought to be learning some manners." The squire shook his head, his face red with indignation at the behavior of his betters.

Burgess! Charlotte's heart banged so frantically that she thought it might dislodge the pillow that was tucked under her breasts. She glanced back the way she had come, but the road was quiet except for a slow-moving hay wagon. Where was Burgess now? "Where did you meet him?" she asked.

"Meet him? Harumph! The man charged upon us like a lunatic," the squire complained.

"Where?" Charlotte asked, unable to stop herself. She did not want to draw her companions' attention to herself, but she had to know. Was Burgess heading toward the coast…or was he behind her even now, gaining on her? Her mount was not fast. She had slept during the night and had wasted precious time sharing a meal with the Titworthys. A man on a good horse could travel so much more quickly… Panic put a hard edge to her question as Charlotte asked again. "Where?"

"It was sometime yesterday," answered Mrs. Titworthy. "Had we just set out?"

"No, it was in the afternoon, after we had the trouble with the coach. Stupid Frenchies gave me a vehicle with a bad wheel! Nearly ended up in the ditch! Lucky we didn't break our necks. They ought to be whipped, the lot of them, preying on Englishmen, taking good coin for shoddy…"

"It was after that little town, the one with the funny name," Mrs. Titworthy interrupted, a hopeful smile on her face.

Charlotte felt her heart sink to her knees. They could not tell her. Burgess was somewhere on the road back there, searching, and she had no idea where. She had a sudden urge to mount up and dash off into the fields in an effort to lose him, but she knew she would only get lost, and without food or money her chances were bleak. Her hands trembling as she tried to still her rising panic, Charlotte forced herself to remain standing next her horse.

"I don't give a damn who he is," the squire argued with his wife. "He better not try to stop us again, or I will show him the barrel of my pistol!"

"We did not realize how difficult it would be traveling alone, just the two of us, you see," Mrs. Titworthy explained.

"Harumph!"

"But now that we have you with us... You will ride along with us, will you not? Say you will, Mr. Linley," Mrs. Titworthy urged.

Charlotte eyed them, their expectant faces awaiting her response, and she managed a shaky smile. Forcing her thoughts away from her pursuer and toward the English couple who were being so kind to her, she nodded. "I would be delighted to accompany you for a while," she said, pitching her tone deep.

The squire harumphed his approval and his wife tittered and chattered, while Charlotte warily watched the road. Somehow, after what seemed an eternity, her companions managed to enter their coach, and Charlotte swung herself up to ride beside them.

She had no choice. She could not go back knowing that Burgess was there, looking for her, nor could she try to find a way through the unfamiliar countryside. She could only go forward, onward to Paris, and she might as well have company. As the third member of a party of English travelers, Charlotte reasoned that she would be less conspicuous, and if Burgess was coming closer... Well, she would rather not be caught alone on the road.

Charlotte tried not to look behind her, forcing herself to keep a fixed gaze ahead instead, but whenever a rider overtook them, she froze, certain that Burgess had come with a couple of henchmen to drag her back to his château. Despite the squire's promises, Charlotte suspected that he could not wield his pistol well enough to stop a madman in full fury.

The afternoon dragged by slowly, making her impatient and anxious to ride faster, to lose her pursuers in one last gallop toward freedom, but she kept to the pace of her companions. She was tempted to take the English couple up on their offer to join them in the carriage, yet she dared not. Although the Titworthys seemed too foolish to see through her disguise, Charlotte knew that she made an awfully pretty young man in ill-fitting garments, and she had no desire to test her acting skills in close quarters.

So she rode, hour after hour, exchanging a few words here and there with the squire and his wife through the window of the coach, but spending most of the time consumed with worry. Once a rider cantered by them, nosing about for a look at the inside of the vehicle. He spoke not a word and took off swiftly, leaving Charlotte to wonder whether she should make anything of the incident or not.

By the time evening approached, she was so troubled that she nearly started at every sound. Perhaps it was the close proximity of her destination. Sanctuary beckoned so strongly that she could almost taste it, and to lose it now when she was within reach would be too horrible to bear.

Although Charlotte was far too anxious to notice her weariness or hunger, the Titworthys were not so distracted. Upon discovering what they determined to be a decent inn on the outskirts of the city, they decided to lodge for the night.

They tried their best to persuade their new friend to join them, but even the offer of another free meal could not sway Charlotte. She had to reach her goal before dark, for the thought of spending the night in a strange, foreign metropolis was nearly as frightening as the promise of pursuit.

"I wish you would not go on, Mr. Linley," Mrs. Titworthy said, a worried expression on her face. "It has been such a comfort to have you with us."

"You will get along splendidly," Charlotte assured them. "I have heard that there is quite a colony of English in the city now."

"Can you not give us your direction, sir?" the squire asked gruffly.

Charlotte hesitated, then shook her head. "I apologize, squire, but I am not certain where I shall be staying." She lied, not wishing to give away anything to those who might come after her.

"Is there nothing that we can do for you?" Mrs. Titworthy asked, a show of genuine concern in her eyes. Charlotte blinked, the urge to break down and pour her tale into their receptive ears so strong that she had to bite her lip. They were a nice couple, kind, if not very smart, but she remembered their disgust at the story of the runaway bride, and she could easily imagine their horror should they find her to be a woman masquerading as a man.

Charlotte swallowed hard, feeling more alone than she ever had in her young life, then she cleared her throat. "I have a friend...who may be coming this way. If you should chance to meet him, please tell him that you saw me."

The couple nodded agreeably. "And the name of your acquaintance?" Mrs. Titworthy asked, smiling.

"Wycliffe. The Earl of Wycliffe," Charlotte said as steadily as she could. "Tell him that...Linley passed through. And now I must be off." She glanced over her shoulder, half expecting to catch the sun moving lower before her very eyes, and strode toward her mount. She dared not look back, for the mere mention of Max had clouded her vision.

Charlotte found it lonely going without the Titworthys, who, however ineffectual they might prove in an emergency, nevertheless provided some kind of moral support. Her apprehension reached a new level, but as she neared the city, the bustle increased, so that she needed all her concentration just to make her way through the press of people toward Paris.

Finding the hotel proved to be the most difficult task she had assumed so far, for the city was a tangle of interweaving streets and alleys. Heady with victory at reaching her destination, Charlotte was not so stupid as to decrease her vigilance. There was always the possibility that Burgess might be lurking right around the next corner to snatch her from the very doorstep of her sanctuary.

Charlotte moved carefully, ignoring the exotic lure of her surroundings, the excitement of a city that under any other circumstances would have dazzled her. She kept intent upon her goal, and finally she found it—the Rue de Clichy, and the fashionable hotel whose address she had put to memory.

Chevalier answered the door and gave her an odd glance before proclaiming that tradesmen were to enter at the rear of the building, but Charlotte had not come this far to have the door slammed in her face. She stepped quickly over the threshold.

"Who is it, Chevalier?" asked a familiar voice, and Charlotte recognized the silken sway of Sibylle's skirts. At the sight of her husband's mother, Charlotte nearly collapsed. The idea of refuge, and above all Max, made her head swim, but she drew upon her last reserve of strength and walked swiftly past the horrified manservant to stand before the dainty dowager. Doffing her hat with a graceful gesture, Charlotte released her hair in a great poof.

"Hello, Mother," she said.

Although Charlotte was close to collapse, it was Sibylle who almost swooned. She took one look at Charlotte—one horrified, wide-eyed look—and flung her hand to her forehead with a dramatic gasp. Chevaliar was at her elbow in a moment.

"My lady, sit down!" He urged her into a crimson damask-covered chair and called for a glass of brandy. *Make that two, please,* Charlotte wanted to say, but she could not find her voice.

"Charlotte, is that you?" Sibylle asked in an agitated whisper.

Charlotte nodded mutely. Overcome with emotion, she could only stare stupidly. She was safe, safe at last...

Her euphoria dimmed as she watched Sibylle's eyes travel from the top of her tangled hair down her travel-stained men's clothes to the muddy slippers upon her feet. The dowager's dainty nostrils flared as though Charlotte's very smell was offensive, and Charlotte realized, with a gulp, that it probably was.

"Is this some wretched joke perpetrated by Maximilian?" Sibylle asked in outraged accents.

Charlotte shook her head. Suddenly, she wanted to cry. She wanted Max. She wanted to fling herself into the arms of her husband or her father or some member of her family, but the only relation available was her mother-in-law who, Charlotte knew, would not welcome an embrace. She blinked back the tears that threatened and swallowed hard.

"I...I was kidnapped—drugged and dragged away from my wedding reception by Sir Burgess. I believe he is quite mad." Charlotte shivered at the memory of his convoluted logic. "He thinks to get my marriage annulled, force me to wed him and petition for some title that is in abeyance. He brought me to France, and when I escaped, all I could think of was to find my way to you."

Charlotte sagged against the wall, certain that her words made no sense and that Sibylle might toss her out at any moment simply because she was not fashionably dressed.

"Oh! You poor child," Sibylle said. Surprised by the sound of sympathy, Charlotte searched her mother-in-law's face. She saw concern and a glimmer of affection. It was not much, but it was enough to make Charlotte hurl herself across the space that separated them. And then she was in Sibylle's arms, her tall frame in filthy men's clothes resting against the dainty dowager's bosom.

That was how Chevaliar found them—Sibylle awkwardly patting Charlotte's back while she sobbed out her relief.

"Come, come, my ladies," Chevalier said. Urging Charlotte into a chair, he handed her a glass and told her to drink. The unfamiliar liquid burned her throat, but warmed her, making her feel much more comfortable. After the servant gave Sibylle her brandy, too, there was still one glass remaining, and Charlotte smiled when she realized Chevalier had brought himself a portion, which he tossed down quickly and without apology.

"Now what, my lady?" he asked Sibylle as he set his empty glass down upon the tray.

"Firstly, we must get her a bath and some decent clothes," Sibylle answered. "She is an amazon, mind you, so nothing of mine will fit her."

"But what if the fiend pursues her here?" Chevalier asked, looking more than a little disconcerted by the thought. Three pairs of eyes turned slowly toward the door before them.

Sibylle was the first to look at the group. "He would not dare," she said firmly. "But, just in case, have Jean hire some men and set up a guard." She paused and glanced speculatively at Charlotte. "I do not think we need fear Sir Burgess, for I believe that your own gallant knight shall soon arrive."

At Charlotte's blank look, Sibylle smiled crookedly. "Surely, you do not doubt that Maximilian can be far behind you."

Max! Charlotte's heart danced at the mention of his name. "Do you think so?" she asked, afraid to hope that he might find her so soon.

Sibylle nodded. "Unlike his father, who was but infatuated with me, Maximilian loves you fiercely...so fiercely that I expect he would lay down his life for you in an instant. Who would have thought that he could become so romantic?" Sibylle shook her dark curls at this seeming riddle and then stared at Charlotte as if the girl in boy's dress possessed some secret she had spent her life seeking.

Chevalier broke the silence that followed. "Nevertheless, I think we ought to send a message to his lordship, in case he has been detained or misled."

Sibylle nodded slowly, gazing at Charlotte all the while. "As you wish, but I, for one, am certain that nothing in the world would keep him from his wife. He loves her, you see, in a way that no one has ever loved me."

When Chevalier said nothing, Sibylle waved him away impatiently. Then she cocked her head in a gesture that reminded Charlotte of Max. "Well, who would have guessed that your little country wedding would result in such excitement!"

"You should have come," Charlotte said softly.

Sibylle pouted prettily. "What? And not be the center of attention? You should know by now that is something I cannot abide."

"Why?" Charlotte asked gently.

The preening pose was dropped for a moment as Sibylle looked at her intently. "You and I actually have much in common," she said, shaking her head in wonder. "I, too, was the beautiful, petted daughter of a scholar. Only I had no patience—or ability—for study. My face was my ticket away from the dusty realm of books into the enchanted world of wealthy society.

"When the Earl of Wycliffe showed an interest in me, I did not care that he was old and stuffy and stodgy." Sibylle snapped her fingers. "La! It was unimportant. I dazzled a proposal out of him, and I was suddenly a countess! And, unlike you, silly goose, I loved it. I adored it." She closed her eyes, as if remembering.

"Oh, the parties! The dancing, the food, the drink, the cards...and the houses! The clothes! The jewels! I wanted it all, but Reginald soon tired of such things. He began to treat me as if I were foolish and unworthy of him. I took lovers just to spite him, but he did not care. Once he had Maximilian... The boy was always his sole property, you know," Sibylle mused. "I think Maximilian was born with the same contempt for me that his father had."

"That is not true," Charlotte whispered.

"Oh, it is true, but no matter. I did not need them. I pursued my own pleasures and made a name for myself. Me, a poor tutor's daughter! Now I am a world-renowned beauty, an unparalleled hostess and an incomparable lover to those upon whom I bestow my favors. I have all that could want!"

Except love. Charlotte felt only pity for the lovely young girl who had never grown up and who, even now, sought attention with her outrageous behavior, like a rebellious child. But Charlotte knew that Sibylle would not welcome her compassion. Instead, she took the older woman's hand and squeezed it warmly. "You are truly a remarkable woman," she said.

"I am, aren't I?" Sibylle agreed prettily.

Several swallows of brandy later, Charlotte was ensconced in a tub of scented bathwater in one of the bedrooms and feeling a twinge of tipsiness. Abandoning the empty glass, she let a chattering little French maid wash her hair, and then she put on the long, heavy robe that had been laid out for her.

It was obviously not Sibylle's, but Charlotte hesitated to ask the identity of its owner, since it was a man's dressing gown. Presumably it belonged to some paramour of Sibylle's, but Charlotte said nothing. She simply rolled up the long sleeves, sent the maid away and sat down before a gilded mirror to brush out her drying hair.

She was relaxing under the gentle strokes when she heard a commotion in the other rooms. Dropping the brush, Charlotte gasped in alarm. Her first thought was of Burgess, for she could easily envision the madman forcing his way into the hotel.

Glancing around the room in panic, Charlotte searched for something with which to defend herself, for she would not go without a struggle. She briefly considered setting him afire with the lamp, but then her eyes lighted upon the fireplace. In an instant, she was across the room, hefting a long, cruel-looking poker high in the air just as the bedroom door flew upon, banging on its hinges with the force of a blow.

The weapon fell from Charlotte's grasp as she expelled a long, pent-up breath. "Max!" She raced into his arms, and he caught her, swinging her up as if she were no heavier than her sister Jenny. He hugged her to him so tightly that she could barely draw in air, while he whispered her name over and over.

"Charlotte... Charlotte... Charlotte..."

The sound of his deep, familiar voice was so wonderful she could have listened forever, but he was squeezing her so hard Charlotte felt her ribs might crack. She was suddenly aware of how much strength was contained within his elegant, aristocratic body, and the knowledge made her shiver in a decidedly pleasant way. He loosened his hold to look into her face. "That bastard..."

"No. Nothing happened. I am fine," Charlotte said, giving him a tremulous smile.

"Charlotte," he said shakily, as if he hardly trusted himself to speak. "You were abducted from your own wedding, at the mercy of a madman for days... You have been traveling alone across France, and... you are fine?"

Charlotte ducked her head and smiled in the face of his dismay. She did not want to talk about what had happened, not now, not when he was finally here and she was in his arms, but Max... He would need explanations. He would want all the loose ends tied neatly into knots before proceeding with anything else. "How did you get here?" he demanded roughly.

She noticed suddenly how the strain of the last few days had marked him. He was pale and drawn, his body tense and his brown eyes stark with worry. She wanted only to hold him, to touch him, but she forced herself to speak. "I dressed as a man again."

At Max's incredulous snort, she smiled. "Well, I did a little better job of it this time."

"And you rode all the way here alone?"

"I was with an English couple today for much of the journey," she said, trying to reassure him.

"They did not see through your disguise?"

Charlotte smiled again. "No, Max. It was all right. Truly." She lifted her fingers to caress his cheek in an effort to comfort him, but he did not appear consoled. He dropped his hands from her shoulders, his eyes shuttered. "Apparently, I have been laboring under a misconception," he said softly, "that you needed rescuing."

Charlotte blinked, astonished by his behavior until she realized that he was hurt because he had not saved her. His male pride was wounded! Despite his constant grousing about it, Max *enjoyed* playing her gallant protector, she decided with some surprise. Swallowing hard, Charlotte lifted her hands to his face. "Oh, Max, I knew you would come, and I wanted to wait for you, but I was so afraid, so dreadfully afraid."

He appeared contrite then, like a small boy who wanted to apologize, and he reached for her again. Charlotte knew suddenly that despite his smooth surface, buried deep in the elegant earl was a child who needed her, perhaps far more than she needed him. She took his beloved face in her hands and looked into his eyes. "I still need you, Max. I shall always need you to extricate me from my scrapes."

He returned her solemn gaze silently, and Charlotte saw, as she so rarely did, the vulnerability there in his dark depths. "Let us hope that there are not many more of them of this caliber, for I do not know if I can stand it," he said at last.

"When I reached the château only to find that you both were gone, I . . ." He did not finish, but gripped her shoulders so tightly that she nearly winced. "I had not realized until that moment just how much you mean to me, Charlotte."

He looked frightened, whether by worry for her or by the force of his own emotion, Charlotte did not know, but her heart swelled to bursting. "Oh, Max," she said. "I love you so." She slid her arms around his neck and felt his own close around her.

She heard him release a raspy sigh against her neck. "You did well, and I am very proud of you. Although I am quite accustomed by now to coming to your aid, it is not something I need to do. . . to prove my manhood." He pulled back to give her a crooked grin. "I can think of other, more pleasant ways to prove it . . ."

Charlotte grinned at the change in his tone. "We had better close the door," she whispered, rather amazed that her organized husband, with his fondness for details, had ignored the gaping entrance to their room.

When Max muttered something that sounded suspiciously like, "Hang the bloody thing," Charlotte shut it herself.

She stopped there, leaning back against the wood, to take a long look at him. He was magnificent. Tall and muscular and dark, his body beckoned her without the slightest movement. The air heated between them until finally he took a step toward her.

"No," she said.

His eyebrows lifted slightly, and Charlotte smiled slowly. "Sit down," she said in explanation, pressing him into the chair before the mirror. She picked up the fallen brush and undid the thong that held back his dark mane. "I have wanted to do this for a long time."

His hair felt like liquid silk in her hands, sliding over her fingers so sensuously that she blinked in surprise at the jolt that shot through her. She lifted the brush and brought it down through the strands, once, twice, and then over and over until she met his eyes in the mirror. They seemed to burn into her soul like dark coals.

The brandy thrumming in her blood, Charlotte set aside the brush and speared her fingers through his hair, letting it fall slowly. Mercy, but he felt wonderful... Her hands dropped to his wide shoulders, and she pressed a kiss behind his ear before leaning over him to untie his neckcloth. She heard his indrawn breath and felt giddy, heady with the knowledge of what was to come.

Without preamble, he pulled her into his lap and looked at her for long moments, while the air crackled between them. Charlotte was so taut with expectation that she felt as though the room itself vibrated with the strength of it. She could feel the evidence of his desire against her bottom, and she suddenly realized that she had on naught but a flimsy robe, while he was fully clothed.

"I want to undress you," she whispered.

He made some sound of assent, his eyelids lowering slightly over dark pools sleepy with the promise of sex as he watched her. He made no movement to touch her, but let her have her way when she pulled at his jacket, sliding it down over his arms. He shrugged out of it quickly.

Charlotte smiled wickedly, but said nothing. Holding his gaze, she slowly unbuttoned his waistcoat, making each movement a provocative caress. She slipped it off and then tugged his shirt from the waistband of his breeches and lifted it over his head.

The sight of his bare chest covered in its mass of dark hair made her tremble deep inside, as if every part of her was alert and attentive to him. Charlotte ran her palms down the length of it, rubbing against the muscles, catching at the hairs with her fingertips, and she felt him grow beneath her. Emboldened, Charlotte sensed her own power, for she suddenly realized that she could bring this strong, elegant, wealthy aristocrat to his knees—even as she joined him there.

With a groan, he reached for her, but Charlotte evaded him to slip from his lap. Without a word, she knelt before him and tugged at his boots. She removed one, then the other, and then his stockings. Finally she held his naked foot in her hand. She ran her hands over the flesh and up his ankle, along his muscular calf, and everything in the world dropped away but Max.

She leaned forward, purposely pressing her breasts against his thigh, and began unbuttoning his breeches. He groaned, and Charlotte felt him grip her hair like a lifeline. She ignored the tug on her locks to finish her task, and his sex sprang out into her hand. She remembered well just how he liked her to touch him there.

"Charlotte!"

Without a moment's notice, she found herself unceremoniously pushed to the floor, the lovely gilt chair Max had been reclining in kicked to the side. Before Charlotte could even catch her breath, he was atop her, his hands sliding inside her robe while his mouth devoured hers. Over and over his tongue thrust inside, meeting her own, as he touched every inch of her body in long, heavy strokes—palming her breasts, her hips, her buttocks as if he were on fire and only she could ease the pain.

When Max broke the kiss to rise to his knees, Charlotte cried out in dismay, but he pinned her with his hot gaze, and she quieted as he opened her oversize robe and spread it wide. He looked down at her with such burning ferocity that she squirmed, but he stilled her with his hands, running them in a long, even stroke from her shoulders, over her breasts, to her thighs. Then he pushed his breeches down past his hips and lifted her to meet him.

Charlotte watched, wide-eyed, while he guided himself inside her body. Her breasts heaved as she struggled to take in air. "Dear God," she sobbed. She had never seen anything like it in her life. Max smiled at her, half in wicked smugness, half in delirious ecstasy as he probed her depths, seating himself firmly.

She wrapped her legs around his hips and clenched down on him, her pleasure peaking in a rush, and she closed her eyes, letting it take her. When she opened them again, her husband had lost his smug smile. Instead, he had the look of someone near death.

His head was thrown back and all his muscles were gathered together, straining as he thrust into her over and over until she gasped with renewed fervor. Her fingers dug into the deep pile of the expensive carpet, and she wept with the force of new release as he joined with her, a deep sound like no other emerging from his chest to break free when his last shudder died away.

He collapsed, rolling onto his back and pulling her with him, and there they lay, neither of them speaking or moving, for what might have been minutes—or hours. When she could finally breathe again, Charlotte opened her eyes to see the bottom of the overturned chair.

"We are on the floor," Max muttered in a rough voice that bespoke his disbelief.

Charlotte smiled into his chest. "Haven't you ever...been on the floor before?" she asked.

Max grunted an outraged denial. "Until I met you, I had no knowledge of the area. Now, it has become a common enough place for me," he complained. "Although, when I think of the myriad incidents in which you have managed to ground me, I must admit I prefer this new technique to your previous methods."

Charlotte smiled, remembering the times he had been felled by spilled food or drink. She bit her lip to prevent the laugh from escaping, but then her thoughts wandered back over those occasions. "Max." She sighed softly. "When we get home, I want to romp naked in champagne..."

Her husband groaned in reply.

"Or something," Charlotte amended. "Champagne might be too expensive."

"Devil take the cost!" Max answered brusquely.

"Good," Charlotte answered, "because it is quite delicious, and I was thinking about licking it from your body..."

Groaning even louder, Maximilian lifted his head as though with great effort and opened one eye to gaze at her speculatively. "My dear Charlotte," he whispered, "I find it hard to believe that you are a vicar's daughter."

Chapter Twenty

"You ought to proceed with your wedding trip," Sibylle argued as she dropped a dainty dollop of preserves upon her toast. "Your wife was abducted by another man and spent days—and nights—in his company. The talk will be vicious. You know that, Maximilian, and you should not subject Charlotte to it."

Charlotte felt their attention upon her, and swallowed the last of her breakfast with a gulp. "I would rather not go," she said softly. She looked over at Max, into those warm, brown eyes, brimming with concern, and tried to divine what *he* wanted. It was not an easy task, for her husband had proven to be much more complex than she had originally suspected.

At one time, Charlotte would have thought him incapable of abandoning his schedule, and yet, in the last weeks, he had been forced by necessity to do just that. Would he mind postponing the trip? "I do not think I would be able to appreciate the beauties of Greece right now," she explained with a rueful smile. "I would rather go home and see my family."

When Sibylle made a sound of disagreement, Max sent his mother a sardonic look. "When did you begin caring about propriety or the dictates of the *ton*?"

Far from taking offense at the indictment of herself, Sibylle laughed. "What will I do now that you are no longer the stolid, boring fellow that you always have been?" she asked, her lips curving into a smile. "Whom will I shock with my behavior, now that your wife has outdone me? I will have to become a recluse, staidly abiding by society's conventions!"

To Charlotte's surprise, Max actually grinned at his mother's teasing, and she felt herself smile at the byplay. The tension that had always been so palpable between Max and Sibylle seemed to have eased during their stay in her Paris rooms. Charlotte knew that she acted as a buffer, smoothing over the worst comments from each of them, but her presence was not the only reason for the change.

Something in Sibylle had softened the night she had shared her past with Charlotte. She began to tone down her flamboyant behavior in front of her son, and when she did, he reacted more pleasantly. It was just a bit of give and take, but it was a beginning, and Charlotte had hopes that someday mother and son would admit they cared for each other.

"Does that mean I must stop doing my best to annoy you?" Max asked, his mouth quirking with his admission. "I suppose I shall finally have to get my hair cut fashionably short."

"Don't you dare!" Charlotte protested in shocked tones, and they both looked at her and laughed. "I do not care if it is not the thing, I like your hair long."

"My wife has spoken," Max said, slanting a teasing glance at her.

Despite her amusement, Sibylle made a sound of disagreement. "You may laugh, but people forgive a lot as long as one is au courant," she said airily, and Charlotte wondered if the dowager spoke from personal experience. Had it been difficult for her to fit into the society she had once so envied? Charlotte remembered her feelings of awkwardness when thrust into the ton, and she realized that the transition from poor tutor's daughter to countess could not have been an easy one for Max's mother.

"I still say you should go on to Greece," Sibylle urged. "Give the talk a chance to die down, Maximilian."

Max shook his head. "Although we could resume our itinerary, I do not feel right traveling with Burgess running loose."

"I cannot believe that you did not kill him," Sibylle said with a frown of annoyance.

"I would have, if the coward had not fled." Max answered so quietly, yet with such vehemence, that Charlotte felt chills dance down her back. Suddenly, she knew that her elegant, rather quiet husband was dangerous. Woe betide Burgess or anyone else who underestimated the earl. "I found no trace of him at the château or on the road," he noted bitterly. "But I still have men searching, and I shall find him, sooner or later. The wretch will never, ever touch my wife again. Be assured of that."

Even Sibylle seemed impressed by the intensity of her son's gaze, and she nodded, wide-eyed, in agreement.

Max seemed to recover himself then, and smiled. "However, it might be best to return home for now, instead of making ourselves a target in Greece. When we visit the ruins of Athena's famous temple, I would rather enjoy them without having to look over my shoulder for enemies. I shall be content to spend some time at Casterleigh, which is far enough away from the biting tongues of the ton."

Charlotte released a breath in relief, glad that her wish to return to England did not upset his plans. All this talk of Burgess made her uneasy, though, and she would happily move on to a new topic.

Sibylle did not seem inclined to drop the subject, however. "Then you expect this man to come after her again?" she asked, looking doubtful.

Max's brow darkened. "I do not know, but I am prepared for anything," he answered. "Although my wife is to be commended for her brave escape, I do not intend for her to be forced to such extremes ever again."

"But how long can you stay in the country?" Sibylle asked, her tone revealing her contempt for Sussex. "What of London? What of your... schedule?"

Max sat back in his chair, his eyes roving over his wife with a warmth that was entirely inappropriate for the dining hall, and Charlotte felt her cheeks heat in return. Abruptly, she was reminded of the long night they had spent in feverish lovemaking.

I have cleared my calendar," he said firmly, "of everything but the vicar's daughter."

They were greeted with complete abandon by the Trowbridges, and Charlotte wept with joy to see her family again. Her father cried, too, when he held her close. Then he kept patting Maximilian on the back, mumbling that he knew his lordship would save his daughter, until Charlotte finally whispered to her husband, "Papa wants to hug, you, too."

With a look of confusion, Maximilian turned to her father, and the old man teared up shamelessly in his awkward embrace. For a moment, Max closed his eyes against the force of such emotion, but his own trembling hands gave him away. He was not unaffected by her family's affection.

Maximilian thought of the cool relationship he maintained with his mother in Paris, of the small circle of friends that awaited him in London, and he knew he had never felt this way before.

These people truly loved him.

It still surprised him, the way they had taken him in without reservation and the way they gave so freely of themselves. Maximilian admitted that he had come to enjoy those hours spent in the rabbit warren of the vicarage, with animals underfoot and children running here and there. Despite their loud voices and sticky hands and quarreling, he was content.

If this was lunacy, then he was a hopeless case.

Still, it was getting late, and after a few hours Maximilian insisted that Charlotte needed her rest, and they headed up to the Great House, where the windows were ablaze in welcome. The moment they stepped over the threshold, he felt a hum of well-being such as he had never known. There was something so right about seeing Charlotte standing in the middle of the foyer...

"Oh, Max," Charlotte said breathlessly as she gazed about the quiet dignity of the building. "I love this house. I know you think it is too small, but let us stay here often," she begged.

Of course, he could deny her nothing, but he found himself in tacit agreement. He was home.

All the servants had turned out to greet them, and Charlotte spoke to each and every one, introducing herself to those she did not know by name and lighting the hallway with her warmth.

Suddenly Maximilian thought of how close he had come to losing her forever, and he felt a searing twist to his gut. He had the odd suspicion that he could not live without the woman with the downy hair and bright smile. He hurried her upstairs and dismissed their attendants. Her mood was still sparkling when they reached the master suite.

"I love this room," Charlotte said, spreading her arms as though to encompass what seemed to him to be an ordinary, if tastefully decorated, bedchamber. He remembered the last night he had spent here with Charlotte, before their wedding, and he looked at the place with some affection himself.

"And I love this bed," his wife said. With a sigh of happiness, she ran to pull back the hangings and leapt upon the covers. While he watched with a smile of disbelief at her antics, Charlotte kicked off her shoes and stood up. "It is the biggest bed I have ever seen," she said, hopping up in the air.

"You are *not* jumping on my bed," Max said in a long-suffering voice.

She grinned at him wickedly. "Now, Max... Come! Try it," she urged, motioning for him to join her.

The idea was, of course, ridiculous. The Earls of Wycliffe did not engage in such nonsense. "If I jump upon that bed, it will break asunder," he said.

"It will not!" Charlotte protested.

Maximilian never really knew what possessed him, but suddenly he was climbing up beside her. He jumped once, twice, while feeling the strangest sensation of freedom, before the entire thing crashed to the floor.

Maximilian lay there among the ruins of his bed, with the posts lying askew and the curtains draping over him, and he opened one eye to see his wife hovering above his face. Her green eyes were huge with concern, and her hair had, naturally, come loose to float about her.

"Max! Max! Are you all right? Say something!" she begged.

He laughed, the sound echoing around the enclosed space that had once been his bed, and felt something give way, in turn, inside of him. "I love you, Charlotte," he said.

Charlotte sat in the garden of the Great House, drinking tea and taking in the lovely summer air. The sky was a pristine blue after several rainy days, and the air smelled fresh and clean. The greensward at the side of the building sloped down to a pond, and the view would have been perfect but for the stiff footmen who stood beside her table.

It had been more than a month since the wedding, and Charlotte was chafing at the restrictions that her husband had placed upon her. Having grown up practically within sight of Upper Bidwell, she had been used to walking alone to the village since her youth. Now, she must needs always have someone with her, even if she wanted to do no more than visit her sister. It was rapidly becoming unbearable.

Although not usually given to venomous thoughts, Charlotte cheerfully wished Burgess to the devil and back, not only for all her past grievances, but for the lingering aftereffects of his deeds. Sometimes she wondered if her life would ever be normal again.

"Halloo!" The sound of Jane's voice hailing her from down the hill made her shake off her grim mood, and she stood to wave a greeting. Rarely a day went by without a visit from some member of her family, and in truth most afternoons found a number of them up at the house for one reason or another.

Charlotte felt a twinge of guilt, not wishing to impose on her new husband, but Max did not seem to mind. She suspected that he liked the company as well as she did, or she never would have allowed her relatives the freedom of her home.

Today looked to be no exception to the rule, for trailing along behind Jane were Carrie, Kit and Jenny. They raced to the pond, scaring up a couple of geese, while Jane stepped near. "Are you ready for the picnic today?" she asked.

"Of course!" Charlotte answered with a smile. She was looking forward to an outing to the village green. For some time, she had not been certain whether Maximilian would consent, but she had finally convinced him that she would be perfectly safe surrounded by family and neighbors. She hoped that the footmen could be left at home.

"Cook has been busy all morning. Shall we see what treats she has prepared for us?" Charlotte asked.

Looking very serious and grown-up, Jane accompanied Charlotte into the huge kitchen of Casterleigh, where Cook was wrapping dishes in linen.

"What delights have you packed away for us, Mrs. Stout?" Charlotte asked the woman. A beefy woman who lived up to her name, Cook took her duties seriously, but she was not above spoiling the younger members of the Trowbridge clan with special delicacies.

"Humph. Six courses and the china, and the crystal, and the..."

"What?" Charlotte looked, disbelieving, to where Mrs. Stout pointed out a row of baskets lined up across one long bench.

"But we are to have a picnic, not a dinner party!" Charlotte protested.

Mrs. Stout rolled her eyes. "His lordship's orders, my lady," she explained with a sniff.

Charlotte burst out laughing with such amusement that even the usually grim-faced cook joined her. "I am truly sorry, Mrs. Stout, but he does not know any better. We shall teach him, shall we not, Jane?'' Charlotte asked. ''Unpack all the china and the crystal and such. Wrap some chicken in paper, some cold ham and fruit... Oh, you know as well as I what is proper fare,'' Charlotte said.

''Yes, my lady,'' Mrs. Stout said with a nod of approval. ''You heard the countess, Lizzy. Put away all that nonsense!''

Max was slightly disgruntled to discover that his usual grand dinner was no more, but Charlotte only laughed, and the children teased him so that he finally sat back and enjoyed the simple food that made eating out of doors a pleasure. They had spread blankets on the ground for their repast, but if he thought it beneath his dignity to be lounging about on the grass with a bunch of villagers, he did not say it, and truly Charlotte thought he seemed at ease.

After the meal, the adults visited among themselves, the children ran freely on the green, and the men got up a game of cricket. ''Shall you play, my lord?'' Thomas asked.

''Yes, please!'' pressed James. ''You must join my team.''

''No, mine!'' Thomas protested.

''No, mine!''

''You can take him, lad, but I don't want him,'' said a burly farmer, with a frown of disgust. ''Too elegant to make a good player. Might muss up his clothes.''

The challenge inherent in that statement brought the discussion among the Trowbridges to frenzied heights until, finally, Max was dispatched to defend his class as a matter of honor.

Charlotte sat back with a slow smile as she watched the years fall away from her husband. Stiff at first, he soon was playing with the abandon of a boy, heedless of his fine boots or the timepiece he had left beside her.

The children cheered him on until they were hoarse, and Charlotte laughed as she packed away the remnants of their meal. ''He is a fine man, Charlotte,'' said her papa.

"Yes, he is, isn't he?" she answered softly, so happy that her eyes grew moist.

"Where is Jenny?" asked Sarah, who was trying to gather the children together. "Kit, run and find your sister. It is growing late."

"We want to stay until the match is finished!" Kit argued, but he was silenced with a swift look from his elder. With a deep sigh, he weaved his way among his neighbors, calling for his sister.

In a short while, he was back without Jenny, but before Sarah could scold him, his papa stood up determinedly. "I shall find her," he said, with a gentle smile that deflected Sarah's frown, and he ambled off among his flock.

"She was not anywhere," Kit said with a scowl. "But I have a note for you, Charlotte." He dropped a piece of paper in her lap, and thinking it was from one of the villagers, Charlotte picked it and unfolded it absently. When she read the words upon it, however, her heart stopped in her breast.

"I have your sister. Come to the elm wood now, and do not tell Wycliffe, or she will die."

Charlotte moaned softly, dropping the paper from her nerveless fingers.

"What is it, Charlotte?" Sarah asked.

Charlotte did not even look at her sister. "He has Jenny," she said tonelessly as she stood up.

"Charlotte! Wait! You must tell your husband. He will know what to do," Sarah protested, reaching for her arm.

Charlotte did not even pause to note just how much Sarah's opinion of Max had improved. "I cannot," she said, shrugging off her sister's grasp.

She moved quickly, weaving her way among the blankets and the neighbors with a single-minded purpose, for all she could think of was Jenny in the hands of that madman. The littlest Trowbridge had always been so sheltered, Charlotte could not even imagine the terror the child must be feeling. She knew just how volatile Burgess could be. What if he hurt her? What if he used the opium? Soon Charlotte was moving at a run, ignoring the fading voice of Sarah, who called for her across the green.

Burgess smiled. Everything was going even better than he had hoped. Who would have thought that Wycliffe would abandon his wife to play cricket? It was almost as though Burgess himself had arranged the game. Perhaps he had. The baron let himself drift off, dreaming of his own cleverness. His dreams, especially when he was smoking his pipe, were so real that sometimes it was hard to tell any more what was reality.

He shook himself. Soon all his plans would reach fruition. He had hired someone to watch Wycliffe and notify him immediately if the man left the match. And he had paid someone to hold the little girl who would draw Charlotte to him. Then he would have her to wife, and his father would finally be silenced. When he saw her breaking through the woods, Burgess smiled softly.

"Where is she?" Charlotte demanded.

Burgess said nothing, but nodded at the young man who had been giving candy to the little girl. With a surly nod, the fellow grabbed the child's hand and stepped forward.

"Billy Hobson! Let go of my sister this instant!" Charlotte said.

"Jenny!" Burgess started at the unfamiliar cry, astonished to see a woman following behind Charlotte. Who was this? The older sister? Before Burgess could move, his hostage was racing toward the ugly woman who spread her arms in welcome.

"Sarah!" the girl cried happily.

"Get away from them!" Burgess ordered, reaching for Charlotte.

"You get away from her, you!" shouted a small voice. Out of nowhere, a furious barking ensued, and suddenly Burgess could feel the sharp teeth of a dog on his leg at the same time a little boy grabbed his arm and bit down hard. Shuddering violently, Burgess tried to throw the child off, but then the ladies were on him, nails scratching and legs kicking. He felt dizzy and disoriented.

Charlotte aimed a foot at Burgess's groin and smiled in pleasure to see him double over. Her triumph was short-lived, however, because Billy drew them all up short with a curt command. "Leave off him, all of you," he snapped, and she stilled, panting in rage and frustration at the sight of Billy holding a pistol on them.

"Put the weapon down, young man." The low, gentle voice could only belong to her papa, and Charlotte turned in surprise to see him approaching. Had the entire family followed her here?

"Don't do it," croaked Burgess. "I am paying you well!"

The vicar ignored the baron. "It is not too late to turn away from those who would tempt you to evil," he said to Billy. "Put it down, and we shall forget this unfortunate incident."

Billy made some sort of sound of argument, but it was cut off by a thick arm that suddenly wrapped around his neck. The gun dropped to the ground while Alf tightened his hold on the errant miller's son.

With a cry of victory, Charlotte retrieved the gun and whirled to face her tormentor, but before she could even lift it, Burgess shoved aside her siblings and lunged for her. Everyone gasped at once, drowning out Patches's frantic barking, as Charlotte stepped back and shut her eyes.

The sound of the pistol firing shattered the woods.

Conscious that the cheers from the picnickers had lessened, Maximilian glanced toward where his wife and her siblings sat. When he did not see her, he halted in mid-stride, panic slicing through him and robbing him of air. Then he noticed that the entire family was missing, and he resumed breathing—until he heard the gunshot.

"Charlotte!"

Maximilian flew in the direction of the sound, racing ahead of the curious villagers and breaking into the clearing like a wild man. He was greeted by the most bizarre tableau he had ever witnessed, for there was Alf, dangling a young man by the scruff of the neck, while Kit, Jane, Sarah, Jenny and Charlotte stood in a circle around their father, who was kneeling beside someone lying on the ground.

With a low oath, Maximilian thrust through the group to see Burgess lying there, white-faced, clutching his chest, while blood trickled through his fingers. His determination to kill the baron dripping away like the man's lifeblood, Maximilian sighed. "Kit, run and get the physician, please," he said softly. Kit nodded and raced through the gathering crowd, while the vicar whispered softly to the man they all knew was dying.

The doctor dutifully appeared, followed shortly by the undertaker and the parish constable, who relieved Alf of his prisoner. The last they heard of Billy Hobson, he was loudly denying his involvement in any kidnapping.

"I remember now!" the vicar said suddenly as the remaining villagers began to disperse. "Burgess! Your mama knew a baron by that name. He had some scheme to gain the Avundel earldom by marrying her, but your mama had no interest in such things, of course. She thought he was a crazy man. The poor boy. If that man was his father, no wonder he was a bit confused."

"Then we really are connected to a title somehow?" Charlotte asked. Maximilian saw the boys perk up their ears.

"Oh, yes. I believe so. Of course, I do not know the particulars. Your mama disdained such things, and no money was involved. Whatever land there was had reverted to the crown."

Thomas sighed loudly. "What good is a title without wealth?" he asked.

"Don't be a noddycock!" James replied. "I would have respect and deference and people calling me 'my lord,' and all that." He glided about the clearing as though he were an Eastern potentate.

"Please do not claim you are imitating me," Maximilian said with a groan.

"Why, I would be as good as his lordship!" James crowed.

"You will be as good as gone if you do not come along to your bed right now and mind your manners about it!" Sarah scolded.

That was the end of the Avundel earldom, Maximilian assumed as he watched the rest of the family troop after Sarah. Soon, only Charlotte stood, pensively staring into the woods and rubbing her arms as if she was cold.

Maximilian stepped behind her and put his hands on her shoulders. "We can probably petition to gain it for him, if you wish," he said, although his mind boggled at the thought of James actually having something to lord over his brother.

Charlotte did not answer, but trembled against him, and her next words rang out in the stillness of the darkening wood with a bitter accusation that surprised him. "Is that why you finally decided to marry me?" she asked.

"What? I knew nothing of your connection to the Avundels," Maximilian answered truthfully. He had first heard of the title when she had told him of Burgess's scheme.

"Really, Max?" Charlotte turned to face him, her features so taut with tension that he felt dismayed. "Really, Max?" she repeated. "Let us be truthful. You always thought yourself far too good for a simple vicar's daughter. And I never knew why you chose to marry me. Tell me. Was it because you discovered that I had a trickle of decent blood in me, after all?"

"No!" Maximilian answered forcefully, although the charge made him feel guilty. She was right. He had behaved badly, arrogant and boundless in his conceit, but how could he explain what had changed his mind? It had been such a myriad combination of factors, with Wroth and Raleigh and Burgess and his own overpowering need for her influencing his decision.

"Forgive me," he whispered. "I was a fool. I was in love with you, but too idiotic to realize it. I wanted you so badly that suddenly I could not stand the thought of anyone else

having you. I had to have you myself. I must have you,
Charlotte, now and always.''

Although difficult for him, the admission must have
pleased her, for she slipped her arms about his waist and
pressed her cheek against his chest. "And what of you?" he
asked a bit harshly. He would have liked to kill Burgess
himself, but Maximilian had to admit that the baron had
met his match in the Trowbridge clan and in the resilient,
redoubtable vicar's daughter. "You certainly do *not* need
me to extricate you from your scrapes."

Charlotte lifted her head. "Foolish man," she said with
a soft smile. "I have loved you since the first moment I saw
you—when I crawled out from under the sofa in the vicarage."

Somehow, they had acquired cats.

Maximilian reached down to lift up a dark one and absently stroked its fur. They were apparently part of a brood
belonging to Mrs. Mew, an ancient beast who reproduced
regularly at the vicarage and whose latest litter had managed to find its way to the greener pastures of the Great
House, aided by the Trowbridge children.

Intent upon finishing up some work, Maximilian swung
open the door to his study only to find another feline asleep
on his desk. He let the one in his arms leap to floor as he
approached this new irritant. "Charlotte!" he shouted.
Deuced, but he did not even want the animals in the house;
he would be damned if they were to be allowed in his study.

Stepping closer, Maximilian found that the orange-striped
cat was not only dozing upon his desk, but had the effront-
ery to have nested itself upon his papers. He leaned over,
and with a low oath realized the creature was lying upon the
new itinerary he had devised for their trip to Greece!

"Charlotte!"

Leaving the cat in its damning position, he strode off angrily in search of his wife. Richardson, the insufferable man
who somehow managed to remain employed as Casterleigh's butler, pointed a finger toward the morning room,

and Maximilian stalked to the doorway, putting a hand on either side of the frame to restrain himself.

"Charlotte!" he growled.

She was wandering about the room, peeking behind the furniture, as if looking for something. "Yes, Max?" she answered, without even glancing toward him.

"I want those cats out of my house! One is sleeping upon my new travel schedule!"

At his words, Charlotte turned to face him. "Oh, Max, about our trip," she said. "I think we should postpone it."

"Again?" Maximilian was momentarily diverted from the subject of the felines by this abrupt change in her attitude. Charlotte had agreed that fall would be a good time to visit the warmer climes, and now that Burgess was put to rest, he had no qualms about leaving the country with his wife. "Why?"

"I am expecting your heir," Charlotte answered with a bright smile.

Maximilian felt a surge of astonishment, pride and pure happiness as her words became clear. He pictured the house overflowing with his own diverse brood and groaned with delight. In an instant, he had captured her in his arms.

"You are not disappointed, are you?" she asked.

"About Greece? Good God, no! Let the cats have the new schedule!" he said with a grin.

"The cats!" Slipping from his embrace, Charlotte went back to circling the room. "I saw two of the kittens come in here, and I am determined to gather them up and put them outside."

Maximilian watched her, a wry smile on his face, for he no longer could summon up any annoyance for the animals. His mind was upon the child his wife carried. He was about to shout at Charlotte to halt her nonsense when she dropped to her knees and wriggled under the jonquil damask of the sofa, trying to reach one, leaving her delightful round rump sticking out from under the edge of the furniture.

For a moment, Maximilian just stood there, staring, as his euphoria was replaced by something entirely different. Then he quietly shut the doors and locked them behind him. The sight of her, he decided, was simply too tempting to resist.

Silently, he moved to kneel behind her as she scooted out from her position. When she backed up into him, she released a small, startled squeak from her mouth and a white kitten from her hands.

"Don't move," Maximilian said.

"But the kitten . . ." Charlotte began.

"Forget it," Maximilian advised. "Shall I show you what I wanted to do the very first time I met you?"

"Certainly," Charlotte whispered in a confused voice.

She was on her knees in front of him, her hair floating about her just as it had that day only a few months ago in the parlor of the vicarage. Drawing in a sharp breath, Maximilian lifted the hem of her gown and ran his hands along her legs.

"But, Max!" she protested, trying to turn.

"No, love," he answered. "Stay right where you are . . ."

"But, Max. . . . Oh, Max!"

Epilogue

"Kit, get down from that pile of rocks before you fall and break your neck," Charlotte called out. She felt a tug at her skirts.

"What is it, Katie?" Charlotte glanced down at the three-year-old who was determined to gain her attention, and her heart contracted. Her children were all beautiful, of course, but Katie...Katie had the silken, nearly black hair of her father, falling in gentle waves until it was caught up with a ribbon that matched her eyes. They were green, like her mother's eyes, but a deeper, more intense hue that was breathtaking to behold.

Everyone noticed them, but Charlotte tried not to pet her youngest child too much. That job was handled nicely by the girl's brothers and sisters, Barto, the oldest; the twins, John and Elizabeth; Sibylle, named after a grandmother who, if not doting, was at least a frequent visitor; Linley, and Kit.

"Me, too!" Katie said, pointing to the ruined Grecian wall upon which, to Charlotte's consternation, Kit was still climbing.

"Kit!" Charlotte scolded before shaking her head in denial at her youngest daughter. Katie pouted for a moment, her rosebud mouth turned upside down, and Charlotte felt it again, that sense that Katie was going to be the most stunning of women. Charlotte sighed for her, for she knew what a burden beauty could be, but she knew, too, that all her girls were going to have seasons and Katie would have no compulsion to marry except for love.

"Papa!" Katie's brief pique was banished by the appearance of her father, who lifted her up into his arms and kissed her nose. Her little hands tangled in his hair, pulling long strands from the leather thong that held them, and he sent Charlotte an amused look that said he would cut it, if not for her dire threats of retribution.

Charlotte smiled smugly in return, for they had a bargain. She would not take the scissors to her own unmanageable mass of pale curls as long as he kept his locks at an unfashionable length.

"Papa, it says in the guidebook that these ruins are some of the oldest in the region," Barto said. He spoke earnestly to his father, and Charlotte watched him with a smile. He had inherited Max's sense of order and responsibility, but his brothers and sisters kept him from being too serious. He would make a good earl.

"Look, Mama! I'm Apollo!" Kit called.

Charlotte glanced up to see her son balanced atop a tilting pillar with a makeshift arrow in his hands. "Max..." she whispered.

Without a word, her husband handed Katie into her arms and strode over to where his youngest son was dangling. "Kit..." He spoke in a tone that brooked no resistance as he swung his son to the ground. "Why must you get yourself in one scrape after another?"

"Don't know," Kit replied with a toothless grin.

"Blood will tell," mumbled his father. Charlotte caught the remark and the pointed look toward her that went with it, and laughed gaily in response.

"Father, it is half past five and we were to be at the restaurant by six. We shall never make it on time!" Barto said, suddenly staring at his watch in consternation.

John rolled his eyes at his brother, while Elizabeth looked slightly worried. "We shall get dinner, won't we, Papa?"

"We shall eat," Max said in a long-suffering tone. "Put your watch away, Barto. It is not wise to adhere too rigidly to one's schedule."

"Come along then, children," Charlotte said. "We had best be going."

"I am hungriest!" Kit shouted.

"Then you run ahead," Charlotte said. He took off, followed by the others in what soon became a headlong race down the hill, leaving Charlotte to walk beside her husband at a slower pace.

"Well, we are finally here, Max, on our long-postponed wedding trip. How do you find it?"

He gave her a wry grimace. "I will let you know after we have fed them all."

Charlotte laughed, for she knew that his love for his family was genuine and overwhelming. Although he often teased, in truth, he had infinite patience with all the children. He reached out to take her hand, and she gripped his fingers tightly.

"Have I ever apologized for disrupting your schedule?" she asked softly.

"Many times," Max answered with a grin. "I seem to recall hearing these apologies every time I extricated you from some insignificant scrape...and every time you presented me with a beautiful baby. And on each occasion, I believe I have given you the same reply."

"There are more important things in life than clocks?" Charlotte asked hopefully.

Max shook his head, his lips twitching with amusement. "I shall simply make up a new schedule!"

* * * * *

Harlequin® Historical

MORE ROMANCE, MORE PASSION, MORE ADVENTURE...MORE PAGES!

Bigger books from Harlequin Historicals. Pick one up today and see the difference a Harlequin Historical can make.

White Gold by Curtiss Ann Matlock—January 1995—A young widow partners up with a sheep rancher in this exciting Western.

Sweet Surrender by Julie Tetel—February 1995—An unlikely couple discover hidden treasure in the next *Northpoint* book.

All That Matters by Elizabeth Mayne—March 1995—A medieval about the magic between a young woman and her Highland rescuer.

The Heart's Wager by Gayle Wilson—April 1995—An ex-soldier and a member of the demi-monde unite to rescue an abducted duke.

Longer stories by some of your favorite authors. Watch for them in 1995 wherever Harlequin Historicals are sold.

HHBB95-1

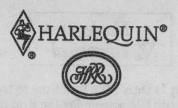

HARLEQUIN®

Deceit, betrayal, murder

Join Harlequin's intrepid heroines, India Leigh
and Mary Hadfield, as they ferret out the truth
behind the mysterious goings-on in their
neighborhood. These two women are no milk-
and-water misses. In fact, they thrive on

Watch for their incredible adventures in this
special two-book collection. Available in March,
wherever Harlequin books are sold.

Harlequin®
Historical

Why is March the best time to try
Harlequin Historicals for the first time?
We've got four reasons:

All That Matters by Elizabeth Mayne—A medieval woman is freed
from her ivory tower by a Highlander's impetuous proposal.

Embrace the Dawn by Jackie Summers—Striking a scandalous
bargain, a highwayman joins forces with a meddlesome young
woman.

Fearless Hearts by Linda Castle—A grouchy deputy puts up a fight
when his Eastern-bred tutor tries to teach him a lesson.

Love's Wild Wager by Taylor Ryan—A young woman becomes
the talk of London when she wagers her hand on the outcome of a
horse race.

It's that time of year again—that March Madness time of year—
when Harlequin Historicals picks the best and brightest new stars in
historical romance and brings them to you in one exciting month!

Four exciting books by four promising new authors that are
certain to become your favorites. Look for them wherever
Harlequin Historicals are sold.